THE SINISTER

Also by David Putnam

The Ruthless

The Heartless

The Reckless

The Innocents

The Vanquished

The Squandered

The Replacements

The Disposables

THE SINISTER

A BRUNO JOHNSON NOVEL

DAVID PUTNAM

OCEANVIEW ((PUBLISHING

SARASOTA, FLORIDA

ISBN 978-1-60809-426-4

Published in the United States of America by Oceanview Publishing

Sarasota, Florida

www.oceanviewpub.com

10 9 8 7 6 5 4 3 2 1

PRINTED IN THE UNITED STATES OF AMERICA

Dedicated to all of those around the world who work tirelessly to combat human trafficking.

CHAPTER ONE

"SOMEONE'S KNOCKING AT the hotel room door. Bruno, can you get the door, please?"

Marie's request wafted out of the steam-filled bathroom of our two-bedroom suite. The scent of lilac mixed with the light fog of humidity that hung low from the ceiling. Marie didn't like to be too far from me, not after all that had happened. Whenever possible, she kept the doors open between us. I couldn't blame her, and when she did leave my view, I tensed until she reappeared. Only time could heal emotional wounds that deep. Turn them to scars, give us some breathing room.

I was standing next to the enormous tousled bed that could double as a regulation wrestling mat, the phone from the night-stand pressed hard to my ear. I had just dialed the hotel's desk to tell them we were finally checking out when the knock came at the door. The nice clerk had said the bill would be "thirty-three thousand, five hundred and thirty-eight dollars and fifty-seven cents." My breath caught. "Can you . . . ah, please repeat that?"

The knock came a second time, not insistent, just a little louder.

"Bruno?" Marie called.

The desk clerk repeated the crazy number, her tone calm and easy as if the amount were a mere trifle, then: "Mr. Jackson, would you like me to put that on the credit card we have on file?"

Credit card? Who could live with that kind of revolving debt? Not at eighteen or twenty-four percent interest. Hell, for that kind of money, we could pay cash for a brand-new SUV and still have enough for the gas to *drive* down to Costa Rica.

"Bruno?" Marie stuck her head out the open bathroom door. "Are you going to get the door? What's the matter? You look like you've seen a ghost." She stepped across the marble threshold and onto the bedroom's plush carpet, dripping water. She held up a thick terrycloth towel to cover her nakedness. Her smooth mocha skin was slick with moisture from having stepped out of a sunken tub filled with luxurious bath salts and piled high in bubbles. She was in her second trimester, five months in, four to go. Soon I'd be a father again. Only this time, at forty-nine years old, I would be closer to grandfather age. I shivered from the prospect of the enormous responsibility. Each and every time, when the thought of approaching fatherhood pinged around in my head, up popped the lovely countenance of my daughter lost, Olivia. God rest her soul.

And, of course, Bosco.

"Bruno, what is it? Who's on the phone?" She grabbed a fluffy robe from the hook on the door and shrugged into it, spooking a small mound of bubbles on her shoulder that sloughed off and gently floated to the carpet. "Who are you talking to?" Fear darkened her expression as she pushed her long black hair out of her face. Her perfectly round tummy bulged in the soft white robe as she tied it closed.

"No. No, it's okay. Just the front desk. That's all. I called them about the bill and to check out."

The knock, yet again.

She stepped over and socked me in the arm. "Don't scare me like that."

I held out the phone receiver as if needing verification of this newest nightmare—this one financial.

She waved it away.

I said, "Scare you like that? I told you we're in the clear. Please try to relax. You just have a case of the nerves because we're almost out of here. We're almost across the finish line."

"No, we're not in the clear. Not until we touch down at Juan Santamaria airport. Not even then. And you know darn well a phone call could be something about the kids. Your dad could be calling. Or . . . or it could be the Los Angeles County Sheriff's Department in the lobby asking you to come down and give yourself up."

I smiled at her wild imagination, her innocence in how the real world worked. "The sheriffs? Really? After we've been here all this time? *Now* they come looking for me, right out of the blue?"

Come looking for the *both* of us. I didn't want to broach that ugly truth to my lovely wife. It would smother the wonderful light in her brown eyes. A twinkle I loved so much, one that of late had gone missing and only recently returned. Law enforcement wanted her as well, though not as badly.

"Sure, why not? It could happen. They could be down there this very minute. And don't give me that syrupy smile. You know it's possible. Especially after—"

I needed to change the subject, get her mind off the horrible events from two months earlier. My new goal in life—helping her to forget how the situation I'd forced upon us had forever changed how we viewed the world. An event that had made it necessary for her to pull the trigger and take a life. The one that gave her night terrors in her sleep. Helping her would also help me try to forget what I'd done. I had shoved it far back into my brain, slammed that door never to be opened again. As if that were possible.

"Thirty-three thousand dollars," I said.

"*What is?*"

"The hotel bill."

Her mouth sagged open. She took the phone from my hand. "How is that possible?" She shook the phone as if trying to wring its neck. "Bruno, how much is that per night? We've been here, what..." Her lips silently counted all the lost time. "Sixty-three days. Two months. Oh, my God, that's five hundred a night? Did you know it was that much? Didn't you get the price when we checked in?"

As if we had a choice. I had to flee the hospital long before I was ready—or risk permanent incarceration. We took up residence in the hotel to hide out and recuperate. I had a couple of bullet holes in me.

I held my arms wide as if to say, *Look at this elegant room, the wonderful view down onto the court of the upscale mall from our third-floor balcony,* but held my tongue. "Sorry, I didn't really pay attention to the price. Initially, we were only going to stay a few days, a week at the outside, remember? This is Glendale. Rooms ain't cheap here, my little chickadee."

"This is terrible. And don't call me that, *Muffin.*" Muffin, a derivative of Snuggle Muffin, okay to use in private, but in the presence of others, it made me cringe and Marie knew it.

I pointed to the phone. The clerk could hear us. Marie put it to her shoulder to smother our words, shielding us from the electronic world.

I wanted to ask her how much she had thought our little *vacation* was going to cost and again chose not to throw my dog into that fight.

Not much of a vacation. The first part of it, I'd been in the hospital for two weeks recovering from a gunshot wound to the chest. The rest of the time laid up in bed or dealing with the blood, sweat, and tears needed for rehabilitation. I'd only been walking unassisted for the last three weeks. Marie, a physician's assistant, still thought I needed to use a cane or risk falling flat on my face. At the time, she'd said, "Go ahead, don't use the cane. A few more scars will only add character to that big boxer's nose of yours."

I didn't have a boxer's nose, not even close. And big? Well, that was just wrong.

She handed me back the phone. The tiny voice of the desk clerk squeaked out of the receiver. Marie said, "Can you deal with this, please?"

The knock at the door again. I spoke into the phone, "Let me call you back." Then to Marie, "I guess we could wait till dark and sneak out the side door. Do the 'ol' smokin' tennis shoes' routine. The room's not in my real name." And what did it really matter, we were wanted by the law for much worse than PC 537e—Defrauding an Innkeeper.

She pointed a loaded finger at me. "We are not criminals. We pay our own way."

I smiled again. I had known her reaction before I'd offered up the unscrupulous solution.

She took another playful swipe at me. "Quit smiling like an idiot, ya big galoot. Get the door. I'm getting dressed. After that we'll deal with the hotel bill." She clapped her hands. "Come on, chop, chop, you have to finish packing. We only have an hour to get to LAX. Our flight is at three, and the international terminal takes a lot longer than the domestic."

All I had left to do was pack my toiletries bag in the suitcase. It'd take two minutes. I headed for the door speaking over my shoulder. "I guess I could get a bellhop job here at the hotel and . . ." Out of deeply ingrained instinct and experience, I automatically stood off to the side of the door, leaned over, and checked the peephole with a quick peek. I took a sudden step back.

"And what?" Marie said from the steamy bathroom. "You know how long it would take you to work off thirty-three thousand dollars at minimum wage? Who's at the door? Is it Karl?"

"No," I whispered to no one. "It's the FBI."

CHAPTER TWO

Assistant Director of the FBI Dan Chulack stood in the hall on the other side of the hotel suite door. He wasn't smiling. Not good. I hesitated and went over the options, which numbered in the negative. We were trapped like a couple of rats on the third floor with our backs to a balcony. I opened the door. He walked in without an invitation.

"Hey, Bruno, how's it going?" He said it like we were old friends and two months had not passed between us since the last time I'd seen him. Two months and four bodies left on the floor of a large open bay garage.

He said, "I just came by to see you off." He checked his watch. "You're running a little behind if you're going to make your flight. That international terminal can get pretty jammed up this time of day."

Hey, how did he know when we were leaving?

I leaned out, stuck my head in the hallway, and looked both ways. Vacant, except for a checkerboard of food trays set on the floor next to random rooms. I closed the door. I hadn't seen Chulack since our unholy alliance to take down an outlaw motorcycle gang's attempt to sell a stolen drone and four Hellfire missiles. A big feather in his cap—a bullet in the chest and hip for me—and night terrors for my

Marie. He'd been promoted from Senior Special Agent in Charge of the Los Angeles office to Assistant Director for The Office of Integrity and Compliance in D.C. He might even make Director one day; he had the smarts and political savvy to climb to the top of that treacherous, backstabbing heap.

But not if anyone caught him in the suite of an upscale Glendale hotel occupied by a fugitive on the Ten Most Wanted List. Not the national list—the LA office's ten most. This wasn't something I had aspired to when I joined the Los Angeles County Sheriff's Department twenty-seven years earlier.

I closed the door, turned. "Well, come on in," I said as I hurried around him to the bathroom to ease the door the rest of the way closed on Marie. I got there in time to block her view as she called out, "Who is it?"

If she saw Chulak, she'd go at him tooth and nail.

"Ah, it's okay, it's just the bellhop," I said. "He wants to take our bags down to the lobby." A little white lie I'd later pay for.

"Oh, good." She opened the door a crack.

Continuing to block her view, I said, "Why don't you go ahead and get dressed. I'll take care of all this." I eased the door closed and held my breath waiting to see if she'd overrule me. She didn't.

I turned back to Dan. "It's not a good idea for you to be here."

His expression fell. "I know."

I'd been a cop for more than twenty-five years and had learned to read people. Something was wrong. My heart took off at a gallop. Was he there to arrest us and didn't know how to say it? That wasn't going to happen, especially not with Marie pregnant. She wouldn't have our child in prison, not as long as I was standing upright.

He wore an expensive suit, charcoal gray with a dark-blue dress shirt and matching silk tie. Subdued. Under the radar. He could be a model in a high-end catalogue for senior executives.

"What are you doing here?"

He looked down at his oxblood loafers that didn't even match. "I guess I feel guilty about what I put you and Marie through. I can't tell you how sorry I am in how it turned out."

He was my friend and hadn't come around during my recuperation because Marie held him responsible for what had happened. And *he did* own a small part of it. But I'd made my own choices and leveled no blame.

Had it taken two months for his guilt to fester and get the better of him? But now? On the same day we planned to leave? Not a chance. Too much of a coincidence. Something else was in play.

"We talked about this right after it happened. That night in the hospital, remember?" I said. "We're adults. We knew the risks. That's all water under the bridge. Thanks for coming by, but we really need to finish packing so we can get home. It's time. We miss the kids and they miss us." I took hold of his elbow, the suit coat material smooth and rich, reminding me of my station in life. I tried to move him toward the door and out into the hall. How long until Marie would be dressed and come out?

He didn't budge. I glanced back at the bathroom door. Marie would have her ear to the smooth painted wood trying to listen. I shifted direction and pulled him toward the balcony, a place we had tried to stay away from during daylight hours. Too many folks moving around down in the Americana Mall. Folks who could look up and recognize me. I'd been all over the news several times in the last couple of years with a big reward stamped in red above my head. Like a devil's halo.

For close to two decades, while on the Violent Crimes Team, I'd hunted murderers with my boss, Robby Wicks. Now I was the hunted and didn't like it one bit. Had Robby Wicks still been alive, he'd have had me in custody or on a slab long before now.

This time Chulack let me guide him. I pulled the curtains aside, opened the slider, and let him pass through first. Outside the ambient noise was louder than in the quiet room. We also exchanged the scent of moist lilac for the smell of warm pretzels and fresh-baked chocolate-chip cookies from the food carts down below. I closed the curtains and then the door. We didn't have a lot of time.

I turned to him. "All right, what's going on?"

Out in the brighter light of day, I saw that he'd aged since the last time I'd seen him. Administrative jobs could do that. Gray streaked his black hair, and the lines in his forehead and under his eyes ran deeper than before. His tennis-court tan had faded. With closer examination, it looked as if he hadn't slept in many days. He moved to the edge of the balcony, put both hands on the rail, and watched down below as the narrow-gauge train carried mall customers in and around outdoor shops like Barney's of New York, J.Crew, Tiffany's, and Urban Outfitters. All the people made the place look like Disneyland. It was the middle of the week; didn't anybody work anymore?

"What are you talking about?" he said. "Nothing's going on. I just came by to see that you and Marie made your flight. I figured I owed you that much."

"How did you know we were flying out today? We haven't told anyone. And I mean not a soul. Wait? Are you tapping our phone?"

"Of course not."

"You didn't answer the question. How did you know?"

"I didn't." He sat down at the end of the chaise lounge chair, leaned at the waist over his knees, and wrung his hands. "I saw your luggage when I came in." He pointed back toward the room.

I pulled a chair closer, sat, and waited for him to tell it. He was scaring the hell out of me. What could possibly make an Assistant Director in the FBI worry like this unless it was to tell an old friend the jig was up and the cops were down in the lobby waiting to spring a trap as Marie had described? It had to happen someday, a dread I barely kept at bay, stored and tamped down in the far reaches of my mind along with that other thing now. Along with Bosco. Not as far down as I wanted it to be.

He wouldn't look at me, adding flame to my paranoia.

"Dan, talk to me. You came here for something other than saying goodbye. You're going to tell me eventually. So, go ahead, get it over with."

He looked up and our eyes locked. It sent a shiver down my back. He reached into his suit coat pocket and took out his phone. He typed in his security code and swiped his finger until he came to a photo. He turned the phone around and handed it to me.

The photo depicted a small, vulnerable child, a young girl with golden curls. Cute as the dickens. She was four or five years old with a sweet smile and big brown eyes. Kids were my Achilles' heel and Chulack knew it. I shoved the phone back to him. "Don't do this. We're leaving today, and nothing's going to stop us. Nothing." Before he took the phone away, I pulled it back and looked again. Something niggled at the back of my memory; I recognized this child from the news broadcasts. "Wait, this is Emily Mosley."

He nodded.

"She's been missing two weeks, almost three. Her nanny was taken as well, right? We've been following it on the news. You have someone in custody. You got him on a failed . . . ransom attempt. Right?"

He nodded again.

"Then what could you possibly want from me? You have to have at least fifty cops and agents on this thing."

"Fifty-five."

I sat back. I'd exaggerated when I said fifty agents. A normal kidnap might have five or six special agents working with the local cops. Ten, maybe fifteen for a sensational snatch. Never fifty. The news had not said a thing about the child belonging to a movie star, or someone politically connected.

"Who is she?"

His eyes welled and his chin quivered.

"Ah, man."

He nodded and swallowed hard. "She's my granddaughter, Bruno."

CHAPTER THREE

"I'M SO SORRY," I said.

He stood, turned away, and went back to the rail. He'd exposed enough of his inner self, his emotions, and needed to pause and gather himself.

All the local news feeds followed the story until a couple of days ago when the family paid the ransom—two million dollars. The cops failed to get the child and her nanny, Lilian Morales, back. On top of that, they lost the money. With nothing left in their investigative bag of tricks, law enforcement had put out a plea to the public for help. Along with a sizeable reward.

There weren't a lot of details of what happened after the failed ransom attempt. Nothing released to the public, anyway. Though it wasn't difficult to figure out. The FBI and LAPD somehow nabbed one of the kidnappers in the failed exchange. The kidnapper wouldn't talk, and now days later, they still had not recovered the child or the nanny. The media hounds had moved on to something inane—like one of those famous sisters who were only famous for being famous.

We both knew what it meant to grab a kidnapper and miss the victim. With the kidnapper in the can, the other coconspirators wouldn't keep a witness alive. Poor Emily. Poor Lilian.

Chulack put his hands back on the rail, leaned on it, and looked down at the mall swarming with people, all of them ignorant of the pain my friend was going through, carrying on in their perfect little world, shopping for things they really didn't need.

What a horrible thing for Chulack to deal with—the loss of a child. I felt his pain.

Most recently with my own son, Bosco.

The curtains parted. A fully clothed Marie appeared on the other side of the glass doors. She wore a red blouse with puffy sleeves, and navy maternity pants. Her smile melted into a scowl when she spotted Chulack. Her hands fumbled with the door as she frantically tried to get it open. She heaved it aside. "What the heck is he doing here?"

I held out my hands, moving between them. "Now take it easy, babe. Wait. Just wait a minute and take a breath."

She slapped at my hands. "Don't tell me to take it easy. We're leaving today. Get out, Dan, and don't come back. I mean it, get the hell out." She raised her finger and pointed to the suite door across the room.

My Marie was the kindest person I ever met. She never had a disparaging word for anyone. Unless that person threatened the welfare of her family; then she turned into a rabid she-wolf. Part of her anger came from guilt. Her entire life she'd studied to be a physician's assistant, took an oath to help people, and never in her life had she dreamt she'd have cause to pick up a gun and shoot a person dead. Let alone two persons. That had been on me. Chulack's duplicity in my lovely wife's venture into my old world, where violence ruled the day, churned her anger and guilt. Venting on Chulack became a necessity to help her heal.

I put a hand on both shoulders and gently spun her around and guided her from behind. She struggled to get free. "No. Let me go, Bruno. Let me go. I won't have it. Get him the hell out of here, now."

I held on tighter and walked her back into the room. I fought to control her and leaned down close to her ear. "His granddaughter is Emily Mosley."

She froze, her back going stiff. In the past two weeks, we'd watched the news about Emily and Lillian and didn't have to say a word about how we'd feel if it had been one of our twelve kids.

We had taken twelve children from hostile homes in Los Angeles and now sheltered them down in Costa Rica where we'd been headed before Chulack knocked on our door. She relaxed. I let go of her. She turned, came in for a hug, and cried. "No, Bruno, no. Not this time. Not again."

I'd made her a promise that when I got out of the hospital I was done. That I would never take up the path of violence again. That nothing in the world could ever take me away from our family. Marie knew when I'd made that promise we had not considered a friend coming to us asking, begging for closure on the kidnapping of a grandchild. She knew I couldn't turn Chulack away, that she, in good conscience, couldn't ask me to. She mumbled into my chest, "Are you going to do it?"

"He hasn't asked me to do anything."

She pulled back and looked up, her eyes wet. "He hasn't?"

Seeing her hurt was like a punch to the stomach.

"No, he's too good a friend. He knows what we've been through. He would never ask. And in any case, I don't know what I could do to help. Not with all that's already happened, the way it went down. There isn't anything left to do but—"

But I knew. Hunt down those responsible and make them pay.

Any law enforcement violent crimes team could hunt them down. The kidnap ransom was over so there was no need to rush. Life was no longer held in the balance.

Not all that long ago, I had been the very best at hunting those responsible for despicable crimes against unsuspecting victims. Wicks and I had been a formidable team.

She opened her mouth to say, "Good," and closed it. Instead, she remained mum. We'd been together long enough to predict what each other would say. Sometimes we had entire conversations without a spoken word. I'd never experienced such a closeness, such mutual love, with anyone before. Except my father, but that is a different kind of love.

Her eyes shifted from tears and pain to confusion. She was remembering the last two weeks, the pictures of Emily Mosley playing again and again on the news feeds. "I didn't mean to be . . . I mean, we didn't know she was Dan's granddaughter."

"I know, sweetie. It's okay."

"I'm a selfish shrew."

"No, you're not. And this isn't on you; this is my decision to say no. You're out of it."

"So, you're going to tell him you can't do it?"

"That's right."

"How do you know he's even going to . . . Yes, he's going to, why else would he be here today. This very minute. Just before we're about to leave for the airport?"

A knock sounded at the door.

She said, "That'll be Karl, to give us a ride to LAX."

"Why don't you get it. I'll finish up with Dan and then we'll go."

"You sure?"

"Yes, I'm sure."

She went up on tiptoes, her tummy bumping into me, and kissed my cheek. "Thank you, muffin." She held an arm around my neck for a long beat, her cheek close to mine. She nodded, kissed me again, and let go.

I watched her move to the suite door. She checked the peephole and opened it. Karl Drago stood there filling the entire doorway. He wrapped his gorilla arms around my Marie and hugged her. Drago had a thing for my wife and acted like an obedient dog when around her. Well, more a rotund lion than a dog. I waved, then turned and went back out onto the patio. I eased the slider closed and stood next to Chulack, elbows on the rail. We watched the people down below. After a moment, I asked, "The guy you have in custody, he wouldn't give it up? Wouldn't give you anywhere to start looking?"

He shook his head.

"You have no leads at all?"

"I had the best interrogator in the Bureau flown out from D.C. to talk to him. Nothing. Not a peep."

"Who is he, this guy?"

"Duane Eldridge. We kept his name out of the press . . . just in case. Well, you know, so if he did decide to talk, he wouldn't face being labeled a rat."

"Ah, man, a Crip from the Rollin' Sixties?"

Chulack's head swung around. "You know him?"

"Insane Duane?"

"Yes. Yes. That's right."

"Yeah, if it's the same dude I'm thinking about, I know of him. I've never met him. Well, that's not true. Me and Wicks were hunting his brother—or maybe they were cousins. I don't remember which. This Duane answered the door to a house where we thought our target was hiding. He mouthed off to Wicks and Wicks slugged him."

What I didn't tell Chulack was that Wicks had been wearing an LAPD SWAT ring, a souvenir from another fugitive hunt when we took down an LAPD SWAT sergeant who'd temporarily lost his faculties over a child custody battle. He killed his wife and then drove to his in-laws and killed them as well, "for having the nerve to birth such a bitch." The ring always left a mark. It was as if Wicks were marking people who'd gone before him so he could readily recognize them down the road.

Chulack looked at the throng of folks below, his mind somewhere else. I reached closer and put my hand on his arm. "You okay?"

"What?" He came out of his trance. "Oh, yeah, sure. Just bone tired. Did you need a ride to the airport?"

"No thanks. Karl's going to take us."

"How's he doing?"

"Good. He healed a lot faster than I did."

The pause hung between us, fat and uncomfortable. He wanted to ask me a favor, one too difficult to comprehend. I wanted to get home to the kids and at the same time wanted to help out an old friend who stood before me like a lion with a thorn in his paw.

I clapped my hands, and the uncomfortable pause collapsed. "I guess we better get going then."

"Bruno?"

"Yeah?"

"Safe travels."

"Thanks." I opened the slider and entered the room. Karl Drago stood with his back against the wall, his thick arms across his chest and an angry scowl across his huge mug. Marie had the suitcases open on the rumpled bed and moved back and forth to the dresser putting the clothes back in the drawers.

"Babe, what are you doing?"

She didn't stop or acknowledge my question. Tears streamed down her face and dripped on the clothes. I looked to Drago for answers.

He shrugged. "I don't know what's going on, pal. But I'll tell you right now I don't like it. What did you do?" He only called me *pal* when he was angry.

I rushed over to Marie. She took shelter in my arms, her face on my chest, tears wetting my shirt. She mumbled something.

"What?" I asked.

"We can't stay here, I mean, at this hotel. We can't afford the room. But if we're not going home, I don't want to change hotels, either."

"You don't have to worry about that. We're getting on that plane and—" I didn't know if I'd ever been so torn. I turned to Chulack. "What do you want from me? What could I do that all those agents and cops couldn't?" But I knew. He wanted me to find his dead granddaughter, poor little Emily. He had to know for sure, put to rest that one iota of hope. For closure. He had to have it no matter what the cost. Even a friendship.

Marie pulled away from my chest and looked up. She'd figured it out long before I did.

Dan had exhausted every possible avenue to resolve this horrible crime that had befallen his family. He'd gone down his list of names to get to me, his last resort.

Marie took a step back. My eyes didn't leave Chulack's. My hand involuntarily went to my right shoulder. Many years ago, when the violent crimes team first started up, my good friend Ned wanted a team logo, a brand to strike fear in those whom we pursued. He'd gotten a tattoo on his shoulder, BMF: Brutal Mother Fuckers. He wanted me to get one as well, and I wouldn't and told him so. Not under any circumstances would I permanently disfigure my body. Especially with a vulgarity of that magnitude. Then he went through a door on a search warrant entry in a position I was supposed to have. Ned was killed in the line of duty. The day of his funeral I stopped at a parlor and had those legendary letters etched in my skin, a tribute to my friend and, most important, a reminder to never say never.

Now Dan wanted the old Bruno back, the Bruno who without malicious intent stepped over into the *gray* area to take down violent criminals, using whatever force necessary. More often than not, resorting to blood and bone.

Only what he was asking this time would require a much darker shade of gray.

CHAPTER FOUR

MARIE PULLED AWAY from me and went back to putting clothes in the drawers. She mumbled, "As it is, I don't know how we're going to pay the hotel bill." She rambled, not wanting to think about what I would have to do to resolve this problem of Chulack's. Only one solution remained. Venture back into the fray one more time after I had told her never again. When would it all stop? When could I play in my own backyard with our children and not have to worry about the violent world on the other side of our own walls?

Chulack stood by the open slider, his hands clenched in fists down at his sides. "I didn't ask you to do anything. I would never do that. You need to get on that plane."

I looked from Marie and back to him. "Yeah, right. You're a real son of a bitch."

He shook his head, confusion and need plain in his expression. "I'll do whatever you ask. Anything, and I mean anything."

Through clenched teeth, I said, "Well, I guess you could pay the hotel bill, that would be a good start."

He reached into his suit coat pocket, took out a thick folded sheaf of papers, and proffered them to Marie. She snatched them from his hand as tears streamed down her cheeks. She opened the papers. From where I stood, I could see it was a copy of our lengthy bill.

"It's been paid. I have an agent down at the front desk taking care of it."

Marie shook the papers in front of Dan's face. "This doesn't absolve you for . . . for . . . ah, the hell with it." She took two steps over and hugged Chulack. He hugged her back as tears welled in my eyes.

Karl, who still stood with his back to the wall said, "This is wrong, man. I'm tellin' you right now, this is the one that's going to—"

"Don't," I said. He shut his mouth.

Chulack, on the verge of tears, said, "I'm also going to pick up the bill for the rest of the days that you are here. No argument. And I'm going to insist that you take a thousand dollars a day, more if you want it. Whatever you want."

Marie stepped away from Chulack, sniffling. "You're not going to pay him for what he has to do. That would only make it worse. That would make it blood money. And I don't want to hear another word about it. As far as the hotel bill, we pay our own way. Thank you for taking care of it, but we will pay you back. We'll send you a check as soon as we get home and move some money around."

The only money we had squirreled away was in the children's college fund. It was quite a bit but not near enough for all of them. We had twelve children with another one on the way. Geez, a kid at forty-nine years old. We needed every penny.

Dan shifted his gaze to me.

I said, "She's right. I can't accept any compensation for this. Now, how do you expect me to operate here in the States without getting picked up for all those kidnap warrants?"

Marie and I had unlawfully appropriated all of our kids from toxic homes in South Central Los Angeles, taken them from parents, all of them crack heads, felons, dope dealers, and child molesters who, if left to their abusive ways, would've eventually killed the children.

Most of the parents didn't care; some did and filed crime reports. That's how I'd made the LA office of the FBI's ten most wanted list. A serial kidnapper. Chulack couldn't do anything about those warrants. They'd just have to stand until the parents died.

Chulack reached into his suit coat pocket yet again and came out with a black wallet. He handed it to me. I opened it. FBI credentials replete with my photo and the name Karl Higgins, an aka I'd used years back while working a sting, where I'd taken down a violent criminal named Johnny Sin. To use those creds would ruin Chulack's career.

Marie quick-stepped over to me and grabbed them out of my hand. Her eyes went large. "This . . . this means you knew exactly what would happen when you came here. You know us well enough that you wouldn't have to ask for one damn thing. That all you had to do was say her name. Whisper 'Emily Mosley' and Bruno would jump through any hoop you put in front of him. I'm surprised you didn't show Bruno a cute little picture of her." She read my sheepish expression and threw the creds at Chulack. "Get out. Get out of our room. I don't want to see you ever again. Bruno will do what you ask, but hear me when I say, Dan Chulack, you are no longer friends of the Johnsons. Now get out. Get the hell out."

I couldn't blame her for how she felt. I followed Chulack to the door as Karl moved away from the wall and went to console my wife, who now openly wept. I should've been the one to console her.

Out in the hall Chulack turned, his expression one of agony. He had not wanted to drag me into this mess. He said, "What are you going to need? I was serious about what I said in there; whatever you want, you just ask."

"It's better that you stay as far away from what's going to happen. It's going to get ugly and it'll ruin your career if any of the stink blows back on you." I picked up his credentials and handed them back.

"You don't understand. I've made peace in what has to be done. I'm ready to walk away from my career. This is my daughter we're talking about, my granddaughter. I'd do this myself, but I don't know the things you know about the street. I wouldn't know the first thing about how to . . . Well . . . Where are you going to start?"

What he meant was that he didn't have the stomach for blood and bone.

"I'll go with the best lead. I'll go talk with Duane Eldridge, Insane Duane."

"In the jail? How are you going to do that? Here, take the creds, they'll get you in."

I pushed them away. "No, I'll take care of it. Like I said, from here on out you need to stay far away from this."

He nodded and pondered it for a moment. "You think you can do it?" His voice came out choked. He couldn't talk about what would happen once I found his granddaughter, her condition, the horrific grief it would cause for his daughter and his daughter's husband. Because right then, as it stood, there was still the tiniest ray of hope. And any hope, no matter how insignificant, was better than an ugly truth.

I ignored his question. "I want every report, every piece of paper law enforcement has generated on this thing, and I want it here within the hour."

He took out his cell phone and punched in the numbers. "What else?"

"I'm not a hundred percent right now, healthwise, so for the heavy work, I'm taking Karl Drago with me."

"No problem, I understand."

"No, you don't. I want your word that you'll give him a get-out-of-jail-free card for everything up to murder and even murder if you can pull it off. I don't intend it to go that far."

He hesitated and was interrupted by whomever he'd called. "This is Chulack," he said. "I want the case file, and I mean everything that's been generated since this started. I want it copied and brought to the front desk of the Americana Hotel in Glendale. You have fifty-five minutes." He hung up and said to me, "I understand what you're asking, and you know if I said I could guarantee this request I'd be lying. I can only promise to do my best."

"That's good enough for me."

"What weapons will you need?"

I smiled. "I know how to get what I need. I want you to get two burner phones, one for you and one for me. That's how I'll stay in contact with you. Leave mine at the front desk."

"Done, what else?"

"Nothing else. We can still be on a plane tomorrow if Eldridge rolls over when I talk to him."

"I don't think that's going to happen. I'm telling you, we tried everything. What can you do different?"

"I won't be reading him his rights."

"Oh . . . right."

CHAPTER FIVE

I WOKE IN a sitting position, my back propped up in bed, a partial clump of papers from the 1,200-page police report lying facedown on my chest. Two-and-a-half reams of paper in total, and with all of those cops out shaking the trees, they couldn't find even one good lead. Marie sat in bed next to me, her legs crossed, her reading glasses perched on the tip of her cute little nose as she read from the same file, the pages scattered out before her. She wore a dark copper-colored silk nightie that accented her skin. She smelled of lilac.

I tried to peer around her to the clock. "What time is it?"

She didn't look over when she answered, "Three twenty-one a.m."

"You shouldn't be reading that."

No reply.

"It'll give you nightmares." I was groggy and hadn't thought that one through. Night terrors still visited her most every night. In them, she stood, gun in hand, debating the most difficult decision of her life. Shoot or don't shoot. And she had to make it in a split second. She turned and looked over the top of her glasses.

I held up my hand in surrender and gave her my best smile. "You know you look sexy with those glasses on." I leaned over to kiss her. She gave me her cheek. Still angry over what had happened the day before. Just hours in the past, really.

I shuffled together the loose pages on my chest. "You find any-thing interesting?"

She took off her glasses. "This whole thing is interesting to me. I've never read anything like it. The money drop debacle is right out of a locked-room mystery, like the ones I read when I was a kid. Right from the pages of Agatha Christie. Well, sort of."

"I haven't gotten that far," I said. "I'm still in the interviews sur-rounding the abduction."

She nodded. "That's some dry reading; no wonder you fell asleep. Nothing there at all unless I missed something. It is odd though—no one, and I mean no one, saw a thing in regard to that child being kidnapped."

"Oh, is that right? You're Sherlock Holmes now?"

"I hadn't thought of it that way until now, but yes, and you're the bumbling Doctor Watson."

I chuckled. "Thanks for that. Tell me, wise ol' Ms. Holmes, what can you derive from the lack of clues in the witness statements?"

She thought for a moment. "Well, if absolutely no one saw any-thing" —she held up a good chunk of pages—"and let me tell you, these guys left no stone unturned. They talked to everyone and ev-eryone's brother and sister for that matter. Then I'd have to surmise that the butler did it."

"Meaning?"

"The nanny, Lilian Morales, has to be involved."

"I only read the ten or fifteen pages before I fell asleep, but in the summary, it said the ransom demand included the return of Emily and Lilian for the two million dollars."

"That's right, but couldn't that be a ruse, you know, a ploy?"

"Is that what you believe?"

She fanned through the pages. "There are some supplemental re-ports from FBI agents who were sent down to Guatemala to interview all of Lilian's relatives. The family is in debt up to their eyeballs, probably due to the cost of getting Lilian into the U.S. That's what one agent thinks. Lilian sends them money every month through Western Union. Lilian's two friends here in the States both say she's the salt of the earth and lives very frugally. She eats beans and rice and vegetables and only allows herself chicken on Sundays. She wears secondhand clothes and sits in the park feeding the pigeons for entertainment on her days off. Every extra penny goes south to her folks."

"Answer the question. Do you think she's involved?"

"That's not fair, Bruno. All I have here is paper. I wasn't there to look any of these people in the eye."

"Based on the paper in your hand."

"The only avenue that makes any sense to me is Lilian being involved. Are all kidnap cases like this one?"

"No." I didn't want to give her the stats on outcomes. Especially ones where the victims aren't recovered after the money drop. "Tell me about the drop."

She shuffled the papers again, came up with what she wanted, and put her glasses back on. "Five days ago, two million dollars in twenties and fifties were put into a specific kind of Louie Vuitton bag, two of them. The kidnapper gave the model and size. Then the kidnapper ran the father, John Mosely, from one location to another to see if he had a tail. Until finally they told him the address in Altadena—311 East Sierra Madre Boulevard. It says here that it's almost exclusively an African American neighborhood."

"Eldridge, the guy I'm going to talk to in the jail in a few hours, is a Crip, and the Crips run that hood. In fact, they run most all of Altadena. Go on."

She handed me some cocoa butter. I knew what to do and started to rub some on her tummy to avoid stretch marks, a nightly activity.

She said, "The kidnapper didn't give the FBI any time to check the address for the drop. On the pay phone, they told Mosely to go inside the townhouse, set the two bags of money down in the center of the living room, and leave. The door was unlocked when he got there. The FBI had the back and the front covered. They watched it for about an hour when this Eldridge character pulled up to the front of the townhouse in a stolen Lexus, a gold four-door. He went in, stayed for less than ten minutes, and then ran out. He jumped in the Lexus and took off at high speed."

I stopped rubbing. "Did he have the two Louis Vuitton bags?"

"Hey?"

"Oh." I continued the massage.

She said, "He had two brown paper grocery-type bags, crumpled up and used. They chased the Lexus around for"—she referred to the report and read from parts of it—"twenty-one minutes. He wasn't running very fast. One agent said it was almost as if Eldridge didn't really want to get away. They never lost sight of him. And there was a helicopter right over the top of him the whole time. The LAPD patrol unit finally did a PIT Maneuver, a Pursuit Intervention Technique, on the Lexus. It spun out and wrapped around a magnolia tree. Eldridge got out and fled on foot. He was caught."

"And the money wasn't in the car?"

"Right. The paper bags contained wadded-up dirty clothes that belonged to the people who owned the townhouse. FBI went back to the townhouse and the Louis Vuitton bags and the money were not there. They tore the place apart looking for it."

"What about the GPS bugs the FBI put in the money and the bags?"

She eyed me. "I thought you said you didn't read that far into the report?"

"It's standard procedure."

"The bugs were left sitting in the middle of the floor where the bags had been left—now gone."

"Okay, tell me. What happened to the money?"

She smiled. "The FBI screwed up. The agent who was covering the back of the townhouses left his position. He said he thought the action was with the pursuit and that Eldridge had to have the money. He thought that logic dictated he jump into the chase. He didn't tell anyone he was leaving his position."

"That was a rookie move. Commanders usually post the rookies at the back or in a position where the least amount of initiative will be needed."

"Anyway," Marie said, "this agent caught himself after only three minutes—or so he says in his statement—realized his error, and went back."

"Three minutes, that's plenty of time to get away."

"But the agent didn't come forward with this mistake until all the agents were called in to be interviewed individually, by this Harold Purdy from D.C. He's the guy who interviewed Eldridge in jail. That's when this FBI agent, Joseph Danforth, admitted to his error."

"You want me to get your thighs?"

"Nice try, cowboy. Just keep on with it, you're doing fine."

I continued to rub. "They suspended him, didn't they?"

"That's right, how did you know?"

"It's the FBI we're talking about. They don't hold with mistakes; they're a black eye on the entire Bureau. And to compound matters, the victims are the Deputy Director's family members."

"Bruno." She shook some of the supplemental reports. "Chulack sent us everything. They have a team watching their own agent. They're following him in a surveillance around the clock. As if they think he might be in league with the kidnappers. Can you believe that? They even did a financial background check on him."

"Dan said they checked everything that could be checked. I don't blame him. Who did the townhouse belong to?"

"The owners were both at work. Nice couple, Simon and Nora Wilson. They checked out okay. The kidnappers just picked out some random townhouse."

"So where did the two million dollars get off to?"

"Good question."

CHAPTER SIX

NINE A.M. THAT same morning, Karl Drago maneuvered the sleek black Monte Carlo in and out of go-to-work traffic, still angry about Marie being upset. I braced my shoulder against the door and put one hand on the dash. "Hey, buddy, can you take it easy, just a little?"

He continued to angry-drive, jerking the wheel, accelerating, and braking hard. He didn't respond.

"You keep this up, I'm going to lean over and toss my cookies in your lap. I'm not kidding here."

I'd been off the pain meds for a couple of weeks and, at Marie's insistence, swallowed one in anticipation of the day's activities. She'd said, "You have to manage your pain. It's always better to stay in front of it." At the door and ready to leave, I kissed her on the forehead. "I love you, kid."

She didn't say it back. A bad sign. She didn't need to pile on the guilt. I had enough of my own to fuel ten lifetimes. The physical pain of being shot in the chest had been nothing compared to the emotional loss of Bosco.

"I can wrap this thing up fast," I had said to Marie. "You'll see—we'll be on that plane tomorrow."

She shook her head. "I'm not going to get stuck here, Bruno. Fair warning."

"What are you talking about? You're right, we're not going to get stuck here."

"After twenty-eight weeks, the airlines won't let me fly international." She rubbed her bump. "And we're getting close to that now. If this takes too long—I love you dearly, you know that—but I will not get stuck here and have the baby away from the kids. It'll keep me away from them too long. We've been gone too long already."

"Okay, I understand, but I prom—"

She put a finger up to my lips. "Don't. Don't make a promise you have no control over. This thing goes more than two weeks, I'm gone. That's all I'm saying. Fair warning." Her tone carried a steel edge to it that I wasn't accustomed to.

"No way will this go two weeks." Those words came out in a half-whisper.

She closed the door to the suite. I stood in the hall staring at it, unable to move. I had it bad for her and immediately started to miss not being in the same room. Who would take care of her if something was to happen and I wasn't there? I closed my eyes and focused, took a breath, turned and headed out to the Monte Carlo.

The pain pill had upset my stomach, and Drago's driving wasn't making things any easier. He wore a triple-X-sized yellow tee shirt with a plain blue long-sleeve button-up over it that pulled tight on his biceps. He had on black denim pants and heavy steel-toed work boots. He'd cut short his mouse-brown hair, which now hung down past his ears and neck covering the more obvious tattoos representing violence from his past life. He let one beefy arm hang out the window and his other hand, a fist the size of a ham, was on the steering wheel. He'd done twelve years of a twenty-five to life sentence for a murder he did not commit during an armored car robbery and didn't like that our first stop of the day was Men's Central Jail in downtown LA.

As Drago drove, I tore open the oversized manila envelope that I had picked up at the front desk. Inside was the burner phone I'd requested from Chulack along with the bogus FBI creds. For a moment, I thought about tossing the creds out the window of the moving car but, instead, put them in my pocket.

Marie's words about leaving me behind in LA echoed in my brain, keeping me from focusing on the problem at hand.

The night before, I had not even dented the 1,200-page stack of the copied crime report left at the Americana Hotel. I got down the basics from the summary, "the where," and "the when," and more important, "the why," in how the exchange got so horribly botched up.

Before all the stress of the day caught up with me, I was going to need some rest. I wasn't anywhere near fully recovered. My little smart-ass subconscious, at the most inopportune times, stood on my shoulder, tugged on my ear, jumped up and down, and yelled, "Bad idea. This is a real bad idea. You can't fight your way out of a wet paper bag let alone take on all The Rollin' Sixties."

I put my head back against the doorframe, closed my eyes, and wondered how I came to be sitting in a car with an angry ex-outlaw biker, racing to a jail filled with criminals who, if given the chance, would take me out in a heartbeat. A jail filled with law enforcement officers all sworn to take me into custody—if they happened to discover my true identity. Why did I do it? If I wanted this kind of aggravation, why not just take out a ball-peen hammer and hit myself in the head with it? The "real bad idea" voice pinged around and around and landed on something Dad had said two months ago before we'd left for the States, mere days before I was shot in the chest. He was sitting next to me on a bench at the clinic in Costa Rica, waiting his turn for chemotherapy. He had a bad type of stomach cancer and had shrunk to a bag of skin filled with loose bones. We were having a similar conversation as to why I did the things I did. Dad knew the answer to everything. His wisdom harkened back to a time without computers and Google, a time when sons worked all day side by side with their fathers in the fields or shops. A time when morals, integrity, and honor were handed down from generation to generation. This day he'd put his hand on my leg and said, "Son, I think you have something inside you, a kind of hunger that every now and then needs to be fed. A need to right a wrong, no matter whose wrong it is, to better the world even if it means stepping on someone's neck in the process."

I had never looked at my life from that perspective and found in it a truth that cut too close to the bone.

The car jolted to a complete stop. I opened my eyes. I'd fallen asleep. My mouth was dry, my tongue thick like it got when I'd been snoring. I shouldn't have let Marie talk me into that damn pain pill.

The thought of Dad, his kind and gentle voice fresh in my memory. I missed him and needed to get this done and get back to him. I struggled up in the seat.

"Hey, Sleeping Beauty," Drago said, "I love ya like a brother but I am not going to follow you into that place." He pointed through the windshield to the large, windowless hunk of concrete, a gray beast that housed 6,000 inmates. Wicks used to say, "All the GUM that gets stuck to the bottom of your shoe, the Great Unwashed Masses. The jail's just one big swirling vortex of criminality and if you're not careful it'll reach up and drag you down with them. It's the Grand Oracle where all the victims' answers are stored."

Drago had pulled into the visiting parking lot of MCJ and stopped us amid a sea of cars. Mostly junkers—cars always at the edge of stalling out or dying on the street when the drivers would simply get out and walk away from them.

"I wouldn't expect you to," I said. "Wait for me." I tugged the door handle and rolled out into the bright sunlight. But I'd forgotten about the bullet in my hip and wilted to the ground. Pain shot up my side and burst behind my eyes. I stayed on my hands and knees until it passed. Drago didn't get out to help and looked from where he sat behind the wheel through the open passenger door. "Hey, bud, that's gotta hurt. In the future, you might try getting out of the car like a normal person." He chuckled.

I struggled up, using the car for support. "Thanks, bro. I'll remember that for the next time." I eased the door closed and headed out between the cars. I left the cane in the car and tried my best not to hobble.

I couldn't stop from swaying as I stood in the visiting line, waiting to be processed through. Sweat beaded on my forehead from the physical stress this simple activity inflicted on my damaged body.

I carried a private investigator's license in the name of Karl Higgins, and the night before I'd called in a favor with Roy Clevenger, a detective who worked for OSS, Operation Safe Streets, LA County Sheriff's Department. Two months ago, while driving on the freeway, I'd stopped to help his wife. She was a California Highway Patrol officer who'd pulled over three bikers. The bikers jumped her. I pulled over and helped her out. Roy said he owed me a large favor. He knew my situation, that I was a high-demand fugitive and on the run.

I had never intended on taking him up on his offer, especially not so soon. He'd said he'd call ahead to the jail and grease the skids to get me in to see Insane Duane Eldridge.

I wore a Dodgers ball cap down low across my brow just above dark sunglasses that wrapped around my face. I'd let my beard grow and kept it neatly trimmed, glistening black with bits of gray. No one would recognize me. At least I hoped not.

My stomach clenched as I was approved by the screening deputy and passed through the barred sally port into the jail where another fresh-faced deputy stood waiting. My escort. Special treatment set up by Clevenger.

Silent inmates dressed in all blues walked the halls with their shoulders touching the walls. The smell never changed, body odor mixed with the fleeting essence of something intangible—a total lack of hope that emitted from wasted lives.

A couple of minutes later, I sat waiting for Duane Eldridge in an eight-by-eight-foot room with solid concrete walls and a beat-up government desk and three resin chairs. The fresh-faced deputy who'd escorted me said it would only be ten minutes or so. After thirty-five minutes, I'd begun to sweat through my shirt.

CHAPTER SEVEN

AFTER FORTY-FIVE MINUTES of solitary confinement in a lonely concrete room, I'd had enough. Sorry, Chulack, my friend, I gave it my best shot. He couldn't ask me to sit in there any longer than I already had, the entire time wondering if some deputy had made me on the way in, saw through my disguise. And, at that very moment, they were toying with their newly cornered rat, waiting to see how long I'd give it, how long I'd sit there like a boneheaded goof before I figured it out and tried to leave. Five or six of the jail's ERT— Emergency Response Team—muscle-bound gorillas were probably right outside the door waiting to take me down. *Face plant me in the highly polished concrete floor. A knee on my neck, a couple more on my back as my hands are wrenched together and cuffed.* That would be it. I'd never again see the light of day, never see my children, my unborn child. Never again see that wonderful light in Marie's eyes. Paranoia ruled the day.

I put my hand on the doorknob, ready to exit the interview room, scared to death of what I'd find on the other side. The nerve to think I could pull this off. The deputies weren't stupid like in the novels and movies. Sure, they had to be waiting on the other side, waiting to laugh their damn asses off. I'd pulled this same trick once before and gotten away with it. Tricked my way into the jail to visit my brother, Noble. That's what had given me the confidence to try it again. Like a bank robber who goes back and tries to rob the same bank twice. What a fool.

Before I could turn the knob, the door swung inward. I jumped back. My legs bumped into the desk. I teetered, almost fell, moved to the left and around to the other side. In came a woman with short brown hair wearing civilian clothes, a white long-sleeve blouse, black form-fitting slacks, and a belt with an empty pancake holster on her hip. Her laminated ID was clipped over her shirt pocket. *Detective Helen Hellinger.* Her intense brown eyes searched for mine without any luck, unable to penetrate the dark sunglasses. She had a light scar, more a line that started on her forehead and curved down the side of her face to the bottom of her cheek. It added a great deal to her character and enhanced an oddly exotic beauty. Her name, that scar, bubbled up from my memory. I knew this woman, not personally but her story. If I was correct, she was a deputy made of case-hardened steel. A living, breathing legend. It had to be her. Her peers tagged her *Wonder Woman.* Cops had to categorize people: good guys and monsters. It made their world easier to understand.

She stood there for a moment, a leather-bound notebook in hand. *Don't panic; she might just have the wrong room.*

She said nothing and stared. An interrogation ploy that I, too, had used often in the past. Let the subject stew as long as possible. See if he or she would break and talk first, give something away, a wedge into their story, something to exploit.

"Ah . . ." I said, "can I help you? I think you have the wrong interview room. I'm using this one."

She didn't smile and opened her notebook to check her notes as the door behind her closed with a finality that took my breath away. My knees, weak from recuperation, or out of fear, eased me down into the resin chair.

She stood in front of the desk and looked up from her notebook. "Karl Higgins? You're a private investigator for the defense of Duane Eugene Eldridge?"

"That's right. Where's Eldridge? I have other interviews to conduct besides this one, and I really need to get moving. I'm beginning to think you guys are holding me up on purpose just because I work for the other team."

She glared at me. "Can you please take off your sunglasses?"

I said nothing, didn't move, and stared back. My Dodgers ball cap, sunglasses, and beard had given me some cover, and to some degree, a false sense of security. I wasn't about to give up one iota of that advantage. I couldn't afford to.

As legend has it, Wonder Woman completed her time working the jail and transferred out to Palmdale, a Los Angeles County Sheriff's substation in the high desert. She finished her training with a TO—training officer—and received top marks. After a year she was promoted to training officer and had a trainee in the car when it happened.

She was driving to a "shots fired" call and had the green signal on Highway 138 and 47th Street. The intersection was clear—at least she thought so when she entered it. A drunk driver on 47th ran the red at high speed and T-boned the patrol car on her side, just ahead of the driver's door. The patrol car spun three times, jumped the curb, and ended up under a gasoline tanker off-loading fuel at the corner gas station.

The airbags deployed, but the intrusion into the patrol car pinned Helen to her seat, the steering wheel pressing into her chest. Gas leaked from the damaged Empire gas tanker truck. Steam from the compromised radiator hissed from under the hood of the crumpled patrol car. The fire department was en route, but no way could they ever get there in time. Not before the loose gas came in contact with the hot cop car. Her left arm was pinned to her side and blood blurred her vision from a deep cut on her face. By her estimate, she only had seconds to live. Her trainee tugged on her right arm, trying to pull her free, too new to this world of violence to see the futility of his efforts. She yelled at him and couldn't get his attention. With her only free hand she slapped his face, hard. "Boot, give me your handgun." He immediately complied. She was pressed over on her side and couldn't reach her own. She told him, "Now, get all those lookie-loos back. Get them all back two hundred feet, you hear me, boot? Do it now." The trainee complied as sirens reached out to her. Still too far. Too late by mere minutes. No way was she going to burn to death. She wouldn't let that happen. She held the gun barrel pressed to her forehead and waited. And waited.

Now, in the interview room of MCJ, Helen took out a slim digital recorder, turned it on, and sat it on the desk. My heart skipped several beats before coming back to normal.

"What's going on? What are you doing?"

"Is this the first time you've been here to interview inmate Eldridge?"

"You know it is based on the visitor log. Was that a test to see if I'd tell you the truth?"

"No, of course not. Why? Should I be testing you? You know . . . you look vaguely familiar. Have we worked together on something before?"

I swallowed hard. "No."

She must be working the Emily Mosley kidnap task force. They'd run out of leads and were grasping at straws. They had Eldridge's file flagged for visitors. When I asked to see him, it set off an alert and the jail watch deputy had called her. That's why it took so long for her to get there. Why I had to wait so long. Why had I not thought of that ahead of time, about the file being flagged?

When she waited again for me to say something else, I stood. "If you don't bring my client here right now, I'm going to file a formal complaint with your watch commander."

"Are you a retired cop?"

"No. But I know who you are."

"Is that right?" She stared at me and allowed the long pause to hang between us.

"Yes, I do," I finally said.

"Then you have me at a disadvantage, Mr. Higgins. Are you just trying to change the subject?"

"Not at all. Now if you're not going to bring down my client, I'm leaving."

She finally let loose with a smile, crooked on one side. The kind of smile a cat has just before it eats the canary. She held up the flat of her hand. "Take it easy. You're acting like a criminal. Just show me some identification, answer a few questions, and you'll be on your way."

"I'm not obligated to answer any questions until you tell me what's going on. And I already showed my ID when I came in through the sally port."

"What's with the belligerent attitude?"

"I don't like being braced without a good reason."

"Ah, *braced* is a cop word. Are you sure you're not an ex-cop?"

Geez, she was good. She was reading me like a book. I couldn't afford to say another word and stood silent waiting for her to make the next move.

She nodded. "How come you don't have a case file to reference when you talk to your client?"

"Case file? Are you kidding? You think the DA has already surrendered discovery on this matter? Eldridge has only been in custody a couple of days. The attorneys involved on both sides still have to do all that legal footwork. You know what I'm talking about. They move round and round each other until the judge says stop."

She nodded. She'd known the answer before she'd asked it. Another test. She was better than good.

"I know what this is," I said. "You're trying to weasel information out of me regarding that kidnap, of which my client has been wrongfully accused. It's because you have nowhere else to look, a go-nowhere case. That's why you're here jacking me up. And I don't like getting jacked up."

She reached over and turned off the tape recorder. "Look, pal, don't get all jacked up over this. I'm not here to box you into a corner. Although, it looks like it wouldn't be too difficult to do."

"Then what do you want from me?"

"Nothing really, just hoping to get lucky. I was already here for the homicide investigation and thought I'd cover all the bases. See if you knew anything."

"Homicide investigation? Know anything about what?"

"Do you know of anyone who would want to kill Duane Eldridge?"

CHAPTER EIGHT

"What's happened to Eldridge?"

"Two thugs up on the tier in 3600 held him by his ankles and dropped him. Landed on his noggin on the bottom floor. DOA."

I realized my mouth had sagged open as I eased down in the chair and said in a half-whisper, "Sorry, Chulack."

"What's that?"

"What? Oh, nothing."

"Now that I've officially informed you this is a murder investigation, I'm only going to ask you one more time: let me see some identification. No bullshit or you're going to find yourself in cuffs getting booked in at IRC, Inmate Reception Center." She held out her hand, waiting, her eyes drilling into my sunglasses.

I reached into my pocket and handed her the mocked-up FBI creds. Glad that I had them and only hoped they worked.

She took them from my hand as she continued to stare into my sunglasses. She didn't like the glasses and was mad I wouldn't take them off. Mad that she didn't have complete control of the situation. She finally looked down at the creds. It wasn't what she expected. Her mouth started to drop open, but she recovered quickly. "FBI? You're FBI? Why did you come in here masquerading as a public defender investigator?"

I snatched the creds from her hand. "Are you familiar with why Eldridge was arrested?"

"Yes, of course I am. Kidnapping. It's still an open case."

"That's right. Do you know whose child has been kidnapped?"

Her eyes shifted from confident to discomfort. For the first time since she'd walked in, I'd taken the initiative. "No," she said, "I'm not part of that task force. I'm just here investigating the jail 187."

I came around the desk, got closer, and leaned in. "Emily Mosely is the granddaughter of *Deputy Director* Dan Chulack."

"I see."

"I don't think you do. Not when you play little chickenshit games keeping me on ice in here when I could be out there looking for the dirtbags who took his granddaughter."

"I . . . Wait just a damn minute. It says in his file that Eldridge lawyered up and that no one could talk to him without his attorney present. What then, are you doing here?"

I leaned in closer yet. "Do I look like your standard tight-assed Feebee?"

She didn't answer. Wonder Woman backed up a step.

"I'm not," I said. "I only get called in on special assignments where . . . well, let's just say I have a gentle touch when it comes to interrogation. I was working a very important caper. I was under deep cover for nine months in Detroit, and they pulled me out to handle this. That should tell you how much emphasis they're putting on this investigation. And you put me on ice in this room for forty minutes? Are you kidding me? Who's your supervisor?"

"Don't you dare threaten me. I've done nothing wrong here. So what, you got detained for forty minutes. I'm investigating a homicide and I have every authority to identify you."

"Well, now that you've accomplished that, let's get on the phone. You call your boss and I'll call mine. Let's see who gets transferred back to the jail working graveyard."

Her turn to come in close on me, her face flushed red, the angular scar standing out white, her breath, Wrigley's fresh. "Mister, last time I checked, this was a Los Angeles County Jail facility. Nowhere does it say FBI has any jurisdiction in here. You're a guest. Time for you to get out, now. Before I arrange a room for you with a complimentary overnight stay."

That was my cue to leave. I'd pushed too hard. I knew from her background and history that it wasn't beyond her anger range to handcuff an arrogant FBI agent and hold him for a supervisor. I couldn't let that happen. "Wait. Let's both just take a breath here."

She spoke through clenched teeth. "I'm not excited or out of control, are you?"

"Do you have a line on the two thugs who picked Eldridge up by his ankles and dropped him on his head?"

"That's jail business and has nothing to do with the *Fan Belt Inspectors*." Then she caught onto where I was going with the question. "So, you're saying that Eldridge was a hit. That he was a loose end in the kidnapping and someone had him whacked?"

I didn't move or answer.

She said, "And now you think your last best lead is the two thug suspects?" She'd eased up a little. Started to relax. This revelation gave her the motivation she needed in her murder and a direction for her investigation that she didn't have before walking into the interview room.

"Yes, that's right." I extended my hand. "And I want to say I'm sorry for coming on so strong. I've been up for forty hours straight. I know it's no excuse, but I also just flushed nine months of deep-cover work down the toilet. Only to come here and find the guy I was supposed to interview turned into a pancake on 3600. Can we start over?"

She didn't take my hand. "The two thugs who did the deed pulled their tee shirt collars up over their noses to cover their faces. They weren't housed in that module. They could be from anywhere in a jail that has seven thousand inmates. We've interviewed just about everyone in the module and we got nothing on the murder. Zip."

Contrary to popular civilian belief, inmates during the day come and go from their cells; they move about the entire jail with impunity. All they need is a pass from the module deputy, an excuse for which there were many: chapel, legal visit, medical, commissary, regular visiting, law library, and the list goes on.

"What about his cellie? Would you mind if I talked to him?"

"I personally interviewed him. He's got nothing. He said he didn't see a thing. Nobody saw a thing."

"Let me guess, he was on his bunk doing hobby craft when Eldridge went over the side?"

"Something like that." Her head cocked sideways at my comment. Only deputies knew that often-used "on-my-bunk-doing-hobby" excuse.

"I came a long way at the behest of some bosses pretty high up the food chain in the *Fan Belt Inspectors*. I'd rather not come back empty-handed. Would you mind if I had a talk with the cellie?"

She smothered a smile. "I can arrange that, but I'm sitting in on it, no arguments."

"I—"

"I said it's not up for debate. Are you feeling okay? You're sweating and you look a little pale."

I put my hand on my stomach as I eased down in the chair. "I'm okay, just a bad taco, is all." I had pushed it too hard emotionally and physically.

"I'll go across the hall to the watch deputy's office and have him send down the inmate."

"You can't just stick your head out the door and yell across the hall to the watch deputy's office?" I didn't want her out of my sight. I didn't want her calling the FBI to confirm my bona fides.

She shot me a crooked smile. "It's right across the hall, just a few steps. If I stick my head out the door and yell at him, he'll think I'm some kinda prima donna, you know like an FBI agent or something. You want a cup of coffee?"

"Sure, that'd be great."

She went out the door. I put my head down on the table to wait and fret. She was going to call the FBI and check. She was too good a cop not to. Now I could only hope she got a hold of Chulack. Anyone else and my goose was cooked. I couldn't help thinking that since the minute I'd walked into MCJ, it was the same as if I, too, were trapped under an Empire tanker truck leaking gas, with a gun to my head waiting for it to light off with a big whump.

CHAPTER NINE

AN HOUR LATER, or it might've been ten minutes, the door opened to the interview room. In walked a white male with a prominent Adam's apple on a neck too long for his body. He wore inmate blues that hung off his thin, five-and-a-half-foot frame. He kept his blond-gray hair shorn close to the scalp. His huge smile seemed permanently affixed, displaying perfectly white teeth that had to be dentures, tops and bottoms. With his big nose and that neck, he looked like a cartoon vulture perched on a branch waiting for his prey to expire. I was about to tell him he had the wrong door when Helen shoved him deeper into the room.

"What's going on?" I asked.

She came in further and closed the door. "What are you talking about? You wanted Eldridge's cellmate. Well, here he is."

"Eldridge was a Crip, a Rollin' Sixties, housed on 3600. That's a Crip module. It's a high Mod. This guy can't be right, he's a low mod." I didn't want to sound prejudiced by adding, "And he's white."

He moved over, stood in the corner, and watched us.

Helen said, "I thought the same thing and checked with classification. That's what took so long. They said this guy is like a ghost and has a history of getting along with everyone." She shrugged.

"With all the overcrowding, that was the cell he drew." Helen crossed her arms under her breasts and leaned back in the other corner to watch.

I pointed to the chair. "Sit." He didn't move and kept the smile firmly in place, his horse teeth peeking out between his lips.

"What's your name?"

"Howard Owsley." His voice came out in a rasp, like someone who didn't do a lot of talking.

The name hit a nerve. "I know you?"

"I don't think so, but I think I might know you."

My heart took off at a gallop. Did this guy know me as Bruno Johnson? I ignored his comment and could only hope he wouldn't elaborate. "What's your street name?"

His smile stayed the same, but his blue eyes glowed brighter. "Whitey."

"Ah, that's right. Whitey Roberts."

"I've been known to go by that name. Don't like it all that much. I prefer the Owl."

Helen said, "You know him?"

"Never met him, but he's been in the papers a couple of times, not his photo or all his names. Just as Howard Owsley, not Robert White. The paper got that wrong. Good thing or he'd probably be dead right now." I turned back to Whitey. "What are you in for this time?"

He shrugged, pulled the resin chair out, and sat down. "What I did or didn't do has no bearing on what's going on right here, right now. I want a coffee, two creams with lots of sugar."

"You really don't want to start out this way, sidestepping my questions. Answer me true, or I'm going to come over this desk, you understand?"

Still with the smile, no fear in his eyes as he waved his hand. "Take it easy. I know this game inside and out. Let's quit wastin' time and get started. What are you offering? Then we'll take it from there. The offer better be sweet, because I got something real good."

Helen came away from the wall. "You know who dropped Eldridge off the tier?"

He looked from her back to me. "Is that really what you want to know or is there something . . . ah, more, shall we say, pressing?"

I got up, came around the desk, and slapped him hard across the face. He fell off the chair.

"Hey! Hey!" Helen yelled. "Don't do that again. I don't care if you are FBI. This is my house. You understand?" She helped Whitey up off the floor, righted the chair, and got him back in it.

Whitey rubbed his face, half stunned. "You're with the FBI now? How's that even possible?"

"Now we on the same page? You know damn well what I want to hear. No more games."

He'd lost that phony smile. The rules had been laid down, the hard way. A small trickle of blood ran from the corner of his mouth down his chin. He dabbed at it with the heel of his hand, his eyes glaring. His bottom lip started to balloon up.

Helen turned back to me. "What do you mean? How would he know? What's going on?"

"Did you run his rap before you interviewed him?"

"Of course I did. Ten arrests, but only two convictions. Ten armed robberies, eight banks, and two jewelry stores, no guns, just notes. And I gotta say this guy does not fit the profile of a 211 artist, even if he used a note. Just look at him."

"Hey?" Whitey said, indignant.

I said, "On those convictions, what were the dispositions? He do any time?"

"Ten months on the first one, and then only six months on the aggravated term for the second. Not very much for either one. Those were gifts, really. They went too easy on him."

"Why do you think?" I asked.

I turned to Whitey before she could answer. "Why don't *you* tell her?"

He just stared.

"Sorry I had to slap you. I don't have the patience or the time for you to yank my chain and try to game us. Now you know where I'm coming from. This is serious business."

"Yeah." He gingerly rubbed his face; it had a red handprint emblazoned across the pale skin on his cheek. "It is all about the business and you said you do know who I am. If you do, then you know that I know the game, and how it's played. I know it better than anyone in this room. So, you want to dance. Let's dance."

"What's going on?" Helen asked.

"This is the White Rat."

"Don't call me that."

I stared at Whitey as I spoke to Helen. "He's a professional rat. Not for money; he doesn't rat for money. He rats for years added to his life. He did rob all of those banks. Each time he was arrested and went to jail, he asked around and identified the most sensational criminal in custody in that particular facility. Then he finagled, begged, bribed, did whatever he had to do to get into that guy's cell. He endeared himself to the poor slob, his cellie, who then confided in him. Then Whitey went to the DA and traded information for his freedom. Did I get that right, Whitey? Isn't that the way it goes?"

He shrugged. "Seems this is your show, you got the floor. For now, anyway."

Helen looked stunned. "How come I've never heard of this guy?"

"He always gets more than enough evidence on who he rats out, which leaves the guy no option but to plead guilty. That way Whitey here never has to testify, and he stays under the radar. His name game helps too. Otherwise, his compadres would find out about it and take him off the board for being a rat. Take him by the ankles and drop him off the tier. That's the only way he can pull it off."

"That's a dangerous game," Helen said.

"Yes, it is. But his game is coming to an end fast. Because the last time, the White Rat screwed up. Didn't you, Whitey?"

He clucked his dentures at me. "I said don't call me that. You do it again and you'll regret it."

I started to come around the desk again, raising my hand, a fist this time.

He flinched backward. "Okay. Okay. Take it easy, big man. Cool your jets."

I moved back.

Helen asked, "What happened the last time he was arrested?"

"He's been on the run for a while. I only heard about it through the grapevine. What was it, Whitey, four years ago? Five?"

Again, he said nothing.

I couldn't tell Helen how I knew. At the time, I'd still been on the violent crimes team and had been asked to chase down Howard Owsley, aka Robert White, aka the White Rat. But he didn't meet the team's criteria. He wasn't violent enough. The DA wanted him real bad. Our targets had to have killed someone, usually several someones. The brass insisted we put him on our B list, which we rarely got to. Multiple murder was a thriving business. Whitey was more a con man than anything else and had evaded arrest by changing his identity and staying under the radar.

"Let me guess," I said. "He was probably arrested for a drunk driver under a fake driver's license and when they fingerprinted him his real name popped up with the warrant."

"Close," Helen said. "Drunk and disorderly in a bar. The warrant's a no bail for accessory after the fact, obstruction of justice, criminal conspiracy, and about seven other charges. The DA must be really pissed at this guy."

"They are. The last deal Whitey made didn't work out. His new cellmate he was ratting on wouldn't plead guilty; the cellmate insisted he was innocent and that Whitey was lying. That meant Whitey had to testify. The cellmate got life without the possibility of parole, solely based on Whitey's testimony. Six months later the marvels of DNA directed the cops to the real killer. Whitey can't pull this stunt to get out anymore. He has no credibility, and if his fellow crooks don't already know, the word will get out. Soon he won't be safe in jail anymore. He was lucky he pulled this one off the way he did. This deal here is definitely his last hurrah."

"So, you're saying," Helen said, "that Howard here found out that Eldridge was involved in a high-profile kidnapping and somehow got himself placed in Eldridge's cell?"

I didn't answer and looked at Whitey.

He yawned. "We going to dance or we going to talk ancient history all afternoon?"

CHAPTER TEN

HELEN'S EXPRESSION HELD no emotion. "He doesn't have anything or he would've told me when I interviewed him. That was only two hours ago. I gave him every opportunity."

Whitey pasted on that creepy smile accented by his overly white dentures and clucked them like a cheap windup toy. "You want to tell her, big man?"

I said, "He didn't say anything when you interviewed him because you can't do him any good. He needs a fed to get him out of a mess this big."

Whitey gave her a smug nod in agreement and shrugged. She didn't like being made a fool. She came closer, sat on the edge of the desk, and gave him the stink eye. "Not even a fed can get you out of these charges, you little dweeb. You have a no-bail hold and the DA's pissed. The DA holds all the cards here, not the feds. You're out of luck this time, pal. This FBI agent can't make you any kind of deal. No way, no how."

Whitey, still with the smile, leered at her, his eyes hungry. He let his gaze drop to her lap. He clacked his dentures, leaned a few inches closer to Helen's leg, and hovered over her hip as he closed his eyes and took in a big whiff.

She pulled back and slapped him harder than I had. His dentures flew out of his mouth, hit the wall, and clattered to the floor. "That's for being a pig." She looked at me. "We done here?"

I shook my head. Whitey fell to his knees, moaning, and crawled after his chompers. "In all my life, I have never been treated this poorly. I swear ta gawd, I'm going to make you pay dear for this, you jack-booted cun—" He caught himself. "You wait and see if I don't." Minus his teeth, his words came out slushy, all of them heavily laden with Ss.

I came around the desk and helped him to his feet. He wiggled his teeth back in without wiping them off. I shoved him. He fell backward into the chair. The chair slid and hit the desk. "Give me something. If you want me to play ball, you have to prove you can produce what you say you can. Give me something right now or I'm outta here and you can find some other fed dumb enough to swallow what you're selling."

He sneered at Helen. "All right. I know who did your boy up on 3600." He held up two fists, opened them at the same time, and made a whistling noise. Then: "Splat! Good luck trying to figure it out, you Dickless Tracy."

I kicked his chair. "Did you hear me? Give me something or I'm going to walk and let you deal with her on your own."

"What do you want? No way am I giving away the store before we've signed a contract with the DA." He slapped his palm with the back of his other hand. "And that contract's gotta state I'm given a get-outta-Hell-free card. A free ride on my charges or it's no soap. I'm nobody's fool."

"You think you got enough info to make that kind of trade? That's a big ask," I said.

He started to stand, this time sneering at me. I shoved him back down.

He rubbed the red handprint on his face. "From what I hear, right now you got nothin', zero, zippo, nada. I'm holding a lot of cards on this one. I got plenty enough to deal. Get the DA in here now, so I can blow this pop stand."

The way he talked, he had one foot in the current day and the other in the seventies B movies.

"Quit bumpin' your gums and give me something, a small part of it to show you're not talking out the left side of your ass. You do that and I'll get you out."

He looked at Helen, then back at me. "All right. The two million, you missed it, right?"

"You know we did. That was in the papers and all over the news. Anyone who can read or watch TV knows that much. You know where the money is? Or at least how it got away?"

He nodded with that perverted smile again. "Have your people check the bathroom in the condo."

"It's a townhouse."

"Tomato, toe-motto."

"It's already been checked."

"Check it again."

Cell phones aren't allowed in the jail. I had to check mine in at the sally port. I held out my hand to Helen. "Let me have your cell."

Helen didn't argue or make an excuse. She didn't ask how I knew she'd smuggled one in and handed her cell over. I dialed the burner number from memory.

Chulack picked up on the first ring and didn't say a word.

"It's me," I said.

"Whatta you got?"

"Check the bathroom."

"Got it." He hung up.

Helen said, "This is a total waste of time. You can't give this perv anything for his information, not if what you said is true. He's made himself unreliable and no DA or judge will give him squat. Trust me on this. He's a useless waste of skin."

Whitey said to her, "How about that coffee, babe. And because of that slap, I want a bear claw or, better yet, a raspberry Danish. And heat it up with some butter."

She leaned in, teeth clenched. "You know what you can do with—"

"Hellinger," I said. She looked at me for a long moment, her eyes angry. She left the room and slammed the door.

Emboldened, Whitey got up out of the chair and sat on the edge of the desk, testing his newfound importance. "I don't know what's going on here, pally. I mean with you being here . . . like this and all, but let's just say, I started out with a handful of information to trade, and as soon as I stepped through that door and saw you . . . Well, now I got a whole bag full of information. A bag full of gold." He grinned that phony white grin.

I took him by the throat, lifting him off his feet, moving him. The knot of his Adam's apple was hard like a walnut against my palm. He flailed as I shoved him up to the wall and squeezed. He choked and sputtered. I got up in his face. I lifted my sunglasses so he could see my eyes, see the last truth he'd ever hear. "You'd be well served to forget whatever you think you know. Because if you put it on the table as part of any kind of deal, then I won't have anything else to lose. You get my meaning?"

His dentures bulged forward in his mouth, the pink tip of his tongue peeking out from in between the chompers. His eyes were wide and white, as his face swelled red. He nodded.

"We have an understanding?"

He nodded again.

"One more thing. I'm not your friend. Don't call me *pally* again. I make this deal, *you will* tell me everything you know, holding nothing back. You understand?"

He grunted, trying to speak.

I let him go. He slid down the wall to the floor, coughing and choking.

CHAPTER ELEVEN

WHITEY WAS STILL on the floor a couple minutes later when Helen returned.

She took one look at him and smiled.

"He fell off his chair," I said. "He's clumsy. You're clumsy, right, Whitey? Get your ass up."

He struggled onto his hands and knees and then up into the chair. "That's right, I'm clumsy." His words came out in a rasp.

Helen handed him a coffee in a Styrofoam cup and tossed a stale cake donut with pink frosting onto his lap. She moved to the corner and crossed her arms under her breasts. "He say anything while I was gone?"

"Tell her, Whitey."

He popped the white plastic lid off the cup and took a sip of the steamless tan liquid. "Tell her what?"

"What she wants to know. Who turned Eldridge into a human cannonball?"

"No. Not without a signed contract from the—"

I stood. "I thought you and I had an agreement . . . an *understanding*."

He glared, trying to burn a hole right through me.

I nodded at him. "You said you know me. If that's true, you know more than anything else, I am a man of my word. Tell her."

He held his glare a moment more, then turned to address Helen. "I only know him as T-Dog. But he's an Avalon Gangster Crip. Some call him Little T-Dog. The other one . . . the other one. I don't know his name, but he's got a tattoo on his forearm, his right arm" —he pointed to his own arm—"that says, 'Police Killa Bitch.' He won't be hard to find with that one. He's a big dude. Real big, and mean as a snake. I hope he kicks both your asses for the way you've treated me. And he will, if you give him half a chance."

Helen looked at me, stunned that he'd given it up that easily. She took out her notebook and wrote down the new information.

Whitey looked at me. "You better be a man of your word and get me out."

Helen looked up from her writing, her eyes saying no way that was going to happen.

Her cell phone rang. She answered it. "Detective Hellinger. Yes, hold on." She handed me the phone.

Chulack said, "We missed it the first time. And we shouldn't have. It was a big mistake. Over the sink in the bathroom, there are some ceiling tiles with light smudges almost invisible. We moved them and found an access, a low narrow access between the drop ceiling and the peak of the roof that runs across the top of all four townhouses. A real tight crawl space. Someone knocked a hole in the drywall into the next townhouse, and the next two after that. The last one is vacant. They simply walked right out the front door with the money. This is great information. You got anything else?"

I looked at Whitey. "I gave someone my word. You need to get him out. I'll personally run with him and make sure he's not blowing smoke."

"What's his name?"

"It's going to be a tough pull."

"What's his name, Bruno?"

"He's going to need a full pass if his info works out. I gave him my word and—"

"His name?"

"Howard Owsley." I reached over and grabbed Whitey's wrist and read his booking number from his wristband.

Chulack said, "When do you want him out?"

"Tomorrow morning at nine. I'll pick him up at the gate."

Whitey jumped up. "Wait. I gotta get out of here tonight."

I held up my finger. He went silent.

Chulack said, "You need anything else?"

"I can't talk right now."

"I understand. Call me later. This is good work. Thanks for this, my friend. I owe you."

"I'll call you." I hung up.

Whitey spoke with pink frosting and cake donut mashed up in his mouth and smeared across his too-white dentures. "I can't go back to my house tonight, not after she goes and jacks up T-Dog. I'll be dead meat."

Inmates all referred to their cells as their house.

I said, "Close your mouth when you talk. Didn't your daddy teach you any manners?"

Helen closed her leather notebook.

I said to her, "You have to wait until nine a.m. tomorrow before you brace T-Dog."

"Wait. Wait," Whitey said. "I still can't go back to my house. What if someone saw me come in here with you two dicklickers. No way. I'm no good to you dead. I need to get out tonight. To-fucking-night."

I was dead on my feet, running on empty, and desperately needed to lay my head someplace safe. "Can you stick him in isolation, like maybe the infirmary on 2000, put an extra duty deputy on him until tomorrow morning?"

"We could do that. Maybe." She turned to Whitey. "Did you see T-Dog and this other guy drop Eldridge, or did you just hear about it?"

"I saw it. I was standing right there when he went over kicking and screaming. It was awful, that noise when he hit. I swear ta gawd it sounded just like a watermelon run over by a big truck. Cut him off mid-scream. I can still hear—"

"He's still not a good wit," Helen said. "His last time in court he lied."

"That's the best you're going to get. It's a jailhouse killing of a kidnap suspect." I fell short of saying "kidnap/*murder* suspect." "Can you do it or not? Isolate him until tomorrow morning?"

"Is he going to testify?"

"Yes."

"Ah, man," Whitey said.

"I'll do it," Helen said. "But I *don't* think the person you had on the phone has the juice to get him out. Not a chance in hell."

"Lady," Whitey said, "you're about as dumb as a box of rocks. Don't you know who you're talking to here?" He pointed to me.

"Yeah, she does," I said. "An FBI agent who has plenty of connections. Quit worrying about it. I gave you my word."

"FBI?" Whitey said, "Oh, yeah, right . . . Right." He'd almost blown my cover.

"I'll see you in the morning," I said. "Now I have to get out of here. You keep your head down, Whitey." I came around the desk and offered my hand to Helen. She shook it. With her other hand, she tried to lift my sunglasses. I stopped her and smiled. "Not today, Detective. Maybe some other time."

"Yeah," she said, "and soon."

CHAPTER TWELVE

I MOVED OUT through the jail visiting exit down the long walk mixing among all the others, who Wicks would have described as GUM, the Great Unwashed Masses. Some coming, some going, very few with any hope left in them. My energy level was zero, my feet heavy as blocks of concrete. I was on the last of my reserves, burning fumes and about to pass out. Sweat beaded on my forehead and ran into my eyes, stinging and blurring my vision. I made it to the parking lot and stopped twice to lean against some random cars to rest. At that rate, it was going to take me an hour to get back to Drago's car. How was I going to get this job done? Today, I'd only been out and about for three hours and it damn near killed me. I had grossly overestimated my recovery and fitness level.

Far up ahead, a door opened and closed. Drago appeared out of nowhere, his hulk shading, blocking out the sun. He took hold of my shoulders and hurried us to the car, my shoe leather barely touching the ground. He didn't like being anywhere close to a jail and moved us right along.

"I'm sorry, man," he said, "about this morning. I shouldn't have acted like some kinda spoiled brat."

"It's okay."

"No, it's not. Look at you. You can barely walk on your own and I'm actin' like some kind of horse's ass. I'm sorry, man. I got my mind right now. I'm with ya, whatever you need."

"Just get me back to the hotel so I can lay down and rest."

We made it to the car. He gently picked me up as if I were brittle porcelain and set me in the passenger seat. He came around, got in, started up, and headed out.

I put my head against the doorframe and closed my eyes.

"You okay, bossman?"

"I'm fine, just worn to a frazzle. Give me a minute to regroup."

"What happened in there? You talk to the guy?"

"No. Two dudes tossed our guy off the tier. He landed on his head. Drago?"

"Yeah?"

"The people who did it might know I came to visit. Work counter surveillance hard, make sure our tail's clean. We don't want anyone following us back to the hotel."

"You rest easy. I got this."

I'd seen Drago's countersurveillance moves; no one was going to stay with us. I wanted more than anything else to let sleep tug me down into the depths of blackness, escape the horrible regret, the horror over what happened to Bosco, escape it for an hour or so. But for that wish to come true I needed dreamless sleep, which had rarely happened in the last two months. This time, being so tired might help. I had a couple of things to do first. I pulled my cell phone from my pocket and hit the speed dial.

Chulack picked up. "Go."

"Did you work your magic? Is Whitey getting out tomorrow morning?"

"Yes. You get anything else?"

"I need you to get a writ and have two bodies from MCJ transferred to federal custody. Hold them at the Roybal Building so I can talk to them later on if I need to."

"Right. Who are they?"

"They are the two who dropped Eldridge off the tier. He landed on his head. He didn't make it; he's 927D."

"*Eldridge is dead?* Hold on one." He held the phone away from his mouth. "Oakley, get over here. Did you know Eldridge was murdered at MCJ?"

"That info's just coming in now." Oakley's voice smaller and distant.

My guess was Oakley hadn't known, and now made his feeble excuse rather than suffer the wrath of a deputy director.

"Get over there. I want everything they got on it."

"Yes, sir."

Chulack came back on the phone. "I'm sorry, Bruno. I'm on it now. You've gotten more information in two hours than these fifty agents and deputies have working it for two weeks. What are the names of these two suspects?"

"Whitey—"

"You mean Howard Owsley?"

"That's right. He gave up the two suspects, but Whitey knows a lot more about the kidnap than he's tellin' me right now. That's why I need him out tomorrow morning. He said the two that tossed Eldridge over the tier were Avalon Gangster Crips. One goes by T-Dog or Little T-Dog. The other is a running buddy, same gang, no moniker, but he has a distinctive tattoo on his forearm, 'Police Killa Bitch.'"

"Okay, that's plenty enough to work with. I'll get it done."

"I got a detective named Hellinger, who's working the murder. She promised she won't brace those two until tomorrow morning. You have until tomorrow morn—"

"I'll have them in our custody in less than three hours. What else do you need?"

"I want them sequestered, no one talks to them, no phone calls. They are my plan B in case Whitey doesn't work out."

"You thinking they hit Eldridge so he wouldn't talk about the kidnap?"

"Yes. It has to be. Anything else is too big of a coincidence. Hold them for kidnap, conspiracy, and murder."

"This is great stuff. Keep it up."

"Not so great. I got cornered in there and had to use those FBI creds. I'm sorry, it's going to put you on the cross."

"I already know about it. Hellinger called. I told you, I got it covered. You just keep doing what you're doing. I don't want you to worry about anything in your rearview mirror. I've got that. You just keep driving forward . . . and as fast as you can."

"That's the other thing, I'm wasted. I mean, I can hardly keep my eyes open. I'm going back to . . . to my crib to sleep." I didn't want to say the name of the hotel over the phone. "I'll be back on it in the morning."

"I understand. Like I said, you have worked miracles already. I've enough here to keep me busy. Call me in the morning. No, call me anytime if you think of something. Anytime, day or night, you call me."

"You got it."

"Thanks, Bruno."

"We're not there yet. Talk to you in the morning." I hung up.

Drago kept his eyes on the road. "You're not talking about Whitey, the White Rat, are you? You can't work with that little puke. You can't trust one damn word that comes from his mouth."

"Thank you, my friend, for being concerned. I agree, and under normal circumstances, I wouldn't even think about using him. But these aren't normal circumstances. I promise to be careful. And besides, I have you to back my play. You can squish him like a bug if he does us wrong."

"With pleasure."

"Now, I need to close my eyes just for a couple of minutes. Wake me when we get to the hotel."

"You got it."

I closed my eyes and fought off the darkness for a moment more. "Tomorrow," I said, "can you get a truck with tinted windows? With the constant pain in my hip, this car is too difficult for me to get in and out of. A truck with one of those jump seats to tote Whitey around in."

"Not a problem."

"And, Karl?"

"Yeah, bossman."

"I'm going to need a war bag, body armor, guns, night scope, binocs, stun gun, at least three sets of Peerless handcuffs, the whole shebang." I opened one eye and caught him looking at me.

"The way you just asked, I suppose you don't want me to tell Marie about it, is that right?"

"That would be great, buddy."

He nodded and didn't answer. I wasn't sure he wouldn't tell her if she asked him outright. Something else I'd have to deal with but only if it came over the plate as a fastball. Even so, I'd still be in trouble with Marie; to her, an omission was the same as a lie.

A split second before I let the darkness take me, I cringed at the thought of what I'd find down in the dark depths of nothingness.

Bosco. My son.

"No, mister, please don't. Don't."

"Bosco!"

I jerked forward. Looked around. I was sitting in Drago's car. I'd slept the entire way from the jail back to the hotel. We were parked in a parking garage; cool mixed with the dim light–almost dark, shadows everywhere. The sudden quiet stillness rang loud in my ears.

Every moment of every day, I tried like hell to shove the image of Bosco's eyes, his words—push them far back into that safe part of my brain, to hide them forever.

Tried and failed.

Sweat soaked my shirt collar, and my chest worked hard to keep up with my breaths. Drago had let me sleep some while he patiently waited.

"Take it easy, boss," Drago said. "You might need to see a head shrinker, you keep waking up like this."

"What? Oh, no, I'm fine. I'm fine." I said it twice like I was trying to convince myself.

The ugly memories always came at me unrelenting in the form of night terrors. They always replayed exactly the same with both violent sounds and ugly smells included. Odors were never supposed to enter into nightmares. *My* brain hadn't been informed of that bit of psychological trivia.

The way it happened, the way it unfolded, seemed simple enough. Events so random and yet monumental always start out so simple.

"You wanna talk about it?"

"What? No ... I ..." I didn't want to tell the tale, to bring it out into the light of day. But maybe that's what I needed to do, talk about it. Drago was a good friend and wouldn't judge. I didn't need someone judging. Guilt already smothered the breath out of me. I closed my eyes, sat back, and forced myself to say the words. I started talking.

CHAPTER THIRTEEN

TWO MONTHS EARLIER, the day was bright and warm as I drove down the freeway headed for a meeting when I spotted a problem on the side of the road. A California Highway Patrol officer had pulled over three outlaw motorcycle gang members. The officer was all alone. I pulled over, deciding to wait until her backup arrived.

In a really screwed-up sort of way, outlaw motorcycle gangs mirror the Boy Scouts. The bikers earn patches to wear on their cuts, their denim vests. Each patch or "rocker" symbolizes an accomplishment they achieved. Dirty, ugly achievements like having sex with a cadaver, armed robbery, rape, murder, and even assaulting a police officer.

Two of the young Visigoths wore new cuts without any patches. They had everything to prove. The older one with the long brown hair, his cut hanging heavy with soiled patches, supervised the other two. He would bear witness to their accomplishments. The young ones would want to make a good show for the older one, thus making the situation that much more dangerous.

They all got off the bikes and stood in a group. The CHP officer stayed too long in her car calling out the stop. If she wanted any chance at all of controlling the situation, she needed to get out right away and start giving orders before the Goths had time to develop a plan and work up their nerve. Patrol tactics 101.

I got out and moved around to the shoulder and stayed by my rental car.

The CHP officer finally got out. She looked to be about five-one or -two and to weigh a hundred and twenty-five with all her equipment on.

The old biker with the dirty brown hair and one of the young ones looked White-Caucasian, but overly tanned to the point of appearing Hispanic. The third one took his helmet off to show curly red hair. He wore his gunfighter handlebar mustache bushy and untamed against a dark complexion. He didn't look ugly like the other two; his angular features and his freckles made him handsome in a boyish kind of way. He displayed an innocence that didn't jibe with his costume or with the men with whom he rode. All three stood at least six feet and weighed in at a buck-eighty at a minimum. Any one of them, alone, would be a handful for the officer.

As soon as she got to the front of the patrol car, the group of bikers started to move on her. She froze, hand on her gun, and pointed with her other hand. "Please step to the shoulder of the road." Over the roar of the traffic on the freeway, I could barely hear her.

Hundreds of cars zipped by, all those drivers unaware of the disaster unfolding on the side of the freeway.

The bikers didn't obey but, instead, continued to step closer to her. I didn't have any doubt. They were going to take her on. I ran a few steps up to the side of her car. The older biker saw me and hesitated. The young bucks followed suit and stopped. The CHP officer chanced it, took her eyes off her threat to look at what had caused the bikers to react.

I held up four fingers and mouthed the words "code-four?" to let her believe that I was a cop and at the same time ask if she was okay.

She barely moved her head, indicating she wasn't code-four, the fear plain in her eyes yet not in her expression. I moved up to the front of the patrol car and stood three feet from her, about six feet from the bikers.

She yelled to the bikers, "I won't tell you again, step to the shoulder of the road, and I want to see some ID."

The two young bikers looked at the older one for guidance. The older one locked eyes with me. "Who the hell are you?"

"I'm just the guy standing here on the side of the road, trying to keep you honest."

"You better step off, nigger. You don't want any part of this."

I shifted my footing, taking a combative stance. "Not gonna happen."

"Move to the side of the road. Do it now," the officer said.

No one moved for a long, fat moment.

Then the old lion took a step toward us, his hand on the side of his belt under his cut.

"He's got a ball-peen," I said. I'd caught a glimpse of it.

"I know, I saw it, too." She drew her gun and pointed it at him, center mass. "Show me your hands. Do it now. Do it right now." Her other hand moved down to the top of her radio and pushed the red emergency button. Her action changed the whole game. Now every cop in a twenty-mile radius would be responding code-three to assist her.

Except that we stood on the side of a busy freeway without easy access, not with all the traffic. Backup would take longer than normal.

Too many cops would arrive in minutes. When they came on scene, they'd ask for my ID. One of them would surely recognize me from all the bulletins put out over the last two years. The FBI wanted me for kidnap and various other felonies. I'd walked head-on into a no-win situation. I couldn't leave and I really needed to get out of there.

The older biker smirked at the officer. "What, the split tail's got the balls to drop the hammer on me? I don't think so. Take her, Dirk."

The young one called Dirk hesitated, then leapt forward, hands outstretched, shoulder down. I took two quick steps to intervene, planted my feet, and gave him a roundhouse right. He saw it coming, dodged a little, but not enough. My fist struck right on his ear and skull and vibrated up my arm. I followed with a quick uppercut to his chin that landed solid, jammed his teeth together, and mashed his lips. He stumbled, shaken to his core. He went to one knee to shrug it off.

The older biker, at the same time, took hold of the young red-headed biker and shoved him into the fray. Both junior bikers acted as cover so he could make his move on the officer.

The redheaded biker shoved hard into me. My footing ended up out of position from the punches I'd just thrown. He hit me at waist level. I backpedaled. We landed on the hood of the car, his chin close to mine, his breath minty fresh. He flailed his arms, trying to slug me, inexperienced. I took hold of his ear and pulled with everything I had, while I watched, helpless to intervene, as the older biker made his move on the officer.

The older biker swung the ball-peen high and wide. The officer, distracted for a brief moment with the fight on the hood of her unit, saw the assault too late. The hammer came down on her arm, the one holding the gun. The bone snapped with a crack. The gun flipped in the air. The older biker watched it as it fell to the ground. If he got to the gun, the bad guys would win with smoke and blood and two broken bodies left to die on the side of the road.

I kneed the redheaded biker in the belly again and again as I yanked on his ear.

The officer yelled, not in pain, but in anger over the loss of her weapon. She charged, shoving forward, her head down, her good arm cradling the shattered one. She torpedoed her head right into the older biker. He saw the move, chuckled, and sidestepped her. He swung the hammer again and caught her on the back of the head.

She dropped to the ground face-first, absolutely still. Her breath puffed the dirt.

I shoved the kid off me and dove for the gun down in the grit and broken asphalt.

I landed on the gun, a Glock nine, groped for it, fumbled it. The older biker kicked me in the face. The world wobbled. The air turned thick like a heat wave. The redheaded biker grabbed my foot, tried to pull me off the gun, and came away with my shoe. He fell back on his ass. The older biker kicked me again. I moved my face out of the way this time and took it on the shoulder. I rolled off the gun when he came at me with the ball-peen. Had to, no choice. His swing took him off balance. The blow struck me on the left arm. White pain shot up to my shoulder and turned my arm numb. Still on the ground, I swung my leg wide and hard, kicking his legs out from under him. He flopped onto the ground.

I struggled to my feet, looked left to the gun on the ground. I didn't have time to make a move toward it. The redhead crouched and sprang at me. I let him come, grabbed onto his denim vest, and fell backward as I stuck my foot in his chest. His eyes went wide as he saw the move unfold. He said it fast, pleaded with me, "No, mister, please don't. Don't."

Three against one didn't make a fair fight. I had to even the odds or die. I flipped him high overhead, right out into traffic.

A black Honda Accord took him. Snatched him right out of the air. He smashed the windshield, flew in the air again, and landed on the hot concrete. The Honda with the shattered windshield skidded out of control and crashed into the three motorcycles on kickstands parked on the shoulder.

I rolled over to the gun and scooped it up just as the old biker came in fast with his ball-peen.

I shot him in the forehead.

Flipped off his lights.

Sirens, still miles away, reached out to me. They'd be on scene in minutes. I didn't feel sorry for killing the older biker. He'd called the game and lost. The redheaded biker, though, bothered me a great deal. His eyes, his voice, the way he pleaded. And I'd gone ahead and done it anyway, flipped him out into oncoming traffic.

I struggled to my feet, my knees weak, not wanting to cooperate. I hurried over to the downed officer and took a set of cuffs from the handcuff case on her belt. Dirk, on his hands and knees, spit teeth and blood onto the sandy earth. I put my foot on his shoulder and shoved him over. I pointed the Glock at him. "You saw what I did to your partners. You want some of this?"

He held up his hand and said, "No, man, no. I'm done."

I put the gun in my waistband, cuffed his hand, and dragged him over to the patrol unit. I ratcheted the cuff to the push bar, securing him until backup arrived.

I went back to the patrol officer and eased her onto her back. Her eyes rolled open. "Hey, kid," I said, "it's all over. You're okay. You understand? You're okay and you're gonna make it just fine."

I unclipped her shoulder mic and keyed it. "Eleven-ninety-nine. Eleven-ninety-nine, shots fired, officer down, shots fired, officer down."

I took her gun from my waistband and stuck it back in her holster. A cop always felt vulnerable without her gun in her holster. "Help will be here in about two minutes," I said. "Just lie still and try to stay awake. It's real important that you stay awake. I don't need you going into shock."

Her color drained as I watched. Shock could kill her faster than any bullet. I needed to elevate her legs. I dragged over the older biker, the dead one, laid him on his side, and put her legs up on him. "It's the best I can do for right now, kid. I've gotta run. You gonna be okay?"

She gave me a barely perceptible nod.

I stood. Far off down the freeway, headed our way, a conga line of cop cars drove the shoulder, kicking up a huge dust cloud. All the cars on the freeway had stopped now. I hadn't noticed at what point that happened.

I ran for the rental, the Ford Escape, got in, slammed it in drive, and steered to the right side of the Highway Patrol car, to the far and extreme part of the shoulder, the only way out.

In the middle of the freeway, on the westbound traffic lanes, two Highway Patrol cars stopped parallel to the incident. The officers pulled their shotguns, jumped out of their cars, and climbed the center divider. They wove their way through all the stopped traffic, approaching with caution as I gunned the Ford Escape.

The black Honda Accord had shoved one of the downed choppers into my path, blocking my way out. I pulled the gearshift down into low and gunned the car. I drove right over the motorcycle. The Escape jerked and rattled. I banged into the right front of the Accord, shoved it out of the way, and made it clear. The driver of the Accord shot me the finger.

I took the speed up to fifty, too fast for driving on the shoulder, zipping past all the stopped cars on the freeway, but if I didn't get away, I would never see freedom again.

That redheaded biker, the kid, couldn't have been more than twenty-five or twenty-six. He had a smooth complexion, with a spray of freckles across his nose. I'd been too close to his face, no more than a foot or so in that split second before I flipped him.

Green eyes. Eyes that had pleaded with me. A grown-up Opie, the redheaded kid on *The Andy Griffith Show*, only with a little darker skin. Not so much a kid really. When I took hold of him, he had muscle under his biker vest, built stout like a weightlifter. A hidden strength most people would miss. I know I did. He didn't try that hard to take me down. As I played it back in my head, he didn't seem to have his heart in what the old biker told him to do. And yet he died for it.

CHAPTER FOURTEEN

I OPENED MY eyes, still sitting in the truck. Drago was staring at me.

"The worst part about it, though, was the kid's eyes. I couldn't shake his eyes. And his last words, as he begged me not to toss him into traffic. Those panicked words continue to haunt me. And I know they will for a long time. Forever."

I couldn't read Drago's expression. I waited for him to comment. I did feel better telling him what had happened out on that freeway, but now I needed his reaction, craved it.

I waited.

Maybe he was trying to digest the unbelievable story before he used his words. I hadn't told him the worst part. Couldn't.

In my nightmare, and in real life when it happened, I had no way of knowing the kid I tossed out into traffic was my son. I didn't find out until much later. His last words to me, the only words ever spoken between a father and son, hurt worse than any bullet to the chest.

"No, mister, please don't. Don't."

If Drago didn't say something then I needed to talk to Marie, tell her again what happened. Purge my soul yet again. She understood that need. She knew just the right things to say to talk me down. Not to make what I did right but to make me understand that at the

time there had not been anything else to do. And most important
of all, her job was to make me believe her.

Drago finally spoke. "They were out to make their bones, those
three. You did what you had to do. You don't need to lose any sleep
over what happened. I wouldn't."

Drago was a Sons of Satan dropout. He hated motorcycle gangs.
I should've anticipated his reaction. And yet his confirmation went
a long way to help ease some of the guilt.

Two months wasn't long enough, that's what Marie had said. It
would get better with time. She promised. But it had to be more
than two months. I wasn't so sure that would work either. If I wasn't
able to shove it behind a closed door in my mind, I didn't know
what I was going to do.

The world as I knew it was broken, never to be repaired.

Sweat soaked my shirt collar. Drago put his hand on my chest and
eased me back. "Take it easy, my friend. Everything's cool."

I patted his hand then removed it from my chest.

He chuckled. "You sure all this fatigue is from your injuries, or
could it just be old age?"

I loved him for his attempt to change the subject and cheer me up.

"Give me a couple more weeks and I'll kick your ass so hard you'll
have to unzip your pants to eat a meatball sandwich."

On my best day twenty years ago, I wouldn't have had a chance
against the likes of Drago, the man-mountain. Size doesn't necessarily matter in a fight, but Drago also had an instinct for violence.
He could strike first with a viciousness rarely seen in the evolved
man. Back a million years ago, he could have torn out the throat of
a T-Rex with his teeth and right afterward sat down for a cup of tea.

"It's a date then," he said. "Two weeks. I'll bring a meatball sandwich, so we can test out this bullshit theory of yours."

"You give me two weeks, you'll see. I'll be back at the top of my game. You can even bring a couple of your friends to help you out. You're gonna need it."

He chuckled some more; it transformed him, exposed a seldom-seen juvenile innocence in his eyes and smile.

"Hold on, let me come around and help you get out."

I held up my hand. "Thanks, I got it. Go pick up the truck and put the war bag together—that's how you can help me most right now."

"Roger that."

I opened the door the rest of the way and this time picked my right leg up, set it out, and then pivoted. I stood, strangely revived after that little nap and telling of the event. To some degree, my strength had returned. I pulled the cane out and chose to use it rather than risk a fall and add scars to my "boxer's nose."

I watched while Drago drove away, then headed for the elevator. I monitored my surroundings more closely than I had in the last two months. No one looked out of place. No one looked like an under-cover cop. I could spot cops easily enough. I worried more about the people involved in the hornet's nest I had kicked at MCJ.

The all-glass elevator dumped me out on the third floor. I hobbled along the hall then around the first corner . . . and froze. Down by our suite door stood a blue-uniformed Glendale cop. He stood guard while something serious went on inside our suite.

Our suite!

Marie? Something's happened to Marie.

The bottom fell out of my world . . . wait. There wasn't any ambulance personnel, fireman, or gurney. This wasn't a medical issue.

Oh, my God. Law enforcement had Marie. What should I do? Turn and flee before the uniform saw me? Then later find a way to get her loose from the authorities? I'd done it before with my brother, Noble. I could do it again. Logically, that was the only option. But with hot emotions in the mix, logic took a flyer.

Adrenaline dumped into my system and gave me superhuman strength. In my condition, it would only have a short half-life. My aches and pains disappeared, my vision and mental acuity sharpened. I could do this. I could shake her free if I just used my head.

Too late. The uniformed cop, a young guy, tall with a buzz cut, turned his head and spotted me standing at the hallway intersection, staring at him. Now only one choice remained.

I headed his way, leaning on the cane more than I needed to, feigning a bigger disability in case I saw the opportunity to free Marie. If it arose, I'd take it. I'd hurt the cops even though it went against everything I believed. This was Marie. She was my whole life.

I'd been a cop—a deputy sheriff for twenty-five years. I knew their vulnerabilities. I could do it. I could get her free if I wanted to. It was just a matter of how far I would go. The degree of violence I was prepared to mete out upon these valiant knights sworn to uphold the law.

I came to the cop who stood in front of the open suite door.

"Can I help you, sir?" the cop asked. His nameplate read *D. Mahoney*.

"I'm staying here in the hotel. This is my room. What's going on? What's happened?" I tried to look around him into the suite, to see my Marie.

He moved with me, blocking my entry and sightline to the inside. Doing his job. "Sir, can I please see some ID?"

I hesitated. Which ID should I show him, Karl Higgins, the public defender investigator, or the FBI credentials? "I . . . ah." Then I remembered the name I'd registered under at the hotel. I hadn't taken that ID with me. "My name is Jackson. This is my suite. I just went for a walk and I left my ID inside. Can I go in now? Is something the matter with my wife? What the hell's going on?" I tried for indignant guest and didn't have to work too hard at it.

He smelled of polished leather and gun oil. Adrenaline heightens all senses, with the exception of the most important one, common sense. This according to Marie. Her voice in my head warned to tread lightly until I found out how bad it was. "Don't just put your head down and barrel through," her voice said.

I took a deep breath. He had not been told to be on the lookout for me so maybe it wasn't as bad as I thought.

"Please," I said. "My wife is pregnant. I need to go to her."

He hesitated, then stepped aside.

If it had been me guarding the door, I would have patted me down for weapons first. This thought made me consciously aware of the fake FBI creds in my pocket. If he had conducted a search, he'd have found them.

I moved down the short entrance hall, past the open bathroom, past the open master bedroom, and into the expansive living area where an elderly black woman sat in a wheelchair talking to another woman sitting on the couch. Marie stood over by the open sliding glass door to the balcony, trying to act calm.

"What's going on here?" I had never seen either of the women before. The one on the couch was dressed business professional in dark slacks and a stylish suit coat. Her hair, a premature gray, was swept back with two barrettes.

Marie saw me and hurried over, took me in a hug. She reached up and pulled my head down, putting her mouth close to my ear. "Play along and do not act surprised. You hear me? Don't do it."

"What?" I said, too loud. She pinched my arm. "Ouch."

She stepped to my side with a fake smile. Out of the corner of my mouth, I whispered, "What's going on?"

She squeezed my hand too hard. "Bruno, this is Ms. Hamilton from State Parole."

"State Parole?" I half-yelped.

She'd jerked down on my hand. That common sense thing had gone missing again.

She held out her other hand like Vanna White displaying a new car on *Wheel of Fortune*. "And this . . . is Beatrice Elliot."

The blood drained from my head and I swayed on my feet. *Beatrice Elliot?* Marie helped me over to the chair, eased me down, and said, "See, I told you, my husband has been terribly sick." She turned back to me with that same disingenuous smile. "I told you, dear, not to overdo it on your walk, and now look at you."

My throat dry, my mouth arid as a desert, the name came out in a rasp. "Bea Elliot?"

Marie squatted by my chair and squeezed my hand. "That's right, dear." She whispered harshly through clenched teeth, "You have some explaining to do, Little Mister." Her feeble attempt to lighten a bad situation. A very bad situation. She did it to help make Bea's presence more palatable for me.

Bea Elliot was my mother's name. A mother I had never met.

CHAPTER FIFTEEN

I NEVER KNEW what my mother looked like, what she talked like, her scent, the color of her eyes, her loving touch; not one thing about her.

Except what my father had told me.

As any child would, I had made up an image born of movies, and books, and stories my friends told me of their mothers. A lady with style and glamor. This woman looked nothing like that mocked-up image.

Dad had only told me about her a mere five years earlier when I had cornered him in a deeply emotional conversation about my grandson, Albert. His great-grandson. At the time, Dad wanted something from me that, for his own good, I couldn't tell him under any circumstances. We made an unholy trade and we both regretted it.

He'd finally told me how, decades earlier, he met Mother coming out of a movie theater with a couple of her friends and was smitten at first sight. He followed her for a short distance until she came back and asked him why he was following them. He mumbled and stumbled over his words. She apparently thought he was cute and wrote her phone number on his sweaty palm. They got together, hit it off, and a short time later were married.

Mother wanted a life Dad couldn't provide. A life of extravagance few realized, a life unfairly portrayed and tantalized in the kind of movies she loved. She wanted to live the life of her favorite stars.

Mother committed a robbery of a telephone man making his rounds picking up all the coins from the phone booths. A petty crime for coins but robbery just the same. Two people also involved in the robbery were killed. Victims of their own avarice. Dad had a tough choice to make and called the police on my mom. After they hauled her off that night, he never saw her again. That's why, when I pestered him all those years, he never said a word about her or what had happened.

Now, through some quirk of fate, she sat in a wheelchair in our suite at the Americana Hotel.

Long ago when Marie had asked about my mother, I told her the truth—that I knew nothing about her. I tried to leave it at that. Marie wouldn't give up easily and pestered me, not unlike I did my dad before he broke down, and we traded information. With Marie, I stuck to my story that I didn't know. And finally, I said that I thought my mother was dead. Why else would she not seek out her son? Right?

I stared at her sitting in the wheelchair. She wore a wrap of brightly colored African-print kente cloth, that matched her square cap atop her gray hair styled in long dreadlocks.

What I needed most was eight hours of uninterrupted sleep. This new menace and excitement brought back the cold sweats and weakness I'd experienced earlier in the jail parking lot. I struggled back up to my feet and took a couple of steps headed for my room to lie down. I swayed this way and that.

Marie stayed at my side. "Come on, babe, you need to sit back down." She gave me a hand, this time over to the couch. I sat three feet from Ms. Hamilton, the parole agent, who smelled of black cherry lozenges. Sweat stung my eyes. I swiped it away with the back of my hand. Everyone stared at each other for a moment. Most, it seemed, at me.

"Is someone going to tell me what's going on?" I asked.

Marie moved and stood across the room by the cabinet that housed the big-screen TV. She glanced to the open door at the Glendale cop who stood outside in the hall, then back at me. She kept her hands clasped, resting on her baby bump. She came off calm and collected, as if cops and state parole invaded our environment every day. But I knew her better. Pent up inside, she was awash in a roil of violent seas. "Dear," she said to me, "you do *know* what's going on; you've just forgotten, that's all."

"I have?" I couldn't take my eyes off Bea Elliot. I had a difficult time accepting who she said she was. Instead of drop-dead gorgeous as Dad had described her, this woman looked more like a Goober raisin with all the chocolate sucked off. An absolute horrible description to be sure, but accurate just the same. A shriveled raisin wrapped in beautiful bright-colored cloth. Age had not been kind to her. Time in prison counted double when it came to hair, and skin. Her eyes were sunken, and the absence of hope hung off her like a feverless ague.

Marie, with her fake smile, said, "Sure, you remember. Our friend Bea said that she wasn't happy in that ugly old halfway house and she asked if it was okay to stay with us for a few days until we can get her fixed up in an apartment or townhouse. You talked to her on the phone, remember? You invited her over. We have the extra room we're not using, and you said it would work out just fine."

The parole agent looked from Marie then back to me. I couldn't tell if she was buying into this lie made up on the fly. I know I wasn't.

"Oh, yes, now I remember. I'm sorry. I've been a little under the weather, as my wife must have told you. Of course, Bea is staying here. Where else would she go? It was the cop at our door that threw me off. Was that really necessary? What's the hotel going to think? We have our reputations to uphold." Words I thought belonged in the conversation but had no part in this real world.

The parole agent stared at me as if trying to decide whether what I said was a truth or a dare. "So, you know all about Aliya Ali?" she said.

I said, "Excuse me? Who?" Both Marie and I looked confused.

Ms. Hamilton grinned. "If Aliya is such a good friend, how come you two don't know she legally changed her name from Beatrice Elliot?"

Bea said, "Everyone deserves a fresh start, don't you think, Ms. Hamilton? Why make a big deal out of it? I converted to my religious roots. I'm Muslim now."

Her first words. The first words I'd heard spoken from my mother. I tried to harken back to that faux memory I'd created—to the tone, the syntax I'd assigned to her, and came up empty. That part of my life was now gone forever.

How come, when my mother first laid eyes on me, she had not said, "Come here, Son, let's have a look at you"? Or "Come here and give your mother a kiss"? I was a grown man and yet I still had that childlike need.

Marie lost her smile. "I don't see how that makes any difference as it pertains to Bea staying here with us. When you came in, all you asked was if Bea was a friend and if she had, in fact, made arrangements to stay here. Now, you've established both of those facts, so I think it's time for you to take your leave. I need to get my husband his medication and into bed. As you can see for yourself, he's on the verge of collapse."

We all stared at Ms. Hamilton, willing her to get up and leave before she had a chance to uncover the obvious truths: the two fugitives, one standing and one sitting right in front of her. And a fugitive mother perpetuating a lie of her own making. The silence hung in the air thick enough to choke on.

Finally, Ms. Hamilton nodded and then stood. "Thank you for inviting me into your nice home. But let me be absolutely clear; as long as Bea is staying here, this is her *residence of record*. That means you give up your right to privacy. I can, at any time, conduct a home visit and search the premises. You understand?"

Marie said, "Of course we do. You're welcome anytime. We have nothing to hide. Now, if you don't mind?" Marie extended her arm.

I knew it hurt Marie to lie like that, but it came out smooth and well oiled, as if she lied every day.

Ms. Hamilton followed Marie out. Marie closed the door after her. The entire suite let out a collective sigh of relief.

Marie disappeared into the kitchen. She returned with a tray that contained a Yoo-hoo chocolate drink in a bottle and two dual packs of Hostess Snowballs, pink coconut that covered chocolate cup-cakes with white cream filling. She came into the living room area and, too harshly, set the tray on my lap. The Yoo-hoo teetered and almost fell over. I caught it as I continued to stare at Bea, who returned the gaze in kind. She was unabashed at the huge problem she'd just laid at our doorstep. Unabashed at meeting her son for the first time. She acted as if unannounced searches of our long-term hotel room by state parole would be an acceptable practice.

I took a long drink. The cool chocolate milk tasted wonderful. I patted Marie's hand. "Bless you, my love. You don't know how much I needed this." With a shaky hand, I unwrapped the sweet confection and took a big bite. In our normal world, back two months earlier, Marie didn't allow such high-calorie treats. Empty calories being "a moment on the lips, a half-century on the hips." But this wasn't our normal world; our life was down in Costa Rica where we'd been headed before Chulack knocked on our door. Since the incident two months prior, I had been losing too much weight, and Marie had allowed me to eat whatever my appetite chose. All the Yoo-hoos and Snowballs I could eat was the one good thing that came out of the previous mess. I had always been a willing slave to my appetite.

Bea finally spoke again. "It's not proper manners, eating in front of your guest. I know Xander taught you better."

The mention of Dad's name by this unwanted interloper came off strange, almost alien, and I didn't like her for it. I wanted her to leave Dad out of it.

I tossed Bea the second pack of Snowballs. Rude, but that's how I felt. She was jeopardizing our very existence. She caught them with one hand, her eyes never leaving mine. Her bleached white teeth tore the package open. She ate in silence without exposing the simplest emotions on her brown, wrinkled countenance.

I didn't know what to say to a mother I'd never met. What could I say? She'd almost gotten us all thrown in prison for life. And yet I had a hundred questions, no, a million.

"You're really Beatrice Elliot?" I asked.

She stopped mid-chew, her eyes drilling into me. "What do you think? That I hired that stuffed-shirt parole officer as some kind of actor and this is all just an elaborate con? Is that what you mean? Come on, I heard you were street smart."

Marie sat next to me, her leg touching mine. She rested her hand on my knee. "Why now? Why come to his hotel, right now?" she asked.

Bea stared a little longer before she finally spoke. "I was in prison." She broke eye contact and looked down at the remaining pink Snowball, her first sign of vulnerability, her first true emotion, shame. "Xander at least told you that much, right?" She swallowed hard. "I went to prison for a couple of murders I didn't commit. I didn't kill those people. They killed each other. The felony murder rule though—what a stupid law. It placed both of their deaths right at my feet. I accepted my penalty, no matter how harsh. My biggest regret, I never got to see my son grow up."

"You're saying you're just now getting out for that crime? That was over fifty years ago. They don't keep people in that long. You should've only done half that time."

She broke eye contact. "Well . . . ah, yes, you're right. I was let out . . . a few years back. For a little while . . . and then had another . . . setback. But . . . that's old news. I'm here now. I've got my life back on track and finally reconnected with my family."

Marie shook her finger. "No. You are not going to just waltz in here and claim some filial right. Not if it jeopardizes us. I won't have it."

Bea let an eerie grin creep across her face. "How would my staying with you for a couple of days jeopardize your welfare? Am I missing something here?"

The way she said it, she somehow knew about our fugitive status. Of course, she did. But how? She could've easily guessed our status based on the fact that we were registered under the name Jackson and not Johnson. But how would she even have access to that kind of information? And lots of folks registered under different names for benign reasons. No, she'd gotten all the information from some other source.

"How did you come to know we were staying here at this hotel, in this room?"

"My grandson told me."

"Your grand—" Marie started to say.

"Bruno," I said in a half-whisper. My brother Noble's son. Noble had named his first son after me.

Her sudden confident smile said I'd hit upon the answer. Bruno had gone missing for a few days, a couple of months back. I'd been too busy at the time to pay much attention. It wasn't like him to disappear. Bea had something to do with it.

He was a responsible, heads-up kind of kid. He was nineteen years old, with a girlfriend and two small children of his own. He was an intern at the South Los Angeles Sheriff's Station awaiting his twenty-first birthday so he could enroll in the academy and become a full-time deputy.

"How did you find Bruno?" I asked.

She took another bite of the pink confection and spoke with her mouth full, her hand up as a screen. "I ran into him on the street."

"Just randomly ran into him? You're lying." The room started to swim. I had to lie down or pass out. A verbal confrontation with a mother I'd only just met was the last thing I needed before I'd had a nap.

Marie sensed the problem. She stood, took both my hands and tugged. "Come on, let's get you to bed."

"No, I can't leave you to deal with this problem. This is a huge mess."

Bea said, "Oh, now your mother's a problem? A huge mess? Really? Well I never in all my—"

Marie rounded on her. "Shut up. You and I will talk after I get him into bed and not before. He's overdone it today and needs his rest." She turned back to me. "Now, *little man*, get your butt up and into that room."

Oh no, not the *little man* treatment. That's what she called the children when they'd done something bad. The air in the room warbled like a heat wave. *Had* I been bad? My thoughts started to swim in the wobbly air. I let her help me up and into the bedroom.

CHAPTER SIXTEEN

"*No, MISTER, PLEASE don't. Don't.*"

"*Bosco!*"

I sat up in bed breathing hard, my heart racing. Marie hurried over with a warm washcloth. "It's okay, baby."

I looked around trying to rectify in my mind how I had suddenly left the side of the freeway under that bright summer light, a place where my son, Bosco, was run over by that black Honda, and I ended up on a plush California King with a beautiful pregnant woman giving me a sponge bath. She wiped my forehead, face, and neck. Then my arms. She unbuttoned my shirt and did my chest. It felt wonderful. Just her touch, her concern. That's all I needed to continue on. To know she cared. That she loved me.

Marie wiped down my chest and arms.

I shrugged the rest of the blankets off my legs, the sheets underneath me damp from sweat. I swung my legs over the edge. My head swooned a little.

"Where are you going?"

"I need to get up and use the restroom."

She took hold of one elbow. "I'll help you."

"Please," I said, too sharply. "I'm not an invalid."

"Right. Of course, you're not. I just . . . never mind."

I didn't want to be weak and sickly, and most of all, vulnerable, in front of my lovely wife. I shouldn't let my ego rule the day. But I'd never been vulnerable in my entire life and now I had been for too long.

I stood for a moment and shook off the residue of deep slumber that contained so much evil as my eyes took in her side of the enormous bed, which was scattered with a collage of color photos. "What's all this?"

"Someone left them down at the front desk in a box. They're copies of the kidnapping investigation. Oh, and Chulack called. Said it was important. I wouldn't wake you. He said he understood."

"Where's the burner phone?"

"Bruno, you only slept four hours. You need a lot more, at least eight, ten preferably."

"Please, let me have the phone. I promise to go right back to bed after I call." I froze, confused for a second as I remembered something else. I pointed to the closed bedroom door. "Ah . . . did we really have that meeting out there with . . . was that real or just another bad dream?"

Marie smiled. "No, you didn't dream it. Your mother, Bea, is sleeping in our spare bedroom. She and I had a nice little talk. I'll tell you all about it after you get some more rest."

I took Marie's hand. "I'm sorry. I really didn't know she was alive."

Marie patted my chest. "I know. But you're still in a lot of trouble with me. Right now, you have enough to worry about. Don't think you're getting off easy. After all this mess is over, you'll get your spanking."

I smiled. "Well, if I've been bad enough to warrant a spanking, maybe I'll take it right now so I won't have it, you know, hanging over my head." I winked.

She gave me a little shove. "I guess you are feeling better."

I kissed her forehead and hugged her.

"Take it easy, you brute, you'll squeeze little Johnny right out of me. I'm not a tube of toothpaste." She pulled back, smiling. I kissed her on the mouth and cut it short thinking about the phone call from Chulack. He wouldn't have called unless it was important. "Babe, where's the phone? Please?"

She moved along the edge of the bed to the nightstand and picked it up. She dialed and held it to her ear. After a few seconds she said into the phone, "You have two minutes, buster, then he's going back to bed." She handed over the phone.

"Yeah, Dan?"

"I'm sorry about the call, but I thought you needed to know."

"It's okay. What's going on?"

"We got there too late."

"I'm sorry. I just woke up. Say again."

"Thomas Adrien Armstrong and Calvin Ivory bailed out of MCJ."

"What? Who?"

"Little T-Dog, and the guy with the tattoo, Police Killa Bitch, were both bailed out before I got the writ over there."

I sat on the edge of the bed on top of some of the many 8x11 color photos of the crime scene. Chulack's daughter's home. They depicted an upscale house in LA now minus a little girl named Emily. My butt crumpled some of the photos.

"Ah, man."

"Yeah, I know. We're on it, though. I mobilized everyone. We're out shaking the trees, but so far they just up and vanished."

I said, "Getting bailed out was their payment for dropping Eldridge on his head."

"That's what we're thinking, too."

"You know," I said, "those two are a loose end just like Eldridge. We need to get to them before whoever's behind this does."

"I know."

"We still good with Whitey, for in the morning?"

"Yes. You need any help with him? I mean with surveillance or in handling him?"

"No, it would be better if—"

"I know. If I stayed out of it. And it's already morning. You have about five hours until he's released, unless you want me to push it."

"No, let's keep it the way it is."

"Okay, anything else?"

I hesitated and looked at Marie, held her eyes.

Chulack said, "What is it?"

"A favor."

"Anything you want?"

"This has nothing to do with the kidnapping."

He said nothing and waited.

"Could you please get me a history of Beatrice Elliot, female, black, about seventy-five? That's Elliot with one 'T.' She should have a CII number for 187."

"Not a problem. I'll have it for you when you wake up."

"Thanks. I'll call you later. Goodnight." I hung up, tossed the phone on the bed, and headed for the bathroom, taking off my clothes as I went.

"What are you doing?"

"I need a nice hot shower to wash off all the jail crud. Should've done it before I laid down."

"I don't think you should be in the shower by yourself."

"I was hoping you'd say that."

"Oh, no, cowboy, this is strictly medicinal. No slap and tickle this time."

She'd caught up, stepped out of her clothes, and turned on the shower water while I continued to struggle out of my pants. The pain in my hip made it a difficult proposition. Marie came over. "Stand up straight. Put your hand on the wall there."

I did as I was told. She squatted, grabbed my pants at the waist, and tugged them down. I wasn't the only one happy she'd volunteered to take a shower. She got bumped in the face with all my happiness. She giggled, then turned serious. "Bruno," she whispered, "your mother's in the next room."

Words from my wife I never thought I'd hear. That immediately took the fun right out of the splash and tickle.

"You're a real buzzkill, you know that?"

She turned me around and slapped me on the ass. "Come on, cowboy, get in there. I'll soap your back."

Standing on my own two feet, the warm water sluicing down my back, the ever-present tension finally eased from my body. I relaxed and let out a long breath. But it didn't matter. For the umpteenth time in the last five minutes, I again tried to shove Bosco out of my mind. And instead, look on the bright side of life. I found it too difficult. Not yet. I still needed distance. The investigation Chulack set at my door helped to take my mind off it and eased, just a little, the regret and deep remorse.

Marie used a big sponge behind me and worked on my back, going easy on recent wounds now turning to ropy scars.

I twisted at the waist, turned, and faced her. She put a hand on my shoulder to stop me. I said, "I just want you to know, I don't have it so bad right now. Nice night, nice hotel room, and the love of a beautiful woman."

Marie said, "Where is she, I'll kill her."

I chuckled. She always knew how to make me laugh. I pulled her into a hug.

CHAPTER SEVENTEEN

NINE FIFTEEN IN the morning, five hours after the shower and another long nap, I'd totally recovered. Almost, anyway.

I sat in the truck just down from 450 Bauchet Street, MCJ's exit for the Inmate Reception Center. I didn't know how long this burst of new energy would last before my ass would again start to drag and threaten total collapse. I had to work fast and get things done. Make things happen. Get back to Costa Rica and the kids. Back to Dad.

And now, as if I didn't have enough to think about, the added emotional load of Bea Elliot floated around in my brain like a lost, wandering child bleating for its mama. The way she looked, the things she said, the way she acted. I tried to shake all of that off and focus on the task at hand. And found it near impossible.

On the seat next to me, Drago had put two different types of binoculars in the war bag: one huge marine pair and the second pocket size. I held up the marine binocs for twenty to thirty seconds at a time, trying to conserve my strength. I hoped I hadn't missed Whitey coming out. I kept the air conditioner running in the new, glossy black GMC truck. It had dark tinted windows to keep anyone from seeing inside and a hard fiberglass tonneau cover over the bed.

I'd left Drago back at the hotel suite sitting on the couch watching *Ren and Stimpy* on Nickelodeon, the big-screen sound turned down low, as he stuffed his mouth with my reserve stash of Snowballs and Yoo-hoo chocolate drinks. I couldn't leave Marie there alone unprotected. Not with Bea Elliot in the next room. I didn't know anything about her. Not enough anyway. At the very least, with Bea's background, someone of ill repute could populate her orbit and put Marie at risk. That wasn't going to happen.

My own mother. What a shocker. And then to think of her that way. As a risk.

Based on what I did know, I couldn't trust her. This wasn't a fair assumption; I was prejudging. When it came to Marie, I wouldn't take any chances.

Marie had been up all night worried about me. I'd left her asleep in bed with a handful of kidnap crime scene photos resting on her chest. She just wanted to help and get this over with as soon as possible. She'd also read more of the report than I did.

Once she woke and found Drago with his pile of torn-up Snowball packaging and empty Yoo-hoo bottles—his feet up on the coffee table—she was going to be mad as hell. Better angry than the alternative, me worrying about her all day. Drago was like a bulldog; he wouldn't let anything happen to her. She liked Drago a lot and didn't mind him hanging around. She'd just be angry at me for not having anyone to back my play out on the street. Especially in my current condition.

At MCJ people came and went in cars, patrol units, and long buses painted black and white with "Los Angeles County Sheriff's Department" on the sides. Every size, shape, and color of sketchy human popped out of the freedom gate. All looked relieved. Some wandered out with their heads craned in wonderment to the bright blue sky. A few immediately took off running to get as far away as possible. One guy in a wrinkled business suit went to his knees and kissed the filthy ground. I knew how he felt. I'd been there.

Five minutes later, out came Whitey. His first step a stumbling trip, almost as if the IRC regurgitated a piece of rancid meat and spit him out. He held all his worldly possessions in a clear plastic bag clutched to his chest as he looked around waiting to be picked up. He wore dirty denim pants and a yellow tee shirt with black letters on the back that read *Will trade wife for beer*. A real charmer, this guy.

He waited exactly eleven minutes and twenty-eight seconds before he rabbited. He hurried down the street, his head on a swivel as he made his break.

He went to the bus stop at the corner, his anxiety high from his perilous choice to leave before I could pick him up.

His angst translated down to his feet; he paced back and forth waiting for the bus. I wouldn't swoop him. Not yet. I wanted to see where he went. See if anyone else was interested in him. Like the Crips.

The city bus pulled up and disgorged more citizens of similar ilk who beelined to MCJ Visiting to see a loved one behind the thick Plexiglas, to talk to them using a black, hard plastic phone placed to their ear. The same piece of black plastic used by tens of thousands of other folks that came before them.

The majority were women trundling children along by outstretched arms; this added load more a drag on their lives than a darling child.

Whitey stepped up onto the bus. His head came out for one last look around. He smiled with his disgustingly white dentures, pleased with himself at the move he'd made. In his pea brain, he'd pulled one over on Bruno Johnson. The door to the bus wheezed closed. The huge beast belched out a cloud of black smoke as it lumbered off down the road retracing the same path in the asphalt, doing it hour after hour, day after day.

Even with only one car in the surveillance, following something dinosaur-sized was easy. Each time the bus pulled to a stop I double-parked down the street, engine running. The other drivers, familiar with discourteous commuters, waited impatiently behind me rather than risk a road rage incident with the unseen occupant of the truck.

Inside the bus, the carefree Whitey sat and talked with a woman, flashing his pearly whites. A regular Don Ameche.

The bus headed south, out of downtown. Thirty minutes later, Whitey disembarked at 60th and Avalon. He had his arm around that same poorly dressed woman who'd been out in the sun all her life, eighty years old, or maybe forty, her dirty brown hair a static halo. They went into a market of sorts, one lacking any signage and covered in gang graffiti. They came out two minutes later, each carrying a forty-ounce bottle of Old English 800 beer. Whitey didn't belong in this area. The Rollin' Sixties Crips owned it. What was going on?

I'd had enough and pulled up to the curb outside the market. Whitey lost his disingenuous smile when he saw me get out. He quickly looked both ways, ready to flee. No way did I have the gumption to pursue. I wouldn't make it fifty steps before I collapsed. I stopped and yelled, "I'm not in the mood. You rabbit, I'll get in the truck and run you down like a dog, then just keep on driving."

He raised his chin. "No, you won't. You wouldn't dare. You need me."

I walked toward him. "Yeah, like I need herpes."

The woman standing shoulder to shoulder with him said, "Baby, what's going on? Who's this smoke talkin' shit? What's he doing here?"

"This, my lovely princess, is the late, great Bruno Johnson."

The forty-ounce bottle slipped from her grasp and shattered. Liquid yellow with white foam covered the grubby sidewalk and spiked it with shards of glass. She backed up until she reached the wall of the market, her eyes wary and filled with fear. She turned and scurried down the street.

"Thanks a lot. You just ruined a real good thing. She promised me a blow—"

I knocked the bottle out of his hand. It shattered, and added to the humid reek of cheap hops that rose off the already heated concrete.

Two cars skidded up and stopped, angled to the curb in front of the market, one a Chevy Malibu, the other a Toyota Camry. Two men jumped out of the Malibu, guns drawn. Out of the Toyota came a third cop. Along with Hellen Hellinger. Two of the men yelled to put up our hands.

How had they found me? I'd been careful about a tail. No way had they followed me.

Whitey complied and whispered, "Now who's in deep shit, Mr. Bruno Johnson?"

CHAPTER EIGHTEEN

I PIVOTED, GRABBED Whitey by the neck, and shoved him, his feet kicking loose under him. I walked him over to the wall, slammed him against it, and pressed a shoulder into him. Sometimes it took two lessons for the concept to take root. I got up in his face and lifted my sunglasses. I gently squeezed his throat until his face bloated red. "You just don't get it. Like I told you yesterday, they find out who I am, I got nothing to live for. You understand? Nothing at all. Nod your head if you understand."

The deputy sheriffs, with their guns drawn, continued to yell they'd shoot if I didn't immediately comply. "Get down on the sidewalk with your arms and legs spread. Do it now. Do it now."

I let go of Whitey. He coughed and choked and went to his hands and knees, down on top of the sidewalk slop created by the Old English 800. He slid the larger shards out of the way with a bladed-hand before going almost prone.

I raised my hands in the air and slowly turned. "FBI. I'm on the job."

The men continued to yell to get on the ground.

"I'm not doin' that. Go ahead and shoot. Let's see how it comes out in the news tonight, huh? 'LA deputies shoot black FBI agent in South Central.' That won't go over too well with your boss."

Whitey looked up, eyes red and watering. "Go on then, show some balls, shoot his black ass."

The men stopped advancing and yelling. They looked to see Hellinger's reaction to this new twist. She didn't move for several long beats, then came around her car door walking over to me. She stopped at arm's length, reached out with her leg, put her foot on Whitey's butt, and shoved him the rest of the way down into the soup. She slowly brought her hand up to remove my sunglasses. I grabbed it. "Not today either, Deputy. Another time though, I promise."

"A word." She turned and moved ten feet down the sidewalk. I followed. She carried her anger hidden well in her somber expression. I stopped and faced her. She took her own sunglasses hanging from her neck and put them on. Tit for tat.

"You screwed me," she said.

I stepped to the side of her and yelled at the deputies patting Whitey down for weapons and handcuffing him, "Leave him be, he's my asshole. Go find your own." I turned to her. "Tell them."

She said nothing.

They trundled Whitey off to the Malibu, as he yelled bloody murder. They put him in the backseat, his clothes wet and stinking of beer.

"Okay, look," I said. "Those other two, they bailed out, so technically I didn't screw you."

"But your buddies showed up with a writ and would've grabbed them if they could. I waited on talking with them because you asked me to. You reneged on our deal. And since I never lose, I'm here to round up the material witness to *my* homicide." She cocked her head and pasted on a smug smile.

I chuckled. "Right, and the sky's purple."

"What?"

"You didn't have to wait and follow Whitey; you coulda snatched him right out of IRC. No. You wanted him to lead you to Thomas Adrien Armstrong and Calvin Ivory. When I swooped Whitey, you had to protect your case." I held my arms out wide. "And here we are at a standoff."

"Armstrong and Ivory are suspects in *my* homicide. They tossed Eldridge off the tier, remember? I have every right."

"No, you're circumventing a federal investigation."

"It's all the same, isn't it?"

"Not if you mess up what I have going on. Whitey's mine. I'm the one who got him to talk. Armstrong and Ivory are ancillary, not the main players in the kidnap, and you know it."

"He's in the back of my cop car and there are four of us and only one of you."

I reached into my pocket and took out my cell phone. "Ah, but you keep forgetting, I've got the juice card. I've been nice so far. You push me anymore, and I'll tell my guy on the other end of this phone to get you out of my way, permanently. Don't make me do that."

She put her hand up to her mouth in mock horror. "I'm so scared." She brought her hand down. "Do it. If my department stands me down, then I guess I'll have to go find another murderer to chase. There's no shortage."

"You're bluffing."

"Then go on, make the call."

Now I was the one who wanted to see her eyes.

I said, "I think you're the kind of cop who'd keep coming even if they did tell you to stand down."

Five years ago, when I was still a detective for Los Angeles County, that's what I would've done. Damn the torpedoes, full speed ahead.

She'd pushed me into a corner without any options. "Let's make a deal."

"Not a chance. We already tried that and you screwed me. You can't be trusted."

"In this new deal, you ride along with your witness. He never leaves your sight."

She said nothing.

"Okay, you'll also get all the resources the federal government has to offer."

She thought about that for a second. "You're going after the kidnap first. I want Armstrong and Ivory."

"They're the puppets. I'm going after the puppet master."

She took another moment then stuck out her hand. "Deal."

I shook it. She grabbed on tight and pulled in close. She raised her sunglasses. "You screw me one more time, and FBI or not, I'll arrest your ass for impeding my investigation."

"*Screw you?*" I said, shooting her my best smile. "Take it easy, Deputy, I'm married."

She tried like hell to hold her somber expression and couldn't. The corner of her mouth betrayed her with a hint of a smile. She let go and moved away. The three men hurried over to her. They conversed while I walked to my truck. One of the detectives opened the back door of the Malibu, let Whitey out, and took the cuffs off. I yelled, "Get your ass over here."

The detectives got back in their cars.

Whitey looked around, a little stunned at the sudden turn of events, and headed my way. Hellinger went to the trunk of the Camry, took out a war bag, not unlike mine, and headed for the truck. The sheriff detective cars left, chirping their tires.

I told Whitey to get in the front passenger seat; I got in the back seat behind him.

Helen opened my door almost as soon as it closed. She took her sunglasses off. "What gives?"

"You're driving. Get in."

Up close she had smoldering brown eyes, the kind of weapon that when wielded properly brought the strongest men to their knees. And that light scar on the side of her face gave her a hint of mystery, an exotic essence rarely seen. It caused a shiver to run up my legs, up my back, and into the top of my head. She nodded, tossed her war bag onto my lap, and slammed the door.

She came around, got in, adjusted the seat, and started the engine. "Where to?"

"Tell her, Whitey." He'd brought his warm body odor into the truck that now mixed with sour hops from the Old English 800. He ogled her as if under a spell. I reached up and flicked the top of his head.

"Huh? What?"

"Where to, dipshit?" Helen said.

"How the hell should I know?"

"What did Eldridge tell you?" I asked.

"Who?"

Helen started to go at him. I held up my hand. "Hold it." She sat back. I said, "Insane Duane."

"Oh, why didn't you say so? I don't know from no Eldridge. What do you want to know about him?"

"Is this guy really that dense?"

"Just take it easy," I said. Then to Whitey, "Yesterday you said you had more information, something else to trade. I got you out—that's my end of the deal. Now give." He wasn't dense, I could see his mind working a million miles a second. He was trying to work the options and how they'd best suit his interest.

"I think I'm going to need money to sweeten the deal. Thanks for getting me out and all, but I'm gonna need to see some green."

Helen said, "You going to let him run a game on you like this?"

"Take it easy." I unzipped my war bag and took out the Taser. "We're on a clock here and I don't need you yankin' my dick." I leaned forward and pushed the button. The Taser crackled; the blue electronic pulse visible between the two electrodes.

He held up his hands and backed against the dashboard. "Okay. Okay. Head over to Roscoe's Chicken and Waffles. You know where that place is over off Manchester, in Inglewood?"

She didn't answer him, put it in gear, backed up, and took off. She drove like an old ranch hand and the LA streets were empty dirt roads without curbs and traffic laws.

I asked, "What's going on at Roscoe's?"

"Insane said, when he got out—because they weren't going to hold him long—they couldn't. He didn't do anything but go into an empty townhouse and then drive away. That's trespass, nothing more. He didn't know the cops were following him—chasin' him. You know what I'm sayin'? They didn't have any evidence that he was involved in the kidnap."

"Anyway?" I said. Whitey somehow forgot to mention the part about the Lexus being stolen.

"After he got out, he was supposed to go to Roscoe's and meet this dude to get paid for leading the cops away."

"Who?" I asked. "Who's he supposed to meet?"

"You're not jackin' me around here, are you? You're not going to dump me off at the jail after you get what you want, are you?"

"Who's the dude?" I put my foot on the back of the seat and shoved hard, twice.

"His name's Colby; they call him Worm."

I looked up to the rearview to see if Helen's eyes said she knew of a gangbanger named Worm. She looked back in the reflection. She didn't know him.

I shoved his backseat again. "Gimme your kicks."

"What do you want my shoes for?"

"Just give 'em to me."

He took them off. A worse smell filled the truck's cab.

Helen fanned a hand and made a face. "Sweet Jesus, you need to see a doctor."

He handed them back. I rolled down my window and tossed them out.

"Hey! Hey! What the hell ya doin'?"

I caught Helen's eyes again in the rearview. I said to her more than him, "I don't want anyone following us."

"Followin' us? What the hell you talkin' about? What's that got to do with my shoes? You're buyin' me a new pair of shoes."

Helen shook her head, letting the corner of her mouth give way to a bit of a smile.

CHAPTER NINETEEN

HELEN KNEW HER job. She drove by Roscoe's Chicken and Waffles three times, scouting the place while asking Whitey questions.
What kind of car does Worm drive? What's he look like? What
gang did he claim? Whitey replied each time with disgust, "I told
ya, I don't know nothin' that I didn't already tell ya."

"Then what good are ya?" Helen said.

She finally parked in the same strip center as the restaurant and
shut down the truck. "How are we going to identify this guy?"

Whitey continued to leer at her and said nothing.

Even with the air-conditioning blowing on high, sweat beaded on
my forehead and ran in my eyes. I started to get the shakes like I had
low blood sugar. I'd forgotten to eat breakfast in my haste to leave
the hotel suite before Marie woke. I got out and opened Whitey's
door. I grabbed his hand and slapped on a cuff.

"Hey? Hey? What gives?"

I threaded the other handcuff through the handgrip on the ver-
tical support beam and cuffed his other hand.

"Come on, man. You can't leave me here like this. What if
someone comes close enough to see me? How am I going to defend
myself? At least leave me a gun. Come on."

Helen opened her door to step out. "If someone takes a shot at you, just duck."

"Funny. You could do stand-up but don't quit your day job."

I closed his door.

With his face right up to the window, his voice came out muffled. "Get me some of them waffles, the kind with that strawberry compote crap on top. And the classic chicken, not the extra crispy. Get the classic."

Helen yelled, "Don't hold your breath," smiled big, and gave him a thumbs-up.

I walked beside her weaving in and out of the cars and said, "You know you have an unflattering little mean streak."

"I won't lose any sleep over the likes of that guy if that's what you mean."

Today she wore distressed denims, a soft blue V-neck blouse, and a starched long-sleeve dress shirt. The shirt was unbuttoned and left pulled out to hide the accoutrements of her profession on her belt and in her shoulder holster. She had on a pair of scuffed brown Timberland hiking boots that she plodded along in quietly. She looked feminine and at the same time carried a hard edge that projected absolute control.

Inside, Roscoe's was packed to the gills with customers. As soon as I opened the door, we were hit with the ambient noise of a couple hundred big people eating and talking.

I wore a blue work shirt with the Pepsi emblem over the left breast and *Tim* over the right. A throng of customers filled the waiting area, sitting and standing in the hungry crowd closest to the hostess podium where a short, fat black man didn't like the look of me and let it leak out of his expression. He had a higher opinion of his restaurant than letting a Pepsi delivery man wearing sunglasses eat at his fine establishment. "It's an hour and a half wait," he said. "You might want to try down the street at the IHOP."

I eased my hand up onto the top edge of the podium and slipped a folded fifty-dollar bill under the edge of his scheduling tablet, leaving enough exposed for him to see. "Worm?" I whispered.

His expression shifted. He looked each way before he tried, unsuccessfully, to slip the bill out of view without anyone seeing. A buxom server walked up and said. "Table six is open and nineteen just needs to be bused."

"Fine, show this man to table thirteen."

She grabbed two menus. "This way, please."

Helen wouldn't go ahead of me and instead lagged behind two steps. I didn't mind.

She whispered, "Fifty dollars, really? Feds have all the money. I did that, it would've had to come out of my own pocket."

I wanted in the worst way to tell her I knew all about the tight purse strings of the LA County Sheriff's Department. How it tended to hinder the pursuit of criminals who put money above all else. Like fishing without any bait.

The server stopped us at a near-empty table. A big booth, one large enough for six and now only seating one. A diminutive black man in a natty green plaid suit with pink highlights, a teal-green shirt, and a salmon-colored bow tie. He looked up through black-framed glasses, and stopped a syrup-dripping wad of waffle about to enter his mouth. A mouth that sported lips too red to belong to a man. His eyes blinked twice. Three times.

I turned, took a step back, and whispered to Helen. "This isn't good, he's a cutout."

She nodded. Whispered, "What do we have to lose?"

Colby, aka Worm, must spend his days at various restaurants passing on verbal messages, orders from the shot callers. A high-priced middleman, in the high-tech world of triggerfish and wiretaps, where criminals found it easier and safer to take a step back three or four decades to more primitive forms of communication.

Colby said, "Can I help you? This booth is spoken for."

I slid into the booth, my hip screaming at the abuse, and moved all the way around until my shoulder touched his. Helen saw the play, entered the booth on the other side, and put her shoulder next to his just as he tried to squirm away from me.

He squeaked, "Who are you? What are you doing?"

I didn't answer, just took a fat juicy drumstick from his plate and bit into it. My mouth exploded in a marvel of savory sensations. No wonder Roscoe's was so popular.

"Hey! Hey! What are you doing? Get out."

Helen slid Colby's plate over in front of her, took a fork from a fresh setup on the table, and cut out a bite from the uneaten side of the waffle. She dipped it in the swirl of whipped cream before putting it her mouth. "Hmm."

"Get out of my booth before I have the police called. They'll throw the both of you out on your ear. I'm not kidding."

The server had not left and stood by with her order pad at the ready. "Are you two going to order something?"

"Yes," I said. "Can I have an order of chicken and waffles to go. Another order of what Colby here is eating and—"

"Apparently, I'm not eating my own breakfast. You are. How do you know my name? What do you want?"

Helen picked up the paper Colby had been reading—the *Economist*, from London. Out slid several envelopes and a cell phone.

He grabbed for them. I slapped his hands away.

"Now just one minute, those are mine. You have no right to—"

Helen raised her elbow, put it in his throat, and pressed backward.

The server tried not to smile. She apparently didn't think much of Colby. "And for the lady?" she said.

"Some hot tea," Helen said, "two slices of bacon, and two eggs over hard." The server wrote it down and left as I grabbed one of the envelopes with one hand while still munching the drumstick. I set the drumstick down and wiped my hands on his plaid blazer. I opened the envelope and found cash, fifties and hundreds. I held it open so Helen could see. She let out a low whistle. The other envelopes held the same, all of them varying amounts. Payoffs meant for gangsters, for services rendered in their games of mayhem and menace.

Helen eased off him, lowered her elbow.

"This is preposterous. Do you know who I work for? If you did, you wouldn't be—"

"Do you know who I work for?" I said, pointing to the Pepsi emblem. This made Helen smile. I liked making her smile.

I said to her, "Did I tell you that I'm happily married?"

"Hmm."

"Pepsi?" Colby said. "You have got to be kidding me. What do you want? What in the world could the Pepsi Cola company want with me? Why would Pepsi employ a knuckle-dragging thug like you?"

Helen handed Colby his own cell phone.

"What?" he asked. "No, I will not open it if that's what you have in mind, and you can't make me. I never in all my life—"

I casually took the serrated steak knife from beside his plate and made it disappear under the table. He jumped and yelped when I stuck the tip up against his smooth round belly.

He grabbed the phone and punched in the code. Helen took it back from him. She scrolled through the recent text messages and phone calls.

"What's that phone number?" I asked her.

She removed a pen from her pocket and wrote on the napkin. I took out my burner phone and dialed. Chulack picked up. "Yes?"

"Dump the phone numbers and texts from this number." I gave it to him.

"I'll call you right back," he said, and rang off.

"What are you doing here?" Colby asked again. "You obviously don't work for Pepsi. What do you want?"

We said nothing.

The server brought our food and set it in front of us. We started to eat. Helen said, "All the texts are in abbreviations and code. It'll take hours, days even to decode. They're no good to us right now."

"Maybe if you tell me what you want, I can help you?" the little man said.

"This is really good chow," I said to Helen. She shrugged. The server came back, put a white plastic bag on the table that contained our takeout, and dropped off the ticket.

I took the ticket and put it in Colby's blazer pocket behind his silk hankie. "Be sure you leave a good tip. Now are you going to tell me what I want to know?"

He half-yelled, "I would. Gladly. To get you two uncouth leeches out of here, but you won't tell me what you want!"

Other patrons stopped eating to look over.

I said, "We can take this outside into the alley if you're going to get loud."

Helen said, "Yeah, just tell us what we want to know and we'll be gone."

"I don't know *what you want to know*!"

I leaned in close to his ear and whispered, "Little T-Dog and Police Killa Bitch."

All the blood drained from poor Colby's face. Now he did look like a worm.

CHAPTER TWENTY

"THIS IS KIDNAP, you know?" Whitey said from the front passenger seat when we came back to the truck. I uncuffed him, set the to-go bag on his lap, and got in behind him. Helen got in and started the truck. She hadn't said a word after I'd walked off with Worm's cash envelopes.

Whitey continued to scream foul until I glared at him.

As far as Helen was concerned, I'd crossed an invisible line of corruption she didn't want to deal with. I might've thought the same thing had I still been a cop with the same burdensome and unnecessary rules to follow.

She backed the truck out of the slot and drove through the parking lot headed for the street exit. My body had accepted the rich, greasy food with relish and now demanded sleep as a form of payment. Fatigue rolled in on me so thick and heavy I wouldn't be able to fight it long and within minutes would have to surrender to its beck and call.

"Hey, where's my compote? Son of a bitch. I wanted me some strawberry compote. I was really lookin' forward to it. My mouth's waterin' and—"

Helen reached over, leaving one hand on the wheel, and tried to snatch the Styrofoam container from his lap. He jerked it away just in time.

"You don't like it, don't eat it," she said, and went back to driving.

"Oh hell, I'll eat it." He picked up the waffle caveman-style and took a big bite. He talked with a mouthful. "You get what you needed from Worm?"

Neither of us answered him. He took a chicken wing, stuck the whole thing in his mouth, and worked it for a minute or two, his mouth making ugly contortions like he had a miniature magician in a straitjacket in there trying to get loose. Then he pulled out two totally naked bones. Whitey might've been one step lower on the evolutionary chain than I was accustomed to dealing with.

"If you got what you wanted, you can let me off anywhere along here." He waved a hand that clung to a drumstick, the chicken grease running down his wrist.

My eyelids hung at half-mast as I continued to fade, sliding toward a slumber I knew would last more than an hour. Not a safe proposition with an unpredictable criminal unsecured in the front seat and a cop, who, if she discovered my identity, wouldn't hesitate to run me into IRC to face charges I could never beat. "How about you work with us a little longer?" I said to Whitey.

Whitey spun in his seat, anger in his eyes. Bits of chicken and waffle flicked from his mouth when he spoke. "We had a deal. I held up my end. You said you were a man of your word. What happened to that, huh? I knew it. I knew you were going to screw me and—"

I reached over and dropped one of the envelopes filled with cash on his lap.

"Huh?" He set aside his breakfast and peeked in the envelope. "Sweet baby Jesus. This some kinda joke? Is this for real? Where're the cameras? Am I on tape for takin' this and you're just gonna arrest me on some kinda entrapment shit?"

"It's yours if you do exactly what I—I mean what *we*—say, when we say it. You do that, you get another envelope when we're done."

His head popped over the seat to look at me. "You're serious?"

Helen watched the road and looked up into the rearview. "He can't help us anymore," she said. "He doesn't know anything else. We might as well drop him right here."

"Yes, I can. I do know a helluva lot. You bet I do."

"You in?" I asked.

"Well, hell yeah, I'm in. Wait. Whatta I gotta do? I'm not gonna kill anyone, if that's what you got in mind. Well, maybe, if you guys say it's okay, I'll do it, sure. But I'm gonna need more than two of these envelopes if that's what you got in mind. This is great. I mean—"

"Whitey, shut up, turn around, and eat your breakfast. I was up all night and need to grab a couple of Zs. Be quiet and don't cause any problems. That's your first assignment."

"Sure. Sure, you got it, man. No problem."

I checked the review mirror and caught Helen's eyes. She shrugged, now maybe more content that I had not intended to keep the cash for myself.

I eased down across the seat and let the sandman crawl up from the depths of the earth, grab me by the throat, and drag me down to a place I didn't want to go.

Bosco flew through the air, my foot on his chest as I fell backward. His green eyes—Sonja's eyes, pleading with me. "Don't do it, mister, please?"

I woke to my cell phone vibrating. I got up confused, looking around for the Honda that had snatched my son out of the air—looked for the dead bikers, the downed Highway Patrol officer. Instead, I found myself in the backseat of an air-conditioned truck, the phone in my right front pocket buzzing.

My mouth was dry and tacky. I struggled to sit up. Helen sat in the front seat with the binoculars braced on the top of the steering wheel, watching the apartment on Willowbrook in Compton, the one Worm told us Little T-Dog frequented. The truck smelled of fermenting beer, body odor, and something else, rotten and dying.

I pulled the phone from my pocket, reached for the door latch, eased it open, and slid out. "Hello?"

"Bruno? Where have you been? I've been calling. I thought something happened. I was about to track your phone's GPS."

"I'm okay." I didn't want to tell him I'd been lying down on the job, but he deserved to know. "I . . . can't go too long without some sort of break."

He paused, taking in that information, and was probably wondering if I could do the job at all. "We dumped the info on that cell phone number. The texts are all in code. I sent it to the guys who handle this sort of thing in D.C. I'll have it back soon. You sure you're okay?"

"I'm good, I promise."

"You . . . ah, got anything else for me?"

"I'm working on it." I didn't want to give him something with no chance of panning out. "I should have something for you soon. Stay by the phone."

Another long, uncomfortable pause while I tried to peer into the truck through the heavy tint to see what Helen thought of my clandestine phone call, and could only see my own reflection. I didn't like what looked back, a broken-down black man with dark circles under eyes sunken into a gaunt face. Someone I didn't recognize at all.

People on the street, in cars, and on the sidewalks, went about their everyday business. They didn't care one wit that a crumpled, slump-shouldered black man in a sweat-soaked Pepsi work shirt stood by a newer truck talking on a cell.

A hundred yards or more down the street, three gang members dressed in street regalia did the gang crouch close to T-Dog's apartment door. Hard-core, experienced veterans. The building was mustard with red doors and trim and a rotting composition roof. All the windows and doors in the entire building had been reinforced with steel bars and framed in thick angle iron.

"I got that information you wanted," Chulack said.

"Huh? What?"

"On Beatrice Elliot."

I stood up straight. I'd forgotten about that request. I wasn't sure I wanted to know the answer. No, I knew I didn't. I put my forehead up against the window of the truck and closed my eyes.

"Bruno, you still there?"

"Yeah, go ahead."

"Beatrice Elliot *was* arrested and convicted of murder but her crime was vacated."

I opened my eyes. "What?"

"It doesn't give a reason why here, but I'll find out."

"She's on parole."

"That's more information than I can get right now. Her jacket has been flagged by DOJ."

"What does that mean?"

"I've seen something like this before. Sometimes it means"—He hesitated.

"What?"

"It could be a WITSEC flag. I have a bureau attorney jumping through the necessary hoops so we can get a peek at it. Tomorrow, maybe."

WITSEC? Was my mother in the witness protection program? Had she given up a major player in some far-reaching criminal conspiracy?

"Okay, thanks."

"You got anything else for me?"

"Ah . . . nothing yet." I turned and looked down the street to the apartment where Little T-Dog was supposed to be. The endless waiting for Chulack had to be taking years off his life. I didn't want to leave him hanging.

"Okay," he said, "let me know if—"

"I do have something. Right now, it's still a long shot."

"Good. Let's have it."

"There's a small possibility—a real small one—that I'm going to need two SWAT teams to hit a house."

His voice rose several octaves. "Give me the details."

The need of a SWAT team meant arrests and arrests meant movement in his stalled kidnap investigation.

"It might not be a 'go.' I won't know for about an hour and then this is only a fifty-fifty that I'll need them. Maybe seventy-thirty that I won't."

"Bruno?"

"Have the two teams stage way out of the area. Too close, and these bangers will get a whiff of it."

"I understand. What's the address?"

I gave it to him.

"What are the circs on this place?"

"It's Little T-Dog. I don't know for sure if he's in there. Not yet. Can you call the Sheriff and have them keep their units out of the area?"

"Sure. Sure, this is excellent, Bruno."

"I have to get back to it," I said. I had enough of my own grief and angst without his transferring through the phone.

"Keep me posted." He clicked off.

That's when I noticed how low the sun hung in the sky, less than an hour until dusk. How long had I been asleep? Several hours at least. Helen must think something was wrong with me.

More important, what was Marie thinking? For sure she'd be worried sick. I needed to call her. No, I needed to get back to the suite. That information about my mom was disconcerting and had to be clarified. And at the moment, Bea was the only one who could do that.

I had to make something happen, and quick. I made my decision and got back in the truck.

CHAPTER TWENTY-ONE

"WHITEY, IT'S TIME for you to earn your money."

"I don't like the sound of that. Not one bit. Doesn't matter, though. I can't do anything till I take care of a little personal bizness. I gotta drop a deuce."

"You're a real pig, you know that?" Helen said.

"Hey, it's a perfectly natural bodily function. I'm not ashamed of it. Come on, get me to a head, I'm starting to turtle."

"Pig."

"I want you to go in that apartment and see if Little T-Dog is in there," I said.

Helen grinned. It came off a little evil.

"No way. Are you kiddin' me? They'll eat me alive."

"You got off that bus at 60th and Avalon. How come? I think it means you're comfortable running around in this area."

He squirmed. "Come on, man, I really have to use the head."

"Tell me why you think you're safe around here."

He shrugged but kept quiet.

"You showed an inmate—a shot caller—how to get out of his case by setting someone else up to take his fall, going to the DA to trade bogus information. Just like you did that last time and got caught."

"No, hell no." He said it without conviction.

"In any case, for whatever reason, someone owes you big. That's why a white boy like you can run around down here without getting jacked up."

"Look . . . Wait. Wait. Maybe there's some truth to that, but that's all over now. I already used up that ticket. The dude told me the next time I was on my own."

"We need this and you're going to do it."

"You can kiss my white ass, if I am."

I leaned back, suddenly tired of all the games. "Listen, you get out and walk down there right now or we'll drive you up, open the door, and drag you into that front yard. We'll make sure those gangsters see our badges while we thank you for all your help."

"No, you won't. That's straight-up murder, the same as if you pulled the trigger, and you know it."

"If you had to, you can talk your way into that place. Get moving."

He looked to Helen. "You're not going for this, are you? It's murder." Maybe he thought he'd built some kind of rapport with her while I'd slept. Fat chance.

She shrugged again. "Look at it this way, they've got to have a toilet in there to handle your *turtle* issue." She shot him a lopsided grin.

I did feel bad about sending him into a place where violence was an everyday staple, the same as a bowl of cornflakes with diced-up bananas. For that matter, probably more common. This was the life he chose. I held up a second envelope of cash.

"Yeah, right. Does me a whole lotta good they gut me like a pig."

"You going to get out and walk up there on your own two feet, or we giving you a ride?"

"Not only no, but hell no."

I nodded to Helen. She twisted back to face the steering wheel and started the truck.

"Okay. Okay." He held up his hands with his eyes closed and took in two large breaths. He opened them. "You know, for a minute there I thought you two were a couple of good Joes and not asshole cops like all the rest. Typical. I'm not kiddin', I should've known better. What was I thinking?" He smacked his head with the flat of his hand.

"Get out," Helen said.

He opened his door. I reached over the seat and put my hand on his shoulder. "You'd better leave your money here."

His expression shifted to incredulous. "You're outta your ever-lovin' mind. Not on your life, asswipe." He got out and slammed the door. He looked at the truck for a long beat before turning around and heading down the middle of the street in typical mope fashion, a saunter that said he had all day to get where he was going.

"You know," I said, "he'll have a better chance without shoes. No narc would walk up to a pad like that in stocking feet." I was only trying to convince myself that I had not forced him into committing hari-kari.

"You're probably right. But those are some dirty socks," she said.

"All the better. Did you tag his shoes with a GPS? That's why I tossed them out the window."

Helen didn't answer, reached into her pocket, and pulled out some folding money. "I got a twenty says he'll need paramedics."

I tried not to smile. "You're one cold broad."

"Oh, like you're not thinking the same thing?"

"Yeah, well maybe, but I'm not putting money on the 'if.'" I put a twenty up on the top of the seat. "Paramedics in fifteen minutes. Because it's a matter of when, not if. I'm taking fifteen minutes."

She threw her head back and laughed. It was out of character for her usual plain-Jane affect and at the same time sexy beyond belief.

I chuckled along with her. "Did I tell you my wife is very beautiful?"

Her laugh ratcheted down until she stopped and continued to stare at my sunglasses. "Take them off. Please?"

"Sorry." I got out of the backseat of the truck and got in the front seat vacated by Whitey. A residual stink lingered, one similar to Limburger cheese. It was thicker than just an essence and had substance to it almost like it was a living entity.

She lost her smile and turned back around to watch Whitey walk the plank.

His shoulders rose and fell out of sync as his stocking feet stepped on bits of grit and small rocks in the street. He took his time. At his rate of travel, it might take him twenty minutes to go the hundred yards down to the apartment.

We watched in silence.

Helen didn't look away from the windshield and asked, "What's your medical issue? Why'd you check out for so long?" She hooked her thumb toward the backseat where I'd napped.

I looked from Whitey down the street to her and waited. When she looked at me, I said, "Two months ago, I was shot in the hip."

She said nothing and nodded as if she understood, as if it wasn't a big deal and for her, everyone she knew took a round to the hip at least once in their lifetime.

"That wasn't the bad one, though. Someone else stuck a .25 up to my chest and pulled the trigger. That's the one I'm having a little problem recovering from." I pointed to my breast.

"Yikes, sorry to hear that, really." Her expression softened for the first time. It changed her into an entirely different person. Exposed a deeply hidden vulnerability. She didn't like to show that part of herself and quickly turned back to watching Whitey's progress. "You get the guy who did it?"

"It was an ex-girlfriend who pulled the trigger, the mother of my son. My wife, Marie, shot and killed her."

Helen's head whipped around. "You're kidding me, right?"

I didn't answer.

She stared for a moment. "That's harsh. I mean really. Remind me never to go out to dinner with you or your wife. Jesus, you play rough." She went back to watching.

Dinner? With her? Nowhere near the realm of possibility.

Whitey made it to the small yard in front of the apartment where the three gangbangers stood guard. All of them wore the same solid black Dickies pants, with black-, gray-, and white-striped knit shirts. They had blue bandanas tied around their foreheads, low, just above their eyes, gang colors. Uniformed soldiers. Two grabbed Whitey and shook him like a rag doll, his arms flapping. They let go and punched him. He went to the ground. They all kicked him again and again. I cringed with each blow. My hand involuntarily went to the door handle to roll out, to run down there and rescue him. No way would I get there in time. What was going to happen would happen and I couldn't stop it even if I wanted to.

Whitey yelled something as he covered up, taking the kicks to his back and head and abdomen.

They stopped kicking and stepped back for a moment to listen to his rants. One of them moved over to the heavily reinforced door and spoke through the screen to someone inside. He nodded. The door opened. Whitey struggled to his feet, brushing off his pants and shirt. Blood ran down the side of his face. I felt sorry for him.

He was all right, though, not too battered and bruised. I kept telling myself this was something that had to be done.

He tried to kick one of the members who'd participated in the beating. The guy easily stepped out of the way. All three laughed. Whitey disappeared inside. The door closed behind him with a heavy clang that reverberated up and down the street. With it came an uncomfortable sense of finality.

Helen checked her watch. "You said you got fifteen minutes for the paramedics. He just proved he's scrappy so I'll take twenty minutes. Hope they didn't literally kick the crap out of him. If they did, he's not getting back in this truck."

She was a little too callous and cynical, especially for a woman. I wanted to ask her what it felt like to sit in a crumpled and disabled cop car underneath a leaking gas tanker, with her own gun to her head, waiting for the big *whomph* that would ignite the thousands of gallons of gas all around her. That had to be an enormous emotional scar, one better left undisturbed. She'd survived physically, but at what cost emotionally? I'd discovered through the years, far more cops carried those types of invisible scars than the public could ever imagine.

We waited some more watching the front of the apartment, willing Whitey to come out.

Finally, she said, "You know, you shouldn't be back to work yet. Not in your condition. How did HR give you a medical release?"

"You're absolutely right. I should still be in bed. This is a special favor for a friend. And for the record, I do appreciate the assistance."

She turned to look at me, her eyes soft again, damp and desirous. "That's some favor."

"He's a good friend."

She held my gaze a moment longer trying to figure me out, then went back to looking through the binoculars.

Twenty-two minutes after he went in, the steel door opened. Out flew Whitey. He stumbled and fell in the dirt scaring up a puff of dust, a third-base runner sliding into home. The three in the front yard chased him to the street. They stopped at the edge of the sidewalk as if long invisible leashes tugged them back. Whitey stood in the street and yelled, swung his arms, and kicked at the air. A fool's errand; you don't antagonize a pride of lions. The gang members ignored him and moved back to their perch close to the door. Whitey regained a smidgeon of bravery and advanced back to the sidewalk, still yelling and swinging his arms. He picked up a rock and slung it at them. The smaller one of the three ran at him, then stopped in the middle of the yard. He raised the front of his shirt, his hand going to the stock of a handgun. Whitey turned and fled. He tripped and stumbled and fell, skinning his hands and knees. He got up and ran a few yards, his head turned, watching his aggressor, afraid of a bullet to the back, before he shifted his gait back to a trot and then a walk.

Helen shrugged and put her money away. "Don't think he's bad enough for paramedics, the bet's off."

"Let's hope Little T-Dog is in there and we didn't send him in for nothing."

CHAPTER TWENTY-TWO

WHITEY MADE IT back to the truck and banged on the passenger window. I eased the tinted window down an inch. "Get in the back."

He didn't move and pointed to the apartment down the street. "You see what those pricks did to me? Those bastards kicked my ass and took my money. Gimme a gun. Come on, man, gimme a gun."

He was too loud and making a scene. I moved the window to halfway down. "Don't make me step out. I said, get in the back." Helen hit the automatic door locks so they made a noise.

Reluctantly, Whitey complied, climbed in where I'd been sitting, and slammed the door. "You gonna do something or not? You can't let them get away with this. They took my goddamn money." He punched the headrest to my seat again and again.

"While you were in there," Helen said, "did you manage to void your bowels of all those wild kingdom issues?"

He glared at her.

"Who's in there?" I asked. "Is Little T-Dog in there like Worm said?"

"I'm not sayin', until you say you're gonna do something about what happened." He jabbed an angry finger in their direction down the street. "I'm workin' for you. You gonna let them do that to your employee? Huh? Are you?"

"Look, I'm tired," I said. "It's been a long day and I want to go home. I'm sorry you got the hell beat out of you, I am. But let's try and stay focused on the job at hand." I took another envelope from my pocket and tossed it on his lap.

He crumpled it in his fist. "I'm so damn mad I could spit." The blood on the side of his face no longer ran and had started to dry with dust and bits of grit sticking to it.

"Is Little T-Dog in there or not?"

"Yeah, he's in there. They just ordered takeout, Chinese. With my money. You believe that? Egg Foo Young and egg rolls with my damn money." He thumped his chest with a fist full of crumpled envelope. "They laughed at me."

It was hard to believe Whitey had pride enough to get insulted.

I pulled out my cell phone and hit the speed dial. Chulack picked up. I said, "Go." The phone went dead. I rolled down the window the rest of the way to listen.

Whitey sensed something important had just happened. "What's going on?" He stuck his head past the seat into our side of the compartment. Helen put her hand on his face and shoved him back. "He said to shut up and listen." She rolled her window down.

In the jungle, when a carnivore, a class-A predator, is on the prowl, everything goes silent. That's what I heard outside the truck window, a stillness, a prelude to violence. A prelude to blood and bone. While hunting men with Robby Wicks, this was something I dearly missed.

Dusk hung in the air thick enough to blur the harsh lines of reality. Three black Suburbans rolled down the street, the kind with aftermarket sideboards to stand on and handrails attached to the roof. Three HRT FBI agents stood on each side wearing full SWAT gear. Eighteen personnel.

Whitey watched in awe. "Holy shit. I wouldn't want to be those bangers in that shithole right now."

Two of the bangers in front saw they were outgunned and fled. The foolish one stepped forward as he pulled up his shirt and yanked out his gun.

Simultaneously, two of the Suburbans stopped on the street. The twelve HRT passengers disembarked, stepping lightly to the ground, machine guns up, yelling, "Get down. Get down. Drop your gun." The lead FBI agent fired a three-round burst. The foolish gangbanger wilted to the ground. A fine mist of red floated in the air where he once stood.

The first Suburban backed up over the curb as all eighteen agents fanned out to cover the door breech. Two ran around to secure the rear of the apartment. The Suburban backed up in the yard and stopped as one agent dragged the dead banger out of the way. Another agent dragged a chain with a hook from the back of the vehicle and secured it to the reinforced apartment door. All the while the other agents yelled, "Search warrant. Search warrant. Demand entry." The Suburban took off, spinning the back tires, filling the air with a rooster tail of dirt.

The chain yanked. The door, the entire wood frame, and part of the wall pulled free of the apartment and got dragged out into the street. The agents tossed in five flashbangs. The lowlight dusk exploded with bright flashes of yellow and orange. White smoke billowed out. They entered, guns up to their shoulders.

Gunfire came from inside.

Then silence.

It all happened in less than thirty seconds.

I turned to look at Whitey. He wore a huge smile.

"Did you see that?" he said. "Son of a bitch, that was really something. You did that, didn't you? You did that with one word. You said, 'Go,' into the phone. And all hell broke loose. You did that.

Son of a bitch. That was like some kind of military weapon. You fired a cruise missile right up their ass and ka-fucking-boom."

Helen put her hand on his face and shoved him back, really putting her shoulder in it this time. He bounced off the back window, giggling like a school kid.

"Shut up," she said. "Didn't you see what just happened? Someone died right there in that front yard. Died right in front of us."

Whitey looked indignant. "Are you kiddin' me? That dude doesn't count."

"Shut up. Shut up right now, or I'll climb back there and *I'll* beat your ass."

Down the street, Chulack pulled up in a plain-wrap undercover car. I got out, stretched, and headed down to meet him as dusk handed off to full dark, no stars. The truck door opened and closed behind me. Helen was coming along to take custody of Little T-Dog. Only she had to know the FBI wasn't going to give him up, not for all the money in the world. I took my phone out, typed in a text message, and hit SEND: *I'm an FBI agent.* To remind Chulack not to call me Bruno. Down the street, Chulack pulled his phone from his pocket, looked at it, and put it back. He waited in front of the apartment for HRT to finish.

He was waiting for me.

CHAPTER TWENTY-THREE

HELEN CAUGHT UP and walked at my side.

I said, "You leave Whitey in there with both our war bags? I got a couple of extra guns and mags in mine."

"I grappled him up. He's not happy about it."

We walked some more. She said, "We're going to be here all night with the shoot team debrief. We're involved whether we want to be or not."

"Wrong. That phone call I gave Chulack was from an anonymous source. That's the way the report will read. We're just going to check in, make sure we can talk to Little T-Dog in the morning—that is if they don't solve this thing right away—and then we'll call it a night."

Darkness masked everything. An agent pulled one of the Suburbans up to the curb at an angle; now the headlights illuminated the front of the gaping hole in the apartment that looked like a speed freak missing two front teeth. Uniformed Los Angeles County patrol deputies arrived and blocked off both ends of the street. No one would be able to pass until late tomorrow afternoon. Paramedic sirens pierced the air.

An agent in a suit came out of the gaping hole carrying a notepad. Residual smoke and the headlights gave him a haloed effect. He beelined to Chulack and got there the same time we did.

Chulack's tailored suit looked fresh, but he was more haggard than the last time I saw him. He wouldn't be able to take much more of this kind of stress.

The agent said nothing as he looked at us and then at Chulack. Chulack said, "They're okay, they're with me. Go ahead, what do you have?"

The agent looked down at his pad. "When they entered, HRT met with armed resistance. They were forced to neutralize the threat."

Wienie words, to protect the Bureau, words that would start as a seed and grow into a plant to help shield them from public scrutiny.

Chulack shook his head, disappointed. He must've told the teams he had to have them alive and talking. "Go on."

"We only have a preliminary ID at this time, but it appears that Thomas Adrien Armstrong is one of the DOAs."

"Damn. You sure?"

"He was ID'ed by his tattoos. It's ninety-eight percent."

The agent smiled.

"What?" Chulack asked.

The agent took out his phone and pulled up a photo. "Sir, inside we found twenty thousand dollars of the ransom money—the serial numbers check out. These are the guys. Whoever gave you that phone tip was right on. We'll get forensics in here and run the whole place down to the last hair. We can also interview the other four inside. We just found our way back into the investigation. We'll get them now. It won't take long."

Chulack allowed himself a small smile, had to be the first one in a couple of weeks. He offered me his hand. I shook it. He said, "Thank you, my friend."

"It wasn't me. This is Helen Hellinger, a detective with Los Angeles County Sheriff's Department. She did most of the heavy lifting."

He shook her hand. "You ever need anything from the FBI, you call me, direct."

She nodded, choosing not to speak, which was not like her.

I said to Chulack, "You can take it the rest of the way, right? I have to get back to Marie. Let me know what happens. But in the morning."

"You got it, Bru—" He caught himself. "I'll call you at eight."

"Make it ten." Exhaustion suddenly jumped on my back and tried to pile-drive me into the pavement. I turned and headed back to the truck. Helen came with me.

"Just like that you're really calling it a night? We just got started. We still have to run down Calvin Ivory, *Mr. Police Killa Bitch.*"

I stopped. "You don't need me for that."

"I thought you wanted to find the kidnappers."

"I do, but the FBI has plenty of leads right now to keep 'em busy. They'll figure it out real quick. I need to get some rest."

In the dark, she nodded. "Okay. Where can I reach you?"

"Why don't I call you?"

"Don't feed me that standard FBI enigma bullshit. I thought we had something going here, some rapport. We're a good team." She pointed back to the damaged apartment. "The suspect to my murder is dead. I need Calvin Ivory to clear my case." She said it like an accusation. "We need to get him off the street before he kills someone else."

She was definitely right about that last part. And in another time, back when I used to hunt men, she wouldn't have been able to stop me from running Ivory down.

I again started walking back to the truck. "I'd like to help you, but I have other problems I have to deal with tonight. I'll call you in the morning. You need a ride back to your car?"

She got ahead of me, walking backwards, skipping every other step to keep up. "We could've taken our time on this. We could've watched that apartment until T-Dog went mobile and took him down in his car. *Alive*."

I stopped walking. "There aren't any guarantees in life. He could just as easily pull a gun on a car stop."

"You know what I'm talking about."

"Yes, I do. And in a perfect world we might've tried that, but like I told you back at the jail, I was brought in to handle this a certain way. Time was not our friend. It's still not."

She pointed back to the apartment. "That's the way you handled it, with two dead, and our best lead to find Calvin Ivory gone up in smoke and lead?"

It was more like blood and bone, but I didn't say it out loud. "What do you want from me?"

"Never mind. Thanks for nothing. I don't want to put you out with what you have going in your personal life. I'll grab my war bag and catch an Uber."

"Hey, I'm sorry. I'll talk to you tomorrow."

"Yeah, right. So that's it then, we're done."

"I didn't say that. I said that I'll call—"

"Yeah, you did. I know exactly what that means. I could say nice working with you, but like Whitey said, you can kiss my white ass."

I wanted to tell her I was sorry, that she had it all wrong, but I was too dog-tired to deal with it. My phone call to her in the morning would dispel all her misgivings.

Back at the truck I found Whitey trussed up on the backseat, his hands cuffed behind his back and his feet secured with a rope-a-dope that hooked to the chain of the handcuffs, effectively hog-tying his hands to his feet. What we used to call turning the guy into a "suitcase." Helen had accomplished this maneuver with amazing speed and agility. I didn't remember her staying behind that long before she followed.

I only wished she'd gagged him. He continued to yell and scream about his rights and lawsuits, and owning the both of us. That we'd be his "dirt slaves," whatever that meant.

She grabbed her war bag, slammed the door, and walked off into the night. I didn't want it to end that way. I liked working with her and realized it wasn't so much a matter of liking her as missing the thrill of the hunt. The day's activities had somehow satisfied something inside me. For the last twelve hours, I was able to feed that need Dad had described, the need to right a wrong even if it meant putting a knee on someone's neck. I didn't drop the hammer on the gang member in the front of the apartment or on Little T-Dog, but like Whitey said, I'd been the one to push the button that fired the "cruise missile up their asses." That brought to mind Helen's reaction to Whitey's overexuberance after watching the kill. She had not acted like any cop I had ever worked with. She had too much empathy, and in the cop job that kind of emotion would erode her core values until she fizzled and popped like a kernel of corn in boiling oil. She'd become a burnt-out wreck at risk of eating her gun. I needed to talk to her about it but didn't know her well enough to broach such a sensitive topic. I'd have to find a way.

I opened the truck door and got in, anxious to get home to Marie.

Whitey's swearing from the backseat helped keep me awake on the drive back to Glendale.

CHAPTER TWENTY-FOUR

By the time I pulled into the parking tower at the Americana Mall and Hotel, Whitey got tired of screaming, his voice going hoarse. The entire drive, I had plenty to think about, but instead I kept coming back to the way Helen had reacted to the sudden dissolution of our partnership. Her anger didn't seem appropriate.

She did have something to worry about, though. In all likelihood, the FBI would take the evidence from the scene, and the interviews of those involved, and run down Calvin Ivory. Who, if taken alive, could give up who he worked for, the rest of the kidnap conspiracy. It could all be over by the time I woke in the morning. Marie and I would then be on the next flight out, headed for the beautiful—but, more important, peace-loving—Costa Rica. To recuperate, to see the kids and Dad. We might just do that anyway, not tell a soul, and leave. I'd done my part. With the type of people involved in this heinous crime, hope for Emily Mosely, if there was any left, had dwindled down into the negative.

I called Drago and told him where to meet me in the parking garage. He lumbered out of the elevator, his head checking right then left, securing his environment before he proceeded. A natural survival instinct important in someone who had angered The Sons of Satan, an outlaw motorcycle gang. The Sons had a shoot-on-sight order out on Drago. Not much chance of Drago being spotted in Glendale by anyone of their ilk. The Sons would stand out like a black cat on a snowbank.

I stood waiting. He came up and handed me a Yoo-hoo and a package of Snowball cupcakes. My stomach rolled at the thought. It was too soon after witnessing the shooting. What I needed was a cold beer and something savory, like a shark steak fresh off the grill. Not this sickening sweetness.

"You look like shit, my brother."

"Hey, good seeing you, too." I twisted off the cap to the Yoo-hoo and took a long slug of the chocolate liquid. It did taste wonderful and at the same time electrifying, reenergizing. I needed it more than I thought.

"How's Marie doing?" But I knew. If there had been an issue, Drago would've called right away.

"Great. No problems."

"And what about the wom . . . I mean . . . my mother?"

"Strange duck, that's for sure." He held up his hands. "No offense."

"I know what you mean."

"She's all right, I guess. It's kind of weird. For some reason, I never saw you as having a mother."

I chuckled. "So you think I just, what, sort of miraculously appeared, walked out of some early morning mist or something like that?"

"Yeah, I guess so." He pondered the image I must've evoked. "I'll tell you what, she never stopped talkin'. I'm not kiddin'. I had to put some wadded-up toilet paper in my ears. Oh, hey." He plucked out the makeshift earplugs. "That's better." He worked his jaw, popping his ears.

He peered into the open truck door and spotted Whitey lying still and quiet on the backseat. "You fill your hunting tag for the year with a scrawny white boy. There's no meat on his bones? You are getting old."

"Who's that?" Whitey craned his head around to see. "What? You're friends with Jabba the Hutt? Figures." He struggled against his bindings. "Come on, get me outta here. It's not funny anymore. I get out, I'm gonna kick all your asses."

Drago made a face. "That smell coming from him?"

"Yeah, 'fraid so. He might've messed in his pants." I took a moment trying to decide what to do with him. "You know, just in case this thing doesn't go well out there on the street tonight, there's an outside chance I might need him in the morning, and—"

"I'll take care of it."

"Can you clean him up a bit and maybe get him some decent clothes?"

"No," Whitey, yelped. "You're talkin' like I'm some kinda dog you're gonna take out back of the barn and shoot. That's what you really mean, isn't it? I know it is. I'm not just anybody's fool, you know. No sir, I'm not goin' anywhere, 'specially not with no fat-assed Marlon Brando who thinks he's a biker. No way. Cut me loose, or I swear to gawd, once I get free, I'll kill all of you. You hear me? I'll do it."

Drago said, "Does he have to be in one piece tomorrow morning?" He said it without humor.

Whitey went quiet for a moment, then said, "Johnson, don't do this to me. I kept your secret today. I did. You know I did."

I reached in and patted his head. "You do what Drago says and you'll be all right. He'll treat you good."

"Johnson? Johnson, no. You can't—"

I eased the door closed, looking around the near vacant parking tower to see if anyone heard the verbal exchange. I handed Drago the keys. "Thanks for all your help."

"No thanks necessary. This is kinda fun compared to what I had planned."

"I'm afraid to ask." I held up my hand. "Don't tell me." I put a hand on his shoulder, which was as much touching as Drago allowed from other men. He'd had a pretty rotten childhood. He never told me about it. I could only assume by little things he let slip during our time together. And from some ancient scars on his ankles and wrists and across his back.

"See you in the morning for a ride to the airport."

"Right, boss. No problem."

I headed to the elevator, eating the Snowballs and swilling the Yoo-hoo like a drunken sailor. Thinking about Marie's smile and that wonderful king-sized bed I wanted to fall into and get lost in along with her.

On the third floor, I turned the corner and this time didn't see a Glendale cop standing down the hall in front of the suite. Small miracles.

Thirty seconds later, I froze, hand on the door latch, and remembered my mother would be in there. The thought made the world tilt to one side just a little. I was a broken-down old man. It was too late in life to be conversing—for the first time ever—with my mother. Maybe she'd be asleep and I could deal with it in the morning.

My mother.

I couldn't shake how strange that sounded. "Mother" continued to ping around in my fatigued brain. I went in.

No luck. The woman sat in her wheelchair almost in the same place I'd seen her the first time. Marie, on the couch, stood up. I raised my hand and said, "Evening." I went into the kitchen area to the reefer where I took out an ice-cold Sierra Nevada pale ale. Marie was standing behind me when I turned. She wrapped her arms around my torso and buried her head in my chest. "You big galoot. I'm so glad to have you back."

I knew she really wanted to ask the more important question about our status and ETA of our upcoming plane ride.

I took a long slug of beer that cooled all the way down and didn't mix well with the Yoo-hoo and cupcakes I'd scarfed too quickly. I kissed the top of her head just as a burp slipped by me. "Oops, sorry."

She looked up at me and smiled, the kind of smile I lived for. "Well?"

She couldn't wait any longer.

"We caught one of them. They'll catch the other one by morning, and we can catch the next flight out."

Her smile grew wider. She leaned up, pulled my head down, and kissed me on the lips. "That's wonderful, babe. It really is." Her expression shifted to concern. "How are you feeling?"

"Like ten miles of bad road."

"You need to get some rest. A lot of rest."

I didn't want to tell her I'd slept a good chunk of the day in the backseat of the truck while she stayed at home worrying about me, stayed with a woman we didn't know.

"Come say hello to your mother and—oh my God, Bruno, what's that odor? You stink. Were you around a cadaver? You're not getting into our bed until you shower."

"Good, I was hoping you'd say something like that."

She slapped my chest and lowered her voice to a whisper. "You be good. Don't forget, we have company."

She guided me into the living room area. I sat on the couch with her next to me holding my hand. She suddenly stiffened. "I'm sorry." She slid down the couch away from me.

Bea watched all of this without a word, without any expression at all. I lost my smile when I looked at her. Fatigue and stress caught up and snuffed out any decorum left in the tank. I was running on fumes. I asked, "What exactly do you want? Why have you come here?"

Marie tried to answer for her. "Bruno, she wants to reconnect with her family. That's a perfectly natural—"

Bea had not taken her eyes off mine. "Let her speak," I said.

Bea waited. Time stretched. Sweat beaded on my forehead.

Finally, she said, "I need to get out of the country. I'd like to go with you to Costa Rica."

Marie's mouth sagged open in shock.

CHAPTER TWENTY-FIVE

I WAS SUDDENLY sick to my stomach. No way would I let this woman traipse into our lives after all the lost years, the lost decades, and make such an absurd request. What the hell was she thinking? That blood relations gave her that right? Not a chance. I struggled to my feet, swaying to maintain my balance as blood rushed from my head. "You're welcome to stay here as long as you like, as long as we are here." I turned and took several steps toward the bedroom, thinking another eight to ten hours and all this would be over. Marie said, "Bruno, wait. Let's talk about this."

I faced the living area and them. "Did you know this is what she wanted?" I asked Marie.

"Of course not. I would've talked to you about it first. I wouldn't have dumped this in your lap. Not like she just did. You know better than that." She turned to Bea, pointing a loaded finger. "You're out of line."

Bea shrugged. "It's always less painful if you just yank off the Band-Aid." She shot us a disingenuous smile, at least that's the way it appeared. I hadn't been around her long enough to know better. I opened my mouth to tell her no way in hell was she going with us to Costa Rica, but Marie's hand came up and covered my lips. She patted my chest. "Let's get you to bed, big guy. We can deal with this in the morning."

"Really?" Bea said. "It's only eight fifteen. The good nightclubs aren't even open yet."

"What the hell—" I said. Marie spun me around and headed me out. She got me in the bedroom with the door closed. "Wait," she said. "Before you say another thing, let me—"

I said, "I don't believe the gall of that woman. How can she—"

Marie held up her hand. "I said wait, Bruno, and I mean it, not another word."

I shut up.

"You were gone all day. I was the one here with her. I can understand why you're angry. The way she acted, what she said just now, that wasn't like her. I got to know her, a little. She's a nice and respectful person. Nothing like what you just saw out there. She's probably tired just like you are, and neither of you need to say something you'll regret."

I sat on the edge of the bed. I bent over to undo my shoes and almost continued onto the floor. She caught me and helped get my shoes off. I said, "Have you thought that she may be gaslighting you and her true self just made an appearance out there?"

She took a step back. "So now you're questioning my judgment?"

"Uh-oh."

"You better believe, 'uh, oh,' little mister. You're the one who took off this morning while I was still asleep."

"About that, I'm sorry. I didn't want to wake you. You were up all night and—"

"Don't. You know we've had this conversation more than once. You know I don't care what time it is; I always want to kiss you before you leave and when you get home. That's one of our rules." She pointed her finger. "And don't try to say you did kiss me but I was asleep. You know I mean when I'm awake."

I whispered to myself, "One of *our rules*—"

She grabbed me by the ear and yanked. "Ouch, okay. Okay. I give." She let go. I gingerly touched my ear. "You know that's spousal abuse and I can have you arrested. Hand me the phone, I'm calling the police."

She tried to stifle a smile at the absurdity of the statement.

I started to undress to get in the shower. I smelled of Old English 800, grease from Roscoe's fried chicken, and worst of all, I emitted Whitey stink. On the street they called it "stank." Marie started to help. "Stand up."

I did as I was told and said, "I don't want to question your great and wondrous ability to evaluate and classify people based on spending one afternoon with them."

She stopped. "Bruno, tread lightly here. Pick your words carefully."

"Okay, never mind."

"No. No, you're not going to do that. Tell me what you were going to say."

I'd started something I really didn't want to finish. "She told you she's on parole."

"That's right, and so are you, technically."

"Ooh, that one hurt me right here." I picked her hand up and held it to my chest as I smiled, trying to get her to do the same.

"Don't change the subject. You were going to say something else. What was it?"

I squirmed a little.

"Out with it, mister."

"Did she tell you she's in the witness protection program?"

For the second time that night, Marie's mouth dropped open. "She's *what*?" She spun on her heel and stormed out of the room. I finished undressing and took my shower, trying not to smile too broadly at the beast I'd just unleashed on dear ol' Mom.

When I came out of the shower, loud talking still came from the other room. I thought about going out there and backing Marie up, but sleep beckoned like a siren on the rocks. I could catch up on all of my absent mother's trash talk tomorrow. I crawled in between the sheets just in time. The sandman came up and jerked me down deep into the void where I didn't want to go. Where I never wanted to go.

"*Bosco. No!*"

* * *

I sat up straight in bed, the room dark except for the glow from the slit between the window curtains. The mall down below never shut off all its lights. Our room was right above the Barnes & Noble, where in the last few weeks I'd spent many an hour reading in their Starbucks, recuperating.

The collar of my pajama top was damp with sweat and my feet itched.

Marie lay next to me on her side, her knees up close to her bump, her arms around a pillow. She looked more beautiful, if that were possible. Angelic in slumber. I wiggled to the edge, slipped my feet over, and stood. For the first time in two months the blood didn't rush downward and make me light-headed enough to swoon. I was healing fast. I eased open the door to the living area and found the soft glow of the television casting eerie shadows on the walls. Bea sat in her wheelchair watching a rerun of *The Andy Griffith Show*, a comical parody of what life is supposed to be like. A bucolic town without any crime and a sheriff who never carries a gun. What would that be like, a life without violence?

"I'm going to get me a snack," I said to her. "You want one?"

"That would be very kind of you. Yes, please." She didn't sound like a hardened con, or someone on the dodge having done something heinous enough to hide out with the US Marshal's Service from a dangerous criminal element.

I poured two glasses of cold milk and put a small pile of soft batch Keebler Elf chocolate chip cookies on two different plates. My mouth watered at the thought of the culinary delight. I put it all on a tray. It wouldn't be long now and Marie would take a pair of pliers and yank out my sweet tooth.

Bea accepted her snack, looking up at me with brown eyes occluded with cataracts. A wonder she could see at all. Her night vision must be nil. Up close she appeared different, no longer a Ma Barker type and more a harmless, emaciated old woman in a wheelchair. She clicked the TV to mute. We sat in the flickering light, ate our Keebler cookies, and drank our cool milk. A wave of déjà vu struck and made my head swirl. As a kid, more times than I could count, I had dreamt about this very moment: meeting my mom for the first time, talking with her, asking her the big question: Why? Now that it had come true, I didn't know how to deal with it. This was more an aberration that belonged somewhere in another life, one in a parallel universe where Andy and Opie and Barney reigned as kings.

At least Barney kept one bullet in his shirt pocket, a small hint of a violent world. He was a buffoon in that story, and yet he had the instinct to survive.

I finally said, "You going to tell me why you're really here?"

"You know, it's really amazing. I mean I can still see in you . . . that little boy from my memories, your features—that same smile. You still have the same smile. It's kind of a huge shock for me to see you so grown. So old. That cute little boy image will always be how I remember you, though."

I hadn't smiled once in her presence. She was blowing smoke up my skirt, to soften her target to the upcoming con—for the pitch. "Lucky you," I said. "I didn't have a memory to hold on to. You didn't stick around long enough for me to even get an image of you." I felt bad as soon as the words left my mouth.

"Go on," she said. "Get all that poison out of your system. You'll feel better, and then we'll finally be able to get down to the business of catching up with the lives we lost."

"Lives *we* lost?" I caught myself this time before I said more, said words I could never pull back. Who was I to throw stones? I had not been the pillar of moral values even though I tried hard to live a life Dad would be proud of. Things happen. *Life wasn't meant to be easy, otherwise you'd never savor the good times.* A platitude Dad always tossed my way when something in life reached up, grabbed on to my ankle, and tried to drag me under.

We sat silent for a while.

She finally said, "Marie's a lovely woman. You did very well for yourself."

"You don't have to tell me. She's the one thing in my life that keeps me going. Keeps me sane."

She nodded, paused, then asked, "Bruno, how's your father? How's Xander?"

"Didn't Marie tell you?"

"I didn't ask and she didn't volunteer it."

I wasn't in the mood to talk with her about Dad.

"Why are you in witness protection?"

"We going to skip the rest of the small talk and get right down to business?" Her voice caught as she piled on the emotions. "That's fine. I don't mind telling you all about it. I'm not in the program anymore. I was, but I left it because I was getting old and . . . and I wanted to see . . . to be with family." Fat crocodile tears rolled down her cheeks. She held her arms out wide. "Look at me."

And yet somehow the tears came off as genuine and started an acid burning in my heart. I did want to have a mother to love and care for, and I fought that ridiculous desire. I didn't know the woman twenty-four hours ago, and yet now felt sorry for her. I moved from the couch to the chair next to hers and held her hand.

She patted mine. "I made some huge mistakes in my life," she said. "The biggest one was not being there to see you grow up."

CHAPTER TWENTY-SIX

THE LITTLE ALARM in my head finally sounded, reminding me that this woman was a con artist, someone who lived her entire adult life in the criminal world, an immoral world I'd only stepped into periodically to grab a crook and then stepped back into the moral one. Lately, though, it seemed I'd stepped across that line once too often and now I remained stuck, partway in and partway out, getting torn in half. My reaction to the two dead gangbangers the FBI put down in that flash of violence was the perfect example of my total lack of empathy.

"What did you do to be put in witness protection?"

She waved her hand, closed her eyes, trying to dismiss the question. "That's old news, miles and miles of dirty water under *that* broken-down bridge."

"Tell me."

She opened her eyes and looked at me long and hard. "All right, baby. I won't sugarcoat it. You're a big boy and I can give it to you straight."

Now she talked like a con and not a long-lost mother.

"You do that," I said.

She looked down at her hands as shame clouded her expression. "I . . . I . . . that's why I'm on parole. I reneged on the deal, and rode the beef. They did put me in witness protection and when it came time to raise my right hand in court . . . facing those two, I couldn't do it. I went to prison instead."

If what she said was true, she'd just gained a few points in my book, for playing the game straight. "What kind of case? It had to be a heavy one to warrant a fed WITSEC."

"It was. You know Boulevard Freddy Banks?"

"Ah, man, you're kidding me." The floor dropped out from under me as my mind spun. I looked to the hotel room door. No way would it be strong enough to keep out that kind of evil.

She said nothing more and waited.

How could she have moved about in my world for so many years without ever coming up on my radar? Boulevard Freddy Banks was the number-two guy in the rock coke franchise for the greater Los Angeles area. He was huge and notorious. He'd murdered his way to the top and had millions of dollars to help keep him there. Wicks, my old boss, wanted a piece of Banks, but no one could ever put a solid case on him. Banks was too far removed from the hands-on part of the business. And there was a reason why no one ratted on him. If good old Mom had been in a position to take down Banks, she was a lot more dangerous to Marie, to our family, than I had ever imagined.

"He's in the fed pen now," I said. "Right?"

She shook her head. "He just got out. Without my testimony, they only had him on some money-laundering thing. That's why I'm here, now."

"He's out?" My face flushed hot with rage. I wanted to sock this old woman, no, my mother. "You dragged your slop into my life and put my wife, my pregnant wife, in jeopardy? What the hell were you thinking?"

More tears. This time they did nothing to penetrate my anger. I fumed, contemplating wheeling her out into the hall and slamming the door. Let Boulevard Freddy Banks have her. She started to wheel her chair from the living area toward her room. I wasn't going to stop her. For the time being it was for the best. At her bedroom door, her back still to me, she said, "I didn't know you were married. I didn't know you had a child on the way. How could I?" She turned her machine around. "I didn't know anything about you. I didn't. What happened . . . I mean, why I'm here . . . a big thug named Deon Rivers, who works for Freddy Banks, came sniffin' around the halfway house where parole placed me. Ruby Two was with him, that's how I knew for sure he was with Boulevard Freddy."

"Ruby Two was the other one you were going to testify against?"

Mother nodded. "I saw them from up the street. They didn't see me. I . . . had nowhere else to go. I'm sorry. I'll move my *slop* on out of here now. I won't be bothering you anymore."

Part of that empathy I thought had gone missing raised its ugly head, this at a most inopportune moment. "Wait."

She froze.

"You can stay till morning."

"That's generous of you, Son." No sarcasm in her tone.

Trying to use *son* to get to me. Instead, it only inflamed my rage all over again. I fought it. This woman was my mother. Marie was about to be a mother. Even though Marie would never find herself in this kind of jam . . . Oh, but she had. We had. Not two months earlier. Those who lived in glass houses and all that crap. "You have any money?"

She wheeled her chair a couple turns closer; her arms ropy with muscle for a woman her age. "Not one red cent. I'm in a real bind here, Son."

I tried to think. I tried to work out all the possible options. There weren't any. This old woman had backed me against the wall. "No way are we taking you with us to Costa Rica."

"I understand."

"Don't do that."

"Do what?"

"You know what I'm talking about."

She nodded.

"How did you find me?"

"I told you, through your nephew, Bruno."

"How did you know about Bruno?"

"Like I said, I was in this halfway house sponsored by Soldiers for Christ, the one in Lennox."

"I know the one you're talking about."

"There was an overdose. Zoey Oliver, that poor girl, took some pills and was finally able to escape this horrible world." Bea made the sign of the cross. "The sheriff came to take the report."

"Bruno's a sheriff's intern at Lennox station," I said, "and he was on a ride-along with the deputy. That's how it happened."

"That's right. I saw his name on his uniform, 'Bruno Johnson.' I asked him about it. I asked him if he was your son. He told me he was your brother's son. I didn't know you had a brother, Bruno."

"That's a long story. His name's Noble. Maybe I'll tell you about it sometime."

"I'd like that. Well, anyway, that's how I met your nephew. A couple days after, that's when Ruby Two showed with that thug. I didn't know what else to do and called Bruno."

"A couple of months back, Bruno went missing."

"Yes, that's when he was helping me relocate. Watching my back. He got me set up in a real nice apartment under an alias. He watched my back for a couple of weeks to make sure I was in the clear."

"What happened?"

She patted the wheels on both sides of the chair. "An old black woman on parole and in a wheelchair is hard to hide. My parole agent found me. She'd have violated my parole had I not come right over here. I didn't know what else to do. When Marie opened the door and let me in, she saved me. I had already called the parole agent; told her this was where I landed after the halfway house. To be honest, I didn't know if it would work. It was a shot in the dark. I owe Bruno, and Marie, for keeping me out of the joint. If I'd have gone back in this time, Boulevard Freddy would've had me shanked for sure."

"You put me in a real jam here," I said.

"I know, and I'm sorry. Like I said, I didn't know what else to do."

I was about to say, "You could have just taken off, ran for it." But the chair kept that from happening. She *was* in a real jam, and I don't know if I wouldn't have done anything different had I been in her place. That didn't mean she was a nice person or make her eligible to join our family as a late miss-out. She'd have to clear herself of any threat before I exposed all of our children in Costa Rica. I couldn't see how she was going to do that. No way could we make it work.

Over on the counter, my cell phone buzzed, doing its little vibration dance going in circles. I struggled to my feet with more energy than I had a right to own. I knew who had to be calling. Only two people had the number, and one of them was in the bedroom asleep. The news wouldn't be good. Not at that hour.

I picked up. "Yeah, Dan."

CHAPTER TWENTY-SEVEN

AFTER ANOTHER SHOWER to wake up and to at least tamp down the last of the Whitey stank, I woke Marie and kissed her goodbye. She roused. "Huh? What? Ah . . . no, Bruno. No."

"I won't be gone long." I hated stretching the truth, but if it gave her just an ounce of solace it'd be worth the consequences.

I'd called Drago as soon as I'd hung up with Chulack. He was waiting down in the parking tower standing next to a different truck, a midnight-blue GMC with a club cab—one with four doors and limo tinted windows. The aftermarket rims gleamed in artificial yellow light.

I walked up and shook his hand. "Nice ride." I didn't want to ask him where he kept getting the vehicles, it wasn't necessary information. Not in the larger scheme of things.

"Couldn't get the stink out of the one from yesterday."

"Thank you. That's one more thing I don't have to worry about or deal with."

He nodded. "Am I going along today?" Hope clearly in his expression.

"I wish you could, my friend. Today, I definitely need you out there, more so than yesterday. The way things are shaking out, there's going to be some heavy lifting, it's gonna be unavoidable."

"Why can't I come? I think Marie's okay here with—"

"My mom's on the run."

"From who? Not the law. Parole knows she's here."

"Boulevard Freddy Banks."

Drago's jaw muscle clenched, turning to the size of a half walnut, working hard as his eyes narrowed. "Who does she think she is, dragging her shit into Marie's world?"

"Take it easy." I tried to put my hand on his shoulder.

He knocked it away. "Don't tell me to take it easy. What's wrong with that woman? This is wrong on so many levels."

I waited for him to fume a little more, for the hard edge to wear off. "Listen, Marie isn't going to want to move and—"

"I understand. I'll handle it. After it's done, I'll call you and give you the new location. You don't have to worry about any of it. I got this."

"Thanks."

There was an uncomfortable pause.

"Hey?" I opened the back door to the truck and looked in. "What'd you do with Whitey?"

"I dropped him off at Starbucks down the street, it's just a couple of blocks south."

"He's gonna rabbit; it's in his blood."

Drago eyed me for a moment until I got the message. "If I can't go," he said, "take this." He took something from his back pocket and handed it to me, a well-worn 415 Gonzales blackjack. I took it, smiling. I slapped it against my hand. No one in the world made a better sap than Gonzales. Thick leather-cut oblong with a one-inch sewn seam all around the edge, the center core filled with lead. There's an old adage, *God made man, and Samuel Colt made them equal*, that applies in equal measure to a 415 Gonzales, maybe more so. I used to carry one as a deputy, and it got me out of many a jam back when my early ignorance led me around by the nose. I'd been jumped by six suspects in one incident and five in another. I would not have survived had Mr. Gonzales not been in my sap pocket at the back of my leg. The 415, when used properly, was one of the most effective weapons a deputy had at his disposal. Public outcry over its overt brutality caused the banning of this great tool, and deputies went unprotected until another one came along: the Taser. Only the Taser is limited to one shot. In a multiple suspect situation, the Gonzales still reigns king.

"Thank you, my friend. This will help." I put it in my back waistband; it wouldn't fit in the shallow denim pants pockets.

"One more thing." He reached into his front pocket. "I found this in your war bag, and another attached under the backseat." He handed me two smashed GPS transmitters.

I smiled. Helen Hellinger. The smile disappeared. Now she knew where I lived. Not good. I left that issue to mull over later, and said, "Don't forget to text me the new location where you move Marie."

"Do I have to take that witch along with us? It'd be better if I didn't. I could dump her off in the barrio over in El Monte."

For one fleeting moment, I thought about telling him to kick her to the curb. "Drago, she's my mom. I'm gonna need you to play nice."

He pointed at me. "Get a DNA check. If she did really have children, she's the kind who eat their young. You're nothing like her, not one iota."

My turn to get angry. I tamped it down. I had no logical reason to be upset with him for impugning my filial obligation or misplaced pride, not when I agreed with him that she was a menace we didn't need in our lives.

Drago handed me the key fob. "One more thing. The White Rat has something he wants to tell you. If he doesn't want to give it up when you ask, tell him Waldo wants him to tell you."

Drago said it with a straight face.

"Waldo?"

"That's right. You got a problem with Waldo?"

Waldo was Drago's 130-pound trained Rottweiler. Smartest dog I had ever seen. Drago could give Waldo verbal, multifaceted tasks and somehow the dog understood what to do, almost as if Drago and the dog had some sort of Vulcan mind-meld. One time I had tried to give Waldo the exact same tasks. He turned his head one way then the other and looked at me like I was ten pounds of uncooked pot roast.

Waldo always wore a spiked dog collar and never barked. Not so much as a growl. I was nervous around him even with Drago's assurance that Waldo wouldn't maul me unless Drago gave him the word. Maul. Most dogs bit people, but apparently not Waldo. He mauled.

"Okay," I said. "I better get going."

"You call me if you need anything. You sure you don't want me to come along? I can get Kato to come watch Marie. You know he's good."

"I'd like nothing better, but under these new circumstances, I wouldn't be able to focus if Marie wasn't protected by the best."

"I understand. You get in a jam, you call me. I mean it."

I hesitated. "That might not be a bad idea. Can you put a couple of friends on standby, a couple of real meat-eaters? Just in case I need that little extra diplomacy."

"You got it."

I gave him the number to the burner phone. Now three people had it. I got in the truck, started up, and headed out.

I drove around the huge block that contained the mall and other retail outlets. I clocked Helen sitting in a Chevy Malibu, a different color from the day before, watching the exit to the garage parking tower from down the street. She'd been watching for yesterday's truck and had missed me when I came out in the GMC.

I kept going down the street to the Starbucks and missed Whitey on the first pass. I thought I'd predicted correctly that Whitey, once unsupervised, had fled, never to be seen again. Then I spotted him looking nothing like the Whitey from the day before. He sat on the bus bench at the corner right outside the Starbucks. His knees were together, and he was dressed in new clothes that didn't match his personality: khaki pants with razor creases and a lime-green pull-over shirt, the kind that had the little emblem embroidered on the left breast. His hair was cut close to the scalp and his abnormal, crane-like neck with its huge Adam's apple served as a highly visible tattoo to help identify him. The cardboard cup carrier on his lap held three large cups of coffee. He was joe citizen waiting for the bus, and not a 211 artist with the morals of a half-rabid dog in heat.

I backed up and honked. He stood, stepped close, opened the truck door. He didn't display any emotion, as if he did this every day and I was his carpool buddy picking him up to work at some egg-head software company. He climbed in and suddenly realized I was driving and not Drago. "Oh, thank Haysoos, it's you." His face broke into relief so pure I felt guilty. He immediately shifted to anger. "Don't you ever leave me with that animal again. You hear what I'm sayin'? If you try it again, you have my permission to just kill me first."

"Hey, you look great"—I caught a whiff—"and you even smell great."

"Thanks, ya fruit. And just so we're clear, I'm not a homo, so stay on your side of the truck. I mean it."

I chuckled as I pulled away from the curb.

"Hey, there's nothing funny about it. Stay on your side of the truck and keep your dick-beaters to yourself."

We rode for a minute or so while he continued to fume over the previous night's indignities.

"The sunglasses and beard?" he said. "You trying to hide out in plain sight? Is that it?"

I didn't reply. He already knew the answer. He was trying to remind me that somehow in his pea-brain he held sway over me.

He said, "Your friends with that animal from last night?"

I ignored his question. "Why'd you get three cups of coffee?"

"I only do as I'm told, mi amigo. So, I don't rate another ass whoppin'. That animal said something about a woman cop who was going to need a cup."

How did Drago know about Helen? He must've clocked her stakeout and put two and two together. Drago was smart and dangerous, a good combination. As long as he was on your team.

I drove around the corner, pulled up, and stopped behind the Malibu. I called Helen's cell phone just as she got out and walked back to my driver's window. She looked great, wearing stretch-to-fit black denim pants, black cowboy boots, and a salmon long-sleeve blouse, tailored and starched. Today her gun, in a pancake holster, rode high on her hip, right out in the open, as did her gold sheriff's star clipped to her belt in front.

I rolled the window down as she answered her phone. She rested her arm on the sill as I said into my phone, her face no more than ten inches away, "See, this is me calling you just like I said I would."

She said into her phone, "You're a real funny man, aren't you?"

"My wife, Marie, thinks so." I closed the phone. "Come on, get in, let's go to work."

CHAPTER TWENTY-EIGHT

HELEN LOCKED HER Malibu. She tossed her war bag on the floor in the back of the truck and climbed in the backseat. I drove down the mostly vacant street as dawn cracked on the horizon awash in grays and blues. She reached around the headrest and lightly slapped Whitey on the side of his head. "Who's this?"

"Real funny, skank. Touch me again and I'll kill ya."

"Whitey?" she said. "Is that really you? I hardly recognized you."

"Funny. See, I'm laughing. Ha. Ha."

I looked at her in the rearview. She smiled at me, content that her little maneuver—planting the GPS—had worked for her. "Where are we going?" she asked.

She didn't mention the new truck.

"Chulack texted me. They have a dead body that's somehow related to what we're doing. He said it was important for me to come by and take a look."

"Is . . . is it the little girl?" Helen asked. She didn't complain about not wanting to work the kidnap. She knew Calvin Ivory was connected in an ancillary way and if we chased down the kidnappers, they would eventually lead to Ivory. Besides, this was her way into a high-profile case that could only bolster her career.

"Ah, man," Whitey said. "I don't wanna see nothin' like that. Not this mornin', it'll put me off my feed. Go ahead, just let me off here. Come on, let me off."

"Don't worry," I said. "I promise, you won't have to see anything too gruesome."

Helen nodded. "Yeah, for someone with your worldly experience, it's all relative, right?"

"Huh?"

"I mean, you did see Eldridge get dropped off the tier and land on his head." She shrugged. "What's a dead body after you've actually witnessed a murder?"

"Yeah, yeah . . . naw. I still don't wanna see nothin' like that. Especially if it's going to be that little girl."

"It's not Emily Mosely," I said. "I checked the news feeds. They don't have anything on it, and they would if it was her."

No way did *I* want to see something like that. If it did turn out to be her, I wouldn't go within a hundred feet of . . . of the body. I didn't need those kinds of lasting images. I already had enough of my own.

"Whitey," I said. "Hand Helen a coffee." I reached over and took one from the cardboard tray on his lap and took a sip, more to take my mind off the ugly pictures flashing through my brain.

She took the offered cup, popped off the lid, and sipped. "What location?"

"It's not far, but we're gonna have a problem with the natty Mr. Rogers sitting here in the front seat. What are we going to do with him? There's going to be too many other cops around with prying eyes to suitcase him again."

"I don't know who this asshole Mr. Rogers is," Whitey said, "but I'm not gonna be no problem. Like I said, pull over and just let me off right here. It's as simple as that. I'm all done with you asswipes. I'm fed up ta here with you two puttin' a clown suit on me."

Helen leaned forward, coffee in hand, and said to me, "You put up with this dweeb all night?"

"No, he didn't," Whitey yelped. "Hell no, he didn't. He handed me off to some psycho wannabe biker who . . ." Whitey pounded the dash with his fist. "Let me out. I'm goin' ta the cops. What he did to me was . . . was a crime against nature."

Helen put her hand to her mouth to cover a smile and sat back. "What'd he do?" she asked, the mirth slipping out in her tone.

"He . . . He's got this big nasty dog with these huge teeth. I'm not kiddin', they're this long." He held up two index fingers indicating about ten inches. "He's part devil, I tell ya. I'm not kiddin' here. This biker tossed me in a shower, turned the water on high, and pulled the handle off, took it with him. You believe that? Took it with him. He told his dog to keep me in there. The damn hot water ran out and turned freezing cold. And *still* that damn devil dog just sat there and wouldn't let me out. I was stark naked for hours shivering my fool ass off. If I don't come down with pneumonia I won't know why. I'm gonna sneak back there, I swear to gawd, I am, and shoot that damn dog."

"So, you know where you were?" I asked.

"Well, no. Not exactly. He kept me all trussed up. He didn't even untie me when we got there. He carried me in the house like I was some kinda piece a luggage or some shit like that. Damn near tore my arms outta the sockets. Man, I've never been so humiliated in my life."

Helen whispered loud enough for me to hear, "Don't see how that's possible."

"At least you smell nice," Helen said to Whitey. "Lilac, isn't it?"

"Foo-foo girlie shit he sprayed all over me. I'm gonna kill him, you wait and see if I don't."

"Whitey," I said. "Chill out. You're already getting on my nerves. Sit back, be quiet, and drink your coffee. Let the adults talk."

His face went instantly livid. "Why I oughta—"

"If you're not good, tonight, I'm going to give you back to Drago and Waldo." He immediately shut his yap, pouted, and sipped his coffee.

Helen leaned forward. "Waldo?"

"That's the devil dog he's talking about."

"Does this Drago take reservations? I have a couple of candidates for his charm school."

"Charm school?" Whitey screeched.

I pointed a finger at him. He again sat back and closed his mouth.

I asked Helen, "The task force get anywhere last night on Calvin Ivory?"

"You already know the answer to that. I wouldn't be sitting here if we had. You still haven't told me *where* we're going."

"FBI is working a body dump in LAPD's area. We're going by to take a look, see what they have, see if there's anything to work."

We rode for a while in silence. Then Helen leaned forward again. "You mad I bugged your truck?"

"Wasn't proper etiquette, if that's what you mean. And yes, I'm not happy about it."

"Humm. You know I flashed my badge at the front desk of the Americana and there's no one with your last name staying at that hotel."

I took my eyes off the road and turned back to look at her. "You think I'd park my vehicle in the same place I was sleeping? You really must think I'm some kind of rookie."

"Humm. Good point."

I went back to driving. "You're just lucky I came back for you today. After planting those bugs I was within my rights to drive off and leave you."

She nodded and sat back.

Fifteen minutes later, I turned down San Pedro headed for 6th Street in Skid Row, a commercial district of Los Angeles rife with homeless, blue tarps that flapped in the light breeze, shopping carts, and cardboard houses the size of refrigerator boxes. And the stink of urine and feces mixed with body odor.

The entire street was blocked with black and white LAPD patrol units and nondescript undercover cars belonging to the FBI. Must have been close to thirty in all. This was something big all right. I parked the GMC and turned it off as an LAPD uniform, an older guy, gray at the temples, approached, his bright flashlight beam washed out by the encroaching dawn. His hand rested on his holstered handgun. His voice came out muffled by the window. "Can I help you folks?"

I rolled down the window with my FBI creds ready. The officer came closer and looked in. He saw the creds.

"Officer? Officer?" Whitey said. "I'm being kidnapped by these two asswipes. Help? I want 'em both arrested. I demand that you arrest the both of 'em."

Helen extended her arm with her Los Angeles County Sheriff's badge she'd unclipped from her belt. With her other hand, she grabbed Whitey's ear and pulled him back pinning his head against the seat.

"Ouch! Ouch! See, Officer? See?"

The officer chuckled. "Well, if it isn't Howard Owsley, aka, the White Rat. In briefing last night, they put out a want on him." He pointed at Whitey. "DA want's *him* real bad."

Helen let go. "How come everyone in this cow town knows this little shitweasel and I don't?"

"Officer," I said, trying to see his nameplate. "Duffy, is it? My boss, the Deputy Director, wants me to take a look at this crime scene. I don't know what to do with—"

"Sure, I'd be happy to babysit while you take a look." He started to come around the front of the truck.

"Don't you do it," Whitey said. "Don't you leave me here with no blue belly, they're meaner 'n shit."

"We'll only be a minute."

Duffy opened Whitey's door with a set of handcuffs in hand. "You want me to just go ahead and book him for that outstanding want? Please?"

"Well, Whitey," I said, "what's it going to be?"

His face flushed red. "We had a deal. You gave me your word and—"

"I guess not, Officer. He's my asshole. I guess you're going to have to go find your own."

Helen and I got out and walked down 6th. Behind us, Whitey berated Duffy until there came a thump and a yelp. Whitey went quiet.

I whispered to Helen, "I guess he was right, those blue bellies are meaner 'n shit."

She smiled.

CHAPTER TWENTY-NINE

A HALF-BLOCK DOWN, between two large industrial buildings, stood a throng of people, most all in suits and ties, some in long London Fog–type overcoats worn more on the East Coast than in balmy So Cal. They were FBI agents in Los Angeles TDY—temporary duty assignment—to work the kidnap. A uniform LAPD officer with a clipboard standing behind yellow stretched tape with "Police Line Do Not Cross" stopped us again. A new guy, making his bones by doing the scut work. "Your names, please? And you're going to have to produce identification for verification."

He wouldn't let us in the crime scene without our names. I didn't want to give him my fake one. I was thinking far down the road to what would happen in court. In the trial, if they could not identify everyone who entered the crime scene, the defense would have a huge hole to exploit. Whoever kidnapped Emily deserved justice. If I couldn't find him, or them, like Chulack wanted, and mete out an appropriate measure of curbside justice, then I didn't want to taint it for the court for their turn at bat.

"I'll just stay right here," I said to Helen. "You go on. Then you can tell me what you saw."

The copper eyed me with suspicion when I didn't want to enter. I put my hand on my stomach and faked a burp. "Bad taco. I don't want to taint the scene; you know what I mean?"

He smiled and nodded, a snarky comment on his lips. He was too new to risk tossing it out.

Helen took hold of my hand and said to him, "Excuse us just a minute." She yanked, pulling us back a few feet. She whispered, "What's going on?"

"Like I said, I ate a bad—"

Her hand came up slowly to remove my sunglasses. I said, "Don't."

She stared me down, or tried to, through the black reflective surface of the glasses that helped mask my identity. "All right, but this isn't over."

She knew I was hiding something. She turned, went to the copper, gave her name and department. He let her pass through. I watched her walk over to the throng of agents and LAPD investigators. I waxed nostalgic, wishing I was still a full-fledged detective with all the rights and access it allowed. I yearned for it like a juiced-out street bum in the throes of alcohol DTs.

I moved over to the rookie who stood at the line with the clipboard. "What's it look like? Can you describe it for me?"

He checked over his shoulder to see if someone else walked up on him and I was just trying to set him up in a surreptitious integrity check.

I held up my hand. "It's okay, take it easy." I flashed him my FBI creds too fast for him to get a name. "Like I told you, it was just a bad taco."

He still hesitated, trying to decide the pros and the cons of talking to me. "It's a woman," he said.

"A woman? You sure?"

"Positive. It was my partner and I who took the call. We found her."

"Not a little girl?"

"No, a woman. I know a woman when I see one."

I let out a sigh of relief. But knew the time would come when someone would find Emily in a similar circumstance. It would be soon now. If she was ever found at all.

Then my mind all on its own shifted to Bea Elliot, my mom, and to the people she ran with. It was a wonder she'd not already been found this way. And if she had, I would never have been notified. Would never have known about it. Would never had met my mother.

"Body dump?" I asked.

"Yes, looks that way to me." He shrugged. "But I'm new at this."

"How was she killed?"

The rookie squirmed in his freshly pressed uniform and wanted to again check behind him. He started to look and stopped. "I think . . . she was throttled . . . ah, I mean strangled. There are finger marks on her neck and petechial hemorrhages in her eyes. My TO pointed out both of those evidentiary points."

"How long she been down?"

He shrugged. "TO estimates a week at least, probably more, but said it would take an expert to be sure."

A tall FBI agent broke away from the throng and headed our way. Chulack.

Some of his entourage tried to follow him, but he waved them back.

He ducked under the yellow police line and shook my hand. "What are you doing over here? Come on, I want you to see the crime scene."

I held onto his hand and moved him out of earshot of the rookie. I let go. "I would've had to give that guy my fake name."

Chulack eyed me.

He looked tired, dead on his feet. Even so he immediately caught the court implication. He shook his head. "I told you, I don't care who finds out about you, especially down the road. And besides, I'm not looking to get these guys in court and you know that. You *know* why I asked you into this."

He'd said it out loud for the first time since this whole thing started. Words that worked around the ugly edge of what he'd asked me to do. I understood and accepted the way he presented it in the hotel suite. I liked it better, though, as a tacit pact between us. The ambiguity, aired like that, made me out as someone I didn't want to believe I had become, and at the same time someone I was trying to bury.

"You know what my specialty is, I *hunt* men. That's what I'm good at." I waved my hand toward the break between the buildings where the dead woman lay. "I was never good at the investigative part of it."

"You and I know better. Come on, I want you—"

A woman's loud voice—almost a screech—interrupted him. "Daddeeey?"

Chulack's head whipped around. His lips moved. Words leaked out. "Oh, dear God."

We both turned. A woman ran toward us. She wore an expensive house dress with a light overcoat and flat house shoes. Her blond hair flowed in the light breeze, her beautiful countenance wet and marred red from days of crying.

Chulack caught his daughter in his arms. "Is it her? Daddy, is it her?"

"You shouldn't be here, honey."

"Is it her?"

He buried his face in the crook of her neck as he pulled her in tight to his body. He whispered something.

She screamed. "Noooo." She turned weak in his arms. He wobbled under the emotional strain.

My world shifted; the air thickened. The rookie on the tape line said it wasn't a child. He said it wasn't a child like he was sure of it.

CHAPTER THIRTY

HELEN CAME UP from behind and poked me in the back. She pointed over to Chulack and the open car door where his daughter Amy Mosely sat on the seat, her legs sticking out. She was bent over with her face in her hands, crying. "What's going on?" Helen asked. "Who's that?"

"It's the mother of the kidnap victim."

"Hmm, I guess she was close to the nanny, then."

"What?"

She hooked her thumb over her shoulder. "The victim back there in the alley is Lilian Morales, the kidnapped girl's nanny."

"Ah, man."

Amy probably *was* distraught over the brutal murder of her daughter's nanny, but the more obvious reason was that if the nanny was dead, where did that leave poor Emily? This zeroed out her chances. It wouldn't be long now before we found Emily in some other alley on the other side of the city.

A man stood off to the side of a newer Mercedes, a two-door coupe worth more than I made in five years as a deputy sheriff. It was parked behind my GMC truck. He wore a wrinkled two-thousand-dollar suit and handmade shoes. John Mosely. He'd not eaten in a while and had dark half-circles under his eyes. Both the ugly beasts, grief and despair, had jumped on his back, had him by the neck, trying hard to drag him down. It wouldn't be long and I'd see him down in that dark place reserved for night terrors. See him with his Emily, and me on the side of the freeway with the dead bikers, the downed Highway Patrol officer . . .

. . . And Bosco.

No hope remained for his daughter, and he knew it.

"Stay here," I said to Helen. I walked over to Mr. Mosely and extended my hand. "Arthur Higgins. I'm an FBI agent working with your father-in-law. I'm sorry about what's going on." His two-hundred-dollar haircut was mussed, and his tennis tan faded on a now pale face.

"Did you see Lilian? Did she suffer?"

"No, I'm sorry, I didn't go over there. It's better if I don't in case . . . I mean when it does go to court. The fewer people who enter the crime scene, the better." A half-truth tossed to a man who needed more than a life preserver; he needed the whole lifeboat.

He let go of my hand and started to wring both of his own. "Maybe I should take a look. I think I'll regret it if I don't. This is all my fault. I shouldn't have let this happen."

"What are you talking about? How could it be your fault?" Most survivors of violent crimes self-assign blame without basis of logic or evidence.

"Amy wanted to go back to work," he said. "We didn't need the money. She just wanted her career back. I should've told her no. This wouldn't have happened. This is all my fault."

Amy appeared. She went past me and hugged her husband, John. They both broke down and wept at the loss of their friend and nanny. And at its mortal implication. Chulack put his hand on my shoulder. "Amy, honey?" She turned in her husband's arms, her face wet. "This is Bruno Johnson, the man I was telling you about."

I cringed and hoped he'd not said my name loud enough for Helen to hear, who stood ten feet away looking on.

Amy said, "Are you the one who broke the case? The one who found those men with the money?"

"I helped to find them, if that's what you mean."

She hesitated, her eyes burning into mine. She broke away from her husband and came toward me. I thought she'd stop and offer her hand, but she kept coming. She gently put her head against my chest, wetting my shirt with her tears, anointing me to her unholy cause. She wrapped her arms around me. I held on, fighting the lump that rose in my throat. She made me want to get on with it, track down Calvin Ivory, Police Killa Bitch. Make him tell me who was involved in this heinous act that had caused all of this grief, put an end to it.

Amy clutched me hard for an awkward and uncomfortable eight . . . ten hours, or maybe it was only a minute.

She pulled back to look into my eyes. She lowered her voice to a whisper. "Thank you." She let out a sigh and took in a deep breath. "Can I ask you something? A favor?"

I knew what she wanted. She viewed me as some kind of black genie granting her a life-changing wish. I lowered my head giving her my ear.

"Please," she said. "Find those who did this. I don't think I can sleep another night or . . . or live knowing they got away with what they did to my Emily."

I nodded.

She lowered her voice even more. "And . . . and can you please . . . make things right?"

My back went stiff at the veiled vehemence in her last words, this coming from a civilized person. Someone who had never ventured far from Rodeo Drive and now dipped a toe into the gutter.

The request further supported my slide into a world where I didn't think I belonged and I realized I'd only been kidding myself. I knew in that moment I'd grant her the wish and do it with relish.

With the death of Lilian Morales, Amy had accepted her daughter Emily's fate. Amy wanted me to stop her pain. To end it with a large dollop of blood and bone.

Chulack came closer. He no longer looked so desperate and needful. He, too, had lost that last vestige of hope for Emily and had now shifted to anger, ready to unleash a pent-up wrath that had been festering for two weeks. The way the whole situation played out, I no longer cared that they wanted to use me as a tool to wield for no other reason than to fulfill their mission, one heavy in hate and revenge. To someone standing on the outside looking in, revenge was senseless and a grievous detriment to both sides involved. But to those wronged, revenge was a wanton lover whispering in their ear with a promise to make all things right again. I only possessed an ounce of involvement and still I encouraged that lover to whisper those fate-filled words.

I took hold of Amy's shoulders and moved her over to her dad, Deputy Director Dan Chulack. "I have to get moving," I said. "I'll call you."

Chulack gently pushed his daughter away. He took out his creds and let them slip from his hand and fall to the ground. "I'm going with you."

Amy and John Mosely watched with great interest in what I'd do.

I picked up the creds with my left hand. I moved closer to Chulack, my right hand extended. He took it. We shook. I put his creds in his pocket. I held on to his hand, leaned in, and whispered, "You try and come with me, I'll handcuff you to the front push bar of the closest cop car. You understand what I'm saying? This is for me to do." I squeezed his hand as hard as I could and let go. I turned and walked away.

Behind me he spoke with tears in his voice. "Bruno, it isn't fair to ask you to do this."

I kept walking toward Helen. "You're not asking me to do anything. I'll call you when it's over."

Helen fell in step with me. She had heard the exchange and knew the rules to this new game and didn't say a word.

I got in the driver's seat of the GMC. She got in on the passenger side. Whitey sat handcuffed in the backseat, seat-belted in, some Starbucks napkins stuffed in his mouth. I took off my sunglasses and tossed them too hard onto the dash. I gave Helen her chance to see all of me for the first time. She looked long and hard.

I said, "You have a problem with me, we'll deal with it after this is over."

"I'm good with that."

I started up and chirped the tires, taking off.

CHAPTER THIRTY-ONE

MORNING TRAFFIC HAD increased just in the short time we were at the crime scene. I drove out of Skid Row, turning south on Alameda, joining the flow of commuters, instinctively headed for South Central, the vortex of crime in LA that resonated outward like a stone tossed in a still pond. After only a couple of miles, I decided I didn't want to drive without a destination so I pulled over and shut down the truck. I swiveled in the seat, leaned over, and removed the balled-up napkins from Whitey's mouth.

He sputtered and spit out little bits of wad. "You sons of bitches, you can't treat me like this. I'm gonna—"

"You're right." I turned to Helen. "Would you take the cuffs off him, please?" She nodded, got out, and opened the back door. He turned and gave her his wrists cuffed behind his back. Once released he tried to push past her to escape. She grabbed his hand and quickly folded it over in a wristlock. He yelped as she walked him back into the truck. She slammed the door. He quickly crawled across the seat ready to exit on the street side.

"You open that door," I said, "and I'll shoot you in the leg. I don't need you ambulatory to get the information I need. You know me, you know I'll do it."

Helen had gotten back into the truck.

Whitey slapped the top of the front seat again and again. "You can't do this to me. You can't. Never in all my life has anyone treated me like this."

I flicked his forehead. "Shut up and sit back. You're giving me a headache."

He sat back. His rapid eye movement said that his brain was searching to find a way out of his predicament. He brought a finger up, pointed at me. "All right, I've had enough of this shit. You let me out right now or I'm gonna tell her. I swear to gawd, I'm gonna tell her. I know what you said you'd do to me, but I don't care anymore. Let me out or I'm gonna do it."

I stared him down. "Do it."

His mouth dropped open in shock. He recovered, thinking over his options—the previous threats of great bodily injury I had twice hung over his head.

"I'll do it." He continued to stare me down. "Don't think I won't."

"Do it."

He turned to her. "He's not really with the FBI. He's some sort of psycho bounty hunter sanctioned by the FBI, and his real name is—"

Helen beat him to it. "Bruno Johnson, wanted on thirteen counts of kidnap and three counts of murder."

I looked at Helen, caught her eyes. They told me nothing of what she was thinking. Her knowing the secret and letting me continue to sit behind the wheel of the truck spoke volumes and made me want to know her better, made me want to know how long she'd known my true name.

"You know?" Whitey squeaked. She finally broke eye contact with me and looked at Whitey. "That's right. You have a problem with it?"

He put a hand on his head. "I'm caught in some kind of night-mare. The law is supposed to be the law. There has to be rules that you guys play by or . . . or I guess we'll all sink into chaos." He poked his own chest. "My team, we don't have any rules. That's the way it's supposed to be. But there has to be rules that the cops play by or how do we know who's on what team?"

If his mind continued to spin out of control, his head might explode. "Whitey, take it easy. We need you to tell us everything you know about Calvin Ivory. He was friends with Little T-Dog. Where did those two caper? Where'd they hang out?"

"Oh, no. Why should I help you two dicklickers? No. I won't do it. Let me out."

"Wait, weren't you supposed to tell me something. That's right, Drago said you were going to tell me something. What is it?"

"What?" He looked at me, his vision unfocused again as he tried to rectify in his brain how he'd operate in a world gone mad.

"There aren't any rules anymore. How are we supposed know what—I mean—"

I snapped my fingers in front of his face. "What did Drago want you to tell me?"

The mention of Drago a second time got through to him and brought him back down to earth. "I . . . ah . . . I . . . no, forget it. I want out. Now. The law can be all screwed up but those people . . . those people for sure will cut my throat if I give 'em up. No." He shook his head for emphasis.

"Waldo said for you to tell me."

The blood left Whitey's face as he turned pale. "You're a real bastard, you know that?"

Helen said, "We can drive you over to Waldo's house right now, if that's what you want."

"Both of you are going to hell. I mean it, you're going to burn in hell."

"Last chance." I put my hand on the ignition.

"Okay. Okay. There's supposed to be another meet today. That's what Little T-Dog told Ivory on the phone before you assholes gunned him. Little T-Dog was supposed to intro Calvin into the group, so Calvin can get his money."

"The money for dropping Eldridge on his head?"

"That's right."

"Where and when?"

He licked his dry lips, still debating what was worse, Waldo or Calvin Ivory—Police Killa Bitch. It would've been a tough call to make even for me. "Look," I said, "I'll sweeten the deal."

His eyes refocused. "I'm listening."

"Those poor folks back there who lost their daughter also lost two million dollars of their hard-earned money. You sign on with us for the duration, and I'll give you ten percent of everything we recover as a finder's fee." Chulack wouldn't mind if it meant ending this thing quickly and putting to bed the people involved in this murderous conspiracy.

In the criminal world, nothing else mattered except money. Money was the grease that powered everything. It kept the thieves, thugs, kidnappers, and murderers actively engaged in their nefarious activities the same as high octane fuel in a Gulfstream jet.

"You're not just yankin' my dick here, are you?"

I raised my right hand. "Word of honor."

"Ten percent of two million, that's . . . that's what, twenty thousand, right?"

"Yep," Helen said. "More money than—"

"No, it's two hundred thousand."

"Two hundred"—he looked at Helen—"I don't like you." He paused for a beat, then said, "What are we waitin' for? Get this heap rollin'. Head down to Crenshaw, down there off of 10th. There's this restaurant, a barbecue joint. We got about an hour. The meet's at ten o'clock this morning."

"Ah, man," I said, as I started the truck.

"What?" Helen asked.

"Nothing. I just happen to know that place."

"And?"

"They're going to remember me. Not in a good way."

CHAPTER THIRTY-TWO

THIRTY MINUTES LATER, I parked across the street from the restaurant and shut down the truck. Cars on Crenshaw moved like one long caterpillar between red and green signals, the morning rush in full bloom. The mom-and-pop family restaurant was no longer, least not the way I remembered it. The place had changed hands, and I could only hope I'd had nothing to do with the cause of the new ownership. The sign now read, "Fat Boy's Pork Palace."

Lowered early model cars with reflective lacquered paint jobs and sparkling rims, lined up in the parking lot. All of them highly coveted gang-member cars.

I used the binoculars to gain a better perspective on what we were up against. Through the long picture window that ran the length of the restaurant, males and females sat around tables, talking and laughing, eating thick beef ribs wet with red sauce and potato fries the size of corn cobs. The occupants all sported blue doo-rags somewhere on their bodies along with standardized clothing: blue or black denim pants, sports jerseys, and black leather jackets, even in the heat. This was a Crip stronghold, and taxpaying citizens no longer patronized the place. Fat Boy's was perfect for laundering drug money. The whole setup was good for Calvin Ivory, not so good for us.

Helen lowered her smaller set of binoculars and looked over at me. "This isn't going to work."

Whitey leaned forward over the front seat. "You don't know what you're talking about, girl. Here, gimme those glasses, let me take a gander at all these swingin' dicks. This ain't no big deal." His breath smelled of soured coffee with a hint of deep-fried something with cinnamon and apple.

Helen put her hand on his face and shoved him back. "Quit breathing on me."

Whitey, like a puppy who didn't know he'd been punished, said, "Come on, man. Bruno, gimme your glasses, let me have a look-see?"

Helen said to Whitey, "What do you think is going to happen here? One of us is just going to saunter in there and ask Mr. Police Killa Bitch who he's working for? Get real."

"Yeah, that's exactly the way I'm guessin' it's gonna happen. No other way. Gimme the glasses."

She handed them over. "Sit back and look from there."

He took the glasses. "You a dyke or somethin'? You hate all men?"

"No, just dweebs who've swallowed a big walnut and got it stuck in their throat."

He looked through the binoculars. "Dyke, for sure. Am I right, Bruno?"

"You better leave me out of this one. And I'd go easy on the slurs. Have you forgotten what she did to you yesterday?"

He brought down the glasses. "Wait, I'm one of you now. I've signed on for the duration, remember? You can't treat me like that anymore. Right? Tell her, Bruno, she can't treat me like that anymore."

"If you don't watch your mouth, just try me," Helen said.

"You better apologize," I said.

"For real?"

I shrugged. "I would, if I were you."

"All right, damnit ta hell. I'm sorry."

I cringed and looked at Helen. She didn't seem bothered by it. "How do you want to handle it?" she asked.

"We don't have a choice," I said. "We to have to sit tight, wait for him to show, then follow him away. Take him down on the fly."

"That's not going to work. He'll rabbit for sure. What's he got to lose? And if he does pick up his money, he's definitely not going to want the police to stop him. That means a car stop is out."

"You have a better idea?"

"No." Her eyes blazed with ambition and at the same time a wet desire she didn't try to mask.

I took out the cell phone and dialed Marie. It rang until it went over to voice mail. She never let it just ring. She was either mad at me and screening her calls for having to pick up and move, or she was in the middle of moving and too busy to answer. "Thinking of you," I said. "I'll call you later. Love you, babe."

"Ah, gag me."

"Whitey," I said. He flinched backward away from me. "I know. I know. Hey, I can go in there and scope it out. If he's in there, I can come back here and you can call in another one of your cruise missile strikes. Huh? How about that?"

"No, you can't, you little dweeb. You'll get your ass handed to you."

"She's right."

"Oh, ye of little faith. I expected that from her, but not you, big man. You know how I work. You know I can do it."

"You going to handle it the way you did in the front yard of that apartment yesterday? Is that what you mean by knowing how you work?"

"Not going to happen," Helen said.

"What? You're afraid I'm gonna outshine you? Is that it? Or is it that you have a thing for me now and you're worried I'll get hurt?" He shot her his biggest denture-filled smile.

"No," she said. "I'm just not in the mood to do all the paperwork your dead body will require when they toss it out onto Crenshaw full of bullet holes."

Whitey chuckled. "Is that right? You want to put your money where your skanky mouth is?"

She spun and went over the seat at him. She grabbed him around the throat and squeezed. "You call me anything but 'Detective' again and we're going to have a problem, you understand?"

His face bloated red. She let go. He coughed and sputtered. "You gonna let her do that to a fellow team member, huh, Bruno?"

"I warned you about your mouth. You really think you can walk into that lion's den?"

"Hell ya, I can." He straightened his shirt. "You watch me. For two hundred thousand I'd even—"

"You can't be serious. This dweeb is expendable and all, but it's going to be a major lawsuit if it goes south."

"You know how I'm going to walk in there? With the universal pass, my friends." He didn't wait to say the rest, got out of the truck, and walked half a block down.

She said, "He's either got more guts than I gave him credit for or he's as dumb as a rock."

I looked at her, nodded. We said it at the same time. "He's a rock."

CHAPTER THIRTY-THREE

WHITEY CAME PARALLEL with the restaurant and jaywalked, stopping traffic. Horns lit up the morning as he dodged in and out of irate commuter cars' paths. Through the binoculars, I could see the gang members close to the windows in Fat Boy's Pork Palace stop talking and eating to watch the spectacle: a pale toreador dodging one-ton metal beasts without horns.

Whitey made it to the front door and paused to straighten his shirt and tuck it into his pants. He looked nothing like the Whitey from yesterday who got tossed out of IRC and then again out of the apartment. He could almost pass as an encyclopedia salesman, only that breed of hawker had gone extinct. The bold, brash way Whitey was acting, he wouldn't be far behind, a new entry on the endangered species list.

Whitey's lips moved as he spoke to the cute, scantily clad hostess. He waited at the podium while she left to pass on whatever cockeyed message he'd pulled out of his hat in a feeble attempt to con his way in. The promise of two hundred thousand dollars and the instinctive need to impress a beautiful woman shut down all logical thought.

I shouldn't have let him go in. I put my hand on the door latch ready to go after him, still debating the pros and the cons of his health and welfare in the balance.

Helen, also looking through her binoculars, said, "You know, I heard tell that the American Indians didn't mess with the mentally impaired. They thought it was bad medicine and if they did, it would bring disaster to their tribe."

She made me smile. She pulled down her binoculars to look at me.

I said, "Geronimo and Police Killa Bitch aren't even in the same universe. But you're right, they may scalp him anyway."

She smiled. "What happened here?"

"What?"

"With you, I mean? You said—"

"Oh I ah . . . tracked a murder suspect to an apartment over off of 10th, right down the street there. I ended up chasing him on foot to this restaurant and—"

"Oh, my God, that was about five years ago, right? That, was *you*? I remember seeing it on the news. It looked like a tornado went through the place. You really tore it up. I mean really trashed it."

I shrugged and went back to looking at Whitey in Fat Boy's, who still waited by the podium.

"And you shot the guy. That's right, he was . . . getting away and you shot him in both of his legs. Point blank. Put the gun right to his legs and shot him. Everyone on the job was talking about that one. The way that place was messed up I thought it had to be ten or fifteen guys fighting in there—the way it looked. It was just you?"

"A uniform was having lunch in the restaurant; he jumped in to help. The crook didn't want to go to jail. He was death-penalty eligible, and knew if I got the cuffs on him it was all over. He'd never take another free breath. He had to get through me to get away, and he tried his damnedest to make that happen."

She said nothing. I pulled my binoculars down and found her staring at me. "You catch any heat over it?" she asked.

"No, I was doing my job."

"Hmm." She went back to watching Whitey.

The hostess returned to the podium with two knuckle-draggers, Crips with hard-core prison builds and tattoos on gleaming shaved heads. Whitey spoke fast, using his hands, trying his best to talk his way out of another beating. One of the thugs pointed to the door. They wanted him to leave. He held his ground. The two moved closer. He held up his hand to stop them. He pulled out a wad of cash, the money I'd given him the day before when he returned to the truck all beat up. The E-ticket to get on any ride in the park. But Whitey made a big mistake. He wasn't in It's a Small World, he was in his own Fantasyland. This gave the thugs pause, but only for a moment. One of them snatched the money from his hand. The other punched him in the face. He staggered back.

The two thugs were heavyweights, ex-cons, enforcers whose job it was to squish mild annoyances like Whitey. Break his bones and toss him to the curb.

I got out and ran into traffic dodging cars.

The horns again.

I didn't take my eyes off Whitey. One thug kicked him again and again while he was down.

A car skidded to a stop and barely nudged me. It still hurt. I used a fist on his hood and kept going. From behind, Helen yelled at me. "Go. Go. Move."

The restaurant door opened. Whitey flew out. He got up cradling his ribs and bleeding from his face. He looked around for something, anything he could use as a weapon. With some difficulty, he picked up a media stand, the kind that held free flyers on gentlemen's clubs and midnight escorts. He struggled to get it over his head and ran toward the window.

I yelled, "Whitey? No!"

He chucked it.

The window crashed down in a million tiny cubes of ice. The two thugs inside spun and came out the front door just as I made it across the wide street and sidewalk. In an instant, they were all over me. In my weakened state, I didn't have a chance with the two rhinos. I yanked the 415 Gonzales and laid the first one out, chucked him upside his head, switched off his lights. The second one was fast. He swung. I ducked, but not far enough. His fist caught the back of my head and set off some minor fireworks. I caught him on the jaw with the backswing of the 415. Small bones and teeth cracked. He went down, flopped on top of his friend, out cold. Pile-o-thug.

That was it for me. I was all done. I'd used up my entire daily allotment of energy. I bent over, hands on my knees, trying to catch my breath.

Angry gangbangers emptied out of the restaurant. Helen, in her black cowboy boots, spread her feet in a combat stance and pointed her Glock at them. "Go ahead, I'll kill all of you. Get back. Get back, now."

The threatened burst of violence from such a beautiful woman even caught me looking. The procession slowed at the door as too many tried to shove their way out.

We backed up to the first row of cars in the parking lot. Cornered.

A short black woman wearing all red satin pushed her way to the front of the crowd, one that was quickly turning into a lynch mob. "Hold it. Hold it. Shut up all ya all." She held her hands high in the air.

They listened to her with an eerie reverence. The noise reduced to a murmur.

Helen eased on back to me, still holding her gun pointed at them. She whispered, "That's Ruby Two." Said it like I was supposed to know that name. And somehow, I did. The name ricocheted around inside my head. I couldn't make the connection and knew it was important that I did.

CHAPTER THIRTY-FOUR

WHITEY HAD MOVED behind me and peeked round as if I were a bulletproof oak. With the heel of his hands he wiped the blood from his eyes. He tugged on the back of my shirt and said loud enough for only me to hear, "He's in there, I saw him. He was sitting at a table by hisself." He let out a groan and put a hand to his head. "Oh, man, those bastards hurt me. They hurt me bad. They wiped the floor with me."

The mob moved until it encircled us. Ruby Two said to Helen, "What is it you want? You can't just come off the street and break out the window of my place. You can't lay out two of my boys and not expect me to do somethin' about it. Tell me what's going on or I'll turn 'em loose on all y'all."

Helen let go of the gun with one hand and pulled out her cell. I moved close to her, put my hand on hers. "No." She was about to call 911. The last thing we needed was the cops. If they arrested Calvin Ivory, he'd go to jail for tossing Eldridge off the tier. There would be no incentive to talk, to tell us who had hired him. Then we'd never get to the kidnappers, never get the money back. Ivory was a hard-core gangbanger; he wouldn't give it up no matter how hard I thumped on him in a restricted jail environment. I needed him on the street where more persuasive interrogation techniques could be employed. Even if she did make the call, this crowd would eat us before the police could arrive. Whitey had boxed us in a corner with his attempt to make something happen. My fault. I'd lost control of the situation when I let him get out of the truck. I still wasn't back to my old self. I wasn't thinking straight.

I held up my hand. "This is on me," I said, looking right at Ruby Two. "I just wanted some ribs. I've been in the joint for two years on an ADW and just got out. They closed down Stops over off Imperial and I'd heard this was the new place for hot links and chili fries."

The crowd noise grew louder. She raised her hand. Silence settled yet again as her eyes narrowed. "She's wearing a badge. If you jus' got out, what are you doing runnin' with her?"

I put my arm around Helen. "She's with me." Helen didn't flinch.

"What about that white boy who ruined my window?"

"Don't know him. Me and Helen just walked up here to get something to eat and your two boys attacked me."

Ruby Two smiled. "Well, then, give up the white boy and you two kin come on in and have yourselves some links and chili fries."

A car started up and took off. The metallic blue Chevy Impala bounced over the curb onto Crenshaw and drove on the right shoulder, half on the curb, half off, all the way to the red signal, made the turn, and disappeared.

Behind me Whitey whispered, "Ah man, there goes my lotto ticket."

"Not today," I said to Ruby Two. "We're going to walk away and we don't want any trouble."

"What about my window?"

Whitey said too loud, "Those two took my money. They robbed me. I want my money back."

Ruby Two raised her voice. "You do know this, white boy. You lied to me." The crowd murmur rose and they started to close in.

"Bruno," Whitey said, "get my money back. I want my money back." He had no concept of the threat, or what was about to happen. He just knew he had to have the cash he'd earned through knuckles and the boot.

Someone in the crowd said, "Dat's Bruno Johnson."

The crowd stopped moving in and froze; it took in a collective breath.

Ruby Two lost her smug smile. "Can't be. Bruno Johnson's dead."

"I'm getting tired of hearing that," I said.

Ruby Two said, "Dat right? Prove it."

I put the 415 Gonzales back in my waistband and pulled up my sleeve, revealing the large tattooed letters "BMF" on my shoulder. Someone in the crowd said, "I'm gettin' the hell outta here. He'll kill us all."

The momentum had shifted. To keep it moving, I reached under my shirt and pulled out two guns, held them pointing at the ground, let them think I was crazy and would start shooting. More of the mob peeled off.

Whitey stuck his head around me. "That's right, assholes, this here is Bruno Johnson. Get back. Get back or I'll turn him loose on you. Heh heh."

"Shut up, Whitey. Come on, Helen, let's get out of here."

Whitey crabbed around me and dropped onto the two downed Crips, his hands fumbling in their pockets. He came out with the wad of bills they'd stolen from him.

Ruby Two said, "Dey's not gonna like you takin' their money."

I asked her, "Can I talk to you for a minute?"

"I got nothin' ta say ta the likes of you."

"You're gonna want to hear this."

She thought it over and shrugged. "All right, come on." She turned her back and moved to the side of the restaurant next to the broken-out window, a yawning maw outlined in a jagged fringe of cubed glass that twinkled when it caught the morning sun.

She wasn't any taller than a middle-school kid and yet she held sway over the mob that had dispersed and now flowed back inside. She wore her hair in tight cornrows with blue beads woven in. She had a black outline tattoo of the Playboy Bunny under her right eye and looked to be about thirty years old. But I'd been out of the business for a while and no longer trusted my age assessment. She could just as easily be a youthful forty or forty-five. She had a round moon face and pale green eyes, eerie eyes like a Siamese cat that toyed with a mouse.

"I want ta get paid for my window."

"I'll take care it," I said. "You own this place?" I peeled off four hundred-dollar bills and handed them to her. She shrugged and the tension in her shoulders eased. The money saved face for her in front of her people.

Customers inside the restaurant looked on, curious as to why Ruby Two would be talking in confidence with someone with my reputation.

"That's right, it's my place, what's it to you?"

"I'm not interested in you or what's going on in this fine establishment."

She pointed a finger. "I don't like what you're implyin'."

I held up my hand. "Let me talk." She went quiet. Some of the bolder patrons inside moved closer to hear, but not yet close enough. I lowered my voice. "You know who I am, right?"

"I heard of you, ya."

"I don't want any trouble with you. I want Calvin Ivory and—"

"He ain't here."

"Listen to me. I saw him split when all this mess lit off. Don't try and lie to me. You don't want me mad at you. I'll come back here with a team of sheriff's deputies and we'll burn this place down. If you know me, you'll know I'm serious."

She squirmed a little, caught herself. Her back stiffened. "So, you want Ivory, then?"

"That's right."

"For what?"

"Doesn't matter to you. He needs to answer for something he did in the jail, and I think you know what it is. Tell me where to find him."

She hesitated, glanced back over her shoulder at the encroaching crowd inside the building, and whispered, "I'll find out where he's layin' his head. Meet me tonight behind the old Sears on Long Beach, at eleven. I'll give up that punk. He shouldn't have brought his stink inta my place."

"I'll be there. Don't play any games. I'm not kidding. I'll come back here and drive a truck right through your restaurant just like I did five years ago."

Her mouth sagged open in surprise. She'd heard the stories. I turned and walked away.

Traffic on Crenshaw had stopped. The commuters had seen the near-riot, the hyenas closing in on the vulnerable prey, and wanted to watch, get some video to put up on social media. Blood and bone.

None of the Crips followed us out into the street as we wove our way in between the cars back to the truck. I needed to rest, my body begging me to lie down and take a nap. Halfway across, Whitey groaned, "Hey, we can't just walk away, not from that kind of money on the table. Are you kiddin' me? You saw that asswipe, Police Killa Bitch—he came outta the place. Someone in there knows about him. I'm not walkin' away from no two hundred thousand dollars. That's more money than—"

"Whitey," Helen said. "Shut the hell up."

I turned to look at him. He'd gone pale. Blood trickled out of the corner of his mouth and into his eyes from a couple of lacerations on his scalp. Combined with the bruises he took the day before, he was starting to look like an extra in *The Walking Dead*.

"Come on, we have to get you to a hospital."

"No, this is all about nothin'. I been hurt worse fallin' in the shower. Let's jack up some of them people in there. What's the matter with the two a you? We got guns, right? Gimme one of 'em, I'll do it myself."

I opened the truck door. "Get in or I'm going to make you into a suitcase."

"Ah, man."

"Get in the truck, dweeb."

He climbed in. "Hey, don't talk to me like that. I got us here, didn't I? Tell her, Bruno, tell her how I got us here."

"Whitey, please, please, just shut up." I closed his door and got in the passenger side.

Helen drove and pulled us into traffic while she talked on the phone. She fed the person she called a license number and hung up.

"What was that?" I asked.

"The license plate to that Chevy Impala, the one the dweeb said Ivory was in when he drove away."

With the mob descending on us, she'd had the presence of mind to memorize a license plate. You don't get more professional than that. After this chase ended would she let me walk away, or was she going to try and take me down?

CHAPTER THIRTY-FIVE

I WOKE SPRAWLED on the backseat, head clouded with sleep, mouth gummy. Helen sat behind the wheel, vigilant, watching the house in Compton where the Chevy Impala was registered. Soft oranges and yellows of the fading day meant I'd been asleep for too many hours. Why was I surprised? My body did what it needed to heal. I struggled up in the seat trying to get my bearings. "Hey, where's Whitey?"

She didn't turn to look at me. "He said he was hungry. He walked down to that market two blocks over to get us some microwave burritos."

"How long has he been gone?"

She checked the time on her phone. "Three hours, twenty-one minutes."

"What? Why'd you let him go?"

"You said he was part of the team."

I got out and got in the front seat. "No movement at the house?"

"No, the car hasn't shown. I would've woke you. We don't even know if the registration is up to date. This place could just be a mail drop. This could be a total waste of time, and by the looks of it, it probably is."

"Whitey's not coming back."

"No big loss, in my book. I don't know why you put up with the likes of him."

"Let's call it for now. Take me to my hotel." That's where her car was. I'd drop her off there and then head to wherever Drago had set up again.

She started the truck and headed out. "So, that's it, we're done for the day?"

"You have any other ideas?"

In about six hours I had a meet with Ruby Two that I had not told her about. Wasn't sure why I hadn't told her. She'd become more like a partner than an adversary who wanted to put me behind bars for the rest of my life.

She shrugged; her eyes focused on the road. Something was different about her. Her mood, a morose brooding. Something was eating at her. Was it a conflict in whether to take me in?

I checked my phone. Drago had sent a text: "When ur done, come back to the suite."

He hadn't moved Marie after all. I ground my teeth. Stubborn, bullheaded woman. She could be persuasive and knew how to manipulate Drago. She had no idea what was going on and had not trusted me enough to pack up and move when I'd asked her to. I wouldn't have asked if it hadn't been absolutely necessary. We were going to have a fight over this one.

"Is it true?" Helen asked, keeping her eyes on the road.

Her question pulled me out of my anger. "Is what true?"

"About you running some kind of underground railroad for abused children. That you sneak up here and rescue two or three at a time and take them back to a big ranch in Chile?"

I chuckled. "Is that what people are saying?"

She took her eyes from the road to look at me. Serious. In dire need of the answer.

"It's not what they're saying," she said. "It's legend. The warrants out for your arrest kind of corroborate that legend. How many kids?"

I shrugged. "Twelve." I didn't correct her on the location. It wasn't Chile, it was Costa Rica.

"Oh," she said.

"What?"

"Well, I just heard it was something like fifty-seven."

"Fifty-seven? I can hardly keep track and support twelve. My wife's pregnant with number thirteen, and I'm up here running down a kidnapper when I should be home taking care of those kids."

She took her eyes off the road for a second to look at me, to look into my eyes searching for modesty, and more important, the truth.

She pulled on the steering wheel, guiding the truck over to the curb.

"What are you doing? I need to get home."

She put it in park, turned, and put her back to the door so she faced me. She did have something on her mind. I waited.

Her expression suddenly shifted; all guile melted away. She turned vulnerable and needy. "I . . . ?" She caught herself and stopped, unable to talk to me, the topic far too emotional.

"What? Just say it."

She shook her head and turned to look through the windshield at the passing world outside. A tear formed at the corner of her eye and rolled down her cheek, leaving a glistening trail of sorrow. It caused a little ache in my chest.

I scooted closer to reach out and put my hand on hers, the one that rested on her leg. "Tell me."

She looked back at me. Her chin quivered. "I . . . In all my life I have never felt so helpless."

I squeezed her hand.

"I need to ask you a favor," she said. "A big one."

My capacity for favors had already hit overload, the needle all the way in the red. "If I can help, you know I will. What is it?"

She shook her head. More tears. Her throat moved up and down to suppress the sobs. I resisted the urge to hug her, afraid it would send the wrong message. I let her work through it. What could bring such a strong woman to open up like this, to need something from me of all people? She had ability and bravado to spare. She knew the world and how it worked. There was nothing she couldn't do if she put her mind to it.

She broke eye contact and looked down at my hand on hers. Her words came out soft, almost inaudible. "I have a niece . . . "

My heart skipped several beats, made me light-headed. Oh, dear Lord. I instantly knew the ask. Marie was going to kill me.

I squeezed her hand. "Go on."

She looked back into my eyes, hers wet and pleading. "I have a niece I've tried to get put in my custody—legal guardianship. She's in a bad way. My sister—she's an absolute evil bitch." She hesitated. "That's not true, it's the meth. She's possessed by it. Child Protective Services have taken little Stephanie away from her twice. The court keeps giving her back. They say a child is better off with the mother even in a challenged environment. *Challenged environment*—you have to see this place, what she has to put up with. I've tried my best to intervene. My sister has to have the welfare money Stephanie brings in every month to support her habit. She took out a restraining order against me. I can't see Stephanie anymore, according to this same cockamamie court. The law did this. The same law I worked all my life to enforce. I don't even know how she's doing. This place in Chile, is it nice, with a good school, and other kids to play with?"

"Of course it is. It's all those things and more. But Stephanie will be away from her mother and that's—"

"No." Helen shook her head. "You don't understand. Stephanie has already had a spiral fracture of her arm, and a skull fracture. Two different incidents. She's emaciated with dark circles under her eyes. Last I saw of her. You, more than anyone, know what that means."

She was right, I did. The violence was escalating. Stephanie had been lucky so far and was now living on borrowed time.

Helen stopped. A sob got away from her and snatched her words. "The place is a dump and my sister has every speed freak in the city coming through there. I don't get her out soon, she'll . . . even if she survives, she'll be ruined if I don't do something soon. Do you understand?"

"Yes, I do."

"So, you know what I'm asking?"

"I do."

"If it's a matter of funds, I'll send you money every month. I'll work overtime, send you more than you could ever need. Please? I'll do anything you ask, just say yes." She openly sobbed.

The large lump in my throat threatened to choke me. While working the streets, I had all too often seen the situation she described and at the time could do nothing about it. I couldn't intervene back then and had experienced Helen's helplessness and despair, over and over again.

But I could also hear Marie's words, "You're only one man. At what point do we say, 'no more'? At what point does the number of children detract from the care of those we already have? At what point do we become the same problem we are trying to correct?" All great arguments. But the bigger one, the most important question, was how do we live with ourselves if we turn one away and something happens? Because something will happen if left up to the evil and unscrupulous. We buy a bigger place. We find the money from somewhere; we do what we have to do to make it work.

She shifted in the seat and put her head against my chest. I held her. "Please?" she whispered. Her warm tears wet my shirt.

I couldn't answer, the lump in my throat choking me. I tried to nod and couldn't.

CHAPTER THIRTY-SIX

HELEN SHUT THE truck down inside the parking tower to the Americana. Secrecy no longer mattered, not with the favor floated between us. I had not told Helen yes or no. I told her I had to think about it. I gave her our suite number and the number for the burner phone.

"Pick you up here in the morning?" she asked. Her tone carried anxiety over the unanswered question regarding her niece.

Her face was in shadowed relief. I couldn't see her eyes, what she was thinking. Not with the hooded light in the parking structure. "No," I said, "be back here at ten."

She nodded and didn't inquire further, though she wanted to.

I said, "We're going to take down Calvin Ivory tonight."

"Good."

Neither of us moved, the hesitation uncomfortable for the both of us. "About that other thing, I have to talk to my wife, Marie."

"I understand. I wouldn't expect anything less."

That uncomfortable pause again. "Maybe," she said, "it might be better if you don't tell her about it and just do it. Sometimes it's easier to ask for forgiveness than permission."

"I would never do that to Marie."

"Hmm."

I wished she'd quit with that kind of response, that tone. It cut me to the quick.

She reached out in the dark, put her hand on mine, left it there for a long beat. Her hand was warm, almost hot. An odd transformation occurred; we'd somehow became linked emotionally, at least that's what it felt like. Not as man and woman but more as partners in a moral dilemma, a proposed criminal act. Doing a wrong thing for the right reasons. She had touched me in that moment for that very purpose and it had worked like a magic potion.

I sighed. "I'm going to hate myself in the morning."

She had not let go and squeezed my hand.

I took in a deep breath. "Where does Stephanie live?"

"You're not going to regret this, Bruno. I'll keep my promise. I'll send you money every month." She started the truck.

"Wait . . ." I had not meant to go back out to recover the child, not at that very moment.

Helen let go of my hand to steer. She backed the truck up, put it in drive, and headed out. "She's in a dump, a real shack in South El Monte."

Once the truck had moved even one foot on this new crusade, I couldn't stop Helen, tell her "no," that we'd do it later after we took down the kidnappers and punished them for killing Emily Mosley and Lilian Morales. Once started, if we stopped and something happened to Stephanie—well, I was just locked in now until it was finished.

What would Marie say? I tried not to think about it.

The truck wove around the circular ramp to the ground floor, the lights a kaleidoscope of flashing images. Helen drove with new resolve, her jaw set, her eyes alive with hope and promise, the scar down the side of her face more an exotic question mark.

"How old is Stephanie?"

"Four, and the cutest little girl you have ever seen. Just wait. You'll agree with me once you meet her."

"Tell me about your sister, the setup, the way this house looks. How many rooms, how many square feet? Doors, windows? Weapons in the house?"

"It's about thirty, forty minutes from here depending on traffic. It's in a barrio where gunfire is common." She stopped at the street entrance and looked over at me, as if saying, "Don't be afraid to use a gun." Or maybe that was my overactive imagination.

"You think your sister is going to be that big of a problem?"

Helen turned onto the street and gunned the truck. The centrifugal force pushed me back into my seat. She wanted to get there fast and recover her niece before I changed my mind.

"Marjory loves Stephanie, no doubt about it, but she loves her meth more and will forsake Stephanie at the drop of a hat if it came down to her daughter over a two-five baggie of speed. It's a three-bedroom, two-bath shack, about a thousand square feet, located on the west side of the street. The front door opens to the living room. There's always a Harley-Davidson parked just inside the front door."

"Ah, man. She's living with someone, Marjory?"

"That's right. Is that a problem? Shouldn't be. Not from the stories I've heard about you. I saw how you took out those two in front of the restaurant."

"I'm not a hundred percent healed. You gotta know that. I slept all day yesterday and today."

"I can handle myself."

"I thought you said you have a restraining order against you. You can't be seen within a thousand feet of this place."

"Screw it. This is Stephanie we're talking about."

"If you're identified tonight, it'll mean your job."

"You just said you're not up to doing this alone."

"First rule, we do it my way or not at all."

She hesitated. "Okay. You tell me what you want me to do and I'll do it, no questions asked."

"Who's the dude she's living with?"

"JD. Johnny Melvin Douglas."

"Hold on, she's living with Wizard?"

Her head whipped around to look at me. "You know him?"

"He's a Devil Dog, an affiliate of the Visigoths."

"That's right. I told you, this isn't a good place for Stephanie. Every day that she—"

"Wait," I said.

She stopped talking and paid attention to the road.

"If Wizard is home, there's going to be blood and bone."

"You backing out?"

"Don't do that."

"Hmm."

"It's not what you think."

"Tell me then."

I sat back and closed my eyes. Images I'd tried to suppress flashed back on me, thick and heavy, laden with enough sorrow to bury a civilization. Bobby Ray had been the president of the Visigoths, the local chapter, and he was also Sonja's husband. Sonja, Bosco's mother, had been the one to shove a .25 auto hard against my chest.

"What's the matter? Tell me?" Helen said again.

I had not spoken of it to anyone, not even Marie. But Marie had been there for it, heard and witnessed the entire episode, something in the last two months I'd tried so hard to forget. The event came most every night in the form of night terrors.

I told Helen. Told her all of it:

I was down on my back in a big garage, gunshot in the hip. Bobby Ray was lying dead in a pool of his own blood not ten feet away. Dead by my hand. Sonja squatted next to me.

Sonja stuck the Raven .25 up against the left side of my chest, her finger on the trigger, and spoke through clenched teeth. "That's right, Bruno, I can see it in your eyes that you've finally figured it out. And if I were really mean and wanted to milk every ounce of revenge outta what you've done, I'd leave you alive. That's right, let you live with what you've done. But I'm not like that. I live for the moment, always have. You know that. And I want my pound of flesh, right now."

She drove the gun into my ribs and gritted her teeth even more. "You tossed your own son out into traffic, Bruno. You killed your own son. That's what I wanted to tell you when I called and asked you to meet me here tonight. I wanted to look you in the eye and tell you that you'd killed your own son, just before I dropped the hammer on you."

She took a deep breath and said it again, said it for the last time. "You killed our son, Bruno."

She pulled the trigger.

The round parted skin and muscle and burrowed past the cartilage between the ribs. The small lead round, fired point-blank, entered my chest cavity with a pain like nothing I'd ever felt before. I welcomed it as the darkness slammed down on me one final time.

"Oh my God," Helen said. "I'm so sorry, Bruno. I didn't know." Her foot had unknowingly come off the accelerator. The truck slowed.

My face was wet from tears. After telling her what had happened, a portion of the guilt, the heavy emotional weight, lifted. Just a little bit of it. Maybe the healing process had finally started by talking it through, by revealing my deepest, darkest secret to this stranger.

CHAPTER THIRTY-SEVEN

THIRTY MINUTES LATER, Helen turned off Lower Azusa Road to Cogswell Avenue and shut off the headlights. She slowed to a crawl. All the streetlights had been shot out, making the street dark and forbidding. The only flickering light came from farther down the street, making shadows cast from trees and cars and people dance to a silent beat on the fronts of the dark and quiet houses. Houses filled with people shut in, cowering, waiting out the night.

"It's on the right about halfway down."

"Stop about three houses north. I'll get out and go on foot."

"You sure you don't want me to go with you?"

"I've done this before. You just keep the truck running and—"

The house came into view. Thirty or forty Devil Dogs, in their greasy denim cuts, black leather, and silver chains, stood around a fire that blazed in a fifty-five-gallon drum in the front yard. The flames licked at the dark sky, billowing oily black smoke. Harley-Davidson motorcycles backed up with their back tires touching the curb took up the entire length of the house. The brightly polished chrome on the bikes flickered, reflecting the firelight like winking eyes.

"Keep driving. Go. Go."

Helen hit the steering wheel with her fist. "Damn."

We passed the house slow with the headlights off. Five of the bikers melted into the shadows going for their guns, just in case. The rest watched us go by, giving us the evil eye.

"We'll have to come back on a night that's not so busy."

She didn't say anything, made the turn, hit the headlights, and gunned the truck, angry.

"You're right," I said. "This isn't a good place for Stephanie. We'll get her out of there, I promise."

I did want to rescue Stephanie from her situation, but at the same time I had also developed a hatred for outlaw motorcycle gangs and didn't mind rubbing it in their face by snatching an innocent they believed belonged to them. A child they planned to corrupt and brainwash.

We rode in silence, each of us in our own thoughts. My stomach growled. I could really use a Yoo-hoo and a couple of Snowballs.

Helen said, "What happened to Bosco?"

"What?"

"Bosco, the—"

That answer was too personal and emotionally taboo. The words clogged in the transfer from my brain to my lips. I didn't know if I'd ever be able to talk about that again. Not the part about Bosco. I hadn't even told Dad.

"It's okay," she said, "if you don't want to tell me."

"No, it's not that. It's just . . ." I let the words trail off into oblivion.

Silence. More road passed under the tires.

"Your wife, you said she gunned Sonja?"

I didn't answer. Couldn't. I was done talking. I didn't look at her and watched out the windshield.

It took a little longer to get back to the Americana. She parked in the same place and didn't turn the ignition off.

"You can keep the truck for now. Pick me up here at ten so we have time to scout the location."

"We'll get Stephanie tomorrow?" she asked.

"No promises. We'll get her as soon as the opportunity presents itself."

"We need *to make* the opportunity present itself."

"Yes, of course. That's what I meant. I'm tired. I need something to eat and a little nap."

"Right, see you back here at ten."

I got out and watched her drive away. We couldn't save Emily Mosley, but we could save Stephanie. The thought of a little four-year-old girl in a nest of vipers like that made me want to get Drago and a mob of his friends with ball bats and chains and go back. But that would do no one any good.

I rode the elevator up shifting gears, thinking about Marie and how she had stayed in our same hotel room. Then I remembered Chulack. I took out the cell and dialed.

"Yeah, Bruno? What have you got?" His tone was resigned and lacking the hope he'd had in other phone calls.

"I'll have Calvin Ivory in pocket, tonight."

"Good. You going to need any help?"

"No, but thanks. After I have a talk with him, I'll give you a call and we can decide on where to go from there."

"I'll have people standing by waiting for your call. I'm also sending over the crime report and photos from the Lilian Morales crime scene. I'll leave them at the front desk, like before."

"With any luck, we'll have this whole thing wrapped tonight." I didn't say the obvious, that Ivory would give up who hired him and we'd move up the line to the kidnappers. We'd persuade them to tell us what they had done with Emily. Then all that would remain would be a sorrowful death notification, something I was glad I'd have no part of.

I clicked off the phone and stuck my card key in the door. I opened it and stepped in. Cops develop instincts citizens don't have or even comprehend. One is sensing whether a house or domicile is occupied. Without stepping in any further, I knew the hotel suite was empty. I stifled Marie's name on my lips, ready to call out to her.

Nothing in the kitchen or living room area was disturbed; in fact, it looked like the place had been recently cleaned. I moved to the bedroom. Nothing but a silence quieter than death. The closet stood open. Empty.

I jerked my phone from my pocket and checked for text messages. Nothing new.

The room's doorway shadowed. I spun, yanking out a gun.

"You gonna shoot me, Hoss?"

Drago.

"What's going on? I thought you said you didn't move from this suite?"

"That wasn't entirely true."

"Not entirely true? Come on, man, you scared the hell outta me."

"You know, your voice just turned squeaky. Follow me." He turned and waved.

I followed him. He stopped at the doorway, stuck his head out, peeked up and down the hallway, then crossed to the door opposite. It opened on its own before he got there.

Marie.

I hurried to hug her and said to Drago, "You moved them across the hall? Really?"

"Still with the squeaky voice?"

We pushed in and Marie hugged me back and closed the door. She said, "It wasn't his fault. I told him we weren't going to move. This was a compromise."

"Some compromise." She poked me in the ribs.

"Works out anyway," Drago said. "I can see if anyone comes by your old place. I'll have the drop on them." He pointed behind the door as it closed to a sawed-off pump shotgun propped in the corner.

CHAPTER THIRTY-EIGHT

DRAGO OPENED THE door and stuck his head out in the hallway. "Hey, what'd you do with that little toothless moron?" He came back in and let a little-used smile creep across his expression.

"He took a flyer."

"Too bad, I was just getting to like him. And tonight, Waldo's going to miss his little play toy."

Marie had wrapped her arms around me, her head in my chest, and had not let go. She held on tight as if I were a pole in a fire station. The public display of affection made Drago uncomfortable. He said, "I was just running out to grab some Cuban food for everyone from that place down the street, you in?"

"How about a couple of burgers instead? That stuff is too spicy."

Drago waited for Marie to look at him, give him the okay on the burgers. Drago didn't make a move without Marie's approval. He also knew about the past dietary restrictions she'd put on me. Knew they'd been suspended for the time being.

Marie sensed the pause. She pulled away. "Go ahead, Karl."

"Be back in a jiff," he said.

He only used words like "jiff" when he was around Marie. It'd be cute if it wasn't so puppy-dog like with syrup on top, coming from a man-mountain who could chew nails and spit rivets.

Drago left.

I needed to tell her about the most recent development in the kidnap case, tell her about Stephanie and take the heat, sooner rather than later. I didn't want it hanging over my head.

The suite was a mirror image to the one across the hall, the one where we'd spent the last two months recuperating. Even so, it still felt alien. Mom sat in her wheelchair in front of the television watching an old sitcom, one of Marie's favorites with John Ritter: *Three's Company.* Canned laughter came from the television, but nothing from Mom. Her face remained stoic. The moniker, "Mom," still had a funny taste to it.

"What's up with her?"

Marie took my hand and whispered, "Come on in here."

She led me toward our master bedroom. I hesitated just as we left the living area. Not wanting to give Mom the wrong idea, I raised a hand and waved. "Hi, Bea."

She said nothing and didn't take her eyes from Don Knotts talking to John Ritter.

Marie yanked on my hand, pulling me into the bedroom, and closed the door. "She's mad because Drago wouldn't let her run an errand today. He said it was a matter of security."

"He's right. Bea should understand that."

"He wouldn't let her use the phone, either."

"I agree with him."

"I do too," Marie said.

"What is it she thinks is more important than her health and welfare that she needs to leave or make a call?"

"She wouldn't tell me. Rude, if you ask me. After all we've done for her. She said we are holding her hostage. At the same time, I can kind of see her point."

This was where I would normally tell Marie she was putting her values on someone else who was coming from an entirely different world, but she'd warned me in the past, under the threat of great bodily injury, not to use that form of logic on her ever again. Well, she hadn't put it exactly that way.

Instead, I just said, "Hmm." A response I'd stolen from Helen. It wouldn't work many more times before I got a playful punch to the gut and an admonishment never to do that again. She tended to mold me into some kind of pseudo-perfect specimen. I didn't mind.

Marie had the kidnap photos and the reports spread all across the huge bed. On the nightstand sat a legal pad filled with notes, page after page of them. It was a go-nowhere kidnap investigation and yet she thought she could solve it as if this kidnap were an inside job and the clues were buried somewhere in all that paper. She was a regular Columbo. Or just bored and the investigation was more like a thousand-piece puzzle that depicted a twenty-acre wheat field.

"There are more reports and photos down at the front desk if you're interested," I said.

When I left in a few hours, at ten, I wanted to keep her mind busy and not worrying about me. I kissed her on the lips. "I missed you, babe."

She gave me another hug. "Come sit. Tell me all that happened today."

I shoved aside the mundane photos, interior shots of the Mosely house, and we sat on the edge of the bed. I was so glad to be back, to see her smile, to see the light in her eyes, the way she looked at me. It recharged the life in me like a giant solar battery, warm and comforting.

"You sure you want to hear this?"

"Yes, I do. Of course, I'm interested in what you're doing."

"Looks like you're studying up on the case."

"I am. Don't change the subject. Tell me."

"You know, I got that phone call from Dan this morning."

"And?"

"It was a body dump."

Her hand gripped mine tighter.

I said, "No, it wasn't Emily."

She let out her breath.

"It was Lilian Morales."

"Oh no, Bruno. No."

She knew exactly what that meant. With the foiled two-million-dollar drop and now the nanny found murdered, no hope remained for Emily. None. There wasn't one reason to keep her alive.

"That poor, poor family." She stood up, emotionally hurt, and wrung her hands as she paced. I watched her.

She started to gather up all the photos and reports, shuffling them together into one big pile, getting the bed ready to sleep.

She stopped, shook her head. She looked up at me. "So, that means we're leaving tomorrow?"

"Baby, I have one more thing to do tonight."

"What? No, Bruno. It's over. You did your part."

"I would agree with you, but I set up a meet with someone who worked for the kidnappers. So only I can do this."

She'd been emotionally battered the last couple of days, holding her breath each time I went out the door, holding it until I came back. She took in this new information without complaint. I couldn't dump the added load of Stephanie on top of everything else. Besides, it hadn't happened yet. And if I'd learned anything from my years on the street, it was that fate was a hungry hunter and laughed in our faces, especially when we tried to plan something to combat the evil imbalance.

"The family needs to know what happened," I said, a weak motive she didn't deserve. When in reality it came down to me wanting a piece of Police Killa Bitch. A physical vent I intended to use to ease two months of emotions that had continued to build and was festering now, ready to erupt.

But at the same time, I didn't want her disappointed in me.

She broke the silence. "Your dad called."

My breath caught.

"The kids are fine," she said.

"You tell him about Bea?"

"I would've, but I didn't think it was my place. I think it would be better coming from you. You need to tell him. He has a right to know."

Of course, she was right. I didn't relish making that call. I took out the cell. Marie squeezed my hand and kissed my forehead. She left the room and eased the door closed.

I dialed the number to our rented villa in Costa Rica.

CHAPTER THIRTY-NINE

ROSA ANSWERED THE house phone, cheerful, happy to hear from me. We spoke at length about all the children and what they'd been up to. The normal, mundane kind of things that happened daily, but I ate it up with relish, like dipping a finger in the chocolate frosting of a sheet cake. Finally, I asked her to get Dad.

I waited on the phone while Dad made his way through the house. The sounds of happy children playing in the background brought on tears of joy. I missed them so.

I had not told Dad what had happened with Bosco. How I had been in a fight for my life and had tossed a son I didn't know I had out into traffic on the freeway. How Sonja, Bosco's mother, had been the one to tell me I'd killed our son. How, out of an act of revenge, she'd been the one to stick the gun into my chest and pull the trigger.

I wanted to tell Dad in person. That had been the reasoning, nothing more than a weak excuse to avoid the pain.

After speaking with Helen earlier, the emotional relief it produced, I realized that telling Dad might further my emotional healing. But I'd be passing on that same emotional load to a man who didn't deserve it. What Marie said made sense. He did have a right to know all that had happened.

He was going through chemo for stomach cancer and was weak, all skin and bones, his body being held together by strength of soul and faith alone. Did I have the right to dump all of this on him?

No.

I desperately needed to hear what he had to say.

I started breathing fast, hyperventilating. Sweat broke out on my brow. I went into the bathroom, closed the door, and slid down the wall to sit on the cool tile floor. I reached up and turned the light off. Inky darkness slammed down with an incongruous kind of pressure that I knew wasn't really there.

I had to tell Dad or let the blackness continue to devour my emotional center until I shriveled up to nothingness.

"Son, is that really you?"

I closed my eyes tight and tried to picture him. All I could conjure was a dad from thirty years ago. A dad, stout and stalwart, who wore tee shirts that displayed well-defined muscles, a tightly cut Afro without a bit of gray, a man who protected me and Noble from all evils that slithered out of the ghetto.

"Dad?"

"Bruno, what's the matter? What's happened?" He'd read my voice, the tone. We'd only told him we were lying low, avoiding the law, and would be home soon. Nothing about being gunshot. What he must think after two months. Better he thought us on the lam than to tell him the truth.

I closed my eyes tighter, trying to put the words together. They wouldn't coalesce. Not about the incident on the freeway or the one in the garage.

"Dad, guess who knocked on our door?"

"What? Who—"

"Bea Elliot." For some reason, I couldn't call her *Mom* in his presence.

His breathing increased. Too easily heard over thousands of miles of phone line and airwaves.

"Hold on. Hold on, let me sit down." A chair next to the phone scraped the floor then banged against the wall, and I could picture exactly where he was in the villa. He was by the entrance to the kitchen. The large paver tiles. The hand-painted mural of trees and flowers on the wall above him. The sweet scents of cinnamon and freshly cooked bread.

"Dear Lord, say that again, Son. I don't think I heard you correctly. I think I had one of my spells, just now."

"Bea Elliot. Right out of the blue, she knocked on our door."

"How . . . I mean . . . I thought she was . . . ah . . ."

He had his own preconceived notions in what had happened to her, the same as I had.

"What . . . I mean . . . I don't know what to say to that."

"She's in a wheelchair." Words that slipped out all on their own. Inappropriate for the moment, but I'd become just as brain-twisted as he was, trying to put myself in his place, what he must be thinking, his mind traveling at light speed pondering the lost years, the lost emotions, the lost love with all the *could've beens*.

"What happened to her?"

I opened my eyes to darkness. I had not even asked her how she came to be in the chair. I guess I only assumed it was brittle bones and lack of musculature that came naturally with advanced age. Or I had just not cared enough to ask?

"I haven't had a chance to talk to her much. She's staying with us for the time being. I've been helping out a friend of mine and—"

"Son?"

"Yeah, Dad."

"When were you going to tell me about you getting hurt? Bad hurt."

He, too, wanted to change the painful topic to something else not so painful. But not the case for me.

I gripped the phone too hard. Noble, my brother, was staying in Costa Rica to help out while we were away. Noble had probably talked with Bruno, his son and my nephew. The same nephew who'd helped bring Bea to our door.

"I'm all better now. I didn't want you to worry." How much did he actually know? Did he know all of it and was waiting for me to say it? To tell him about Bosco? No way could he know that much. Marie wouldn't have told my nephew. She wouldn't have told anyone.

Silence.

"We all miss you and Marie. Son, come home as soon as you can."

That was it? That was all he was going to say about Bea? The wife he hadn't seen in forty-seven years? He must've made peace with that relationship, probably a long time ago. Or maybe he just needed more time to process it. It was a big lump of emotion to swallow.

"Dad, it's good to hear your voice. We'll be home soon. I promise. How are your treatments coming along? How are you feeling?"

He chuckled. "Can't keep my pants up anymore, my belt's too big. Gotta get me some of those old-man suspenders, I guess. I'm feeling better. I think it's working. I think I'm through the worst of it. I better be."

"That's good. That's really great, Dad." A big load lifted off me. Too much guilt had plagued me for the last two months. The trip had originally been for a couple of days and had stretched to a couple of months. All lost days I'd been away from my father and the children. Missed opportunities for spending our lives together, making priceless memories for the ages.

"We'll be home in a couple of days, I promise."

"I'll look forward to it. Give that lovely bride of yours a kiss for me. Love you, Son."

"Love you, too, Dad."

He clicked off, too soon. I could've talked to him for hours. I *needed* to talk to him for hours.

CHAPTER FORTY

I STRUGGLED UP from the bathroom floor using the wall as a support, turned the light on, and squinted at the brightness.

In the living room, Mom had not moved from the television. I went to the kitchen area and opened the refrigerator door. Marie sat on the couch knitting a blanket with soft pink yarn for the new baby. She thought our new child would be a girl. Whenever I told her no way, had to be a boy, she'd shoot me a coy smile and say, "You're just being silly." Which I didn't understand, how that was silly. I was serious. Leastwise, I thought I was. My deep and abiding love for her tended to skew my outlook on the world. In a good way.

I said, "I'm having some Snowballs and a Yoo-hoo, any takers?"

Marie didn't look up; her fingers continued to knit one, purl two. "Drago's bringing you burgers; you'll spoil your dinner."

"Thanks, Mom."

Marie and Bea both looked up. I cringed.

The suite door rattled and started to swing open. I spun, my hand going under my shirt to the stock of the .357. In walked Drago with three white bags spotted with grease. With him came a heavenly aroma that caused my mouth to water and stomach to growl.

Marie got up, set her pink blanket aside, and wheeled Bea over to the dining room table. Neither spoke.

Somehow, Bea seemed more vulnerable than the first time I'd seen her. She still had not said a word. I brought out some plates and flatware as I watched Bea's eyes. She wouldn't look at me. She didn't like being a hostage.

Drago brought food for six people, but the way he ate, it probably wouldn't be enough. I unwrapped the two giant cheeseburgers, set them on my plate, and had to wait for everyone else to get dished up. I sucked down some Yoo-hoo in the interim. I did not relish the upcoming dietary restriction soon to be reimposed. I was surprised it hadn't already landed.

Finally, I picked up the luscious burger and took a bite. I closed my eyes and savored the wonderful flavors of melted cheese, red grilled onion, a quarter pound of burger, four slices of bacon, all smothered in mayo. I tried to stifle a groan and couldn't.

Our little town in Costa Rica didn't have any place that served American food. When we'd first arrived in town, I'd put forth the idea of opening a burger joint and Marie had said, "Dear one, you'd go broke. These people are smart; they eat healthy, fresh fruit, rice, chicken, fish. Not burgers of all things."

"You can't say that for sure. They don't know what they're missing. It could be crazy-popular."

"You want to be the man who single-handedly brings down the country's longevity rate?"

She wasn't fun to debate; she always went for the throat to shut me down early.

Drago spoke around a mouthful of spicy Cuban food and pointed his fork at me. "That was you on Crenshaw today, wasn't it? Saw it on the news."

I stopped mid-chew and cringed, my eyes automatically going to Marie. She looked at me with an expression I couldn't read as she continued with her dainty bite.

Drago said, "Saw those two assholes getting loaded up on a gurney and—"

"Karl, language, please?" Marie said.

"Oh, sorry. I mean those two shitbags. And that big window knocked out. That was you, right? They called it a near riot."

I wouldn't lie in front of Marie by denying it, and instead, just shrugged.

"That was the same place, wasn't it?" he said. "From about five years ago? You told me about it, remember?"

I gave him the stink eye, trying to get him to shut up.

"Oh, sorry." He picked up another white carton and ladled out more of the spicy rice. He'd gotten both spicy and mild. With her pregnancy, Marie had a problem with too spicy.

I swallowed first. "I didn't see the news broadcast," I said, "but yes, I was out on Crenshaw today. And we did have a little dustup. Nothing big, though."

I looked over at Bea, who had only been stirring her food around on her plate. Now she stared at me. "Was that Fat Boy's Pork Palace?" She said it like she also knew the place, knew it well.

"That's right, why?"

Drago said, "Wish I'd known. I woulda called ya, had ya pick up a couple orders of pork and beef ribs. They got the best in the city, I'm tellin' ya. And the chili fries, man oh man."

I couldn't picture Drago walking into that nefarious den of Crips and ordering ribs, not without causing a problem larger than I had.

I said again to Bea, "Why?"

My phone buzzed in my pocket. Marie looked up from her plate. It had to be Chulack. Something else had happened. I pulled it out and stepped away from the table. I touched the Call icon and answered it without looking at who it was. "Yeah, Dan?"

"Son?"

"Dad?"

"I'm sorry, Son. A little while ago you caught me off guard with . . . with that information. Godamighty, you darn near stopped my heart. I wasn't thinking straight."

"That's okay, I understand."

"No, it's not okay. That was no way for a grown man to act and I apologize."

I turned my back to the dining area and lowered my voice. "Dad, you should have seen my reaction when I came into the suite and found her here. I understand. It's okay."

"I feel better already talking to you about it," he said. "Now, I think it best I talk to Beatrice."

My breath caught. I'd not been expecting that. Dad had more integrity and moral fortitude than anyone I knew. I wished I could be more like him.

"Sure, just a minute."

I went to the dining room and stood by the wheelchair where my mother sat. I held out the phone. For some reason I couldn't say, "It's Dad." Instead, I said, "It's Xander."

Her face lit up with a huge smile that made my world swim with nostalgia. Had I somehow remembered her smile from all those decades ago? She snatched the phone out of my hand, held it against her breast, and waved with her other. "Come on, move me out of here. This is private. Come on, don't stand there with your mouth open catching flies. Move it."

I wheeled her into the other room. I moved away as she said into the phone, "Xander? Oh, Xander, is it really you?"

Boy, what I would have given to hear both sides of that conversation. I sat back down, picked up my burger, and took a bite. It didn't taste nearly as good.

In the living room area, Bea faced away from us. Her shoulders shook as she wept. In between sobs I could barely make out her saying, "I'm so sorry . . ." and "Can you ever forgive me?" Then she listened, nodding and not saying much of anything else while Dad spoke. Only what could he be saying? You'd think she needed to be the one to dig herself out of such a deep hole. A pang of jealousy hit; I wanted to be talking with Dad like that.

Marie reached over and squeezed my hand, her eyes wet. I didn't feel elated over the reunion. Too much had happened in the last few months to be able to examine any additional heated feelings.

Somehow Dad found it within him, a way to talk to a loved one over the phone about something powerful and intimate. Where I found it impossible to tell him about Bosco and had used the feeble excuse that it needed to be done in person.

Drago didn't like all the emotional soup served with his dinner. He stood with his plate and left the suite to finish eating standing sentry out in the hall. I picked up my burger, ready to join him, but Marie froze me in place with her eyes.

"Right," I said. "Maybe I'll just finish eating right here."

"Hmm."

Now she was doing it.

CHAPTER FORTY-ONE

I MADE IT out to the curb at the parking entrance to the Americana, five minutes before ten, just as Helen pulled up in the big GMC truck. I got in.

"Where to?" she asked.

"The Sears that's closed down on Long Beach Boulevard in Lynwood. The rear parking lot. We need to scout it first, see if anyone is out there already set up and waiting for us."

I already knew the layout. I'd been there for a meet, two months earlier. A meet with Jumbo. In my wanderings in the world of criminality, I found all criminals tended to swirl around in a vortex of the vile and loathsome, using the same cohorts and frequenting the same locations. Especially if that location had worked out okay in a prior meet. Criminals, like normal humans, are creatures of habit. But some of them rise above the level of *creature* and into the *pure beast* category where kidnappers of little girls trod always watching over their shoulders for people like me.

Helen drove off without comment.

After a time, I said, "You get any rest?"

"That party on Cogswell is still going strong."

She'd gone back to El Monte in the hopes the biker party would break up early and allow an opening to rescue little Stephanie. Those kinds of odious biker get-togethers usually went all night and deep into the morning. The dawn of the new day would find some of them in the dirt hugging empty Jack Daniel's bottles and near-naked groupies with cheap empty beer cans scattered all around. The reek of sour beer, body odor, and urine rising on the morning mist.

I said nothing.

She said, "I called El Monte PD anonymously, told them shots had been fired at the location. They drove by, hit them with the spotlight, and just kept going. You believe that? I gave them all the probable cause they needed to raid the place, and all they do is spotlight it."

"As a street cop, I'm not sure I wouldn't have done the same thing." She'd been so concerned with how to get into the Cogswell house, she had not considered the danger to Stephanie by sparking a violent confrontation between the police and the bikers.

She took her eyes off the road. The streetlights going by gave little snapshots of her expression—of that exotic scar on the side of her beautiful face. I withered under her glare. She'd thought different of me. I'd let her down. I should've been old enough, mature enough, to understand and not to care. But I did. I wanted her to believe I had a big "S" on my chest. A natural instinct, like a peacock strutting chest out with all his brightly colored feathers displayed in a fan.

We rode in silence until she said, "Ruby Two told you to meet her here? Is that it?"

"That's right. She's going to give me Calvin Ivory."

"You know this is probably going to be a setup."

"Yeah, maybe."

"Then why are we going?"

"No matter what happens, there will be people here we can talk to. Crooks who will have information to move our way up the ladder to the next level. That's the way it works." She'd operated within the confines of the law too long and didn't know this other world. How to bypass due process, skip right to the heart of the issue at hand, using a little blood and bone.

"Hmm."

"You up for this?"

"You don't need to worry about me."

"You can't be familiar with this kind of situation, and that's okay."

"Oh, really? You think I'm not?"

"Don't get your back up. I know you can handle yourself. But here's just a suggestion. It goes down wrong, you don't give them a chance. You don't yell 'Police,' or 'Freeze.' There aren't any rules in this kind of game. You just shoot and keep shooting until no one's left standing, you understand?"

She took her eyes off the road to look at me again. "I thought you wanted to talk to some of these *people*? They're the ones responsible for dropping a witness off the tier and for dumping the body of a nanny on Skid Row. We shoot and keep shooting like you say, who's going to be left to tell who's pulling the strings?"

"When it goes to shit, the talking part takes a backseat."

"So, then we take dying declarations?"

"That's right. If it goes that way. Park three blocks north, we'll both walk in. There's a fence around the perimeter in the back with thick overgrown vines. You stay in the shadows of that fence to the rear and watch my back. Don't let them know you're there. You're my ace in the hole."

"Hmm."

Twenty minutes later, she pulled to the curb in a residential area, north and east of the defunct Sears, and parked. She climbed half-over the backseat to her war bag, her left hip close to my face as her body wiggled. She smelled of sweet soap. Her shirt pulled up, exposing a delicate tattoo of a winding vine with small yellow roses scrolled across the small of her back. Delicate flowers juxtaposed against a worn leather sheath clipped to the inside of her pants, a sheath that held a dirk, a double-edged knife, an illegal weapon according to Sheriff policy and procedures. A last-ditch, down-and-dirty weapon. It meant she subscribed to the old adage "better to be judged by twelve than carried by six."

She came back over with two extra magazines for her gun, two more sets of handcuffs, and a mini Maglite. She pulled her Glock, ejected the magazine and checked the loads, reinserted it, and press-checked the chambered round. "You ready?" she asked.

"Let's go," I said. She wore a black cotton long-sleeve shirt, black denim pants, and black shoes with crepe soles.

We got out and walked down the sidewalk. It was ten-thirty.

Helen peeled off as soon as we made it to the back parking lot and disappeared in the shadow of the fence line, following it around in an arc. I could barely make her out, and wouldn't have had I not known exactly where to look.

I walked straight into the defunct shopping center boarded up with industrial-grade plywood and painted over with gang graffiti.

My cell rang. I answered it. Helen. "There are two cars that have gone by twice out front on Long Beach, a Gold Lexus and an early model Caddy, fire-engine red with aftermarket rims. There they go again. They're early. It's a trap just like I thought. Get out of there, now."

She was back far enough in the lot where she could see both ends of the building, past the north and south sides, and out into Long Beach Boulevard.

"I'll keep my phone on," I said, "and in my shirt pocket so you can hear. If it goes down bad, you take out the guy farthest from me and work your way in. You understand?"

"I don't have a long gun. All I got is a pistol."

"Do the best you can."

"Damnit, Bruno. I start shooting, you hit the dirt."

"Take it easy. They can kill us but they can't eat us." It was a saying Robby Wicks tossed out every time "the shit was about to go loud."

"Oh, that's just perfect."

At least I got her to come off her standard "Hmm."

"Sssh," I said, "here comes a car now." Headlights lit up the back parking lot. The gold Lexus. It stopped, the lights cutting a swath across the weed-infested asphalt reaching out to me and not quite making it. I stepped out of the shadows of the building. The car rolled slowly toward me.

"I'm too far away, Bruno. I have to move closer or I won't have a shot."

"Stay put. You're my ace in the hole, remember? They see you, it'll ruin everything. Now, shh."

The Lexus rolled up slow. Gravel popped and snapped under the tires. Ruby Two was driving. The car stopped ten feet away. Her window whirred down. "You're a lot dumber than I gave you credit for," Ruby said. "Comin' ta the back of dis place, the middle of the night like dis. Heh heh." She brought a gun up and rested it on the windowsill pointed right at me, not ten feet away.

"Hold your fire," I said for the benefit of the phone in my pocket.

One other male occupied the front passenger seat. Big. He got out on the far side and swung his arm across the roof of the Lexus; his hand held a gun. Police Killa Bitch—Calvin Ivory. I wanted a piece of him.

"Real easy," Ruby Two said. "Take yo gun out and let it drop."

CHAPTER FORTY-TWO

WITH TWO FINGERS, I pulled the .357 from under the shirt in my front waistband and set it on the ground.

"We ain't fools, we know you got yourself another one. Go on, take it out, put it with the other one."

I pulled my second .357 and set it down with the other, the stock set in a favorable position. They had me. Now it was up to my ace.

Ruby said, "Calvin, go on then. He's all yours. Now we're even. Just make it fast, hon, and don't make a lot of noise like you did wit dat guy on Peach last month. Ya dang near brought the whole world down on our heads wit all dat screamin'."

Helen's tinny voice came through. "I'm moving closer."

"What was that?" Ruby said, still sitting behind the wheel of the Lexus, holding the gun pointed at my belly.

I held up my finger. "Don't move." Meaning for Helen to hold her position. We still had a few precious seconds before it lit off. I could still get some information from Calvin Ivory while he thought he had the upper hand.

He *did* have more than the upper hand. He had me cold until Helen could intervene. I needed to get him talking, and fast.

Had Robby Wicks, my old boss, been there, he would've been calling me all kinds of a fool. And he'd have been right.

"Don't move?" Ruby said. "What's the matter wit ya? The damn fool's a nutcase."

My guns were still at my feet. If it came down to it, if Helen caused a big enough distraction, I could still dive for them. I'd have better than a fifty-fifty chance. In the old days, I lived for those low percentages, the thrill of it. But now I had a child on the way. *A little girl, silly boy.*

"Not yet. Hold. Hold," I said.

"What are you talking about?" Ruby Two said. She was catching on. Her head moved quickly, checking her mirrors. The lizard part of her brain was sensing a trap. She was ready to hit the gas at the first sign of trouble.

Calvin came around the car; his body shadowed the headlights. He wore a dark blue tank top to show off heavily muscled shoulders that gleamed from being freshly oiled. They bulged from recently working the weight pile. He had a gold ring in his nose and a tattoo that peeked out the top of his tank top depicting a gang member who wore a mask and pointed a gun with a Cadillac Escalade in the background. On his thick right forearm was the tattoo "Police Killa Bitch." He liked to kill cops, or so he wanted people to believe. "You lookin' for me?" he said. "Well, I'm right here, nigga. Now what's ya gonna do?"

"That's right, I am looking for you," I said. "You're under arrest for murder. Turn around and put your hands behind your back."

Ruby Two let out a cackle and slapped her steering wheel. "Dis is great. I can't wait ta get back ta the Palace, tell the homies all about dis fool. The balls on this guy."

"Hey."

Helen's voice.

For real this time, not over the phone in my pocket. She came close and stopped on the other side of the Lexus just in the glow of the headlights, her hands held open at waist level. Another gang member in shadow behind her pointed a chrome handgun at her back; his teeth gleamed in his smile. He'd gotten the jump on her and walked her in.

"Hey, Ace," I said.

"This isn't funny, Bruno," Helen said through gritted teeth.

I turned to Police Killa Bitch. "Just tell me what they did with Emily Mosely and I won't have to hurt you."

He'd been coming for me around the Lexus, his hands down low, fingers splayed. He wanted to go hand-to-hand, squeeze or beat the life out of me. I wouldn't stand a chance, not with all that muscle, not with his thirst for mayhem and dismemberment.

He hesitated. "What are you talkin' about? I don't mess with no little girls. Ruby, what's he talkin' about?"

Calvin Ivory didn't know all of it. "Who hired you to drop Eldridge off the tier? Tell me that much and I might let you walk away."

"Shut him up fast, Calvin," Ruby said. "We gotta get the hell outta here. No time for jaw jackin'. Get it done."

Calvin Ivory looked back at me and took another step my way. His hand shot out and grabbed a handful of my shirt as his other big fist pulled back to knock my block off.

My hand snaked behind my back for the 415 Gonzales sap. I wasn't fast enough. I'd have to weather some broken or lost teeth and split lips and hope he wasn't good enough to ring my bell.

Before I could yank the sap, and before he let go with his teeth-shattering fist, headlights splashed into the parking lot.

Ruby Two said, "Hold it." She let her gun slip down below the edge of the sill and out of view. The gangster holding his gun on Helen did the same, putting the gun down behind his leg.

The headlights stopped and sat still at the driveway opening to the street, the motor on idle. Adrenaline heightened everyone's senses, and at least for me, it made the quiet hum loud enough to wake the dead. All of us watched and waited for an eternity, maybe ten or fifteen seconds. The car suddenly moved, doing a little arc turning around to head back the way it had come. The profile gave away the model, an older Caddy, candy-apple red. Everyone watched.

The Caddy stopped. White condensation puffed out the tailpipe. An old seventies song, muffled by the closed windows, came from the inside, something about love on a bright summer day. The souped-up engine gave off a low rumble like the purr of a large cat.

The backup lights flashed on.

Ruby had time to utter, "What the—"

The right rear tire spun, throwing out burning white smoke and kicking up bits of gravel and grit. The Caddy jetted toward us, trunk first. Everyone scattered. I leaned down, scooped up one .357, and shoulder-rolled out of the way. In my peripheral vision, I caught a snapshot of Helen making her move. She pulled her dirk and spun, slashing her distracted captor. His hands went to his face as he screamed. Blood oozed through his fingers. She kicked him in the knee. And kept kicking. He dropped his gun. She scooped it up and fired at the Lexus.

The trunk of the Caddy slammed into the front of the Lexus with a rending of steel and shattered glass. The force shot it backward.

The slashed gang member crumpled to the ground and howled in pain. Police Killa, at a full run, disappeared into the shadows of the building. Ruby Two's head reappeared behind the wheel of the Lexus as she sat up. She backed up, doing a screeching Y-turn, and left the parking lot at high speed. Helen banged away at the fleeing shadow of Police Killa until her gun clicked empty. She went after him on foot.

I didn't have a shot and stood up on shaky legs.

The window whirred down on the Caddy. Whitey's face came out; his dentures in the ambient light glowed in the dark. His large Adam's apple bobbed when he spoke. "You lookin' for a ride, cowboy?"

I ran around and jumped in the Caddy.

CHAPTER FORTY-THREE

"YEE HA," WHITEY yelled. The Caddy bounced onto Long Beach Boulevard and threw me back and forth in the seat. He turned south, the same direction as Helen, slewing the rear end. Calvin Ivory was nowhere to be seen on the street or sidewalk. Helen stopped running and shrugged as we drove past.

"Pull over, pick her up."

"Naw. She needs the exercise to burn off all that man-hating spunk. She's a real man-eater, you know what I mean?" He continued south to Mulford and turned left, then made another quick left on California.

"Where are you going? You don't know which way he went. He probably kept going south on Long Beach."

"This is the way I'd be going." He turned off the headlights and slowed to a crawl, looking right and left, his eyes those of a predator. Whitey was pure crook from the top of his head right down to the bottom of his dirty little toes.

"How did you find us?"

"I wasn't looking for you, pally. I was following the money. I sat out front of that cheesy barbecue joint for hours waiting for that sleazy broad Ruby to leave. I knew she'd take me to Ivory and she did. I figured since you wanted to talk to him so bad, he'd be the one to take me to the money. Didn't know she was comin' to meet you. I want that ten percent reward. That's two hundred grand. You'd have to rob fifteen banks to get that kind of dough. The great thing about this money, no one's going to call the cops about it and it's tax-free. The same as if I dug it up. It's all about finders keepers, right?"

"Like you're worried about taxes."

"I could be worried about taxes."

Up ahead brake lights blared red as a car pulled to the curb. A shadow came out of the dark and got in.

"Go. Go," I said. "Get up there to that car."

Whitey gunned the Caddy. The acceleration shoved us back in the seats. "This car's got some real balls," he said.

I put my hand up on the dash. "Yeah, and the owner's not going to appreciate the way you're treating it."

"Quit your whinin'. Two hundred grand, baby. I get my money, first thing I'm gonna do is buy me a real clean 1973 Fleetwood Eldorado convertible, white with red leather interior."

The car of movie legend every sneak thief, burglar, and armed robber talked about.

We came up fast to the back of the car. The Lexus. With Ruby driving. Whitey didn't let off the pedal and rammed them at speed. The collision jarred my teeth. The Lexus' trunk lid flew open as the car slewed out of control. It caromed off a parked car, over the curb, and slammed into a large elm tree in the front yard of a house with a spectacular crunch of metal, glass, and steam.

The occupants didn't wait even one second. Ruby and Ivory bailed out and ran.

The Caddy's engine rattled and banged when Whitey put his foot on the accelerator to give chase. The front grille must've shoved back into the fan. The engine seized. I bailed out and ran after Calvin Ivory. I yelled at Whitey, "Go after Ruby." I couldn't take the time

to look and see if he did what I'd asked. I had a limited supply of
energy and wind and if I didn't overtake Ivory in the first minute or
two, the odds were I'd never see him again.

He was young and bold and highly motivated. He pulled away,
leaving me far behind, the both of us running in the street. He was
getting away. I stopped and leveled my .357 at him. But a pistol shot
at that range, in low light with a moving target, would do nothing
but make him run faster. And in the residential area, the miss would
jeopardize the safety of unsuspecting citizens.

Headlights came up behind me. I spun. Out of instinct I pointed
the gun at the windshield. The car skidded to a stop. Bent over,
taking in huge gasps of air, I yelled, "FBI, I need your car."

A heavyset African American woman, about twenty-five, looked
scared until I said FBI.

"FBI? Hell no, you're not taking my car. I paid—"

I pointed at Police Killa, getting farther away by the second.
"That man is wanted for murder and he's getting away."

"Why didn't you say so? Get in."

"I need to dri—"

"Get your ass in the car."

I ran around and squeezed into the older Toyota Tercel. She
gunned the car. The four-cylinder engine didn't have the horse-
power to get out of the way of itself, but it did have enough to gain
on Calvin Ivory. That was all that mattered. He'd started to slow.
He cut the corner southwest at Imperial Highway across the parking
lot of Bobo's Burgers and running west.

"What's your name? Mine's Bruno."

"I'm Sheila. What do I do when I catch up to him?" Her knuckles
blanched white on the steering wheel.

"Hit him."

Her head whipped around.

I put my hand on the wheel, still trying to catch my breath. "Watch what you're doing."

She did. "I don't know if I can hit—"

I pulled on the wheel and turned us into the parking lot of Bobo's. We entered the steep driveway hard and bounced. My head banged on the roof. A man and woman carrying a bag of burgers with a cup carrier containing chocolate malts abandoned their meal, tossing it in the air, and dove out of the way. We ran over their late-night snack. Mashed it into the asphalt.

Up ahead Calvin ran onto Imperial Highway, cutting across. Cars stopped for him.

We bounced out of the parking lot onto Imperial and had to wait for the stopped cars to move out of the way. Calvin ran west, widening the gap. "Go. Go."

Sheila's Tercel jumped out in front of oncoming eastbound cars that skidded to a stop to avoid broadsiding us. "Sweet baby Jesus." She eased into westbound traffic that also stopped. Imperial was an alternate tributary to LAX and always had cars.

Calvin Ivory gained a full block on us, but he was out of breath and slowing. We were almost back to where we'd started, Long Beach Boulevard. He cut into the Yum Yum Donuts. Sheila slowed, hesitating, not knowing what to do, not wanting to think I'd been serious about running him down.

He made it to the sidewalk and into the parking lot of Yum Yum. I again took hold of the wheel and pressed my foot down over hers on the accelerator. Police Killa heard the engine pitch shift and looked back over his shoulder, fear plain in his expression a second before the Toyota slammed into him.

He flew up, crashing on the hood and denting it, and then smashed into the windshield, which instantly spread into a milky spider web. He rolled off and thumped hard on the asphalt.

I jumped out and slapped the roof. "Thanks for the ride. Your federal government owes you a huge debt."

Calvin Ivory struggled to his feet and staggered off in a drunken sailor's gait.

"What about my car?" Sheila said. "Look at my windshield—it's all caved in."

I pulled out the last envelope with money, took out ten hundreds, reached in, and handed them to her. Her face lit up. The entire car wasn't worth five hundred.

I took off after Calvin.

CHAPTER FORTY-FOUR

CALVIN STUMBLE-RAN ACROSS the back parking lot to a two-foot picket fence that bordered the first house north. He tried to go over, lost his footing, and crashed through it, leaving a smear of blood on a white slat. I stepped over the debris. He held his ribs with his right arm and crawl-hopped on the left using his knees. He moved right into the arc of an oscillating sprinkler, a last instinct to put distance between him and the threat. Me.

The water had been on too long in the same place and puddled the lush green grass.

I circled him, afraid to get too close, the sprinkler wetting my clothes on each go-round. Animals were most dangerous when wounded and cornered. I pulled a Spyco knife from my pocket, flicked it open, leaned down, and cut the hose. I wrapped the loose end around my hand and swung the sprinkler head on a two-foot length of hose. "Calvin, my man, save yourself a lot of pain and further injury. Tell me what I want to know."

"Go fuck yourself." He turned and sat on his butt in a puddle of water cradling his ribs, his eyes emitting a hateful vehemence I have rarely encountered. If I got too close and he got a hand on me, it would be all over. He'd tear me apart. I had no sympathy for him. He was a killer.

I swung the sprinkler. It whistled through the air and struck him on the side of the head. He flopped on his side with a groan.

"Where's Emily Mosley?"

"I don't know who you're talking about. I told ya, I don't mess with no little girls."

I swung and hit him again. This time he just lay there and grunted. Either he'd been hurt worse than I thought by the Tercel or he was trying to lull me in closer.

Back in the day, while chasing the most violent men Los Angeles produced, I gave back everything they gave and more, but I never gave them any extra. When they were down, I backed off, game over. Now I found it difficult to continue with this line of questioning even though Emily was still out there waiting to be found and put to rest.

The lights in the house went on. The front door opened. A disembodied voice drifted out. An elderly African American woman said, "I called the police."

"We'll be gone in a minute, ma'am. Sorry for all the noise."

I said to Calvin, "Tell me who paid you to toss Eldridge off the tier."

"Go fu—"

I thumped him hard again with the sprinkler.

The woman in the house muttered, "Oh, dear me" as she closed the door.

He leaned over and swung a feeble arm. "Damn you."

"Tell me."

He quit holding his head up and eased down into a puddle, his mouth half in the water, blowing bubbles with each breath. He *had* been hurt by the Tercel and wasn't faking. "You already know," he said.

"Tell me. Say the name."

The next thing he said bubbled in the water, but I understood. "Ruubieee."

Distant sirens came from the west. I tossed the sprinkler down and walked away. I pulled my cell and dialed 911. When the call-taker answered, I told her there was a man wanted for murder and where to find him. I told her he was armed and dangerous and to approach with extreme caution. I hung up and crossed Imperial Highway, the way we'd come minutes earlier. I watched and waited until the first Los Angeles County Sheriff's unit pulled up with its rotating overhead red lights reflecting off the front of the businesses and houses. The deputy put the unit spotlight on Police Killa still down in the front yard, a soaking pile of garbage. The deputy pulled his shotgun, racked it, pointed it at Calvin, and waited for his backup to arrive. Protocol. Good solid tactics. I walked down California Avenue headed back to the Sears parking lot, my clothes wet, uncomfortable.

Ten minutes later, I stopped at the corner of Sears on Long Beach Boulevard and peeked around the corner of the building. A throng of cop cars, a fire truck, and an ambulance encircled the downed thug, the one Helen had slashed and kicked. They were getting ready to put him on a gurney. Helen was going to take it on the chin for using an unauthorized weapon on a gangster with a gun. Although justified, she'd take some days on the bricks. I didn't know how she was going to explain what she was doing there in the first place. I'd left her in a real jam. I dialed her number. She answered, "Yeah."

"You okay? Can you talk?"

She looked around for me and couldn't pick me out of the shadows. "Yes and no, I can't. Did you get him?"

"Yes, one of your patrol guys has him up on Imperial."

"Excellent. He give you anything?"

"Nothing we already didn't know. Ruby hired the Eldridge murder done. She's in it up to her nose."

"Yeah, figured as much."

"You going to be okay? You going to be able to talk your way out of it?"

"Don't worry about me. If you want to help, you can take care of that little favor you promised."

"You never let up, do you?"

"I thought you already knew that about me." I could hear the smile in her voice.

"You did a good job tonight. I'll catch up to you later, Ace. Call me."

"Keep your head down, Bruno."

"Yeah, see ya, kid."

I rung off and dialed Dan Chulack as I continued down Long Beach on foot getting as far away as possible. That time of night a large male black soaked to the skin looked suspicious.

"Yeah, Bruno, what do you have?"

"LA County just took Calvin Ivory into custody on Imperial. Get some of your people over there to debrief him."

"Did he tell you anything?"

"He did. And I'll take care of it."

"Tell me."

"I said, I'll take care of it. I think we're only one step away from finding out what happened. I'll let you know. Listen, I need another favor."

"Go."

"When we took down Ivory, I was with an LA County detective. You remember Helen Hellinger? She went above and beyond doing her job. She's in the grease and—"

"I understand. I'll take care of it. I'm en route there now. You call me when you get something else and I mean the minute that you know."

"Thanks, Dan. This will all be over soon. Tomorrow at the latest. I'm going to end it tomorrow, I promise."

He didn't say goodbye and clicked off.

I dialed an Uber and waited five minutes. A clean, older model Ford Explorer pulled to the curb with a cute little Hispanic gal driving. I got in the back. She headed out watching me in the rearview more than she normally would.

My phone rang. I checked it this time before answering.

"Yeah, Dad, what's going on?" He must've been excited about re-connecting with his ex-wife and wanted to talk about it.

CHAPTER FORTY-FIVE

"Son," Dad said, "I have to ask you something and it's something I don't feel I have the right to ask. I tried to sleep and couldn't. I know I won't sleep until I talk to you about this."

The Hispanic gal driving the Ford Explorer, my Uber ride back to Glendale, continued to watch me in the rearview.

"Sure, Dad, go ahead. It's not about one of the kids, is it?" My mind wouldn't leave the trouble I'd heaped upon Helen to deal with on her own. Not enough to focus on what he was trying to say. I was a real heel to leave her alone like that to face the music.

"I . . . I . . ."

"Dad, what is it?"

"I'm just going to say it. Don't think ill of me, Son. I'm not long for this world. Even if I do beat this cancer. I've had a lot of time recently to think things over. Think about . . . regrets and . . . missed opportunities."

I knew he felt I'd wasted the last two months when I should've been home with the children during the most formative time in their lives.

"Dad, it's okay. Just tell me. I'll do anything you want. Anything."

He paused. Too long. Oh, dear God, this was going to be bad.

He said, "I wouldn't ask you if . . ."

"Dad."

"It would be a wonderful gift to me if you'd bring Bea here with you when you come. There, I said it. She's definitely interested in coming—we've already talked about it. She said she wouldn't come unless she has your blessing."

I sucked in a deep breath and held it. I could only hope he hadn't heard the embarrassing reaction.

How could he ask something like that? Bea had been immersed in a criminal world for decades. How could we expose our children to that kind of influence? That kind of menace?

"Son?"

"Yeah, Dad. Just a minute. Just give me a minute to process this. It's a lot to take in all at once."

There wasn't any better influence on the children than my father. He knew best and would never jeopardize the children. He was wise and had more common sense than anyone I knew. He would not ask such a question without thinking it through.

Was I prejudging Bea? Had my aversion to all things criminal automatically influenced my decision? Did I really believe the common dogma that no one could change? That once a criminal always a criminal?

"Dad, I'm not saying no, but let's talk about this for a minute."

"All right, I'm listening. But first, do you remember what I told you all those years ago?"

"Sure, Dad, but remind me anyway." He'd told me a lot of things that I cherished, advice and moral rules that had molded my life.

"A judging brain requires a listening ear."

He'd somehow read my mind. I had to step gingerly here. "You don't know her, what's she like and—"

"You're absolutely right." His tone shifted, sharper with an edge.

"Wait, just hear me out. Of course, I will do whatever you think best. Whatever you want. I just want to be sure this is what you really want . . . that you . . . you understand all the ramifications."

He paused again. "Bruno, I didn't think you'd ever find love. Not with the kind of life you lived."

I closed my eyes tight. He was going for the emotional throat of this thing, not at all trying to work up to it.

"Until, that is, you found Marie. Then I knew. Just by the way you look at her, the way you two act toward each other. So maybe you can understand just a little bit of what I'm feeling here. How I'm thinking."

"I do, Dad, I really do." Marie was my entire life and most recently a flickering candle flame in a night dark as pitch.

The Hispanic gal driving the Explorer went back to watching the road; my conversation with Dad must've put her at ease. She took the on-ramp to the freeway. We still had a twenty-minute drive.

"Let me think about it a little more," he said. "I'm just glad your agreeable and wouldn't mind if she came. You're right though. I'll give it some more thought. It's a big decision."

I had not said I was amenable, nothing even close, but wasn't going to correct him. I'd meant it: if he wanted her to come to Costa Rica, he'd earned that right, ten times over. A hundred times over. He was also right about love. I knew firsthand how it could cloud one's perspective. Millions of people had died from that over-the-moon emotion; wars had been started over it. Dad still remembered those bygone days before Bea took the wrong path. He wanted that feeling back. I couldn't blame him. If something happened to Marie, it would be no different than if someone cut off my right leg. Both legs.

"Okay, then," I said. "You call me and let me know. I'm almost done here. I'm going to end this thing tomorrow one way or another, so you have a couple of days to decide. We'll be coming home day after tomorrow."

"Thank you, Son. This is a big load off just knowing you'll go along with it . . . I mean if I decide to go that way. I think I'll be able to sleep now."

"All right, Dad, call me as soon as you decide. I'll have to arrange for her passport, plane ticket, and all of that."

"I'll talk to you tomorrow then, good night. Love you, Son."

"Love you, Dad."

I rang off, put my head back, and tried to envision how Bea, in her wheelchair and with her gruff exterior, would interact with the children. How she would integrate into our household.

My eyes shot open.

I'd forgotten all about Marie. What was she going to say? I already knew. I could already hear her words, see the flames coming from her eyes as she burned me to the ground like a dragon with fire-breathing breath.

I needed to rest, close my eyes, and grab a catnap, but couldn't. Too much conflict swam round and round in my head. I eased back in the seat and caught the driver's eyes in the rearview.

She said, "I didn't mean to eavesdrop, but it sounds like you have a pretty nice relationship with your father."

"Yes, I do."

The yellow sodium vapor lights on the sides of the freeway flashed by. I said, "You really shouldn't be doing this kind of job at night, especially in the neighborhood where you picked me up."

"I'm real careful. Besides, I grew up here and I know what to look for."

"Oh yeah, what streets?"

"Platt and Birch. On Birch, just down from Platt."

"By the park, south of St. Francis hospital."

"That's right." She said it with a smile in her tone.

"I used to work at Bullis and Century."

Her eyes went to the rearview mirror when she spoke. "The Sheriff's station?"

"Yes. It's closed down now. They moved it over off Alameda. I grew up in the Corner Pocket with my brother, Noble Johnson."

"I thought you looked familiar. I must've seen you around."

"My father was a postman for forty years and—"

"Oh my God, Xander Johnson?"

"That's right."

"My mom loved your father, waited at the mailbox every day to talk to him. Made him chocolate chip cookies and lemonade on summer days, and in the winter, hot cocoa and oatmeal and raisin cookies. Mom said he is the nicest man she has ever met. She was heartbroken when he retired."

"I don't disagree with her."

"I can't wait to tell her that I gave you a ride."

"What's her name? My dad still has a razor-sharp memory."

"Martha Sanchez."

"I'll tell him." I hoped she hadn't heard about Xander's fugitive son, Bruno.

She smiled big in the mirror.

Twenty miles rolled under the tires on the uneven concrete freeway. She got off, drove the surface streets to the Americana, and stopped out front. I gave her a big tip on my phone. I got out and hesitated at her open window. I offered her my hand. "I don't know your name."

She smiled hugely and took my hand. "Alisha."

"Bruno."

I took the envelope from my back pocket that still had three thousand dollars in hundreds. "Here, you're a nice girl and shouldn't be driving at night. Maybe this will keep you on day shift for a while."

"What? No." She tried to push it back to me. I walked away with a hand waving over my head.

CHAPTER FORTY-SIX

I ENTERED THE Americana through the parking garage to the side rather than the front door and came into the lobby from the garage entrance. I pushed the button for the elevator with my back to the wall, watching the front desk area, automatically on high alert for interlopers. The elevator door opened.

Over in the lobby, a man stood. "Bruno?"

He knew my name. *He called out my name.* My hand, all on its own, went under my shirt to the stock of the .357.

He came around the couch where he'd been sitting and headed my way with a huge smile. A flicker far back in the memory banks identified him as a friend, not a foe, but I still couldn't place his name.

He noticed my hand under my shirt and my expression. He continued coming closer, his head whipping quick from side to side checking to see if anyone was watching, and kept his hands away from his body. "Hey, take it easy, it's me, Kato."

"Kato, geez, you scared the water out of me."

He'd cleaned up, had to in order to sit surveillance in the Americana. He was Drago's friend, who wasn't afraid to pull the trigger. There were many people who carried guns and thought themselves ghetto gunfighters, but when it finally came down to blood and bone, they dropped their guns, turned and fled. Kato wasn't like that and had proved his worth on more than one occasion. He normally dressed like a sixities hippie, a perfect cover for his junkyard-dog mentality. He was medium height, thin with his brown wavy hair pulled back into a severe ponytail. He wore blue denim pants and a gray blazer. No wonder I hadn't recognized him.

The elevator door started to close. I stuck my hand in, stopped it. "Come on."

Kato got in; the doors closed.

"You shouldn't have called me by name."

"Oh, yeah, sorry. My bad, it won't happen again."

"Drago's got you staked out here?"

"Yeah, all's quiet, nothin' movin' at all."

"Where did Drago go?"

Kato broke eye contact, no longer looking comfortable in his blazer.

"What?" I said.

"Don't be mad. Drago said you'd throw a mega conniption."

"What?" I fought the urge to grab him by the throat. "Did something happen to Marie?"

"No. No, nothing like that. She's fine. No problem there."

I let out a long breath. "Okay, what is it, then?"

"The old broad in the wheelchair apparently took a flyer."

"She's gone?"

"Yeah, that's why Drago thought you'd be mad. He said he was supposed to watch out for her. Don't know why. She sounds harmless enough. He put me down here to keep an eye on things while he went to look for her."

"Drago didn't say I'd have a *conniption*, did he?"

Kato smiled. "No, he said you were going to squeeze out a litter of kittens."

"*Squeeze?*"

"Okay, shit a litter of kittens."

The doors opened on the third floor. He put out his hand to hold the doors open. "I'll go back to the lobby and do what the big man asked me to do."

Something flitted across the back of his eyes.

I stepped out of the car. "What? You're not telling me something?"

He stuck his head out and checked both ways to make sure no one else heard. He whispered, "I'd be real careful when you open your door."

"Why? Is Marie that angry?"

He shook his head.

"Good," I said. "For a second there I thought I was in trouble."

"No, Drago doesn't like to screw up. You know all about that. So, he hedged his bet. He left Waldo in the hotel room to protect Marie. I don't know about you, but that dog gives me the damn willies. Those eyes, the way he looks at me like I'm some kinda White Castle cheeseburger." An involuntary shudder shook his whole body. That shiver somehow transferred to me in an electric chill that sizzled up my spine. Ridiculous. I'd been around him before and he wasn't like—

Just before the doors closed all the way, Kato leaned forward and said through the crack, "Good luck with that devil dog."

I moved down the hall, smirking at his last comment. "Devil dog. Waldo's nothing but a big cream puff. What's the matter with everyone? I get along just fine with that dog." Before I made it to the door, the one across the hall from our old suite, sweat broke out on my forehead. I had nothing to be afraid of, right?

Who was I kidding? I let go of the doorknob, took out my cell, and dialed Marie.

"Hey, you. Are you on your way back?" she asked.

"I'm outside the suite door. Is it safe to come in?"

"Oh, you big baby. Waldo's just a big overgrown puppy. Get in here."

"Could you take hold of his collar until he can get a sniff of me. I wouldn't want his jaws to, you know, go off accidentally. He's got a hair-trigger."

She giggled. "Get in here."

I opened the door. She stood across the room in the living area. Waldo, a hundred and thirty pounds of muscle, fur, and teeth, sat on the floor next to her, his eyes on me. I'd never experienced it before, but now I did: *The White Castle cheeseburger effect*. The door closed behind me with loud finality.

Marie said, "Waldo, alert."

Waldo let out a bellow of a bark that was more of a roar and leaped forward. I turned and tried to get the door open but my hands fumbled on the latch. Any second the jaws of death would clamp down on my ass, tear a hunk off for a rump roast. Marie said, "Waldo, out." Three feet away, Waldo stopped and sat. Marie bent over laughing, her hand to her mouth.

I slowly turned back around. "That wasn't funny. I almost wet my pants."

CHAPTER FORTY-SEVEN

MARIE ASKED, "HAVE you eaten anything? It's important you keep up your strength for your continued recovery." Her medical world peeking out. I loved it that she cared so much.

"No, but I'm okay."

Her question was also in code. What she really wanted to know was whether I'd finished the job and had I found Emily Mosley. Whether we were finally going home. She wanted to know, yet she didn't. The sadness in that final outcome would be a horrible end to an already horrible trip to the States. The same emotions had darkened my every waking moment since Dan Chulack walked through our door. I was helpless to change that outcome and needed to do something, anything to moderate that feeling of helplessness. I could no longer help Emily Mosley, but I could help someone else in dire need. All of a sudden that thought shadowed everything else.

"I'll fix you an omelet with ham and cheese and a couple of crepes."

I knew better than to argue with her about eating. I sat on the stool at the kitchen bar and watched her work her magic. She made the best omelets, fluffy and light as air, and crepes that would make the top chef in France bow in homage.

Waldo came over and sat next to my stool, looking up at me with those big brown eyes. I reached down to pat him on the head. The way his eyes followed my hand, I stopped midway and retracted my fingers before they disappeared down his gullet.

I looked back at Marie. "So, my mom took off?"

"Hmm. Drago's out looking for her."

I tried to ignore Waldo but could hear him breathing and slurp every now and again from too much slobber. I'd never had a problem with him before. It was that damn Kato talking smack . . . and Whitey had done the same thing. Transferred hysteria, that's what it was, pure and simple.

I waited for Marie to say something else, to be angry that Mom had been disrespectful, leaving without a word, leaving after we'd opened our home to her. She'd taken up Helen's "Hmm" response, one Marie copied from me, a dialogue tic passed around like a flu virus.

Marie started humming "Greensleeves" as she clanged the pans, clinked the bowls, and whisked the eggs. She paused her musical interlude. "You going to tell me what you've been doing while I do this?"

"We caught up to the guy we were looking for."

"Did he tell you what you wanted to know?"

"Yes. We'll be done tomorrow for sure, and on a plane for home the day after. So, you can start packing."

She looked up. "That's good."

She didn't say "that's great," or seem the least bit elated. She didn't ask if I thought there was any chance at all for Emily. She already knew that answer. It'd been too long since the failed money exchange. There was no other possible reason why Emily had not already been returned.

But there was. Just the one.

And nobody wanted to say those words out loud.

I had to tell Marie about Dad's request to bring Bea along to Costa Rica. The stink of it hung over the kitchen, a black cloud threatening at any moment to turn into a category-five hurricane. I couldn't keep it from her. I watched her work, the way she moved, the way she kept her hair. She looked up and caught me. "What?"

"I love just looking at you, that's all. I love your delicate hands, your cute little button nose, the color of your hair, your eyes. I love everything about you."

She shot me her famous coy smile. "Oh, stop it." She went back to cooking.

"Babe?"

She stopped fussing with the egg concoction in the saucepan and looked up at me.

"Dad called."

She waited, neglecting the omelet.

I took a breath and let it out. "He wants us to bring Mom home to San Jose."

"Hmm." She went back to tending my breakfast.

"That's it?"

"What do you mean, *that's it*?"

"You're not going to . . . you know, bite my head off?"

She smiled. "What? Now you think I'm a praying mantis or something?" She thought about it for a second. "The female only eats the male during mating. You want me to put this aside for now and we can go into the bedroom?" She couldn't hold her solemn expression. The corner of her mouth let a smile peek out.

"No. No. I just thought that you wouldn't think it was such a good idea, that's all."

"*I don't* think it's a good idea. But if that's what your father wants, I think we should honor his wishes."

She'd come to the same conclusion I had but had done it in an instant. Another reason why I loved her.

"I love you, babe."

She deftly flipped the omelet in half. "Ditto."

I was destined for "Dittos" until we stepped off the plane back in Costa Rica, where I would officially be forgiven for extending our stay in the States.

Waldo jumped up and ran to the hotel suite door. Seconds later it opened and in walked Drago. I did feel better having Waldo around to protect Marie; he might even be better than Kato.

Drago wrestled with Waldo. Waldo growled and played rough. They rolled around on the floor until they both tired of the game. Drago took the stool next to me just as Marie finished putting two crepes on a plate with the omelet. My mouth watered. She set it in front of Drago. "Thanks, Mrs. J." He took a fork and dug in.

"Hey," I said. "What am I, chopped liver? I thought I needed my strength for recuperation."

"Lately, Karl's been here more than you have. To the victor go the spoils."

Drago smiled while he chewed. Marie leaned as far as she could and patted Drago's hand. Did it on purpose to get my goat. Then she started making more food for me.

Drago paused. "Sorry, bro, about losing your moms."

"Wasn't your fault."

In between chews Drago said, "I went looking. Couldn't find her. Looked all over. Checked with some friends, put it out on my network. They'll be watching out for her. I'll get a call soon, you wait and see if I don't."

"It's not your fault. Who would've thought she'd take off like that? She was safe here and she knew it."

He dropped one of the crepes. Waldo caught it in midair and gulped it down. "Thanks for being understanding, bro, but I screwed up, I know I did. I'll fix it, count on it."

"Come on," I said. "Let's take a ride."

He crammed the remaining half of the omelet in his mouth as he nodded and stood.

Marie pointed a loaded spatula. "You should get some sleep, Bruno, you need your rest. You overdo it, you'll find yourself back in the hospital."

I held up my hand. "Take it easy, Kemosabe. I'm just going to ride around with Drago, looking for an old woman in a wheelchair. No big deal. We'll be back in a jiff." I used Drago's word on purpose, the one he'd used earlier.

Drago slid off the stool but hesitated, looking at Marie for permission to go outside and play.

She nodded.

Drago said, "I'll leave my partner here to take care of you. We won't be long." He said something to Waldo in German. Waldo watched Drago carefully until Drago finished talking, then went over by the door to the suite and lay down. Drago had just activated a muscle-covered fur and fang land mine. Enter at your own peril.

CHAPTER FORTY-EIGHT

OUT IN THE hall, walking to the elevator, Drago said, "I guess we can just drive around some more, hit a few places I already checked. But like I said, I got the word out on the street. I should get a call soon as someone spots your moms."

He wore heavy brown Wolverine boots, denim pants, and a black and white Raiders football jersey. The jersey, two sizes too big, could conceal every sort of weapon short of a bazooka.

The word "mom," coming from his mouth, sounded alien. I had for the larger part of my life wanted to say it. Wanted to with all my heart. Now that I could, well . . . not so much. That fact made the world a shade darker, additional coloring I didn't need, not with all that had recently happened.

I pushed the button for the elevator just as a wave of fatigue washed over my entire body. My knees went weak. Along with the fatigue came a serious urge to lie down right there on the floor in front of the elevator and sleep for ten years. Marie had been right: I was pushing the edge. Maybe I'd already gone past it. Was in a free fall, and didn't know it.

In the elevator car, I stared at the floor numbers overhead. "We're not going to look for Bea, not right now, anyway."

"What are we doing, then?"

"A favor for a friend." I gave him the address on Cogswell and nothing else. Not out of spite. My mind had automatically shifted to the problem of extricating little Stephanie from under the noses of twenty-five or thirty drunken, partying Devil Dogs. Tightrope-walking debilitating fatigue also had a hand in my lack of explanation. I needed to close my eyes even if it was only for a few minutes.

In the parking structure, he guided us over to a tricked-out Dodge truck, an old one. This was his personal vehicle, teal green with a diamond plate aluminum toolbox in the back bolted down next to the cab. The box didn't contain any *working* tools, per se. It did contain tools of *his* trade, though, the kind used in the unholy issuance of blood and bone to those who deserved it.

I eased down in the seat to close my eyes for a bit. "Wake me when we get close and I'll fill you in." All energy left my body as I slipped into the inky black, slipped into the warm waters of night terrors. I wouldn't have gone so easily had I not been so dog-dick tired.

I landed flat-footed on the side of that freeway with the bikers and my son, Bosco, as they confronted the female Highway Patrol officer. This only moments before I tossed my son out into traffic.

Damp, cold air woke me with a start. The truck door stood open. Drago had parked down from a streetlight under the cast of a large tree that darkened the night. He leaned in with a cut-down ball bat with duct tape on the handle, nudging me. "Hey, Hoss, it's time to rock and roll."

"What?" I grabbed the bat. The core had been drilled and filled with lead and made the bat a lot heavier than it looked.

"We're here. We need to move before one of those assholes spots us. We're parked about five houses north. They're still movin' around and they have two lookouts who are sober. Come on, let's go."

I rubbed my eyes as I scooted up and looked around. We were parked on Cogswell, but how did he know what we were going to do?

He tossed in some body armor. "Put this on. I want to be able to tell Mrs. J. that I did everything to talk you outta this and protected you the best I could."

I shook off the sleep, unbuttoning my shirt and shrugging out of it. "Drago, you don't know the play. You don't know what we're even here for."

I slipped into the body armor, pulled tight the Velcro straps, and put my shirt back on over it. Body armor doesn't do you much good tactically if the bad guy sees it. He'll only adjust his aim and shoot you in the head. Or in the leg first, then the head.

Drago stuck his big pumpkin head into the cab. "The address you gave me is crawlin' with Devil Dogs. They're thick as maggots on rancid meat. Doesn't matter what we're here for, we have to go through them before we do anything else. Might as well get at it while we still have the element of surprise." He didn't need an excuse to mow through his enemy. He just needed to be directed their way.

He stuck out his black-gloved hand that held a roll of quarters. With his other, he handed me a half-used roll of gray duct tape. I took it and taped the quarters to his palm. This still gave him the use of his fingers for grasping "assholes," or the piece of three-foot galvanized steel pipe he'd wield like a knight's broadsword. And at the same time, as a last resort, have a hand chock for punching.

I tore off a strip of tape and smoothed it down in his palm. "There are too many Devil Dogs for the two of us."

He let out that creepy grin he normally kept under tight wraps. "Too long in the tooth, old man? Too old to run with the big dogs?"

"You know better. But there's a little girl in there, and if we stir up that hornet's nest—"

He stopped and looked down the dark street through the back window, as if he could see the house. "You didn't tell me there was a kid in the mix. How old?"

"Four years, a little girl named Stephanie."

His jaw locked. He punched his gloved fist into his palm, testing the hand chock. "So that's why we're here, to get her?"

"That's right."

"No little kid deserves to live around this kind of vermin. She'll get eaten alive."

"I know."

"What's your plan, then?"

"We need a distraction."

"Like what?"

"You got a couple of real meat-eaters who ride Harleys and who live close by?"

He let out that creepy smile I'd grown to love. He took his cell phone from his pocket and dialed.

CHAPTER FORTY-NINE

I MOVED DOWN the sidewalk in the deep shadows cast by the trees. A mist with a slight chill moved in as nighttime handed off to early morning. Drago was behind me, but I couldn't hear him. I stopped next to a tree with a large trunk, two houses up from the Cogswell address, the last one that afforded enough cover. I couldn't go any farther without risking exposure. Now all we could do was wait.

I wore black gloves, not for fingerprints but to protect my hands. It didn't matter if the police found any evidence. Odds were the police wouldn't be called. I'd put a bandage across the bridge of my nose to break up my features and kept the ball cap down low over my eyes. I didn't need the Devil Dogs identifying me and come looking. Drago didn't care. Preferred it if they did. "It's always better to have your prey come looking for you than to have to go out and find them. Take them out while in the comfort of your own home, that's my motto."

I held the cut-down ball bat in my left hand, leaving my right available to draw the .357.

Music thrummed from the front yard of the Cogswell house, heavy metal. Head-banging noise. The neighbors couldn't be happy.

The front door stood open, emitting a large wedge of yellow light. Denim-clad thugs in black leather jackets came and went, briefly passing through that light and back into the darkness. One of them, out by the sidewalk, unzipped and urinated in the dirt parkway while tilting back a Foster's beer. Cans and bottles and fast-food wrappers littered the dirt front yard. The majority of the bikers stood around the fifty-five-gallon drum with flames leaping and biting at the early morning darkness. The scene resembled one from a million years ago when troglodytes first discovered fire and gnawed on ptero-dactyl bones as they celebrated no longer having to live in caves.

Three of the bikers started yelling and shoving each other. One threw a punch. All three went to the ground writhing, kicking, socking, and biting. The others gathered around and cheered, throwing in a random kick when the throbbing mass of assholes rolled too close.

From behind us the roar of loud motorcycles echoed down the street. Two fellow bikers, friends of Drago's, pulled up in front of the Cogswell house, stopped, and put their feet down to balance their hogs.

The three thugs on the ground in front of the house stopped rolling in the dirt. The dust hung in a cloud above them. The new silence from the onlookers had stifled their gladiatorial event. They struggled to their feet and stood with their cohorts.

The back passenger on one of the bikes, another biker, had long dirty blond hair pulled back and tied with a blue bandana. He wore a black leather jacket with lots of silver-colored zippers and held a tall, square liquor bottle filled with an amber liquid. Gasoline. A long dirty rag hung down the side.

The group in the yard collectively grunted and involuntarily took a half-step back as the lizard part of their brains alerted them to this new threat. At the same time, they tried to justify how this could be happening. Not to them. How could these three punks be doing this to *all* of them? Were they batshit crazy?

The passenger biker with the bottle took out a Zippo lighter and flicked it, the flame inches from the wick. The bikers in the yard scattered, bellowing expletives.

He lit the wick. Blue-yellow flame jumped up along the rag. He threw the Molotov cocktail at the running thugs. The square liquor bottle tumbled end over end in slow motion before crashing to the ground. The glass shattered and spewed burning fuel among the running black boots and legs.

Drago's friends yelled, "Sons of Satan" and roared off.

They weren't Sons of Satan members.

Three of the bikers fell to the ground rolling on the flames, frantically tamping them with their hands. All screamed bloody murder and ugly words not fit for the common man. The rest of them quickly regrouped, ran for their bikes, mounted, started up, and roared after their attackers.

I took a step. Drago's hand, from behind, grabbed my shoulder. "Not yet, Hoss. Give the rest of 'em a minute to play lemming."

The three on the ground got their flaming legs out, then stood and yelled, pounding their chests. They, too, ran for their bikes. Out of anger, one stopped long enough to kick over the fifty-five-gallon drum. Flaming wood and ash and smoke spilled out mixing with the flames from the shattered Molotov, making shadows dance on the front of the house. They got their bikes started and took off.

"Now," Drago said.

We walked in long deliberate strides and sidestepped around the fire, which was already reduced by half from the lack of fuel and containment. The burnt smoke was acrid in my nostrils. Two drunken thugs late to the fleeing war party stepped out of the house side by side.

Drago skip-stepped to gain the right footing, swung the long steel pipe, and struck them both at the same time across the face with a mushy thunk. Both fell straight down. "Go. Go," Drago said. "I'll take care of these two."

We both had zip ties to bind the leftover threats, but Drago didn't believe in them. He went to work, swinging the pipe, striking the prostrate thugs. He thumped and battered and broke bones. I had to jump to the side to keep out of his frenzy.

A breeze came up, blowing smoke into the house as I entered.

Broken-down secondhand furniture sat on crusty, outdated gold shag carpet with large crankcase oil stains from the Harley parked in the center of the small living room.

A biker, the biggest of the lot, stood next to a straggly woman who wore a tank top and had too many ugly tattoos. She was missing a couple of teeth on one side. Both stood over by the entrance to the small kitchen. I recognized the male. Wizard, the guy who lived there. One of the top Devil Dogs. The woman was Helen's sister, the mother of little Stephanie.

"Get out of my house," the woman raged, her fists clenched down at her sides.

I squared off. "Give us the meth and we'll be outta here. No one else has to get hurt." Our ploy, so they wouldn't know our true mission.

Wizard had his head shaved in a short Mohawk with tattoos on both sides of his exposed scalp: knights with swords and valiant steeds, and white supremacist acronyms. "You don't know who you're messing with." He stuck out his bare chest and pulled a long Bowie knife from the sheath at his side, ready to do battle with the black thief who'd just intruded into his secure domain.

"Sure I do. This place belongs to some kind of save-the-dogs group, right? The Hush Puppies, or shit like that? Well, we're here to shut down the kennel. This is your last chance, where's your meth?"

Wizard took a step toward me just as Drago stepped in, the long galvanized steel pipe in his hand smeared with Devil Dog blood.

Wizard stood a little taller and took a half-step back. He blurted a harsh whisper. "Drago? What are you doing here?"

"You heard my partner, the meth. Where is it?"

Wizard took another step back and pulled his woman in front of him as a shield.

Drago twirled the long steel pipe as if it weighed nothing at all and said to me, "You look for the meth. I'll take care of these two."

"You sure?"

Wizard's big Bowie knife blade glinted as he held it out at the ready.

"I got this. Just don't take too long. We don't have much time."

I spun and headed down the hall cluttered with dirty clothes and discarded trash. Someone had punched and kicked holes in the walls, all previous signs of anger that still oozed from the dark indentations.

I checked all the rooms, under all the beds and piles of clothes. I checked the two filthy bathrooms. No Stephanie.

What had happened to her? My mind flitted to an imaginary image, a fresh mound of dirt out in the backyard. I shook it off and headed back to the living room, hoping Drago hadn't put the hurt on them to the point they could no longer talk.

CHAPTER FIFTY

DRAGO HAD WIZARD on the floor, striking him with the pipe using a two-handed overhead swing. The woman crawled into the corner and huddled there, her eyes wide in terror from the knowledge that her turn came next.

"Where's the meth?" I yelled. I didn't want the meth but didn't want to blow our cover either. I didn't know what else to say. The yell stopped Drago mid-swing. Blood ran down the pipe, across his glove, and down his forearm. Wizard groaned, only semiconscious, and didn't move. Drago stepped over to the woman, grabbed her by the hair, and yanked her to her feet.

The woman screamed and clawed at Drago's arm. He shoved her. She bounced off the wall and slid to the floor. I'd have had a twinge of remorse had I not known this woman kept Stephanie in this kind of environment for no other reason than to collect the welfare stipend.

In a lowered, urgent tone, I said to Drago, "She's not here."

"You sure? We can't stay much longer. Those assholes are going to be rollin' back here any minute now. When they get here, it's going to go loud, and I only brought this pipe, not my sword. Check that closet right there."

Sword? Did he really have a sword?

"The closet? What clos—" I spun. Of course. I'd seen it, but at the same time had not. Little girls were never supposed to be kept in closets. I pulled the door open. Out came a barely perceptible whimper. More like a mew from a small kitten. I pulled a small flashlight from my back pocket and lit up the interior.

And wished I hadn't.

One of those images that would forever haunt and reoccur at inopportune moments.

Curled up in her own feces, Stephanie cowered on the floor in the corner among greasy Craftsman wrenches, empty oil cans, and dirty rags. A silent rage rose inside me. I wanted to crush and kill those responsible.

She flinched at the bright light. "Sssh, it's okay, Stephanie. I'm going to take you out of here. I'm going to take you to a nice place with other kids and—"

She tried to pull back even more but couldn't. She wore a soiled dress, worn thin, her skin splotched with dirt, her face streaked with tears. In her golden hair was a blue ribbon, incongruous with the rest of the horrific scene. As if the little blue ribbon made up for all the other ghastly treatment.

I got down on one knee, going slow, not moving toward her, not yet.

From behind me, over by the kitchen, Drago said, "You got her?"

I waved an arm outside the closet at him to be quiet.

"Old Hoss, we got to get on the road, like right now."

"Stephanie, my name's Bruno. Your Auntie Helen sent me to get you. I'm a friend of your Auntie Helen."

"Aunt Helen?" Her blue eyes perked up. A flicker of hope returned. She wasn't too far gone after all. She could still be rescued, brought back from the brink of permanent emotional meltdown.

I moved in slowly. "Come on, give me your hand."

She tentatively reached out.

"That's it. That's a good girl."

Drago's phone rang. He answered it. "That's the rabbit—the dogs are on the way back."

I laid gentle hands on her. Her skin was hot to the touch, probably from an infection. I started to lift her. She cried out as she tugged to a stop. I took out the flashlight and shone it around. I turned angry all over again. The sons of bitches had wrapped wire around her ankle and then bolted that wire to the wall. A wire leash. The wire had cut into her flesh, making it purple and red and swollen. Another few hours and she'd have lost the foot. Still might.

"It's okay, sweetie. You're safe now. I got you. I promise no one is ever going to hurt you again." I took out the Spyco knife and used the serrated edge to cut the wire midway between the wall. There wasn't time to take it off her leg. The wire had cut so deep, surgery might be needed to extricate it. Marie would know what to do.

I picked her up. She glommed onto me, the last life preserver in a sinking ship. I stood, the anger-adrenaline giving me renewed strength. I stepped out of the closet into the light. Drago came toward us until his eyes landed on Steph's poor swollen foot.

His eyes turned large. Drago rarely reacted to anything. "Sweet Jesus—"

He spun, took two large steps over to the woman, picked her up with one meaty hand, and flung her against the wall ten feet away. She collided with a yelp and a thud and slid to the floor. Drago picked up his pipe and headed for her.

"No," I whispered, trying not to spook Stephanie, whom I kept sheltered away from what was happening.

Drago froze, pointed a gloved finger at me. "No, you're not going to stop me. Not this time. This time it's payback."

"Don't." I said it a little harsher. An order. "Tell her. Just tell her."

He looked confused for a second, then realization crossed his eyes. He stepped over to the woman, grabbed a handful of her hair, and yanked her head back as she tried to pull away. "We're taking your daughter. You can have her back when we get the meth. We'll call you with a time and place for the trade."

The ruse, a cover story, so they were less likely to involve the police.

"Now come on," I said, "let's roll."

We made it outside as the roar of twenty-five motorcycles echoed in the neighborhood. We crossed the yard and down the sidewalk into the darker shadows cast by the trees just as the mob of bikers rolled up. I held Stephanie close to my chest, her body hot with infection. We got in the truck. Drago pulled a U-turn and didn't switch on the lights until we took two more turns. We'd made it out alive with the little girl.

Sometimes miracles did happen.

Or maybe it was just time for Stephanie's luck to change.

CHAPTER FIFTY-ONE

HALFWAY THROUGH THE drive back to the Americana, Stephanie raised her head from my chest to look around. She moved in my arms closer to the window to watch the passing landscape, the late-night cars, the streetlights. Entranced with this wondrous world outside the hell she'd been subjected to most of her life. In the dim light, her pale skin took on a deathly pallor. Dark half-moons under her eyes added to the effect. I opened the ice chest on the floor where Drago kept cold the chocolate drinks I liked so much—Yoo-hoos. I opened one. She grabbed it from my hand and drank from the bottle like a recently rescued sailor from a desert island.

"Whoa there, little girl. Not too fast. You'll make yourself sick." I gently pulled down on the bottle and let her continue to drink at a slower rate. From the ice chest I took out a package of Hostess Snowball cupcakes and opened it. She snatched one from my hand and took a huge bite. Tears burned my eyes. This poor little girl. I'd seen a lot of abused and damaged kids but this one—

Or maybe I thought the same thing each and every time I came across an endangered child. The world's vulnerable and exploited.

She finished the Yoo-hoo and the two cupcakes in no time at all. She let a little burp slip out and eased her head back down on my chest. She fell instantly to sleep. A restless slumber filled with night terrors. I stroked her hair and whispered reassurances.

I covered her in Drago's huge leather jacket, a mock-up of one worn by World War II pilots. Drago had always wanted to fly planes but was afraid of heights. For part of his life when he was four and five years old, he lived in a high-rise tenement in Harlem. His dad made him stay out on the fire escape twenty floors up, shivering in the winter with one thin blanket and sweltering in the summer, watching the little cars and even smaller people far below move around like ants.

He parked in the hotel parking tower. We got out and headed for the elevator. This was the first time in real light since we'd left the hotel. Blood covered the front of Drago in long lashes of spatter from the pipe he'd wielded back at the Cogswell address.

"Hey, bro?"

He stopped. Blood splatter freckled his face, neck, and arms.

"You can't go up like that."

"Huh?" He looked down at his arms as if seeing them for the first time.

"It's all over your face, your hair, and ears."

"Yeah, I can't let Marie see me like this. She'll know we've been out capering. I'll run home, shower and change. I'll be back in twenty or thirty minutes."

"Not in a jiff?"

He gave me a rare smile and let slip a smidgen of shyness. I had to be the only person he let rib him. He headed back to the truck.

"Hey, Drago?"

He turned.

"Thanks for being there for me. You're a good friend."

He swallowed hard, the emotion plain in his expression. He nodded and walked back to the truck. I held Stephanie with both arms and totally covered in Drago's jacket. I didn't want anyone to see me carrying her in. She weighed fifty percent of nothing. I pushed the elevator button and waited. What was Marie going to say about another kid for the Johnson extended family back in the Rica?

In the hall at the suite, I couldn't reach my card key and softly kicked the base of the door. Waldo had to be on alert; the noise would raise his hackles. I waited.

Finally, a shadow covered the peephole—Marie checking the ID of the unannounced guest. She'd have a small Smith and Wesson .38 in her hand, ready for anything. I hated that she had to live this life.

The door swung open. "Don't you have your own—"

I pulled back Drago's coat a little. Marie's eyes opened wide along with her mouth. "Emily? You found Emily?"

I hurried past her. "No, this is Stephanie. She's in a bad way."

Marie got ahead of me, stood in my way, and pulled the coat all the way off. *"Oh my God, Bruno."*

I held Stephanie while Marie did a quick medical assessment. When she came to the wire around Stephanie's ankle, her head whipped upward to look at my eyes. I could read her mind.

I said, "The appropriate amount of comeuppance was meted out." I didn't want to go into it further for fear the sleeping Stephanie might hear. In the past, I found that some kids, even though abused, remained fiercely loyal to their parents, especially their mothers.

"Here, give her to me," she said, shaking her head. She carried Stephanie toward our bedroom. "She's burning up with fever." Over her shoulder, Marie said, "It'd be all right with me if you went back and gave them an extra dose of comeuppance. They deserve it and more. Come in here and help me."

Marie laid her gently on the bed. "First thing we have to do is get that wire off, and I mean right now. I cannot believe anyone—" She caught herself and turned from mother back to professional. "Run some warm water in the sink. Get a washcloth and some soap."

I stood there for a moment staring at the wall to the master bedroom. Marie had taped up every photo from both crime scenes: the Mosley house where Emily was last seen and the Skid Row body dump of Lilian Morales, a depressing tableau of a little girl lost. Emily.

We saved one.

At least we saved one. That mantra continued to echo in my brain.

Marie had seen the detective shows on TV and in movies where they put the reports and photos up on walls. She thought that it would let her see the big picture and allow her to solve the crime. Her stubborn drive could be so endearing and at the same time caused a little ache in my heart.

"Bruno, get moving."

I headed for the bathroom. I didn't know how to tell her that I wouldn't be able to help take out the wire embedded in the flesh of poor Stephanie's ankle. I had seen every form of mayhem perpetrated upon the human body while working the streets: shootings, stabbings, bludgeonings, car accidents. Even an abundance of blood and bone I'd personally meted out. But when it came to children, I didn't have the stomach for it. Not so much as a minor glimpse of a child suffering. I didn't know how Marie did it.

She got her medical bag and laid out her medical instruments on a sanitary paper towel on the bedspread. I brought a soapy warm washcloth and wiped down the sleeping Stephanie's face and arms. Wiped the damp cloth through her golden hair. Her delicate features, cute and angelic, gave off an odd illusion: a cherub swaddled in a halo of innocence and vulnerability. I half-whispered, "How could anyone in their right mind hurt a child like this?"

"That's the key. You just said it. Those animals aren't in their right minds. They're unstable and a detriment to society."

I didn't like it when she waxed pessimistic. Most of the time her world was viewed through rose-colored glasses. But lately we happened to travel on the edge and too often stepped over to the other side and then jumped back. At least that's the way it was for me. More and more the thought bubbled up that one day I would step across that line and not be able to come back. I'd take too big a bite of criminality and choke on it.

In the other room, Waldo growled. Seconds later, the suite's doorbell rang. Marie looked up at me. In that brief moment we had a wordless exchange.

"No way anyone followed us. You keep on with what you're doing. I'll handle this." I pulled a .357 from my waistband and held it down by my leg. I closed the bedroom door behind me. Waldo stood staring at the suite door waiting like a lion in the Coliseum for a Christian to be tossed out.

I put my hand on his back to let him know I was there. He growled. I jerked my hand back. Yikes. That damn dog. I moved to the peephole.

Helen Hellinger stood out in the hall staring at the peephole.

Stephanie's aunt.

I opened the door. Helen pushed in. She reached down and patted Waldo's head, not really even paying him any mind.

What the hell? How did he not take her hand off with a chomp of gnashing teeth? He didn't know Helen, this new intruder to our domain.

"I went by the Cogswell place," she said, "and the party's all broke up. They made a helluva mess. Almost burnt the house to the ground. Come on, now's our chance, let's go."

"It's probably not a good idea to go anywhere around that place for a while."

She turned angry, stuck a finger up in my face. "You promised. We had a deal, remember? You're not going to renege on it."

"Helen, wait—"

She shrugged out of my grasp. "I'll go myself, you chickenshit coward."

Marie opened the bedroom door to see what was going on. Helen saw past her to Stephanie lying asleep on the bed.

Helen's mouth dropped open.

CHAPTER FIFTY-TWO

HELEN JUMPED ME. Wrapped her arms around my neck and buried her face next to my ear. "Thank you. Thank you. Thank you," she whispered. "Whatever you want, you got it. I owe you. I mean it. Whatever you need, I'm there for you." Her tears wet my cheek and neck.

I stood there, not knowing what to do with my hands, and held them out away from the both of us. Marie shot daggers at me with her eyes. I said, "This is Stephanie's aunt. She was the one who asked me to—"

Helen pulled away from me wiping her eyes with the heels of her hands, sniffling. "I'm so sorry. I'm acting like some kind of high schooler. I'm not normally like this, really." She wiped her hands on her pants and offered one to Marie. "I'm Helen Hellinger. Your husband is a prince among men. Really, I mean it."

That was all the attention Helen gave us. She hurried into the master bedroom to check on Stephanie.

Marie came over close, her expression still angry. It shifted to a smile as she went up on tiptoes to kiss me on the cheek. She whispered, "Just as long as he remembers he's *my* prince."

"Oh my God. Look at her leg," Helen said from in the bedroom. She stormed out of the room, headed for the door to the suite. I grabbed on to her. She tried to shrug away. Marie jumped in to help and took hold of Helen's arm.

Waldo barked.

"Let me go. I'm going back there and—"

"And what?" Marie said. "Your niece needs you here. What good will it do her if you go to prison? You're the only one who cares about her."

Helen froze. The scar on the side of her face stood out bold and white where the rest was red. Her chest moved in and out too fast.

She relaxed. Marie and I let her go. She calmed; her breathing evened out. "That's why you did it without me, isn't it?"

I shrugged.

"Not just a handsome prince but a smart one as well."

Marie said, "You up for helping me? I need an extra pair of hands to get that wire off her leg."

"My wife is a doctor."

"Not a doctor, a physician's assistant."

"Whatever you need, just tell me what to do," Helen said.

Marie put her arm around her. "Come on, then."

I said, "I'm just going to lie down in here on the couch. Give a holler if you need something."

I lay down, unable to sleep, the adrenaline like an obstinate genie who refused to go back into the bottle. The violence from the Cogswell rescue continued to play out in my head. Phantoms and apparitions flitted around in the ether behind my closed eyes. So many things could've gone wrong but didn't. Someone was watching over little Stephanie. I closed my eyes. How did that work, exactly? The random fate of it. How did Stephanie catch a lucky card and Emily Mosley roll snake eyes?

I woke, twenty minutes, an hour, two hours later, to Waldo scratching at the suite door a moment before it burst open. In came Drago, large and intimidating.

He came right over to me. "Bad news, bro."

I sat up rubbing sleep from my eyes. I'd been sleeping far too much lately. My body needed it and said to hell with my mind, which was supposed to be the one giving the orders.

"Give it to me," I said.

"Word on the street, Ruby Two has your moms. Your moms went to Ruby Two, trying to help you out with your problem with Calvin Ivory. That's the way I heard it."

Helen and Marie came out of the master bedroom, Marie wiping her hand on a clean towel. "What's going on, Karl?"

Karl spun, turning to put his back toward the wall.

I said, "A gangster by the name of Ruby Two has Bea."

Marie shook her head. "When's it going to end? I'm going home tomorrow, Bruno. With or without you." She turned, went back into the bedroom, and closed the door. Trying hard to shut out the violent world that continued to pursue us.

"Who's Bea?" Helen asked.

Drago said, "She's Bruno's moms."

Helen looked from him to me. "She's your mother and you call her Bea? You seem awful calm for just finding out a street gangster has your mother."

"It's a long story." I turned to Drago. "What does Ruby Two want? She has to want something."

"Two million. She says she wants her money back. The money you took. Did you take two million from her? That's a lot of Benjamins, bro."

I whispered, "Whitey."

Helen came closer. "What?"

"When the Lexus crashed into that tree, I took off after Calvin Ivory. I yelled at Whitey to go after Ruby Two. The money from the kidnap payoff was probably in the trunk."

Helen nodded. "So, he didn't go after Ruby—he took the money and ran. Now Ruby wants her hard-earned cash back."

"We have to find Whitey, and fast."

Drago turned toward Helen. "I know a couple of places to look for that little shitweasel."

The back of his football jersey was soaked in red from mid-back down to his waist. He'd been wearing a leather jacket when we hit the house on Cogswell.

"Hold it, big man."

"No way are you going to keep me out of this one." He knew I'd just seen his injury.

"Marie?" I said loud, but not a yell.

The door reopened. Out popped Marie. "What's going on?"

Drago had spun around to face Marie so she couldn't see. She looked from him to me. "What?"

"I have to go out again. Drago wants to go."

"I'm okay with Waldo here," she said. "Go ahead, just be back by tomorrow or you're going to find this place empty."

"Tell her, Drago, or I will."

"What's he talking about, Karl?"

"It's not a problem, it's just a scratch."

"What?" Marie said, venturing out a little farther. "Karl, come here, show me."

He dropped his head like a scolded child and turned around.

"Oh my God." She hurried over and raised his shirt. He had tried to cover it with a poorly applied bandage, three Kotexes strapped down with duct tape, the whole rig now soaked through with blood. She gently pulled it off to reveal an ugly gash that sagged open. He didn't just need stitches; he probably needed surgery. Wizard had tagged him good with that Bowie knife while I had searched for Stephanie.

Tears filled Marie's eyes. "You're not going anywhere, Karl. Go in the bedroom and lie on the bed on your stomach. Try not to move around too much. You've lost a lot of blood."

Drago said, "I gotta go with Bruno."

She raised her arm and pointed to the bedroom. He shuffled along, doing as he was told.

She turned to Helen. "I'm going to need your hands again to help me clean and close that wound."

"I have to go with Bruno. He's going to need help."

Marie didn't hesitate, just nodded.

From the open door to the bedroom, Drago said, "Take Waldo." He spoke German to his faithful sidekick. Several long sentences.

Waldo listened, his eyes alive and anxious. I could've sworn that damn dog nodded. As if a dog could understand a string of orders like that. Who was Drago trying to kid? Not me, that was for sure. I wasn't buying it.

CHAPTER FIFTY-THREE

OUT IN THE hall, I stopped. Helen almost bumped into me. "What gives?"

Waldo sat and looked up, awaiting orders. I guess he understood at least a part of what Drago told him. What kind of dog acted that way? It was eerie.

I said to Helen, "Drago's my friend. Marie would not have said she needed help with him if she really didn't. I need you to stay here and help her."

"I'm going with you."

I didn't have the time or the energy to argue. "Not five minutes ago you swore to do anything I asked. Well, I'm asking."

"This is the wrong move and you know it."

"Maybe," I said. "When you're finished, call me and you can catch up."

"You sure this is the way you want to play it?"

I nodded, leaned back, and reopened the suite door for her. She put her hand on my shoulder. "Keep your head down. Listen for my call. I'll be coming the minute I'm done."

"You got it."

She disappeared into the suite. I hurried down the hall to the bank of elevators before Marie could run out and try to play commander in chief. Squash the new orders I'd given Helen.

Waldo stayed right at my side.

In the parking tower, I got in the big GMC, with Waldo in the passenger seat looking out the window for someone to chomp. My back turned damp from Drago's blood, which had soaked into the seat. I drove the circular route in the parking structure to the exit. Inside the truck smelled of Drago's favorite scent, bubble gum or tutti frutti and now mixed with a hint of dog.

I hadn't known Whitey long enough to call him a friend, but I did know his type from many years of chasing bank robbers, carjackers, and murderers. Bank robbery was Whitey's main vocation, and bank robbers are a breed apart. Unique in the way they think and act.

The majority of bank robbers go dry for days, weeks at a time, starving, fighting the urge to commit a robbery to again risk getting thrown back in the joint for decades at a stretch. Once they make the decision, risk the gamble, score a big bag of loot, they always go hog-wild with the money in celebration of their success. And continued freedom.

So I asked myself, if I were a bank robber and just came into more money than I would ever see—even if I robbed twenty banks (more like fifty) on the same day—what would I do with two million dollars?

First and foremost, I'd want to show off. Show my friends my new Big Man status. That is, if I were a bank robber.

The easiest way to accomplish this was to go to a bar where everyone knew him, buy drinks for everyone, hand out cash like it was dirty paper he no longer wanted. I drove to the dive bars in the area he frequented, some of which happened to be in the Crips area, the Rollin' Sixties, and farther south in South Central LA, my old stomping grounds.

Sometimes luck shines down on you like a bright ray of light from heaven. Maybe it was karma for taking Stephanie from that deadly environment.

Or more likely it just came back to that vortex of criminality that continued to swirl round and round in the same areas, pulling in and destroying everything in its wake like a black hole. In any case, the fourth bar I scoped out, me and Waldo hit pay dirt. Out in front of the Crazy Eight on Central at 81st Street sat a clean 1973 Cadillac Fleetwood Eldorado convertible, white with red interior. The top was down. It sparkled like new and was out of place like the proverbial sore thumb. This was the same car Clint Eastwood drove in the movie *Thunderbolt and Lightfoot* after he had recovered a shit-ton of money from a previous score, the robbery of a bank depository.

Thieves, thieves, tramps and thieves. Many professional criminals continually spoke of that movie, of that car, how cool it was, and how they'd buy the exact year and model if they ever hit a big score. A symbol of their exceptional success. No one ever did it, though.

The parking lot to the rear of the Crazy Eight brought back too many memories. Five or so years ago, I'd almost lost a good friend there, Nigel Braddock. He was literally beaten to within an inch of his life.

I entered the back door and stepped into a short hall with male and female bathroom doors on either side and waited until my eyes adjusted to the dark. Waldo stood at my side, ready for action.

Ralph Ledezma, the owner-operator—if he still owned it—kept the place dark. His clientele didn't want to see life pass them by while they hid in a bottle of watered-down liquor. What Nigel called "plastic vodka," because it came in cheap plastic half-gallon jugs.

I stepped in farther and found nothing ever really changed in the ghetto. Ledezma stood behind the bar wiping down elbow prints and bits of peanut shells with a dirty rag. He always kept his red curly hair cut close to the scalp, but now he sported a bald landing strip right down the center. One of his blue eyes worked; the other never followed along and must've been glass from a bar fracas that occurred years before. So many freckles covered his hands they looked suntanned.

He always wore a blue bowling shirt with "The Crazy Eights" embroidered over the pocket and scrolled large across the back in now-faded yellows and oranges. He nodded when he saw me as if all the years I'd been gone never happened.

Fifteen or twenty patrons, more boisterous than I ever remembered of this crowd, drank top–shelf type drinks instead of cheap beer. Five more came in the front door. The word had gone out and in a couple hours or less the place would be assholes and elbows with mooches and leeches coming from far and wide for the free booze and to help celebrate the big score. I bellied up to the bar, nudging the stool aside, choosing to stand. Sitting takes away a huge advantage if someone comes at you. Not having your feet on the floor leaves you without balance and support.

Ledezma put a draft beer down in front of me with white foam overflowing the rim. I took up the mug and drank down half of it. It tasted wonderful and went down too easy. I wasn't a big drinker and used to only imbibe at the conclusion of a takedown when I worked with Wicks, my old boss on the violent crimes team. To celebrate another murderer taken off the street.

I set the mug back on the bar and wiped the foam from my mouth with the back of my hand.

Ledezma leaned in, his breath rancid with the reek of Slim Jim meat and cheap bourbon. "No dogs. We're not going to go through this again, are we?" He hooked his thumb over his shoulder. "Get him out, or I call the cops."

The last time I'd been in the bar, I'd brought my dog Junior Mint in with me. Junior had trashed the place by pulling over a free-standing refrigerator that I'd tied his leash to. Shattered all the cheap bottled beer inside. I missed ol' Junior Mint.

"Not my dog. *You* tell him to get out. See how that works for ya."
I took up my beer and moved down the bar, inserting myself between all the other patrons who surrounded the man of the hour,
Whitey.

Whitey's head wobbled on his shoulders, his eyes glassy with
drink. If he wasn't seeing double, he soon would be. "Hey, take it
easy, stranger, there's plenty to go arou—" His eyes focused on me
and went wide. He did a staggering spin and tried to flee.

I turned to the bar, my back to him to drink the rest of my beer,
and said, "Waldo, guard."

Behind me came a deep-throated growl. Whitey yelped. "Keerist,
not the devil dog. Not this crazy-assed dog, again." Waldo growled
again. Whitey stood frozen by the door, not moving. "Bruno, call
him off. Call off your damn dog." He'd sobered, his speech no
longer slurred.

Ledezma said, "Hey? That is your dog."

"He's not my dog," I said. "Whitey, come back over to the bar."

"Okay. Okay. Just call him off."

"Waldo, out." Waldo went from alert to sitting. He was still close
enough to "take a bite out of crime," if the need arose. Whitey
looked back at the bar, then at the door, calculating whether or not
he could make it before the land shark reacted.

"Not a good idea. You rabbit, Waldo's going to have a rousing
game of fox and hounds with you being on the receiving end. Get
over here. Waldo?"

Waldo let go with another low rumble easily heard as the bar had
gone quiet to watch what happened next. Like lookie-loos at a bad
car crash, craving the blood and bone.

I could get used to having Waldo on my side.

Whitey came over to the bar and slapped it with his hand.
"Gimme a vodka."

I shook my head at Ledezma.

"Sorry, Whitey, the man says you're cut off."

Whitey shoved two over-beveraged patrons out of the way and came right up to my face. "What did I do to you? Tell me. What did I ever do to you for you to treat me this way?"

I took a last sip of beer that had lost its bite and pushed it away. I watched his reflection in the dirty mirror behind the bar. "You stole my money."

His expression fell as he flinched and blinked. The barflies moved back a couple of feet, fearful of impending violence. Afraid of being swept up in it.

Whitey recovered, turned aggressive, but this time kept his distance. "That's not your money. It's . . . it's finders keepers and you know it." He pointed at my face. "We talked about this. You know we did."

"It doesn't belong to you and it doesn't belong to Ruby Two."

"Okay wait. Just wait, what about . . . what about the ten percent finder's fee. You did say . . ."

"I'm a man of my word. You know that. Where's the money?"

He looked around, fear again filling his expression as he pictured all of his newfound riches slipping through his fingers like hot sand on a beach. "Ahem, ah, can we take this outside?" He didn't want to give away the location in front of all his sketchy peers. Say in front of witnesses that he'd acted the fool and hidden two million dollars in the trunk of the 1973 Fleetwood Eldorado parked out front at the curb.

Thieves, thieves, tramps and thieves. Crooks were as easy to read as the TV guide.

CHAPTER FIFTY-FOUR

I TOOK HOLD of Whitey by the scruff and escorted him to the street-side front door; his feet skipped and shuffled to keep up. Waldo's paw nails clicked on the dirty floor behind us as he followed along. I would have sworn he had a huge smile on his mug. He must've thought it was feeding time.

Whitey writhed and struggled under my grip. "Why you treatin' me this way? We're partners, remember?"

I opened the door and shoved him into the early morning darkness. Out on the sidewalk, I said, "We're partners, are we? I had to come looking for you. Real partners don't run off with all the money. You were supposed to go after Ruby Two, not snatch up the money and run."

"And what? What would I have done if I caught her? She'd kick my ass for sure."

"You got a point there. Gimme the car keys."

He spun around and put his back to the car, hands spread wide. "No. I've seen the way you drive. You have no respect for fine machinery. This is my baby. I'll drive."

I let my eyes drop to Waldo, who sat on his haunches waiting for the order to chomp Whitey's leg, crunch it like a hot and spicy chicken wing.

Whitey saw me look at the dog. "Damnit, Bruno, I just paid three times what this car was worth when it was new."

"I can't help that you're a fool. The keys." I held out my hand. He slapped them into my palm.

"Now get in." Then I pointed to the backseat and said, "Waldo." The dog jumped in the back.

"Ah, man. Look. His claws, the paint. That's the original leather, for cryin' out loud. He's sitting his dirty ass on it."

"Get in the car, Whitey, or I'll have you-know-who get out and assist you." He went around in the street and got in the passenger side. He slammed the door.

I used the key and opened the trunk. Like a good little crook, Whitey had transferred the money to different brown paper grocery bags, just in case Ruby Two had put a GPS in the previous containers. He probably thumbed through all the bills as well. I took out bundles totaling a hundred and fifty thousand and slammed the trunk. I tossed the money on his lap when I got in.

"What's this?" He didn't stop moving as he asked, stuffing the money bundles inside his button-up shirt.

I stuck the key in the ignition, started it, and pulled away from the curb. "You're end of the take minus what you paid for this little gem, and what you spent back there in the bar."

Waldo had his rump on the backseat and let his chin rest on the front seat next to the headrest as he watched Whitey's every move. A little bit of slobber ran down the seat.

Whitey opened his mouth to protest, then shut it. He opened it again. "Ah, man, look what your beast is doin' ta my car."

"You know," I said, "this *is* a big car. I think there's plenty of room up here in the front for all three of us. Whaddaya think?"

"You would, wouldn't ya? Bring that beast up here with us?"

"Then give all the jibber-jabber a rest. I need to think."

Now that I had the money, my first instinct was to drive over to Fat Boy's Pork Palace on Crenshaw, but it was too late; the place would be shuttered for the night. Or would it? I pulled a U-turn and headed north, up toward the twenties.

Whitey opened the glove box and reached in.

I said, "Take it easy. Your hand comes out with a gun and your gonna know what it feels like to instantly lose ten pounds of ass to you-know-who."

"You're all talk. You need me or I wouldn't be sittin' here."

He'd had time to evaluate his situation and figured something out I had only known subconsciously. Whitey had surveilled Ruby Two and had the most recent information on her. His hand came out with two huge cigars. He gave me one. Just the feel of it in my hand made my mouth water. Marie would kick my ass if she smelled cigar smoke on me. What the hell, I was in the grease already. I bit off the end and spit it over the door out into the passing street. I leaned in so Whitey could light it. After he first lit his own, of course.

Back in the day, while working patrol, I had developed a real taste for good cigars. Some cops put a dab of Vicks Mentholatum under their nose while investigating overripe and bloated dead bodies. Not me. I kept a cigar in my posse box, the kind sold in sealed aluminum tubes. I always lit one up to cover the gagging reek that permeated the uniform, ruined it until it was dry-cleaned. Sometimes it took several cleanings. I never developed a lasting addiction for cigars. I came to associate the smoke with grief and regret from a life lost. As I did now, driving the big Eldo. Even so, I still savored the smooth taste, the warm glow in my stomach given off by the heavy concentration of nicotine you only got from an expensive cigar.

Whitey put his head back, pursed his lips, and blew smoke like a steam engine chugging up a mountain grade. "This is the life, ain't it?" He reached out and put his hand on the dashboard, patted it.

"With all these yuppie electric cars zipping around like annoying little gnats, this baby is like riding in an aircraft carrier. Ain't it? And we're just floating along on an ocean of concrete."

I did love the velvety ride in the big car, the wonderful taste of a good Cuban while driving with the top down on a warm LA evening. "Since when did you become so poetic?"

He smiled and pointed at me with his smoking cigar. "Look at you. You look just like a Negro Clint Eastwood."

"You just ruined it. You were doing so good, too."

"Take it easy, big man. I didn't mean anything by it."

"So, you did see the movie?"

"Of course I did. What? You think I'm just some kinda twit that goes out and buys a rig like this for no good reason?"

I wanted to say, *Yeah, and buying it because it was in a cult classic movie was an acceptable justification.*

"If I'm Clint Eastwood, then you know what I did at the end of that movie to Jeff Bridges."

I pulled over to the side of the street and started to reach across him to open his door.

"Come on, man. Quit messing around. This is my car. You can't kick me to the curb, just like that."

I leaned back in front of the wheel, headed back down the street, and spoke around the cigar in my mouth. "Then knock off the Negro Clint Eastwood crap."

"You got it, Clint." He smiled. "Where we goin'?"

"You tell me. I need to find Ruby Two and fast."

He puffed on his cigar as he thought about that. "You know, she's not going to be happy with me. I took her money."

"She doesn't know that it was you. We'll tell her it was me."

He grinned. "You know, you'd make a good Negro Clint Eastwood."

I pulled over and kicked him out.

CHAPTER FIFTY-FIVE

I DROVE DOWN four or five blocks, made three right turns, popped back out on the street, and waited for him to catch up and get back in. Angry, tight-lipped.

I said, "Now quit messin' around and tell me how to find Ruby Two, or I'm gonna drive this aircraft carrier at high speed into a freeway abutment."

"Okay, okay, take it easy, big man, Jesus H."

"Spit it out, now, Whitey."

"Grrr" from the backseat.

He flinched forward away from the fur and teeth. "Hey, take it easy. I only followed her to one other place. I think it's where her beau lives."

"And?"

"If I tell you, you'll get out and gimme my car back?"

I came to a red signal, stopped, and blew on the cigar's cherry trying to keep it alive. "We're not negotiating here. Tell me or I'm going to pull into the closest dark alley and yo mama won't recognize you when me and Waldo are through."

"Okay. Okay. You're nothing like Clint Eastwood, you know that? You're more like Bela Lugosi."

"Whitey!"

"Hundert and twenty-ninth and Grandee, the cul-de-sac, all the way at the end in the apartments. The purple ones, ground floor, first one on the left by the pool."

The signal turned green. I gassed the big car and whipped an intersection U-turn, headed back south.

I pointed my cigar at him. "If you're lying to me, I swear it's going to be your ass."

"Why would I lie to you?"

"Because you're in good with the Crips and that whole block is a Crip stronghold. They keep two derelict cars at the opening of that cul-de-sac in case the Bloods or any other fool tries to ride on them. They block the street with the two cars after they drive in."

"Yeah, so I guess you do know the place."

"Last chance. You really tail Ruby Two to that location? 129th Street, not 129th Place?"

He raised his right hand. "I swear on my mom's eyes."

I held up my cigar. "Gimme another light." He lit the cigar while I puffed and watched the road.

"Hey!" He flipped his Zippo closed. "Where we goin'? You can't drive down that street, they'll kill us both."

I smiled. "Don't sweat the small stuff. They can kill us but they can't eat us."

"That's not funny, Bela. It's not."

Less than ten minutes later, I pulled over and stopped on 130th west of Wilmington. Darkness covered the street like a cloak, all the streetlights shot out by gangsters. We got out. I came around to the sidewalk and grabbed Whitey by the scruff.

"Hey! Hey! What gives?"

I unlocked the big trunk.

"No no no. You can't. Come on."

I shoved him in on top of the grocery bags filled with money. "Now, I'd be real quiet if I were you. You make a lot of noise, it will draw attention to you and if someone comes to your aid, well, I think they'll be more inclined to take the two million and leave your sorry ass in the gutter."

"What'd I ever do to you. Just tell me that much. What'd I—"

I slammed the trunk. Not a peep came out of Whitey. Waldo sat on the grass parkway watching my every move. The night was quiet; not even a cricket chirped. "You stay here and make sure no one steals the car. You understand?" He gave me that dumb-dog stare. "Come on, jump in the back and wait for me. I won't be long."

Nothing but that same stare.

Damn dog.

"Okay, but you cannot, and I'm serious, you cannot bite anyone unless I tell you to. You got that?"

Muffled words came from inside the trunk. "Hey, Negro Clint, are you really talking to that she-wolf? I knew it, you're cuckoo for cocoa puffs."

I slapped the trunk lid hard and took off at a fast clip with Waldo trotting alongside me.

I opened a short chain-link fence gate, entered the front yard to the residence, and followed a concrete walk down the side into the backyard. A cedar plank fence bordered the adjoining house. I kicked two of the planks out and slid through the new opening into the back of the house located on the opposite street—had to be 129th Place; 129th Street would be the next one. Waldo stepped through and followed me across the street, into the front yard of the next house, which was run-down and fighting a blight of weeds and entrenched gang members. No lights burned inside or out, the place dark as a cave.

Neighborhood dogs sensed the intruder, caught Waldo's scent, and barked. We came to a chain-link fence. We had to be quiet now, this was the back of the apartments Whitey had described.

My cell phone rang. I silenced it. Helen. She wanted to catch up and help out. I was already committed. The little man on my shoulder kicked me in the head, said it was the wrong choice and to wait for her.

I started to climb over the fence and realized my unwanted side-kick wouldn't be able to get over. No way did I have the strength to lift him up and toss him over, not a hundred and thirty pounds of fur, muscle, and sharpened teeth. I wouldn't put it past Drago to have sharpened those teeth with a rat-tail file. I could only imagine how trying to pick up Waldo would go; he'd bite off my nose as a joke.

"You wait here. I'll be right back for you." I grabbed the upper crossbar, hoping I had enough strength. I climbed halfway up, my one shoe stuck in the chain link for a foothold as I heaved upward.

Waldo growled. He jumped up and grabbed onto the cuff of my pant leg.

"Let go. Let go, you damn she-wolf." He was going to pull me off. I'd flop on the ground and that would be it. I wouldn't have the strength left for another attempt. I held on and shook my foot. My pants tore and I shot upward. I swung my leg over the crossbar and rested, catching my breath. I whispered, "Bad dog. Bad dog, you tore my damn pants." I swung over and dropped to the ground. "If you're not here when I come back this way, I promise I won't be sad." He stared at me with that White Castle cheeseburger look.

I waved from the other side of the fence. "Catch ya on the flip." I took off, hurrying to get this done before my body decided to shut down, to tell me it was again time to lie down and curl up for a nap.

CHAPTER FIFTY-SIX

I CREPT DOWN the side of the stucco carport to the rear of the apartments, the front of which sat on the street. The only light came from the stars and a sliver of a moon that looked like a smile. I stopped long enough to catch my breath and watch. No one lurked in the broken asphalt alley between the building and the carport. I stepped out and crossed over to the building. Out in the center of the apartments a throng of Crips laughed and joked and swung fists at each other as they drank from brandy bottles and fifths of beer, playing grab-ass. They made plenty of noise to cover my movement.

Someone from behind snuck up and stuck a gun to the back of my head. "Don't move, nigga." He shoved me up against the wall. The gun barrel on one side drilled my cheek into the stucco on the other. His free hand reached under my shirt to my waistband and pulled the first .357. He stuck it in his own waist. He'd missed the second one. He pulled back and clubbed the back of my head with his gun. Bright lights sprang into my vision a split second before my head collided with the stucco.

"What's you doin' back here? And carryin' a gat ta boot? You thinkin' a rippin' us? Is that it? You gonna rip us, huh?" He hit me again. Not as hard this time.

I held my hands up to protect my head. "Take it easy, I work for Ruby Two. She's not gonna be happy you treatin' me this way."

"So, you here for Ruby and you come in sneakin' yo ass over the back fence?" He eased off just a little.

I turned around and touched the back of my head. My hand came away wet and looked black in the moonlight. "That's what I just said. If you gimme my gun back and take me to Ruby, we can forget the way you been treating me." He had to have been standing deep in a carport for me to have missed him. They had someone watching their flank. They were more organized than I had anticipated.

He shoved me. "Let's go." I stumbled and put a hand to the wall to catch my balance. "We'll jus see what Ruby has ta say 'bout dis."

I should've called Helen. No one knew where I was.

We came out from the side of the apartment. The other thugs saw us and hurried over. "Who dat? Who you got, Rodney?" But he said it, "Rot-ney."

"Found this nigga round back with a gat." He pulled it out of his waistband and showed them, a bonus to his hunting trophy. A couple of them shoved me. One tried to kick me but I caught his leg and shoved him hard. I'd had enough and pulled the 415 Gonzales. I swung and caught Rodney across the ear. He wilted to the ground, out cold. I bent to scoop up my .357. They all attacked at the same time when I should've had a couple seconds while they regrouped. These were prison-hardened gangsters who knew how to survive on the street. They slugged and kicked in a standard prison beat-down. I swung and caught one with the sap. He yelped and backed away. One of them caught me solid on the jaw with his fist. My lights winked out then back on again in static flashes. All the strength left my legs. I eased to the ground as the kicks came in earnest. I turned numb, not feeling the pain. They took hold of my hands and pulled me along the ground like a piece of meat. Past several apartments to an open apartment door and then inside. The place was vacant and smelled of human urine and rotted garbage. This was where they handled all their business dealings, the kind they didn't want out in public view. The dope deals, the gun deals, the beatings.

The murders.

A naked light bulb hanging from the ceiling came on and swung back and forth. Bright graffiti covered all the walls, dense and blinding in bright, mind-numbing colors. Names of streets, and monikers, and descriptors like "RIP" and "Police Killa."

Three of the thugs, dressed in black and blue, waited, lording over me while they laughed and grabbed ass.

We waited some more.

I crawled over, put my back to the wall in a sitting position, and assessed my injuries. I didn't think anything was broken, but I'd be sore as hell tomorrow. If I lived that long.

I stuck a finger in my mouth and found a cut inside my cheek and some loose teeth. "You boys really did a number on me."

"Shut yo face or we'll do it again."

I nodded. "Yeah, you can do that and I wouldn't be able to do anything about it. But I came here to give Ruby Two a couple a million dollars and this is the way you treat me? I can tell ya right now she ain't going ta be pattin' you boys on the back, that's for damn sure."

"You knocked the shit outta Rot-ney. He still out cold. Dat the way you come lookin' to give away money?"

The other one said, "Two million? Yo flyin' high as a kite, nigga. Two million?" He shook his head and smirked.

The door opened. In came Ruby Two. All three lost their grins and straightened up.

"Two a you get out there and watch the street." All three started to move.

"I said two, you dumbasses."

The biggest one stayed behind, a real beefy thug with three piercings in his right ear and one in his nose. Ruby yelled for them to close the door, one made of cheap wood, the kind easy to kick in.

Ruby came over and squatted on the heels of her Nikes. She wore black denim with a red satin blouse unbuttoned midway down to her navel. She wasn't wearing a bra and wasn't self-conscious about it. She probably should've been. She moved her sunglasses up. Her eyes were bloodshot and lined with age. "You bring my money?"

"That's right. Didn't expect this kind of reception, though." I started to struggle to my feet.

She pointed her sunglasses. "You sit right back down and don't move. You were supposed to wait 'til we called. Why'd you slither in through the back? You plannin' to take the old woman back without givin' up the money?"

I eased back down.

"You don't look like you got the money on you," she said. "Where is it?"

"Let me see the old woman. You can have the money after you let her go."

She let a creepy grin out of its cage to slither across her face. "I don't think that's the way this is going to work."

"That's the only way it's going to work or you're not getting your money. Now where's the old woman?"

Ruby nodded to the thug. He went to the door and opened it. Bea Elliot in her wheelchair rolled herself into the abandoned apartment. She saw me, turned angry, and rolled closer to Ruby. "You said you wouldn't hurt him."

Ruby stood from her squat next to me. "Back off, you ol' bitch. Wasn't our fault he come in here the way he did. My boys didn't know what was goin' down. Him comin' in the back like that, thinkin' he's Shaft or some shit. He laid out Rot-ney. Plus, the two others from in front of my restaurant earlier today. He needs ta learn his place in this world. Now tell him to tell me where the money is or I'm gonna get mad. And you don't wanna see me mad."

"I said, I'll give you the money after you let her go."

Ruby chuckled, came back over, and again squatted close to me. She took a straight razor out of her back pocket, flicked it open, and ran the warm blade along my cheek. The edge bristled against whiskers, clearing a path. "Now, Mr. Bruno Johnson, maybe back in the day you were really somethin', but you're in my house now, and if I don't pay you back a little somethin' here, my boys are gonna see me as weak. I won't cut you too bad, I promise. You'll be outta the hospital in a couple a weeks. I've done this enough I'm gettin' real good and win the pot most times. We take bets." She moved the blade down to my neck. "It don't have ta be this way," she said to Bea. "Tell yo son here to give up the money. Do it right now. We made a deal. The money for takin' you outta the jackpot with Deon."

I looked at my mother. "You made a deal? This whole thing was all your doing?"

CHAPTER FIFTY-SEVEN

"Yeah, what'd you think was happenin' here?" Ruby said, the straight razor's edge sharp against my throat.

"I guess I should've known." I glared at Bea. She'd traded money that didn't belong to her to get her name off the hit list. And I was fool enough to come looking for her as if she were the victim. She'd made me her patsy. Her only son, a patsy.

The door opened. In walked a tall, thin man with his black shiny pate shaved clean. I recognized him from photos, Deon Rivers. The head dude, Ruby's boss. He'd been on the run for years, a ghost Robby Wicks could never dig out of his hole. And Robby had tried. No one on the street would give up Deon. Everyone was too afraid of him. And for good reason.

He had to be the one to order the death of Lilian Morales and have her dumped on Skid Row. The one who'd organized the kidnapping of Emily Mosley.

The old birddog in me went on full alert. I wanted Rivers, even though I no longer worked for Johnny Law. Old habits die hard.

He was already on the run hiding out. What difference did it make if he kidnapped the granddaughter of an FBI Assistant Director? It would only raise his street cred.

Ruby eased up, standing from her crouch, and held the straight razor down by her leg out of view, but still at the ready. She didn't trust Deon.

Deon moved over and put his back to the wall where he could see everyone in the room. "Thought I told you to call me when this shithead showed up?" He nodded toward me.

"I was gonna, Deon, I was. I wanted ta get the money for you as . . . as a surprise."

"Sure, you're right. Anyone in this room believe she was gonna give me all the money once she got it?"

"Deon, wait. It ain't like that."

"Shut yo piehole, bitch, and stand over there." Ruby did as she was told. The beefy thug who'd stayed behind looked uncomfortable. He worked for Ruby but knew Deon's reputation and didn't want to go against him. A conflict of leadership.

Deon sauntered over to the wheelchair. "Been a good long time, BeeBee, my girl?"

"Yes, it has." My mother looked up at him, defiant, ready to take her medicine.

"Way back when, you took somethin' important from me and now we've come full circle, haven't we? It's finally time for a little payback, ain't it?"

I said, "She arranged to get you two million dollars. That was the deal. You need to stick to it or no one will ever trust you again." Like that mattered to someone like Deon Rivers. But I had to try.

"This is none of yo bitness, Oreo. Stay out of it."

"Bruno, he's right. This is on me. Stay out of it."

"Bruno, huh? Is that right?" Deon came toward me nice and slow, his eyes taking me apart. He crouched down. Reached out and pulled up my sleeve, exposing the upper arm with the tattoo BMF.

"Heard the rumor you was still alive. Didn't believe it, though." He looked at the beefy thug. "Willis, you know who we have here?"

Willis, who was big enough to bench press a Volkswagen full of people, was scared and said nothing.

"This right here is the infamous Bruno The Bad Boy Johnson." Deon looked back at me, lost his evil grin, and turned angry. He took my forehead in his hand and slammed my head against the wall. He slid his hand down to my jaw and moved his face close to mine. "You remember me, boy?"

I said nothing and returned his stare. I had the other .357 Rodney had missed once he found the first one. When the thugs out front put the boot to me, the gun had slipped down inside my pants into my crotch. If I went for it, Deon was too close and would just take it from me. I had to bide my time. I needed a distraction, a good one to give me enough time to yank it out.

"I know of you," I said. "But we've never met."

"Dat right? What do you know, then? Tell me."

"You raped and murdered that little girl in Boyle Heights. You heard the cops had your teeth impressions when you bit her arms, legs, and breasts. So, you took a pair of pliers and pulled out all your own teeth. Those there in your mouth have to be dentures. You've been on the run ever since. Ducking and dodging."

"Heh, I started that rumor my own self." He tapped his front teeth. "These babies are all mine. Didn't think that dumbass rumor would take. Foolish damn people." He stood, pulled his leg back, and kicked me hard. He pointed a thick finger down at me. "You and that asshole Wicks ran me ragged. You took a lot of my kin to jail for not talkin'. I had to spend a lot of money hidin' out 'cause a you two. I always said I'd catch up to you, and lookie here." He turned to Ruby Two. "Jus' before I came in, you were about to take care of some bitness with that razor."

Ruby grinned. "Dat's right, I was." She brought out the straight razor and held it down by her leg. The yellowed light from the hanging bulb glinted off the blade.

Bea said, "Don't do it. You cut him up, you're not going to find out where that two million is."

Deon said, "I seen Ruby work. She'll get it outta him. You watch if she doesn't. Right, Ruby?"

"Oh, I'll get it outta him. No problem there."

Ruby moved toward me. I'd take a few cuts, squirm around a lot on purpose, fighting the pain and the blood while I went for the gun. I figured the odds were less than fifty-fifty. I wouldn't be able to use my hands to fend off the razor. I'd need them to pull the gun. I'd have to give her my face as the distraction. Take a slashing. I put my hands on the dirty concrete and sat up straighter, then let the one hand rest on my belt buckle, ready to undo it as soon as the cutting started. My guts cramped with fear. I needed to talk, say anything—that or risk laying over to the side and tell them every-thing they wanted to know. Where to find the money. "Tell me," I said. "What did you do with Emily?"

"Who?" She stopped short as she stood over me at the ready. The razor hung loose in her hand. I could see my reflection in the shini-ness. I couldn't take my eyes from it.

"Emily Mosley. I have a right to know what you did with her."

She smirked. "I don't know what you're talkin' about? Who?"

"The kidnapped girl. The girl and the nanny."

A large grin again crept across her face. She turned to look over at Deon. "Dat was Deon's idea. We didn't have the girl. Never did. We jus' heard she was taken. We heard on the news no one came for-ward wantin' money fo' her so we did it. We called 'em and said we had her when we really didn't. Sweetest deal I ever seen. Free money jus' for the takin'. Two million dollars fo' doin' nothin' at tall. Ain't dat right, Deon?"

I whispered to no one. "Are you kidding me?"

But I believed her. She had no reason to lie.

We'd been chasing our tails all this time while the real kidnapper/killer was still out there. While Emily was still out there. Alone. Waiting to be found. Not anymore, though. It had been too long.

"Git to it, girl," Deon said.

Ruby Two raised the razor over my head, poised to slash downward.

I wanted to close my eyes to wait for it but couldn't. I was mesmerized by the glint of the blade.

CHAPTER FIFTY-EIGHT

BEA SAID, "DON'T you tell them where the money is. If you do, they'll kill us both."

"Thanks for the great advice, Mom." Words I never in all my life thought I'd say.

Deon chuckled. "She your moms? For real?" He laughed.

I'd slipped and given them something else to use against us.

"Son," Bea said, "that wasn't too smart. What the hell's the matter with you?"

"You're talkin' smack to me? You're the reason we're here."

"I didn't ask you to come looking for me. You were just supposed to drop off the money and be done with it. You didn't have to sneak on up in here like you did."

Deon stopped laughing and faked a yawn. "Time to get down to bitness, Rubeee."

Outside the apartment, something bumped into the door.

"What is it?" Deon yelled at the door. "Leave us be and stand your lookout like I tolt ya or there's gonna be hell ta pay."

The bump again. Accompanied this time with a murmur that might've been a low growl.

Ruby Two asked, "What the hell was that?" A tinge of fear crept into her tone.

Bea, with a plain expression, didn't look at me, her eyes on Ruby. "It's a chupacabra. Don't open that door if you know what's good for you."

"A chupa what?" Deon said. "You're talkin' out your ass, woman."

The door bumped again. Then scratching on the other side.

Deon started for the door.

Ruby Two held up her hand, her eyes gone wild. "Don't open the door. Not if it's *a chupacabra*."

"It's a full moon," Bea said. "They come out on full moons. I know, I've seen them. Whatever you do, don't open that door."

It wasn't a full moon.

Bea must've known about Ruby Two's superstitious fears and was using it as a tactic against her.

"Oh, for fuck's sake," Deon said. He headed for the door.

"Don't! Don't!" Ruby's voice went up several octaves.

Before he put his hand on the doorknob, he looked over his shoulder one more time at Ruby, who transferred some of her hysteria to him. He pulled his gun from his waistband. "Bunch of superstitious bullsh—" he threw open the door.

Waldo leaped up and bowled him over. Deon's gun discharged as he went down on his back.

I rolled to the side, sticking my hand down my pants going for the .357. Ruby screamed, dropped the razor, and pulled a gun. "*Chupacabra. It's a Chupacabra.*" She fired wildly. The blasts echoed in the small confines that immediately filled with gun smoke.

Willis pulled a gun and tried to get a shot in at Waldo. But Waldo and Deon continued to roll around, Waldo chomping Deon's arm, shredding it.

Ruby fired wildly in the direction of the writhing mass of dog and man.

I got the .357 out. "Ruby!"

She turned, gun in hand. I shot her in the chest. I didn't wait to see the results and lined up on Willis, who fired simultaneously at the dog. Our shots echoed as one. Waldo yelped and rolled away trying to bite at his own withers, biting at the sudden pain that came from out of nowhere.

"You shot my dog," I yelled.

I'd hit Willis in the back. He spun around. I fired again; the muzzle flash snatched at my vision, creating holographs that flash-burned into my memory. He fired and hit the wall next to my head. Chipped plaster splattered my face, blinding one eye. I fired again and again until my gun clicked empty. The rounds thudded into Willis. He staggered back two steps then fell forward flat on his face.

Deon struggled to his feet, looking around for his gun. He found it and bent over to pick it up with his good hand. Carnage all around him. One arm hung limp at his side. Blood flowed in a constant stream down his hand to his pant leg. "Damn dog. Where the hell he come from?"

"From his mom. Where else?" Bea said. She shot Deon in the head.

I struggled to my feet.

Gun smoke hung from the ceiling in an even bank, a thick fog. Three people lay dead, along with a severely wounded dog. It had taken no more than three seconds, maybe four.

The door opened again. One of the thugs outside stuck his head in long enough to see the bloodshed, their dead leaders, and popped out. Seconds later, car doors slammed and tires squealed away.

I headed over to Waldo and said to Bea, "Where'd you get a gun?"

"Those dipshits don't like to search crippled women. Especially old ugly ones."

"You had the gun all the time and didn't use it when Ruby was about to cut my face. And you didn't use it then?"

"You're welcome."

"This isn't over. We're gonna talk."

She smirked. "Figured as much. *Typical* male response."

I knelt down next to Waldo. He'd saved my life. I stroked his fur. His breathing was labored and blood seeped from a hole in his side. I put my hand on it to try to stanch the flow. I took my shirt off, bunched it up, and gently pressed down. No way could I lift a hundred and thirty pounds. Not in my condition. And the police would be there soon. We had to go.

"We have to scram," Bea said.

"I'm not going without Waldo."

Bea wheeled over. "It's just a damn dog."

I looked at her. "That's not a *typical* woman's response. I'm not going without him."

"Well, then, damnit, pick him up and put him on my lap."

"He's too heavy."

"Ah, ya big nancy boy, quit being a—" She stood, took a couple of steps, and knelt down to help.

I sat back on my heels, stunned. My world spun a little. "You're not—"

She stopped trying to pick up Waldo. "What? Oh, get over yourself and lift. Five-O will be rollin' in hot any second now. Come on, get the damn dog in the wheelchair."

CHAPTER FIFTY-NINE

I EASED OUT of bed, trying not to wake Marie, every muscle in my body sore or bruised from the beating the night before. I crept on light feet toward the bathroom, needing a cold shower to reduce some of the heat my injured body radiated like a bad sunburn. Sleep had evaded me the three hours I'd lain there cuddled up to my wife. The words I needed to explain to Chulack about what had happened wouldn't come. How could I tell a man what had to be said? The horrible mistake everyone made taking the wrong path in the investigation.

Behind me Marie spoke. "Bruno?"

I turned. She watched me with sleep-laden eyes and a solemn expression.

"Yeah, babe?"

"I love you, Bruno."

I blew her a kiss. "Love you, babe." She was glad we were finally leaving for Costa Rica.

I got in and stood in the shower, my head bowed under the nozzle. I let the cold water sluice over my body. "Ahhh."

My mind continued to spin. Every asset Chulack had thrown at the kidnap of his granddaughter, all those man-hours, had been wasted chasing a false lead. Had they not gone in that direction and stayed on track, would they have discovered what had really happened to poor little Emily? Could they have intervened before they killed Lilian Morales and saved them both?

Fate, the turn of a card, the roll of the dice.

I got out, toweled off, and put on one of The Americana's big fluffy white robes. I walked back into the bedroom drying my head. I stood for a moment and watched Marie sleep. She was such an angel. My eyes shifted to the nightstand next to her. There was a yellow legal pad with half the pages rumpled and marred with notes and doodles. The end result of her investigation from the reading of all the reports, the hours of staring at all the photos taped up on our bedroom wall—several hundred of them. I smiled and picked up the pad, thumbed through the pages, some stained with coffee mug rings, and sugar from a plum Danish. The first few pages listed fact after fact. The back pages listed possible scenarios based on the facts. I loved her dearly, but none of them made any sense. Ridiculous television and movie solutions that rarely, if ever, translated to the real world. She'd been the only one to stay on track trying to solve it instead of chasing her tail as we'd been doing.

I dressed and went out into the living area of the suite.

Over in the corner, on a large towel, sat Stephanie petting the semi-sedated Waldo. Stephanie cooed to the wounded Waldo, telling him it would be okay. The scene brought tears to my eyes, the wounded consoling the wounded. I sat on the couch drinking a Yoo-hoo chocolate drink and wondered if Wicks, my old boss from the violent crimes team, had somehow been reincarnated into Waldo the dog. A good explanation based on how the dog acted: mean, yet loyal to the bone. Silly. That idea lived in a world far removed from mine.

Stephanie had her leg wrapped in a white bandage and already looked a hundred percent better. Waldo, still feeling some of the effects of the anesthesia—his eyes not entirely focused—also had a wide white bandage wrapped around his middle. The emergency vet had insisted that Waldo wear one of the white cones around his head to keep him from messing with his sutured wound. As soon as we'd gotten Waldo in the truck, Drago had taken it off and told the dog in German not to mess with the bandage. Waldo had made me a believer. Some dogs really could understand human words.

Drago was out getting a minivan for our ride down to Tijuana. We could no longer fly, not with Stephanie. We'd have to drive into Mexico and catch a boat, one with a questionable charter, for an expensive ride down to Costa Rica. I was elated to be going home, but at the same time, a large black cloud hung over my soul. I did not want to tell Chulack, see his eyes, see his world destroyed with my words. Destroyed more than it already had been.

"Hi, Stephanie."

She looked up and saw me for the first time since I'd entered the room. She cowered back a little, deathly afraid of men. She'd be like that for a while and had every right to be. Waldo, even in his semi-anesthetized state, brought his head up and growled, a low rumble, a warning not to mess with his charge. Drago must've whispered to Waldo in German before he left, put him on alert to protect Stephanie. I raised my hand. "Not a problem, big dog. I'm not coming any closer. Go back to sleep."

He eased his head back down and closed his eyes.

I finished the Yoo-hoo, stood, took hold of the roller travel bag filled with one million eight hundred thousand dollars, and headed for the mall courtyard down below.

I met Chulack under the bright sun. He sat on a concrete bench next to the pretzel vendor, the same place we talked when the whole mess started two days ago. Seemed more like two years. The heavy aroma should've made my stomach growl, but I didn't think I'd be hungry for a very long time.

We sat next to each other soaking up the sun, not talking. He knew what I had to say wasn't going to be good news. He wore khaki slacks and a long-sleeve blue chambray shirt and brown leather shoes. No suit. Another sign that his instinct somehow had told him the investigation was over and the outcome wasn't favorable.

He finally let out a deep breath. "I guess this couldn't be said over the phone?"

"No, it couldn't."

"This have something to do with the three gunshot homicides on 129th Street?"

"Yes."

He took off his sunglasses and stared at me. "Tell me the rest of it."

I slid the roller bag over to him. "I got your money back. Most of it. I had to pay out a finder's fee."

He kicked the bag. "I don't give a damn about the money. Tell me. Tell me what happened to Emily."

I swallowed hard. "Those people . . . they weren't involved in the kidnapping. It was a crime of opportunity."

I didn't have to explain further. The meaning hit him like a sledgehammer. His fatal mistake, the wrong turn in the investigation that had left Emily out there all on her own with no one actively hunting for her. All of it appeared in his expression, his eyes.

I said, "Anyone would have believed that ransom phone call was legitimate. It wasn't your fault."

"My God, Bruno. My God, what have I done?"

He understood, as anyone else in law enforcement would, that with the death of Lilian Morales, the nanny, and without any other contact—no other ransom request—it all meant little Emily was gone for good.

"Those people on 129th got what they had coming. I got the money back. That part of it is over." Senseless words under the circumstances, but I didn't know what else to say. I didn't want to say that he should have taken a hard look at his daughter and his son-in-law, and now would have to do just that. Once the kidnap had been eliminated, the statistics pointed to them as the prime suspects. His own daughter. He knew he'd have to do it. I did not envy him one damn bit. Subjecting his own daughter to a polygraph. That would be my next move if I ran the investigation. His daughter and her husband. Hard words coming from a loving father.

My friend Chulack looked away, stared off into the crowds of people moving here and there shopping, enjoying the day. Tears welled in his eyes and rolled down his tan skin, leaving glistening streaks. Probably the first time he'd let his guard down on his emotions since his granddaughter went missing two weeks earlier.

I put my arm around his shoulders. He let his head rest on my shoulder while he silently wept.

CHAPTER SIXTY

I WOKE IN the Americana suite bed for the last time. I had lain down to sleep, to grab a quick twenty-minute nap before our long trip down south. Marie sat on the edge of the bed with her hand resting on mine, patiently waiting for me to wake. She wore her best maternity clothes.

Everything else was ready and packed in two small wheeled bags. Now that we had to change our plans to take Stephanie along, we had to travel light. Marie left a great many things, mostly clothes, neatly folded in a stack over by the window with a note for the housekeepers to do with as they pleased, along with items we'd accumulated over the last two months: books, puzzles, games, and toys we had planned to bring home to the children but no longer had the room. On the nightstand sat a fat white envelope with the name "Megan," our regular housekeeper from the hotel. There would be a nice thank-you note from Marie with a thick stack of U.S. currency. Marie always over-tipped.

The light from the sun had moved across the room's floor, making it about three o'clock in the afternoon. I'd slept more than four hours while she'd gotten everything ready. I got up, kissed her on the cheek, and dressed in the clothes she'd laid out for me. I groaned with pain as I slipped my arm in the shirtsleeve. At the same time, I couldn't help but look at the wall of photos she'd left up for house-keeping to take down. Hundreds of photos of the dual crime scenes: the one of Emily's house, and the place where Lilian Morales' body had been dumped on Skid Row. Marie had taken down the awful photos of Lilian's body and destroyed them. All the rest were still up. Left there for a last-minute pondering while I slept.

"I'm sorry it turned out the way it did," Marie said. This, the first time we'd spoken of what had happened since I'd come through the door eight hours earlier, along with Drago carrying a recovering Waldo.

"Hmm," I replied.

"I don't know if I like you saying that." Her voice was low, almost inaudible.

She must've figured out where I'd gotten it from—Helen. "Sorry, I won't use it again."

"I'm so glad we are finally going home." She squeezed my hand.

"Me too, babe." I sat on the bed to put on my shoes.

"That's it," she said. "No more, right? We are going home this time and never coming back."

I stuck my arm around her shoulders, pulled her in close, and kissed the top of her head. She smelled of lilac. I took in a large whiff, closed my eyes, and held her. "Never again."

"No more of this," she said. I couldn't tell by the tone if it was a statement or a question.

"Bruno?"

"No. You're right. We are putting that world behind us for good. No more. Never again."

"Promise?"

I said nothing.

"Bruno?"

"Babe, I don't want to lie to you. What if . . . what if a rabid dog goes after one of the kids. Rabies isn't as controlled in Costa Rica as it is here." I said it with a smile in my words. "Come on, let's get on the road; we got a long trip ahead of us." I took her by the hand and helped her up. She mumbled something I couldn't hear. She hesitated and took one last look at the wall of photos. I watched her eyes take it all in one last time, not stopping on any one photo.

Chulack would be backtracking the entire investigation trying to find the path he'd missed, interviewing his daughter and son-in-law. Maybe he would find the answer, maybe he wouldn't. Too much time had been spent on the false lead, the phony ransom request. Now the odds worked against him.

"Come on," I said. I tugged her hand. "Let's leave this all behind."

I wheeled the two bags out into the living area. Helen sat on the big couch with Stephanie's head resting on her lap. Stephanie was asleep while Helen gently stroked her blond hair. Helen looked up at us with pleading eyes. She didn't want us to leave with Stephanie. The world just wasn't fair. All the reckless and foolish rules that would separate loved ones who needed each other didn't make any sense at all.

Drago sat over on the floor with his back against the wall, Waldo's head in his lap as he gently stroked the big dog's fur. Drago shouldn't have been leaning against the wall with the sutures in his back. A twinge of guilt clouded the room; Waldo had been hurt protecting me, a debt I could never repay.

Over by the door to the second bedroom sat Mom in her wheelchair. She had wanted to continue with her ruse of being wheelchair-bound. She'd saved my life and I couldn't go against her wish. If Marie ever suspected and asked, I'd tell her the truth, but for right now, I'd keep mum on Mom. I went over and extended my hand to her. She took it. I gently squeezed and smiled. "I forgot to tell you thank you."

She smiled. "Well, that's more like it. Give us a kiss." I bent at the waist and kissed her wrinkled cheek. I whispered, "Dad really doesn't know what he's in for."

"Son, you can just keep that little gem to yourself."

She'd called me *son*.

She smelled of White Shoulders perfume, sparking an ancient memory that couldn't really be there. I'd been far too young when she left to have a valid impression.

I let go, turned to Helen, and said, "You can come visit anytime you want. You're always welcome."

Helen nodded. Her chin quivered a little as she tried hard to hold in her feelings.

Drago grunted too loud.

"You too, big man. You can come visit anytime you want. As soon as you get taken off the no-fly list." I smiled.

He frowned and then smiled at my joke. He struggled to his feet. "I'll take the bags down to the minivan."

Helen eased Stephanie's head off her lap and stood. She hugged Marie and whispered to her, "Thank you so much for doing this. I promise I'll send you money."

Marie didn't answer. Her eyes stared off into never-never land. Helen took a step back and looked at her. "Are you okay?" Helen looked to me for help.

"Babe?" I said, starting to get worried, moving toward her. The baby. Was the baby coming?

Still in a trance-like state, Marie turned and hurried back into the master bedroom. Everyone watched her go.

She came right back out seconds later. She held photos pulled down from the wall in both her hands. Her mouth sagged open; her eyes wide. "Bruno? Oh my God, Bruno!"

CHAPTER SIXTY-ONE

MARIE LOOKED DOWN at the eight-by-ten photos in her hand. Blowups of individual items, both mundane, insignificant shots taken from the two different scenes: Emily Mosley's home and the lot on Skid Row.

"What is it?" I hurried to her side and took them from her.

She said, "It can't be that simple, can it? Bruno, does it work that way? Can it be that simple?"

"What are you talking about?" At first, I didn't see it. I looked at them like all the other investigators must have looked at them. The one photo showed a crumpled receipt found amongst all the debris that littered the field close to the body of Lilian Morales. Everything in the field, especially in close proximity to the body, was photographed, gathered, and saved as evidence. It could have come from anywhere, from anyone at any time. Not necessarily from Lillian Morales. In all likelihood, it hadn't. The next photo showed the same receipt smoothed out, a close-up of the items purchased:

The A to Z Handyman Store
Norwalk Town Square
11633 The Plaza, Norwalk, CA 90650

15 ¾-inch lag bolts with corresponding nuts
15 Lock washers
1 Spackle
1 Roll drywall tape
1 Quart white paint
1 Stud finder

"Babe, I don't see it. What are you talking about?"

She didn't say a word and pulled the other photo out from behind the others and pointed to an insignificant item on the Mosley refrigerator held there by a magnet in the shape of a miniature watermelon slice. A to-do list. Item two said, "Finish putting up shelving in the garage."

My world spun for a second from a heavy dose of vertigo. Marie was right. *Could it be that easy? That simple?*

I shook off the vertigo. Marie looked up at me, her eyes large and pleading. She wanted me to do something to ease the mystery, the pain of the unknown. I walked over to Drago and held out my hand. "Come on, give me one."

This time he read my eyes and didn't look for Marie's approval. He reached under his triple-extra-large Raiders football jersey and pulled out a huge Desert Eagle .44 Magnum. He tried to hand it to me. I waved it off. "Come on, man, that's way too big and you know it."

He reached down to his ankle as he lifted his foot. He pulled a blue steel revolver from his ankle carry holster, a gleaming model 19 Smith and Wesson .357. The sister model to the model 66 I was used to carrying. He took a speed loader with six more rounds out of his pocket and handed it to me.

Helen had come over to Marie and was looking at the photos. "I don't know what's going on, but whatever it is, I'm in. I'm going with you. You can explain on the way."

"Good. We're on our way to The A to Z Handyman Store. Drago, stay with Marie and Stephanie. We won't be long." I headed for the door.

"Bruno?" Marie said.

"Oh." I came back and kissed her. The kind of kiss that could easily transport a person to the other side of forever. I turned and headed for the door to hunt down some truly sinister thugs.

CHAPTER SIXTY-TWO

WE TOOK HELEN'S county car, a plain-wrapped Chevy Malibu, blue with stock rims. The whole package screamed cop. She used the GPS to navigate us to Norwalk. Without traffic, the device said it'd take forty minutes. But not really, not the way Helen drove. Maniac came to mind as a sound description.

My foot bounced on the floorboard, a nervous condition caused by the time and distance needed to put this to rest. In my mind, I fought over calling Chulack and telling him. Maybe he or one of his crack investigators had already spotted this lead, investigated it, and it had turned out to be nothing. Or maybe they had not looked that hard because this entire time they had the criminals from the ransom demand in their sights. If I called Chulack, told him, and this turned out to be nothing, it would only cause him more turmoil and grief. He'd had enough of that in the last two weeks to last three lifetimes.

"Well, you going to tell me?" Helen said as she whipped the wheel in and out of traffic, only stopping at red signals long enough to clear the intersection before blasting on through.

"Pull over, let me drive. You're going to kill us both."

She scowled at me and ran another signal.

I held up the photo with the receipt from the hardware store. "This was found in the field where Lilian Morales was dumped."

She didn't look, couldn't without risking a crash. "I saw that, but my friend . . . and I don't want to be the bearer of bad news . . . that sales receipt could've come from anyone at any time and most likely did. There's nothing to link that receipt to Lilian."

I held up the other photo of the refrigerator in the Mosley home. "This is a to-do list."

"Bruno, I got all of that. Tell me something I don't know or I'm going to drive us over to Augustus Hawkins and get you fitted for a straitjacket. 'Cause this is a little beyond crazy. It's the same as buying a lotto ticket, thinking-you're-going-to-win kind of crazy."

"That's right. It is just like a lotto ticket. This all comes down to three simple numbers. This is what everyone missed, and Marie spotted the numbers. Marie's mind must have taken in the information and mulled it around and around until her subconscious, all on its own, locked in on it. We saw it the moment that happened for her."

"Three numbers?" Helen braked hard. The front end of the Malibu surged down and stopped inches from the crosswalk where a homeless man pushed a shopping cart. She didn't wait for him to clear the crosswalk and blew through the red signal. The homeless man kicked out trying to dent the Malibu but missed. He spun around and almost fell.

"Three numbers." I held up the photo of the receipt again and pointed to them.

She pulled her eyes away from her mad dash through LA, but not long enough to see. "What is it. Tell me—Wait," she said. "It's the date, right? That's what you're pointing at? It's the date on the receipt." She paused. I let her think it through.

Realization crossed her expression. "It has to be the date Emily disappeared."

"That's right."

"Son of a bitch. And your wife . . . I mean, Marie, figured it out. That's really something. I'm not kidding, Bruno, that's really something." Helen drove a little faster, if that were possible.

Twenty-seven minutes later, we pulled into the A to Z Handyman Store parking lot. The place shared parking with the You Mail It postal annex store, a Hole in One Donuts shop, and the Advanced PayCheck business, where people could get money advanced on their paychecks. The donut shop had one person sitting inside nursing a large Styrofoam cup of coffee and nibbling on a cake donut with pink frosting.

Most of the cars in the parking lot were clustered close to the Advanced PayCheck business, which tended to draw sketchy people. It was the kind of place that preys on obsessive-compulsive folks who find it difficult to hold down a regular job and spend their hard-earned cash on drugs, gambling, or sex.

Fat cracks ran throughout the neglected parking lot's asphalt, along with litter that migrated with each new breeze.

"You want to watch the Handyman for a while before we make contact?" Helen asked.

"Pull up in front. This lead's been on the back burner too long already."

She did. We got out. Posters for sale items covered the window to the Handyman so we couldn't easily see inside from the parking lot. As I approached the double glass doors, I tried to peek through the posters. One employee tended the shelves while one manned the checkout counter. Both wore red aprons and looked to be in their late seventies with gray, untended mops of hair. I didn't know what

I expected, maybe some sinister-looking thugs with angry tattoos who worked behind the counter and used the place as a money laundry. Anything but a regular hardware store barely hanging on and run by mom and pop.

I pulled the door open and let Helen go in first. The white-haired man at the counter smiled at us. I got ahead of Helen and flipped out the FBI credentials. The man with HERB embroidered on his red apron said, "Oh my."

I put the photo of the smoothed-out receipt down on the counter. "Herb, I need help with this receipt," I said. "What can you tell me about it?"

He stared up at me for a long second, fear in his eyes. Not fear from being caught doing something illicit but more intimidation by a large black FBI agent who'd been rude and had skipped the introductory pleasantries, getting right down to business.

He put on the readers that hung from a chain around his neck as the last vestiges of hope bled out of me. This was going to be a dead end. What had I been thinking? Of course, it wasn't this easy. It would have taken a miracle for it to have worked out. The angels were not looking down on us today.

The old woman who'd been tending the shelves came over. "Herb, what's going on?" The name MAY was embroidered on her apron.

He took off his cheaters. "These folks are from the FBI and want to know about one of our sales receipts." He held up the photo. She grabbed it from his hand. "Well, hells, bells, he can't remember what he had for breakfast this morning."

"I do, too; it was eggs and sourdough toast and some Little Smokies."

She smiled and gently knocked on his head with her knuckle. "Hello? You had oatmeal with wheat toast."

"I did?"

She turned her attention to the photo and put on her own cheaters, which hung from a decorative chain around her neck. Her eyes were occluded with cataracts. May scanned the receipt for just a second. "Sure, nice-looking Mexican gal with a little girl."

I sucked in a breath, a hesitation long enough for Helen to say, "That's great. What can you tell me about her? About what happened that day. Did anyone come into the store with her? Did she leave with anyone?" Helen came off too brusque with her rapid-fire questions.

May put a hand to her chest. "Oh, my land."

"It's okay," I said. "It's just that this is real important."

She looked again at the photo and pointed to the date. "Herb, that was the day they had that flea market across the street."

"Oatmeal? You sure you're telling me straight? She tends to mess with me, if you know what I mean."

"Flea market?" I asked.

"Yes, and everyone that shops there loads up our parking lot with their cars and walks over. Drives all of our customers away. That's how I remember—we hardly had any business that day. Can't say that I remember anything special with this young gal, though. Other than she was real nice. Real polite."

"May?" Herb said. "What about the computer?"

"The computer?" I said.

"Oh, for heaven's sake, sure. Come on, follow me."

We followed her into the back, my feet too clumsy, wanting to move faster, held up by their slow pace.

The computer?

CHAPTER SIXTY-THREE

WE PASSED THROUGH a small receiving area filled with stacked boxes yet to be unpacked and shelved, and on over to a closet-sized office with a glass window. The whole place smelled of Lysol. May sat down at a desk cluttered with invoices and junk mail. She placed her hand on a mouse, moved it. The computer screen came to life. Herb stood behind his wife. "Some nefarious characters robbed us twice last year, so we bit the bullet and put in this expensive security system. Cost us an arm and a leg. It hurt the bottom line; I can tell you that much. Our accountant said we can—"

"A CCTV camera?" Helen said. She gently took hold of Herb by the shoulders and eased him out of the way so she could stand behind May.

May looked over her shoulder and over the top of her cheaters. "What was that date?"

I told her. She typed it into a program. Helen, looking at the screen, said to me, "It's a six-camera system that includes the perimeter of the building and parking lot. It's color with high resolution and a segmented screen."

"Yes, it's brand spanking new. What's the time on the receipt?" May asked.

I told her.

She used the mouse to scroll to the correct time. Helen said, "Start about an hour before so we can see all the activity."

"Excuse me," Helen said as she nudged poor May out of the way and took over the mouse. She artificially reversed the rotation of the earth and moved through the time on the screen, with people and cars acting like animated cartoons going backward. She'd clearly done this a few times before and knew what to look for. She suddenly slowed the world back to normal speed and caught Lilian Morales and Emily coming into the store, moving from one camera shot to another. They picked up the items listed on the recovered sales receipt and put them in a basket. They paid for them and exited the store. Lilian held Emily's hand as they turned the corner and walked between the buildings where a dark gray panel van waited in the aisle among the other cars, engine running. The driver wore a nylon stocking over his face with black leather gloves on the steering wheel.

May put her hand to her mouth. "Oh my dear Lord."

I agreed with her and ground my teeth, wishing what was about to happen wouldn't.

Lilian and Emily still headed for the car, unaware of anything wrong.

Two other men ran up, guns in hand, also wearing nylon masks, and black zip-up jackets. Lilian grabbed Emily and stepped in front of her. The men pulled off their masks and looked around, frantic, not knowing what to do about this new, unplanned wrinkle: Lilian and Emily.

The side door to the panel van slid open to a man without a mask. He had a narrow acne-scarred face and a ponytail. He yelled something. The two men with guns grabbed Lilian and Emily. They put their hands over their mouths and dragged them into the van kicking. The van door slid shut and drove off.

The abduction happened in seconds. Less. No one saw what happened. And just that quick, they were gone.

"It was a robbery," I said. "And they were witnesses. Wrong place, wrong time."

"Wait a minute. That's right," May said. "There *was* a robbery that day at the bank across the street. It happened during that flea market, and the robbers ran away. Ran right through that big crowd. Oh my dear Lord. They were parked on the side of our building the whole time."

"Can you get the plate of that van?" I asked Helen. But it wouldn't have mattered; the van would have been stolen.

She backed up the time past the part where the van drove off, to where Lilian and Emily were grabbed.

"Wait, you passed it."

She stopped and froze the screen where the man inside slid the door open—the man without a mask. She poked the screen hard and said through clenched teeth, "We don't need the license plate. I know that dirtbag. Come on."

CHAPTER SIXTY-FOUR

"His name is Leroy Lazard," Helen said, as she again jockeyed the car in and out of traffic. She took a second to look over at me. "We going to call this in and ask for backup?"

"I really want a piece of this Leroy Lazard," I said.

"I was hoping you'd say that."

"Give me the rest of it," I said.

"Lazard is the guy who sets up bank robberies. He had a guy named Hank Cobo—a real turd—pulling the jobs with a crew. Lazard scouted, organized, and took a third of the take. All of this is according to Cobo. I believed him, though."

"I remember that name, Cobo. He did a bank job in Santa Fe Springs and gunned down some people. That was your case?"

"That's right. I got Cobo to roll. He gave up Lazard, the shot caller of the jobs. Only I couldn't make him. Not enough for the DA, anyway. I had the Crime Impact Team watch Lazard's operation for a while. After two weeks and nothing happened their captain pulled CIT."

"Where're we going?"

"He runs his whole operation from one of those pick-a-part places, a wrecking yard where you go to dismantle the part you need from derelict cars. It's in Compton."

"Compton?"

"Yeah, why?"

"It just seems like everything always comes back to Willowbrook, Compton, or Watts."

"Yeah, I think that whole area was built on an Indian burial ground." She went back to focusing on her driving, picked up Alameda, and headed south. She pulled over just north of Pine. I knew the area well. She shut it off and turned toward me. "How do you want to handle it? I say we just go in and yank Lazard's chain."

"I'm guessing he knows you. I mean, he'll know you on sight?"

"That's right. Is that a problem?" Her tone shifted to defensive.

"This kidnapping is high profile. He's going to be sketchy. He'll jump out of his skin if someone so much as drops a wrench."

She shook her head. "Not necessarily. He'll have been watching the news and know someone hijacked his crime and demanded a ransom. He'll think he's in the clear."

"Do we want to risk that?"

"What are you trying to say?"

I opened the Smith .357 to check the loads and eased the wheel shut. You never flip your wrist like in the movies and snap it closed. You risked damaging the alignment of the cylinder and the forcing cone. "I'm saying, he doesn't know me. I'm saying I go in and scout it, get the lay of the land. I'll have my phone on like we did before so you can hear everything. I make sure he's there and give you the code word. You roll in hot. We take him down together."

"I don't like it."

Most cops worth their salt wouldn't. She didn't want to miss out on the action, and with me going in alone there was always the chance of the situation lighting off without her.

She looked into my eyes. I said, "Think about it. You know it's the smart move."

"All right, damnit."

I got out. She popped the trunk and got out on her side. I met her at the back of the car.

I watched, not wanting to ask what the hell she was doing. She unlocked a Remington 12-gauge riot gun from the rack, pulled down the slide, and checked to make sure a round was seated in the chamber before snapping it closed. She read my expression and said, "You have this tendency to get on the wrong side of people. I just want to be ready."

I nodded. I took out my phone and called her. She answered and turned up the volume as I did on mine before I put it in my shirt pocket.

"What's your safe word so I know when to roll in?" she asked.

"How about, 'get your ass in here'?"

She smiled. "Works for me."

In the CCTV footage there had been four bank robbers: one driver, two thugs dressed in black, and Lazard inside the van. Four against two.

We stood looking at each other. The moment stretched from here to next week.

"All right then. See you in a few minutes." I turned and started down the street.

"Bruno?"

I stopped and faced her.

"Keep your head down."

I smiled. "You just watch where you're pointing that blower."

She again smiled that crooked smile and nodded.

I walked along the dirt shoulder eastbound from Alameda. Scars on my back itched. A few years earlier, a good friend, Judge Connors, saved my life by shooting a gun thug with an Ithaca Deer Slayer shotgun. The thug had been about to shoot me. I took some of those pellets from the judge's gun in the back.

Potholes freckled the asphalt on Pine, a dirty little street without curbs and littered with junked derelict cars dumped off without paperwork. The whole area had a post apocalyptic air about it.

The wrecking yard had at least two hundred feet of frontage. An eight-foot-tall fence of corrugated steel blocked any view from the street. The double-wide gate stood open revealing inside: row after row of cars and trucks, forlorn carcasses that over time were slowly being picked apart by scavengers. In the middle of one wide row sat a semitruck parked straight in with a forty-foot sea container on the back of a flatbed.

The office, positioned in the middle of the street frontage, was a small, single-story house, dilapidated and in need of paint. It seemed as if the ground now worked hard to gulp down the structure. The roof sagged. The windows were boarded over with weather-worn plywood, and the wood siding drooped in places, revealing the interior bones of the structure. I stepped inside. A bell out back dinged loud. I stood at a grimy Formica counter and could see down a short hall out the open back door into the wrecking yard. The office smelled of cigarette smoke and reeked of grease and solvent and sour body odor. Car parts stacked in piles left only warrens to move around in.

A big dude in grimy blue bib overalls came into the back of the house wiping his blackened hands on a red rag. He wasn't happy to see me. "Hey, sport, we're closed."

"Are you ever open? I mean, I was here last week and you said the same thing. What's going on here? Are you really a legit business, or is this just some kinda front?" My abrupt aggressiveness caught the man off guard. I didn't recognize him as being one of the four men in the van, but I'd only watched the brief bit of video twice at the A to Z Handyman. Even though at the time I tried to act professional and only look at the thugs, my eyes had been inextricably drawn to

Emily and Lilian. The stark fear in Lilian's eyes. Maybe it had been my knowledge of how she'd end up, discarded like so much garbage in an empty field in Skid Row. The image brought on the anger.

These people at the wrecking yard were responsible.

He stopped wiping his hands on the rag. "Whatta ya need, sport?"

"A right front quarter panel to a 1979 Chevy Nova."

"Sorry, fresh out a those." He took a large crescent wrench from his back pocket and let it clunk down on the counter. A threatening move.

I pointed toward the back. "I saw one through the gate when I walked up. It's in the second row, right there on the left next to that semi."

The man's lined and overly tanned face was smudged with grease. He let loose a grin that displayed yellowish, crooked teeth. "Okay, smartass, five hundred up front, and you'll have thirty minutes to unbolt it. You don't get it off in thirty minutes, I kick your sorry ass out on the street and keep your money."

"That's three times what it's worth."

"You want it or not, sport?"

I needed to stretch out my visit until I found out how many crooks we were up against and whether or not Lazard was on the property. "Yeah, I'll take it." I reached into my pocket for the cash. He lost his smile. He'd thought the exorbitant price and his obnoxious demeanor would scare me off.

I thumbed open the folded bills and started to count them out. I looked up in time to see Lazard come through the back door. He froze when he saw me.

I couldn't help it; anger and hate jumped into my expression, into my eyes. He read the inference and knew what would come next. He yelled, "Harold, he's Five-O. Five-O, God damn you."

CHAPTER SIXTY-FIVE

LAZARD PIVOTED AND fled out the back door. Harold started to back away from the counter. I leaned over and grabbed onto the front of his bib coveralls with both hands and yelled to be heard in the phone in my pocket. "Get your ass in here."

I pulled Harold toward me. He snatched the wrench and backed up, dragging me over the counter with him. He couldn't get a full swing and clubbed me on the side of the head. Bright pain lit up my entire world. I held on as he continued to back up. I gained my feet on the other side.

Lazard was getting away. I butted Harold in the bridge of his nose with my forehead. His cartilage crunched. Blood flowed. He went loose in my hands.

I'd promised Marie no more violence. No more blood and bone.

I kneed Harold in the groin. He crumpled to the floor, both hands going to protect the violated area. I kicked him in the face hard as I went on by him pulling the .357. "Helen? Helen?" I yelled as I came out the back door.

A motorcycle roared to life and appeared down one of the long aisles of wrecked cars. Lazard. He drove at high speed, the engine winding out, the back tire kicking up a tall rooster tail of oil-soaked soil.

He was going to get away. We'd never find out what happened to Emily.

Helen appeared in the opening to the double wide gate. She held the shotgun down low at her hip leveled at the motorcycle approaching her at high speed.

"Don't kill him," I yelled. I raised my .357 and fired at the front tire of the motorcycle and missed.

Off to the left, the big shotgun bellowed again and again as Helen racked the gauge holding the trigger down. The big gun kicked up in her hands.

The front tire of the motorcycle dipped forward. Lazard flew through the air with no helmet, his arms limp down to his sides. An unguided missile. He slammed headfirst into the side of the sea container on the flatbed and dropped straight to the oil-soaked ground.

I looked over at Helen. Smoke curled out of the shotgun barrel, the gun still held down by her hip. She said nothing. Didn't have to. Her eyes said it all. "You got something to say?"

I answered her out loud. "No." I knew what had happened. Helen had needed an emotional release. A little revenge served cold over what had happened to Stephanie, who'd been locked in a closet with her leg wired to a wall. Lazard had harmed Emily. He became the perfect outlet for Helen's anger. This time Lazard was in the right place at the right time.

The motorcycle's rear tire spun, the engine winding out. Helen shot the bike with the shotgun. The engine sputtered, billowed white smoke, and died just like the driver had. With calm hands she reached into her pocket and fished out fresh shells, fed them into the shotgun, racked it, and put on the safety. I came down the porch steps covering Lazard with the .357.

The side of Lazard's head and face was deformed, his one good eye locked open staring at the sky. Buckshot pellets peppered his *Motorhead* tee shirt with little or no blood. He'd died instantly. He wasn't going to be able to tell us what he'd done with Emily. Her final disposition.

I squatted next to him and searched his pockets for his cell phone. Helen came and stood close, cradling the shotgun in her arms the same as a bird hunter would.

I couldn't be angry with her. Not for what she had done, but maybe a little for cheating me out of doing it.

In his back pants pocket, in a thick black wallet, I found a one-way ticket to Thailand and fifteen thousand dollars cash. The heat of the robbery, the kidnapping, and the murder had gotten to him. He was fleeing to warmer climes to wait it out. Not today, pal.

I stood, my knees cracking from old age. More than ever, I needed to get back to Costa Rica, to the kids and my hammock in the back-yard. I was sick to death of all this violence and killing.

"I guess I better call this in?" Helen said.

"You better get out of here." She tossed me the keys to the car. I caught them and nodded. "Yeah. Hey, there's a guy in the shop, he's unsecured."

"I'll handle it."

I stopped next to her and took up her hand in mine. "I'd say, it's been fun."

She smiled. "Take good care of Stephanie for me. Give her a kiss for me every night, okay?"

"I won't let her forget you. And I'm sure you'll be down there to visit every—"

While I had been talking, somewhere in the back far reaches of my brain, I had been processing the entire scene, all that had happened. Going over the minute details.

Helen read my stunned expression and spun around, bringing shotgun to bear on the unseen threat.

"Oh my dear Lord," I whispered.

"What?" Helen said too loudly.

My mind shifted into high gear, not believing it. Not for a second could I believe it possible. I frantically looked around for something, anything heavy enough to break a lock, and spotted a rollaway tool chest. I ran over and yanked open the drawers.

Helen followed. "What? What's wrong? What's going on? Have you lost your mind?"

In the large bottom drawer, I came across a short-handled sledge-hammer, grabbed it, and ran.

"What are you doing?"

At the back of the sea container, Helen caught up and spun me around with her free hand. "Tell me!"

"He had tickets to Thailand."

"And?"

"This sea container is going to Thailand. Look at the customs tag on the lock."

Her eyes lost focus as she thought it through. It took less than a second. "Sweet baby Jesus. *Human trafficking*." She tossed the shotgun to the ground, yanked the short-handled sledge from my hand, pivoted, and clubbed the lock. Again and again.

I couldn't wait for her. I moved her out of the way and took the hammer. I hit it with everything I had. The locked popped open. She pulled off the damaged lock, and I lifted the long handle to open the door. Light flooded in.

Emily.

She sat up and crawled backward toward two stolen cars. Her arm came up to shield her eyes from the light. Next to her was a gallon jug of water and two large packages of Hydrox Oreo cookies on an old swatch of gold shag carpet. Enough food and water to get her onto the container ship.

Hot tears burned my eyes. The sea container floor was at chest level. I reached in with open arms. "Baby girl, come here. It's safe now. I'm here to take you to your grandfather. Grandpa Dan."

I looked at Helen. Tears streamed down her cheeks.

I turned back to Emily. "Come here, Emily, honey. I'm going to take you to your mommy."

"Mommy?"

"That's right. Come here."

She came to the edge. I picked her up. She glommed onto me, her arms around my neck, her mouth close to my ear. "Thank you."

I hugged her and whispered, "I guess there are angels looking out for you."

Helen said, "Yeah, and his name is Bruno Johnson."

"Gimme your cell phone." Helen handed it to me. I held Emily with one arm and dialed.

"Dan," I said. "It's me, Bruno. Hold on. No, just hold on a minute, would you." I handed the phone to Emily. "Here, it's your grandfather."

She took the phone. "Bampa? It's me, Emily. Bampa? Bampa? Don't cry, Bampa. I'm okay. Really."

AUTHOR'S NOTE

During my first night working as a jail deputy, an inmate was dropped off the tier onto his head and killed—murdered by someone from another module. I soon came to realize the jail could be every bit as dangerous as the street and just as complex.

That first night, I watched how the inmates were fed "chow." With fifteen thousand or so inmates, chow is a major undertaking and difficult to keep under control. Two deputies are in a chow hall rotating the inmates through and keeping order while another stands guard at the hard door to the chow hall, watching. My escort that first night told me that if a fight breaks out, the guy at the door had orders to slam and lock it. I asked, "What about the two deputies inside?" He shrugged. "They have to keep the inmates off them until the crash team gets there."

* * *

There is a famous news story that has always sparked my interest. Robert White never spent much time in jail or prison. Every time he was arrested, he'd look around inside and find out who was in for the most sensational crime and get close to him. White was ingratiating and easily liked. He'd get the crook to talk about his crime, tell details that could only be known by the true perpetrator. White would then swap his information for his freedom.

*   *   *

Twice in my career I commandeered a car. Once it was a van. I borrowed it from a driver who had stopped for me as I stood in the street bent at the waist trying to catch my breath. I chased down a crook who'd run off with our buy money. I sort of crashed the van. Just a little. Knocked off the driver's mirror and scratched the side. When the team sergeant came to ask me if I had borrowed a van, I shrugged and didn't answer, hoping it'd just fade away. If I hadn't caught the crook with the buy money, the entire team would've been in the grease. The sergeant gave the van driver two hundred dollars out of the seized money. The cost of doing business. The guy was happy.

I also commandeered a house twice in my career, both after lengthy foot pursuits that found me deep in Compton, a different policing jurisdiction. Without a handheld radio, I needed a phone.

The thing about the 415 Gonzales is true. I was jumped twice by multiple suspects and the 415 Gonzales saved me.

Throughout my career, I had cause to work with many canine handlers on common problems and critical incidents. Twice, I ran into situations where the dogs were smarter—by a factor of two—than the handlers. There is no doubt in my mind those dogs—on more than one occasion—kept those handlers alive.

Compton is listed by the FBI as one of ten most dangerous cities in America.

And:

While working Career Criminal, my team was called out to Highland for a kidnapped child. When we arrived on scene, we took over the incident and it became our responsibility. The child, a toddler who was too young to talk, had just disappeared and the fear was he had been kidnapped.

Before widening the investigation, we started from the beginning and searched the family home top to bottom. In the past, children have been found under a bed where they had crawled and fallen asleep. Next, the house next door was searched. It was vacant and for sale. The belief of patrol was that the toddler could never get over there on his own. We searched it anyway, just in case. Patrol was not happy with our lack of trust. Patrol said that they had searched it.

I wanted to be sure, so I searched it with two other members of our team. It was a three-bedroom home with two bathrooms. The house was devoid of any furniture and was easy to clear. Walking out, I spotted a closed door. "Hey, anybody look in here?"

The other two detectives mumbled, "It's clear. A baby in diapers couldn't get all the way over here."

I started to walk out, then went back. I opened the door. The baby screamed and scared the hell out of me. The front door to the house had been left open by neighbor kids playing where they weren't supposed to. The toddler had been left unsupervised by the parents and had wandered off. Had the child not been found, he would've most likely died of exposure.

NOTE FROM THE PUBLISHER

We hope you enjoyed reading *The Sinister*, the ninth novel in the Bruno Johnson Crime Series.

While the other eight novels stand on their own and can be read in any order, the publication sequence is as follows:

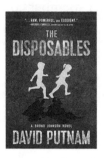

The Disposables

(Book 1)—Bruno Johnson, ex-cop, ex-con, turns vigilante—nothing will stop him and Marie as they rescue battered children from abusive homes.

"I really loved *The Disposables*. It's raw, powerful, and eloquent. It's a gritty street poem recited by a voice unalterably committed to redemption and doing the right thing in a wrong world."

—Michael Connelly, *New York Times* best-selling author

The Replacements

(Book 2)—Bruno and Marie, hiding out in Costa Rica with their rescued kids, are pulled back to L.A. to hunt a heinous child predator.

"While laying low in Costa Rica, former LAPD detective Bruno Johnson must return to California—and risk everything to stop a ruthless kidnapper. The action won't slow down." —*Booklist*

The Squandered

(Book 3)—Again, Bruno and Marie leave the kids in Costa Rica with Bruno's dad to intervene in the L.A. County prison system—and face a murderous psychopath.

"Putnam puts his years of law enforcement experience to good use in *The Squandered*, a shocking and intense tale of brotherly love and redemption realized in the midst of moral decay. It's a raw and gritty story I couldn't put down."   —C. J. Box, *New York Times* best-selling author

The Vanquished

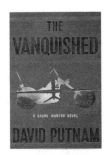

(Book 4)—A woman from Bruno's past lures him and Marie back to L.A.—the result is an unspeakable tragedy that will haunt Bruno for the rest of his life.

"Bad Boy Bruno Johnson comes out of hiding to battle a vicious biker gang that threatens his family. Bring an oxygen tank with you when you read *The Vanquished* because you'll be holding your breath the whole time."
—Matt Coyle, Anthony-, Lefty-, and Shamus Award–winning author

* * *

The Innocents

The first of the young Bruno prequels (Book 5)— Bruno is a new cop when he's handed a baby girl, becoming a single dad. Meantime he's working a police corruption case—infiltrating a sheriff's narcotics team involved in murder-for-hire. Family and professional life for Bruno collide violently.

"*The Innocents* is a terrific read, reminiscent of the best of Joseph Wambaugh. David Putnam provides an insider's knowledge of the Los Angeles Sheriff's Department. His characters and settings are rich and authentic, and his dialogue is spot on accurate."

—Robert Dugoni, *New York Times* best-selling author

The Reckless

The second of the young Bruno prequels (Book 6)—Bruno tackles the roles of the single dad of a two-year-old daughter and an L.A. County Deputy Sheriff in the Violent Crimes Unit. He is assigned a law enforcement public relations nightmare—apprehend a gang of teenager bank robbers without killing them or getting killed.

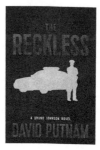

"Reading a novel by David Putnam is almost as good as riding shotgun in a patrol car. He writes what he knows and what he knows is that justice on the mean streets isn't always black and white."

—Robin Burcell, *New York Times* best-selling author

The Heartless

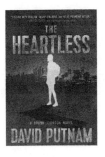

The third of the young Bruno prequels (Book 7)— Bruno has stepped down from his beloved position in the Violent Crimes Unit to be able to spend more time with his teen daughter, Olivia. Now a bailiff in the courts, he gets a frantic call to extricate Olivia from a gunpoint situation in an L.A. gang-infested neighborhood—thrusting him back into violent crime mode.

"David Putnam's *The Heartless* is terrific—a smart, well-written, relentless account of a battle against evil, fought by a protagonist who has a real man's flaws, but also shows us the kind of heroism that's real."

—Thomas Perry, *New York Times* best-selling author

The Ruthless

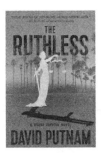

The fourth and last of the young Bruno prequels (Book 8)—Bruno is plunged back into the Violent Crimes Unit when his friends, a judge and his wife, are murdered. Bruno's daughter is now the mother of twins; and the father of the babies is a drug-addicted criminal—abusive, and brutal. This is the setup for Bruno's time in prison as he takes justice into his own hands.

"Dark, disturbing, and all too believable, this is the tale of one man's quest for atonement in a world where innocence is a liability."

—T. Jefferson Parker, *New York Times* best-selling author

We hope that you will read the entire Bruno Johnson Crime Series and will look forward to more to come.

For more information, please visit the author's website: www.DavidPutnamBooks.com.

Happy reading,
Oceanview Publishing